ELENA

THOMAS H. COOK

ELENA

BOSTON

HOUGHTON MIFFLIN COMPANY

1986

Library of Congress Cataloging in Publication Data

Cook, Thomas H.
Elena.

I. Title.
PS3553.O55465E4 1986   813'.54   85–11762
ISBN 0-395-35632-6

Printed in the United States of America

V 10 9 8 7 6 5 4 3 2 1

For Ron Blackwell, Greg Bush,
Cliff Graubart, Norman and Mary Levine,
Janine and Richard Perry, and Susan Terner
New Yorkers

And for Gerard Van der Leun,
who kept his steady eye upon this text

When what we hoped for came to nothing,
we revived.

—Marianne Moore

At the end of the room, the books were arranged in a tall pyramid on a long table. Elena's face adorned the cover of each volume, giving the entire configuration an oddly shattered appearance, as in a cubist portrait, each facet at once secretive and revealing.

Jason Findley stood next to me, still tall and straight, not in the least stooped by age. His manner remained as thoroughly Arthurian as it had ever been, and when he moved, gently lifting his glass to Elena's portrait, one could almost hear the soft creak of his armor.

"It's the perfect picture for the book jacket," he said.

"It will do," I said. Actually, I thought it overly posed, for our unbuttoned age. Still, it did convey a sense of what my sister was like at forty-five, the luminous face against a field of black suggesting something self-sustained, formidable and grave.

"I didn't expect to outlive her," Jason said, his eyes still locked on the imposing tower of books that stood only a few yards from him.

I glanced about. The room was beginning to fill now. Publishing parties are often crowded, everyone wanting to see, be seen; everyone relishing the privilege of being among the scribblers, as if writers were the ones who made the world, as Elena herself once said, rather than the ones who simply marked it down.

Jason turned to me. "Have you read the book?"

"Of course. In galleys."

"And?"

"It's thorough enough," I told him, "but it certainly won't be the last biography of Elena."

"No, I suspect not," Jason said softly. "She was so . . . protean." He smiled. "Whatever that means." The serenity with which he now spoke of my sister sharply contrasted with the tumultuousness of their experience together — the early hope and later anguish.

I looked at the portrait once again. Elena's face stared back at me from a hundred separate angles, her eyes frozen, utterly inanimate.

Of those present at this reception, only I could recall the first flashing of those eyes, the way they searched a room, always latching onto color, movement, any change of light. And I remembered how, later, they seemed to draw the world into them, filter it through her restless mind, then release it back to us, more ordered, perhaps a little tamed.

"Are you still living on the Cape?" Jason asked.

"Yes."

"Beautiful up there."

"Yes, it is."

"That house on the bay," Jason said. "We had some fine times, didn't we? Planting that flower garden of Elena's, remember?"

I could see the three of us struggling with that sandy, unforgiving soil, Elena with her battered hoe and Jason crouched on the ground, digging furiously with his spade.

"We had good times," I said, remembering the bad.

For a time, Jason and I stood silently together. Then he spotted another old friend across the room and excused himself, walking away, his hand grasped tightly to a cane which appeared more hindrance than support. At that instant, he seemed to represent for me everything that totters toward its end — so different from Hart Crane diving over the rail of the *Orizaba* and into the sea, or Matthiessen climbing out the window of the Manger Hotel, figures in that loss which is as perilous to look upon as to avoid, and which, as Elena wrote, "is perfectly rendered, in all its protest and derision, by the first eleven words of *Howl.*"

From behind, I heard a stirring in the crowd. I turned and saw Martha Farrell, the author of Elena's biography. She was beaming at the people gathered around her. This was her day, her party, her book. The polite applause was hers, as well as the brief esteem it represented. But there would be none of this, not the book, the author, or the celebration, without first the life, Elena's.

Christina Waterman walked steadily beside Martha. She was in charge of Parnassus now, the inheritor of the legendary press her father had founded. Though dead now, Sam Waterman, Elena's publisher, was alive in the decor of the room, its towering windows and overstuffed chairs. They were like the man himself, larger than one would expect, and more generous. Christina seemed little more than a mild liqueur after the banquet of her father.

"So happy you could be here, William," she said as she stepped up and embraced me with one of those quick, glancing motions young women use on old men, dodging the smell of camphor. "I understand you wrote a very appreciative letter about the book."

"Yes."

"Very complimentary."

"Martha worked hard. She deserves some credit."

"Any compliment from you, William, is something I cherish," Martha said as she joined us.

As a sentence, it worked rather like a swoon, one of those graceful dips women make in romantic novels when the masculine presence becomes too much for them. Perhaps there was a time when her inflated deference would have appealed to my vanity. But I am old now, and such remarks serve only to make me feel like a piece of crumbling statuary.

"Actually," Christina said quickly, "I was thinking of using a couple of quotes from your letter as part of the promotion." She eyed me cautiously. "Would you have any objection to that?"

"None."

She smiled. "I don't suppose it would be appropriate for you to review the book yourself?" she asked.

"I think not," I told her. Oiling the motor is one thing; pushing the car is quite another. "It'll be reviewed everywhere. *Times*. Front page, I'd say."

"Oh yes, of course," Christina said, "I'm sure of it." She glanced at her watch. "We'd better get started," she said to Martha.

The two of them bustled off to the front of the room, where a microphone stood like a thin, lonely guard before the table of books. Christina stepped up to it, and the crowd grew quiet and attentive.

"Everyone knows we're gathered here today to honor one of the great literary figures of our time," she said. A small burst of applause rose briefly, then drifted down like the last bits of confetti. Christina took one of the books from the table behind her and lifted it to the crowd. "It is entitled *Elena Franklin: A Life*," she continued. "And that is what it is, the story of a great and honored life." She smiled. "In Elena Franklin, there was nothing to debunk."

No, I thought, nothing to debunk. Martha's book was relentlessly thorough, monumentally detailed. But there was something missing still: I had read over six hundred pages about Elena Franklin, but had not, even for the briefest moment, felt the breath, heard the voice, sensed the heart, of my sister. And so it seemed to me that all of Martha's labor had come to nothing, that Elena now lived imprisoned in a book, her soul flattened under page after airless page, and that some breeze should be called forth to sweep away this vast, accumulated dust, a small but feeling wind to set her free.

EARLY WORKS

The first thing I remember is how small she was, and I think now that part of what I always felt for Elena — wrongly felt — resided in this first impression of her smallness.

I had not been well for the last few days, and so I had not been permitted to accompany my father to Dr. Houston's clinic to bring my mother home. My Aunt Harriet stayed with me, a large, sour woman, who moved ponderously under her black floor-length dress. Her life had been bedeviled by an erratic, drunken husband, and I suppose that the bit of advice she endlessly repeated to me that morning was the very sort she had given herself for twenty years: "You'll have to adjust, William, you'll just have to adjust." She meant that I had to adjust to no longer being an only child, but beyond this, I think, she also meant a larger adjustment, the one that must be made to the infinite quirkiness of life, its randomness and disarray.

I was only five years old, of course, hardly capable of understanding any but the most blatant ruminations. Still, from the painful way in which Aunt Harriet spoke of my coming adjustments, I gathered that having a sister was to be a most unpleasant circumstance. So I watched out the window, my face near the glass, waiting for this new intrusion upon my life, this ominous arrival.

She came in a black hansom cab, one of the last to grace the streets of Standhope, Connecticut. The driver sat rigidly on top of the coach, his gloved hands pulling back the reins. In his elegant black coat and top hat, he looked determined to ward off the clanging vulgarity of the motorcar.

My father stepped briskly from the coach, turned back, and lifted his hand to my mother. She took it and eased herself down to the ground, the tip of her shoe dipping into the freshly fallen snow. She held a small bundle in her arms, which she hugged to her breast.

And so Elena came home. She was wrapped in a large pink blanket, and it wasn't until my mother had placed her in her crib and my father had lifted me into his arms that I could see her.

Lying on her back, she did not look much larger than a rolled-up newspaper. Her hands were balled up into two tiny red fists about the size of half-dollar pieces. Her cheeks were flushed with the cold and seemed much too large for her face. Her eyes were tightly closed, so I did not bother to say hello.

"This is your sister," my father said. "Ain't she a pip?"

My mother leaned over the crib and unnecessarily adjusted the frilled collar that encircled Elena's throat.

"Where'd you get her?" I asked.

My father and mother exchanged knowing glances.

"From Dr. Houston," my father said quickly. "From his clinic."

"Is she going to live here now?"

"From now on."

I looked down at her again. So this was Elena, my sister. She appeared too small to be a real person, and I could not imagine that she would ever become one, that she would grow large like me, run and play and make noise as I did. Perhaps she could sit on a table like a vase of flowers, or move very slowly, like the last efforts of a wind-up toy. But that she would ever be fully alive, know her mind and speak it, seek a way in the world that was her own and no one else's — this was beyond my most distant imagining.

From the beginning, everything belonged to Elena. She owned space, and no place was safe from her invasion. She plowed through closets and cabinets, scattering everything in her wake. She pulled clothes from their drawers and lamps from their tables. She ripped at magazines and pulled down curtains, covering herself so completely that I could hardly hear the giggling underneath.

She owned time, and night meant nothing to her. She raged against the way it confined and limited her, and for hours I would lie in my bed listening to the tiny squeak of the rocking chair as my mother tried to soothe Elena into the sleep she hated.

Elena had nothing to recommend her. She slobbered her food out of both sides of her mouth, dirtied herself almost hourly, was always sticky and malodorous. And yet, my mother and father adored her. They washed and dressed her, powdered her behind and cooed lovingly into her small, pink ears. They showed her off to everyone, and these other people, sometimes total strangers, fell immediately under Elena's spell. Their faces lit up with broad, beaming smiles, their voices turned high and affectionate. I had never experienced anything so utterly bizarre.

As the months passed, Elena grew larger and more tyrannical. When I tried to walk away from her, she managed to follow me, her legs shooting out in all directions, her feet scuffing against the wooden floor, her head often banging into chairs or low-slung tables. She did not so much toddle as lunge, her arms beating against the air or flapping at her sides like unfledged wings.

She also began to speak. The babble of grunts and moans became isolated words. The first one was "more," and it was directed at some milky squashed substance in her bowl. "More!" she shouted, opening her mouth to its full, red width, her voice almost rattling the dishes in the cabinet over her head.

Through little skips in time, Elena's hair lengthened and grew darker. She began to rope words together into short sentences. Her eyes, instead of turning brown like mine, deepened into a darker blue. She cried less often, though she would still startle suddenly in the night and rouse herself to a terrible frenzy.

In response to Elena's loss of infancy, my mother became less indulgent with her. She slapped at her hands when Elena grabbed for her sewing, scolded her mercilessly for spills, and sometimes darted away from her so quickly that Elena was left wobbling uneasily on her feet, staring at my mother's retreating figure with a look of great confusion and abandonment.

For a time, my sister reacted to these new circumstances by withdrawing from the rest of us. She would sit by the window or retreat to her room and play there, quite determinedly alone. It was a pattern, this self-contained withdrawal, that would recur throughout her life. "There's a part of me that doesn't need anyone else," Manfred Owen says to his daughter in Elena's last book, "a part that floats away from all the rest, though it's not at all an airy thing, more like a stone with wings."

When Elena was five, my father took a job as a traveling salesman for a Midwestern toiletries manufacturer. It became his fate to roam up and down New England, hawking cleanliness and sweet smells to a people already so deodorized and sanitary they were dying of it. He drove about in a dusty, battered Model T, which must surely have been one of America's first "company cars." There were days when Elena and I would sit by the window for hours, our ears cocked for the first sound of that sputtering engine as it turned the corner onto Wilmot Street. Then we would rush out the door and wait for him, our hands intertwined, staring up the street like two marooned orphans scanning the sea for a rescue ship.

But when he came home, the rewards were few. Something had taken hold of him. In an interview in 1969, Elena described our father as having suffered from "the rapture of the road." As a consequence of this condition, he never looked more ill at ease than when returning home. Again, from the interview my sister gave in 1969: "I think my father was very different from the sort of weary, downtrodden salesman, the Willy Loman type, or R. J. Bowman in Eudora Welty's wonderful story, different from those characters in that he was a romantic nomad, the sort who falls in love with long distance, as Tennessee Williams put it in *The Glass Menagerie*. It is easy to think of his life as pointless, of course, but I'm not so sure that's proper, and I know it's presumptuous. There's this problem intellectuals have, this ancient problem of believing that an unconsidered life is the same as a miserable one. You can take that too far, and intellectuals often do, filling up the world with wasted, blasted lives the way the Fundamentalist mind stacks up souls in hell."

I do not believe that Elena ever managed to convince herself on this point. "Whatever you do, William," she told me on the day I left for college, "stay away from large black traveling cases." She meant the ones our father carried with him on the road.

When he was at home, however, Elena tried very powerfully to attract his attention, at first by grabbing playfully at his legs or quietly crawling into his lap as he sat indifferently reading a newspaper. Later she baked him cookies or cupcakes, once even a large cake, which she dedicated to him, signing her name in pink frosting. When these ploys proved unsuccessful, however, she switched to reverse tactics, and for a time all sweetness died in her. She spilled ink all over his order forms one evening, and he was up all night rewriting them. On another occasion, she crawled into his car with muddy feet and left her tiny footprints from seats to ceiling.

But nothing worked. He simply cleaned the car, laughing and shaking his head as he did so. Then he would be off again, gone for weeks at a time, leaving the rest of us behind, feeling each absence, as Elena would later write in *New England Maid*, "like a little touch of death."

In an early poem, written when she was fifteen, Elena described a bird that could not find its resting place. It tirelessly flitted about from limb to limb in a towering tree, but it could never get a hold, for the tree's thin, insubstantial branches were always breaking under it or drawing away from its approach. For years I thought the bird, neurotically leaping about, was our mother during her emotional crisis of 1920, and that the swaying tree was our home during that time. Later I realized that the bird was Elena, and that the tree, with its remote and ever-shifting branches, its refusal of all that is secure and battened down, was our father, and that this portrait of his eternal restlessness was the way she chose to praise, rather than to blame, him.

W̅hen imagination fails," Elena wrote in *The Quality of Thought in American Letters*, "the mind naturally descends toward the statistical." I lived in Standhope, Connecticut, for the first eighteen years of my life. I was born there, as was Elena, and I suppose it can be said that I was "formed" by it, as much as anyone is ever formed by an environment that is essentially indifferent, insisting that the general civilities be observed but steadfastly avoiding, as Elena wrote, "the question of what life, liberty, and the pursuit of happiness actually are." Elena, of course, was able not only to imagine her hometown, as she did in *New England Maid*, but to portray it powerfully. For me, however, the statistical approach is best, offering at least the candor of fact, though not the glory of supposition.

When Elena was born in 1910, Standhope was little more than a few shops built around an unassuming square. It was a rectangle of woodframe buildings, all of which looked out onto a dusty park which the town fathers reseeded every year, though without much success. Last year, when I returned to dedicate a small bronze plaque in Elena's honor in that same square, I found that the grass still did not grow in those places where it never had. All else was changed and modernized, but nature had remained intractable here and there, asserting its authority in one bare spot or two.

The square itself was very modest indeed in 1910. There was a harness shop, its windows filled with leather goods, bridles and reins and a single, shining English saddle that no one ever bought. Two Italian brothers operated a barbershop, complete with twirling peppermint pole. Their cousins worked as cobblers in the rooms above the shop. Directly across the square, though obscured by the enormous willow that grew beside the bandstand, stood Dickson's Dry Goods, a large general store that distributed everything from Pape's Diapepsin to a fully prepacked steel garage. Dickson's was continually buzzing with the latest town news. None of it ever seemed very engaging to me, or, for that matter, to Elena. "They spoke in monotones of deaths and taxes and the 'Catholic threat,' " she said in *New England Maid.* "Only a little was worth hearing, and nothing was worth remembering." In addition, the town square boasted an apothecary, a haberdashery, and a gun shop sporting a huge wooden sculpture of a Colt .45.

Standhope was situated about halfway between Hartford and New Haven. In the sense of one-room schoolhouses and covered bridges and austere stone walls, it was not really typical of New England at all. By 1910 it had a population of over three thousand, a great deal larger than the New England village of popular imagination. It had paved streets and motorcars, and not long after Elena was born, there was even very premature talk of a trolley. There were enough Irish, Poles, and Italians to construct a small Catholic church, but not enough Jews for a synagogue. There was a hat factory near the river, and a bell foundry behind the general store. There was no hospital, but Dr. Houston maintained a clinic. There were a number of lawyers, even a small accounting firm.

And yet, for all of this, Standhope was deeply Yankee in attitude and affiliation. Those who were not foreign, as Elena later wrote, distrusted foreigners; those who were Protestant distrusted the Catholics and the Jews. Though the small police force was Irish, it enforced Yankee law. In everything there was Yankee pride and Yankee confidence. School and church taught Yankee values. The bankers were Yankee, as was the single insurance agent. Thus Elena really was a New England maid, though one born, as it were, along that borderland which existed almost like a buffer zone between the heat and noise of New York and the laconic chill of Maine.

Had Standhope been less inland, it would have formed part of that beautiful shore drive which once stretched from the northeastern reaches of New York City to Rhode Island, and which provided the traveler with lovely inlets on one side and softly rolling hills on the other. Standhope was landlocked, however, the distance to the sea being just enough to raise doubts about the trip. Elena was eight years old before she saw the Atlantic Ocean, although relative to most other Americans of the time she lived practically upon its beaches. Similarly, the town was just far enough from New York to avoid the smoky clutter that was already engulfing Greenwich and Bridgeport. Thus, as Elena wrote, "Standhope rested near two great powers, New York and the sea, far enough from the former to escape a sense of its own provinciality, and too far from the latter to know a true humility."

In terms of culture, of course, Standhope left a good deal to be desired, particularly for someone like my sister. She described the cultural life of her hometown as residing "somewhere between the general store and the cave." This is a harsh evaluation, for Standhope was not Paris or New York. It was not even Hartford. It was simply a mildly prosperous town in southern New England, ready for progress, though not slavering for it, deeply Yankee, though helpless, as Dr. Houston once said at a town meeting, "before the immigrant horde," a village that had quite recently become a town and would never become a city. Its people lived, like most of the world, between glory and debasement, and if they did not produce great works of art, neither did they produce a Savonarola to burn them in the village square. It had a town band, which shattered the peace of summer evenings with wheezing renditions of hymns, patriotic melodies, and, infrequently, some tune that had wafted up from Tin Pan Alley, which the audience usually greeted with the closeted thrill of the faintly disreputable. It had a group of local singers, mostly conscripted from the Congregational choir. There was an unstable flutist who sometimes sat cross-legged in the park, tooting madly at the birds, and who was finally committed to Whitman House, the large asylum which served as the town's chief employer. It had no painter save for Mr. Webster who did signs of various sorts, and whose greatest work was the enormous representation of a Bethlehem stable that served as backdrop for the annual Christmas play in the school auditorium. It had no writer, except for Mrs. Tompkins who wrote "meditations" on mountains, streams, the willow tree on the town square, and the endless charity of a loving God. It had no sculptor of any kind. Even tombstones had to be purchased elsewhere. And except for a single black-haired Italian anarchist who asked loaded questions at the town meeting, Standhope had no philosopher at all.

It did have a few old homes, however, very stately and universally admired. From time to time a rushed New Yorker would find his way to Standhope and stare wistfully at the Potter house at the edge of McCarthy Pond, or the Dutton place, with its spacious porches, or the old Tilden house, whose gambrel roof towered over a capacious attic. There was a small stone house not far from the bell foundry. It was said to be the oldest structure in the town. It was certainly the steadiest. Even the garden gate was hinged to stone.

The largest house in Standhope, though not the oldest, was owned by Dr. Houston. It was a sprawling structure and seemed to sprout new rooms each year. Dr. Houston's wife was named Mabel, and she had insisted that her daughter be called by the same name. When she was thirteen, Elena dubbed the Houston domicile "The House of the Several Mabels," and she called it that for the rest of her life. For his part, Dr. Houston wrote a fiery denunciation of *New England Maid* when it was published. "Had I known that those little white fingers would ever have written such a book," he declared, referring to the time Elena had smashed her fingers in the door and my mother had taken her to him for treatment, "I would never have mended them." Early adversaries, they remained wary of one another to the end. "There is a kind of beauty in the unforgiven wound," Elena says in *The Quality of Thought in American Letters*, "one which warns away all further wear, the ragged hem, the splintered edge."

Our own house was among the more modest structures in Standhope. It was on Wilmot Street, in easy walking distance to the town square. There were several other houses on the block, all equally undistinguished, though with ample yards for the children. Our house was made of wood with a brick foundation. It had a small porch with wooden stairs and a little two-person swing in the eastern corner. It was painted white with dark green trim, as was most every other house in Standhope, and it was shaded by two large elms. A narrow stone walkway led from the street to the front steps. In the back stood a dilapidated structure, which creaked terribly in the wind, and was either the fallen-down remains of a small stable or a large potting shed.

The inside of the house was as unassuming as the outside. There was a small living room with a fireplace and wooden mantel. The floors were of wide, varnished pine. There was a large kitchen and a small room behind it which my father used as a makeshift office, complete with roll-top desk and wooden filing cabinet. Elena and I each had our own bedroom. For art, there was a portrait of George Washington in my father's cramped backroom office and in the living room a large seascape with gulls in the air and clipper ships. For music, there was an old upright piano which my mother had inherited from her family and which no one ever played. For literature, there was my collection of back issues of *The American Boy*, fifteen volumes of *Beacon Lights of History* — by means of which my father had proposed to educate himself but never had — and an assortment of romantic fiction, all belonging to my mother, novels that ran from Scott to his crudest imitators along the single line of blighted love.

But over all of this — the town itself, the people, its modest culture and small attainments — there was a pervasive sense of comfort and repose. "Its shade was deep and its water pure," Elena wrote in *New England Maid*, "and the one thing I will not take from Standhope is its beauty."

It really was beautiful, and even though I scarcely remember anything of the town's history or politics, I do remember the loveliness that remained in every season, as if all that was unbecoming in the town, the prejudice and ignorance, was but a momentary blemish, or, as Elena called it, "a hasty, ill-considered stroke upon the larger portrait of a great ideal."

But of all those aspects of Standhope which Elena saw so clearly, she felt most strongly for the mute and painful isolation at the center of each individual life. In the passage on Robert Frost in *Quality*, she wrote that "the notion that good fences make good neighbors can only be true of a society that has already resigned itself to a terrible demarcation." In this, I think, Elena became a victim of the thing she mourned. A photograph taken when she was seven suggests her own isolation, renders it clearly, as if it were a part of her own strange mass, the impregnable wall against which the electrons beat. She is standing in front of a large tree, clad in a white short-sleeved dress, which gathers around her like a swirl of snow. She is wearing a pair of white gloves, buttoned at the wrist, and her hair is pulled back and held in place by an enormous bow. Her shoes are black with large metal buckles and her socks white, one of them drooping a little below her ankle. She does not smile; but her face is not expressionless, for she is staring very pointedly at the camera, as if trying to outwit it, give it a wrong turn. Her lips are parted slightly and I can almost feel her small, moist breath. This is one of the photographs she will choose to illustrate New England Maid, and in it I can sense that invisible solitude that held her all her life.

After 1914 the United States moved slowly toward war while the young men of Europe slaughtered each other in unprecedented numbers. From time to time the enormity of what was going on in France intruded on Standhope. I recall seeing pictures of bodies strung out in the hard embrace of concertina wire, their arms and legs thrown out antically as if they were no more than clowns furiously entertaining invisible children on vast, muddy fields. Place names were mentioned in conversation at Dickson's — Verdun, the Somme, Chemin des Dames — but it was impossible to gain any emotional, or even visible, sense of what was going on there. Town opinion held that it was terrible, terrible, and that we should stay out of it.

Then, in 1917, Standhope intervened in the Great War. The people gathered for patriotic musicales or stood in the grassless park listening to the exhortations of politicians and old war veterans (quite a few from the Civil War), who feverishly insisted that Europe must be saved from the ravages of the scowling Hun. German atrocities were lavishly detailed by army recruiters who stood on caissons, their arms flung toward the sky.

It is difficult to believe how much war fever can be generated in a small town. The fierceness, with which Standhope embraced the war effort would have seemed impossible only a few seasons before. Prior to 1917, the flag simply fluttered over the square as it always had and, everyone presumed, always would. Men in uniform were vaguely distrusted, presumed to be sex crazed, and suspected of coming from disreputable backgrounds. And of course, in staunchly Republican Standhope, no one believed that Woodrow Wilson had any intelligence at all.

But everything changed after the United States entered the war. Flags and bunting decorated the town in swirls of festive color. Soldiers marched by smartly in their olive-green uniforms and round doughboy hats, their feet prancing to the beat of military bands. Elena stood beside me in a light blue dress with a large, dark blue sailor's collar, watching the parade pass by. She asked if a circus were coming. I said no, a war.

"Someday I'll go to war," I added bravely.

"Me too," Elena said.

I laughed. "You won't ever go to war," I told her. "Girls don't go to war."

Elena's eyes followed the retreating parade. "Maybe I'll be in the band, then," she said.

I granted that she might be able to do that someday, but that she should rid herself of any thoughts of battle.

"Is Papa going to war?" she asked me.

I shook my head.

"Why not?"

I shrugged. "Maybe he doesn't want to." Certainly at that moment, I could not have imagined why anyone would not want to go to war. It seemed the greatest adventure possible, and I had dreamed of it ever since hearing about the exploits of the Lafayette Escadrille.

"I want to fly a plane," I said.

Elena crinkled her nose. "I want an ice cream, William."

I fished in my pocket and withdrew a small change purse.

"Let's see if I have enough," I said. I opened the purse and counted the money. "Okay," I said after completing a very complex series of calculations, "but only one scoop."

We made our way across the street to Thompson's Drugstore, Elena gently tucking her small hand in mine, a gesture she would repeat from time to time throughout our lives and which gave me a sense — a false sense, I think — of being in command.

We sat down at a small wrought iron table with a white marble top. Across the room I could see the tall dark shelves of the apothecary, its huge tun-bellied jars filled with brightly colored liquids.

"I think maybe I'll be a doctor," I said absently.

Elena glanced quickly toward the soda fountain. "I want a chocolate ice cream."

I smiled, stepped over to the counter, and brought back two scoops of ice cream, each resting rather forlornly at the bottom of a huge fluted glass.

Elena had almost finished hers when Bobby Taylor walked into the drugstore. He looked splendid in his uniform, his hat held firmly on his head by a sleek leather chin strap, the gleaming boots rising almost to his knees, a rifle slung romantically across his shoulder.

I watched him admiringly. "I wish I were older," I said to Elena.

Bobby walked to the counter, then turned slowly in our direction. He must have been eighteen, an age which strikes me now as only a little beyond infancy. He had a lopsided grin that spread over his face with an innocent and unhindered openness. No doubt he had just experienced one of the most uplifting moments of his short life. He had marched down Washington Street and kept his eyes manfully forward while the girls blew kisses at him or waved white handkerchiefs. Only days before he had been an inconsequential teenager, but now he was a soldier, one of those stout lads his country had summoned to beat back the German hordes. The transformation must have been dizzying. One could almost sense his feet rising from the floor.

It took all my courage to address him.

"Hello," I said.

Bobby took his glass of soda from the counter, and walked over to us.

I cleared my throat nervously. "I saw you in the parade."

"You did," Bobby allowed casually. He lowered one of his hands onto the stock of his rifle, a gesture which was no doubt meant to convey the gravity of the task before him. "Where were you standing?"

"Just across the street."

"Got a good view then, I guess," Bobby said.

Elena was indifferently finishing her ice cream, as if nothing at all had happened, as if Bobby Taylor were just another ordinary mortal, not a gallant knight.

"That ice cream looks pretty good," Bobby said to her.

Elena looked up. "Do you like ice cream?" she asked.

Bobby laughed softly. "Sure."

"Bobby's a soldier, Elena," I said.

Elena glanced at me scornfully. "I know *that.*" She turned back to Bobby. "Does that gun have bullets in it?"

"Sure it does," Bobby said.

Years later I learned that soldiers on parade do not carry loaded weapons.

"I'll bet you're a good shot," I said.

"Fair, I guess," Bobby said modestly. He patted the stock gently. "Got to be, where I'm going."

"Yeah."

"Where are you going?" Elena asked.

Bobby shrugged. "Don't know for sure. Wherever the war is, I guess."

"The war is in Europe," I told him.

Bobby chuckled. "Well, I know that much. But I don't know for sure where in Europe I'll be going."

"Bobby's going to go help whip the Germans," I told Elena solemnly.

Elena studied Bobby's face. "Do you have a dog?" she asked.

Bobby reached down and touched Elena's hair. "Used to have one," he said, "but it died a few months back."

I watched his fingers as they gently caressed a strand of Elena's hair. For a moment he seemed to draw away from us, lost in his own thought. Then he opened his hand and allowed Elena's hair to fall from it.

"I'd better be going," he said, though his eyes remained on Elena for a few seconds longer.

"Give those Germans a licking," I told him manfully.

"They'll get what's coming to them," Bobby said. Then he turned smartly on his heels and strode out of the pharmacy and down that road which would take him to Belleau Wood and Château-Thierry, to become one of those brave boys who would break the Ludendorff offensive.

Standhope sent nine boys to Europe and all of them came back alive. One of them had his arm in a black sling, but aside from that he looked just fine. For a while, these returned soldiers were the toast of the town. The mayor gave them a luncheon, and there was another celebration in their honor at the school auditorium. For a few weeks after that, a soldier or two could sometimes be seen squatting in the park. I remember hearing one of them talk about a horse he had seen trotting across no man's land with forty feet of its intestine dragging along behind it. Then the uniforms disappeared along with almost everything else redolent of the war.

In *New England Maid*, Elena wrote that "the flags and bunting and uniforms held their own for a while in what appeared to be a rear-guard action on behalf of memory. But normalcy was a more powerful foe than anything confronted in the Great War, and in the end all the symbols of that struggle faded as if embarrassed by their own eccentricity, fashions that no longer suited the times."

Of all the people who fought that "rear-guard action on behalf of memory," Bobby Taylor was the bravest. He had been gassed twice and shot once, but except for a hard, dry cough, he looked more or less as he always had. There was a drawn quality to his face, a certain wildness in his eyes, but these could be assigned to the extremity of his experience.

It was his behavior, not his appearance, that aroused speculation about him. He would sometimes burst out crying in the middle of a conversation or laugh inappropriately, and in a high, thready manner which sounded almost girlish. Dr. Houston blamed these aberrations on the residual effects of mustard gas and prescribed withering purgatives which left Bobby weak and feverish. Pastor James went by to see Bobby and offered the comforts of Christian endurance. Nothing availed, however, and within three months after he came back to Standhope, Bobby Taylor placed a note on the mantel in his living room. It said: "Thank You." Then he walked into the back room of his house, took off his clothes, crawled into bed, and shot himself between the eyes with his father's pistol.

Elena and I were together playing croquet on our front lawn when the bell began ringing down the street at the Taylor house. We ran toward the sound of the bell as fast as we could, both expecting to see dark smoke rising in the distance since the bells were almost always used as fire alarms. But when we saw no smoke, we slowed our run, then finally stopped a few yards from the house. We could see Bobby's mother talking intently to her neighbor, Mr. Parks, in the front yard. Mr. Parks looked briefly toward the house, then drew her under his arm, lowering the side of his face into her hair.

For a long time Elena and I stood on the walkway watching people hurry past. Then Mr. Parks came over to us. His face was flushed. "Go home," he said, rather harshly. "There's nothing for you to see here."

We went back to our own yard. I picked up my croquet mallet. "Want to finish the game?" I asked.

Elena shook her head, glanced back down the street, then turned and walked inside. She was clearly subdued, though only briefly so, for in an hour or two she was romping about the yard again, though even then, from time to time, she cast secret, fearful looks toward Bobby Taylor's house.

She was only eight years old. What could she possibly have known of war? But knowledge is partly what we choose powerfully to remember, and Elena never forgot Bobby Taylor. He surfaced not only in her actual description of his death in *New England Maid* but also, more subtly, in her section on Stephen Crane in *Quality:*

> At the end of *The Red Badge of Courage,* Henry Fleming has his badge, a piece of cloth stained by his blood which serves as a blindfold for his mind. For what has he lost in gaining it? Surely the greatest soldier is not the young combatant but the old warrior who has come to understand that the color of courage is not always red. Fleming has no such understanding, and it is the central intellectual loss of his experience. Perhaps it is also Crane's, for he seems unable to understand that the illusions which so puff up Fleming in the final passages are identical to those for which the Swede will die in "The Blue Hotel." One is no less suicidal than the other, and both ensanguine the earth from Jericho to Flanders Fields.

In January of 1918, my mother gave Elena a birthday party. She invited several of the neighborhood children, who arrived dressed rather formally, the girls in dark cotton skirts, the boys in starched shirts, knickers, and black knee socks. They seemed happy enough, as Elena described them in *New England Maid:* "Theirs was the unbounded pleasure that precedes experience, the openness that precedes caution." In this somewhat mannered line, one can detect a faint hint of envy. Perhaps Elena was able to sense that the playfulness so natural to childhood had somehow escaped her, at least in part. This is not to say that Elena was a somber child, old before her years, pondering man's tragic fate while watching other children skip rope. She was merely a sober child, curiously self-contained, though in no obvious way particularly gifted. Her gift was in her attraction to the shrouded and ambiguous, a keen moral perception, and a sense that that which is awry deserves more attention than that which is well ordered. She would later write that the greatness of Joseph Conrad resided in the directness with which he approached that which he already knew to be unapproachable. This was true of Elena, as well.

In her biography, however, Martha saw it differently: "Elena's childhood was darkened by the long absences of her father, the disintegration of her mother, and the final betrayal that involved them both." In this line, of course, one observes Oedipus and Electra dancing while Freud pipes the tune. No doubt at all, we had family problems. My father's absences contributed to them, as did my mother's derangement. But if every disordered family created a great mind, then we would have a good deal more intelligence on hand than we currently do.

Thus, rather than offering a portentous description of Elena's formative years, I prefer to suggest what might have been noticed about her at this time.

She was somewhat lonely. She missed her father. She missed him intensely and would brood for quite some time after his departure. She was fascinated by anomalies, stared with inhuman concentration at a five-legged cow a farmer once displayed in the square. Each spring she was usually the first child in our neighborhood to find a four-leaf clover. She was interested in nocturnal creatures, such as owls and bats. Ordinary animals rather bored her, and at no time in her life did she have a dog or cat, goldfish or canary. She had few friends and tended to play either with me or alone. She read slightly more than other children her age, and was especially drawn to stories about calamities — children caught in fires, floods, earthquakes, and hurricanes. She was particularly resistant to cold and often played outside in the dead of winter. She enjoyed long walks, and then, as well as later, such strolls encouraged a talkativeness in her which ended abruptly when the trek was over. She often pushed herself into situations of limited danger, while carefully holding back from anything truly threatening. Her eyes were particularly sensitive to light, so that she often chose to play in the shade or under the eaves. The shack in our back yard was a favorite spot because its roof shielded her from light. She preferred enclosures, and played in the house more than other children not out of insecurity — the most obvious interpretation, I suppose — but because open space offered too much distraction for one whose early aim was concentration.

None of this in any way suggested my sister was extraordinary, and it was not until a particular incident during her eighth birthday party that I began, however vaguely, to suspect something exceptional about her.

We were all sitting at the kitchen table, myself, Elena, and the children my mother had invited to the party. My mother was rearranging dishes in that white painted cupboard which forever occupied her. The front of her dress was still wet from having clumsily emptied the water pan beneath the ice chest, but she had refused to change. Her preoccupation with the cupboard was a disordered priority, the visible tip of what was to become an immense derangement.

We were waiting for my father to come downstairs. He bounded in a few minutes later, shaven and refreshed. He had become something of a dandy, favoring flashy ties and gold stud pins. I was thirteen then, and I hated his good looks, energy, and particularly his physical grace, which was such a maddening counterpoint to my own teenage awkwardness.

"We've been waiting for you, Harry," my mother said icily.

My father flashed his big let's-close-the-deal smile and slapped his hands together.

"On with it, then," he said jubilantly. "I can't wait."

My mother lit the eight candles on Elena's cake while the rest of us watched.

"Okay, blow them out, Princess," my father said.

Elena stared at the cake as if it were not really there but only a photograph in a magazine, something that had nothing to do with her.

"Make a wish, then blow them out," my father said.

Elena lowered her eyes slightly, then glanced up at the candles again.

"Come on, Elena, blow them out," my father repeated happily.

Elena did not move. There was a peculiar heaviness in her face, a sense of being distracted.

My mother touched my sister's shoulder. "Elena?"

"What's wrong, Princess?" my father asked.

Elena said nothing.

"Come on now, make a wish."

"I don't have a wish," Elena said.

The other children laughed, thinking it a joke. My father laughed along with them, but I detected an uneasiness, as if all his long neglect had finally broken over him in a malignant wave.

I looked at my mother and could see the panic rising in her.

"Please, Elena," she said softly, "blow out the candles." In *New England Maid*, Elena described our mother's voice as having "a tone of penitence and beggarly complaint," and so it did that day.

"Please," my mother said again. "Please, Elena, we want it to be a nice party."

Elena closed her eyes, leaned toward the table, and blew out the candles.

Relief swept into my mother's face.

"That's a good little princess," my father said. "Good girl. All your wishes will come true."

The rest of the children cheered loudly, then joined my mother and father in a rousing rendition of "Happy Birthday."

When they had finished, my father drew out his watch, glanced at it casually, then returned it to his vest.

"I'd better be on my way," he said. Then he headed for the door and the road.

My mother did not look at him. She began methodically slicing the cake, tearing into it with dreadful energy.

I looked at Elena. She was staring across the table at me very sternly, and for the first time I sensed the strange bond that only siblings may feel, the relentless embrace of a shared and unshirkable history, an intimacy so compact it seems to press in on the brain.

I tried to smile.

"Have a piece of your cake, Elena," I said.

She shook her head, got out of her seat, and walked into the living room. I waited until the other children had finished their cake, then joined Elena in the living room.

She was sitting in a chair near the front room, staring out at the street.

"Dad has to go to work," I told her. "He couldn't stay for the party."

Elena continued to face the window.

I lowered myself to the floor and curled my legs underneath me, Indian-style.

"Want to play a game?" I asked.

Elena shook her head.

"We could go outside, then," I offered. "We could play croquet. All your friends could, too."

"I don't want to," Elena said.

The other children drifted into the living room and then on out the front door. In a few minutes, all of them were gone.

"I'm sorry you didn't enjoy your party," I said.

Elena did not answer and after a time I also wandered out of the house, leaving her still sitting silently in her chair.

I ended up in a park several blocks away, and as I shuffled about, kicking at the dust with the toe of my shoe, I stumbled upon a small turtle. It struck me that I had not given Elena a birthday gift, and the turtle looked like just the thing to lift her mood. I picked it up and ran home.

"What's that," Elena said as I came back through the front door.

"Something for your birthday," I told her.

Elena slid out of her seat and walked over to me. She delicately moved her finger over the shell.

"It's very pretty," she said.

The turtle, of course, had withdrawn its entire body into the shell.

"Want to see its head?" I asked.

"It won't come out," Elena said. She continued to glide her finger over the shell.

"I can make it," I told her. "Come with me."

Elena followed me into the kitchen. I set the turtle down on the small table near the sink and withdrew a box of matches from the drawer.

"What are you going to do with those?" she asked, staring at the matches.

"Get the turtle's head to come out," I told her. "Watch." I struck one of the matches and laid it on top of the turtle's shell.

Elena's eyes widened. "Don't do that!" she cried.

"Have to," I said. "When it gets hot, it'll stick its head out."

I struck another match.

"Stop it, William," Elena insisted.

"Well, you want to see its head, don't you?" I asked. Elena's squeamishness was beginning to irritate me.

"No, I don't," Elena said frantically. "I don't want to see it."

I lowered the match over the shell. "Yes you do."

"*No!*" Elena shrieked. She grabbed the turtle from the table and rushed from the room.

"Come on, Elena," I shouted, "you're crazy." I darted after her.

She was already through the living room and I could see her running about in the front yard as if unsure what she should do next. I ran out onto the small porch.

"Bring me that turtle," I said. By then I had quite forgotten it was a gift for Elena.

Elena hugged the turtle to her. "No. I won't."

"Bring me that turtle, Elena," I repeated.

Elena shrank back. "Please, William."

"Hand it over," I demanded. I took another step.

She stepped back again, squeezing the turtle tightly to her chest. "No."

I bolted forward and Elena rushed away from me. She was running frantically but I was gaining on her quickly. Then she suddenly veered to the right as she reached the edge of the sidewalk and I flew past her. As I whirled around, I saw her step into the middle of the walkway. She raised the turtle high above her head, and in one fierce movement she slammed it down against the pavement, cracking the shell with the blow.

I stared down at the broken turtle, horrified.

"Are you crazy, Elena?" I said. "Why did you do that?"

Elena stood trembling on the sidewalk. For a moment she watched the insides of the turtle ooze out from the shattered shell. Then she walked silently back to the house, her long hair swaying left and right as she made her way through the thick covering of leaves that blanketed the yard.

Years later I related this incident to Jason. We were sitting in his apartment in the Village and he was looking very stately, pipe in hand, the smoke curled about his head.

"It's an odd story, don't you think?" I asked.

"Yes."

"I've never been able to figure it out, exactly. But I've never been able to shake it, either."

"Perhaps that's only because Elena is so famous. Every little thing matters."

"But I kept remembering it long before that. It's one of *my* childhood memories, not just one about her."

Jason nodded. "What is it that pesters you, William?"

"I don't know, exactly. The contradiction, I suppose. The idea of destroying a thing in order to save it."

"You mean the turtle?"

"Of course."

Jason smiled. "You've got it all wrong, William. Elena didn't throw that turtle down to save it from its pain. She threw it down to save you from your cruelty."

I leaned forward slightly. "So she was just behaving like a sister?"

Jason nodded. "A dutiful sister, yes."

Jason had the gift of giving everything he said the sound of indisputable authority, and yet I think that his interpretation may not have been correct. For her part, Martha related this same incident in her biography and used it to suggest Elena's early rebelliousness against male authority, first my father's, then my own. But I have come to believe that Elena would have rejected any gift from me. For she was acting in defense of something far more important: the mood of thoughtfulness that had overtaken her, and which she would not permit to be stolen from her by small devices. All her life, my sister believed that she had an absolute right to her unease, that it was the central resource of her intelligence. "There is a kind of anxiety that debilitates," she wrote in *Quality*, "and a kind that ennobles, that offers resistance both to the inward and to the outward misery, that cries out for reformation, as the voice of Captain Vere does from the decks of the *Indomitable*, both within the life of one and within the lives of all."

There are times now when I gaze at all those many photographs I have of Elena, and in each of her changing faces this basic seriousness remains, as if it were the single line she threw out to the world, her determined gravity.

Martha ends her chapter on Elena's birthday party with a dramatic interpretation of it, describing Elena's refusal to blow out the candles as "a gesture of resistance and refusal in its initial childhood phase." She says that in the end my sister was made whole, at least as an artist, "by various episodes of psychological disjunction, which, added together, argue for the general diagnosis of periodic childhood depression."

But something of my sister's life is already missing in Martha Farrell's report: her ordinary needs, the ones that bind her to the rest of us. She needed to leap into McCarthy Pond, dress up like a witch on Halloween, take a hay ride to MacDougall's farm, sing all those boring childhood songs. And then, of course, there was that one further need, which rose in her at this time, one that did not so much darken her childhood as give it greater ardency. It was unmistakable. It lived in everything she did: in the way she hesitated before entering the shed or kept the door to her room slightly ajar. It stared outward through her eyes, and was, I suppose, most simply embodied in that lock of Lewis Carroll's creation, that creature of tightened bolt and unbending steel who beats about tirelessly, searching, searching, as it says, for someone with the key to me.

Her hair was almost the color of strawberries, and her name was Elizabeth Brennan. Her eyes were green, and they moved continually. Elena described her in *New England Maid:* "She was sitting in the school yard, cross-legged on a bench, methodically chewing a piece of Wrigley's. She was wearing a blue dress with a white lace hem and black shoes, dusty from the playing field. Her hair was red and hung freely to her shoulders. She had taken out the bow and now twirled the ribbon through her fingers with a strange, unchildlike dalliance. Her eyes never came to rest, and everything they fell upon, they singed a little."

It was Elizabeth who first had the key to my sister. She moved to Wilmot Street not long after Bobby Taylor's death and lived there with her father, a large, heavyset man, who spent most of his time sitting morosely on the front porch of their house, a mug — not a glass or cup, but a mug — of whiskey in his hand. He drank in this fashion all the time, publicly, his legs sprawled out in front of him, his head drooping down, the mug balanced so uneasily in his hand that the whiskey sometimes sloshed onto the unpainted wooden floor.

In 1919 few people referred to alcoholism as a disease. It was a moral failure, a willful dissoluteness. "Your father is a sot," Dr. Houston told Elizabeth bluntly the afternoon she finally dragged her father to his office after a bout of coughing blood. "He's a drunk," Dr. Houston went on, the voice of his time, "and he will remain a drunk until he makes up his mind to stop drinking."

But Mr. Brennan couldn't stop, and so for endless hours he sat out on his porch, outrageously shirtless even in the fall, and sipped at his great brown mug until his eyes finally closed and the mug slipped from his fingers. Then Elizabeth would rush out to him, clean up the mess, rouse him into semiconsciousness, and with great effort maneuver his large hulking body back into the house.

They had moved from Boston, where Mr. Brennan had worked on the docks for many years. No doubt he had pilfered enough unguarded goods there to ease himself into a sodden retirement. "There was an air of lost criminality about him," Elena wrote in *New England Maid,* "of small virtues abandoned for the larger one of survival. It was as if life itself had gnawed at him ceaselessly, stripping off the flesh, leaving only bare and shattered bone." But along with these remains, there was a bit of spirit, too, and when Pastor James came around one morning in a reforming mood and asked him if he believed in hell, Mr. Brennan had the strength of character to reply, "You mean, after this one?"

The house they moved into was only a few blocks down Wilmot Street from our own. It was of modest size, though certainly large enough for two people. It had weathered gray shingles, white clapboard siding, and a dormered roof with one window for each of the two upstairs bedrooms. Mr. Brennan never bothered to furnish it with anything beyond the bare minimum required for human habitation. The living room had one hardwood-and-rattan occasional chair, one press-back armchair, and a single worn settee of more or less Shaker austerity. In his own room upstairs there was a simple metal bed and, oddly out of place, an enormous hall mirror chair upon which Mr. Brennan piled his clothes, leaving the tiny closet empty. There was a wooden half-bed in Elizabeth's room. It was painted light blue, and some sort of Polynesian jungle scene was carved into the headboard and painted in florid reds and greens. Several short barrister bookshelves stood against the walls, the volumes arranged neatly and catalogued by subject. The floors remained rugless, the windows curtainless. "That house was Mr. Brennan's monastery," Elena once said, "and his god was gloom."

All the work of this disordered household fell to Elizabeth, and she performed it with tireless dedication. She made the meals, dusted, mopped, poured the water from the ice chest, and swept the porch. And despite all this drudgery, she never appeared unhappy. Elena called her Jennifer in *New England Maid,* and said that for her "life was the grand rich uncle of whom one is never to ask a favor."

Elizabeth's one great pleasure was reading, and in this her father fully indulged her. I would often see the two of them making their way to the Standhope Library, Elizabeth skipping ahead while her father trudged heavily behind in his baggy gray pants. He would wait for her outside the library, slumped on the steps, smoking a cigar or wiping his sweaty pink face with a dark blue handkerchief. He would wait for as long as necessary, listlessly staring down the street as if waiting for some signal to begin his life again. Then when Elizabeth finally came through the door, he would grasp the bannister and pull himself to his feet, sweep the large stack of books from Elizabeth's arms, and walk her safely home.

As might be imagined, Elizabeth's reading served her very well indeed. Most children in Standhope had little interest in learning more than was minimally required for progressing to the next grade, and so from the first day of her arrival at school, Elizabeth stood out from the rest. For her mind was not only quick but filled with a curious assortment of information that no one else seemed to have.

"She knows everything," Elena told me excitedly after their first meeting.

I was aimlessly sitting on the front lawn. I looked up and saw that Elena was smiling very brightly.

"She knows the names of all the trees," she added quickly, "and she knows about strange animals, too. Did you know there's a fish that lives in a cave and it's so dark that the fish don't have eyes?"

"Of course I knew that," I said, lying through my teeth.

"You never told me about them," Elena said. She looked offended, as if I had purposefully kept something from her.

I shrugged. "Why should I? They're just fish."

"You should talk to Elizabeth sometime, William," Elena insisted. "You really should. You'd like her a lot."

I grunted doubtfully, then waved my hand, dismissing the idea.

"You could meet her this afternoon," Elena said happily.

"Some other time," I said. I began fiddling with a pair of goggles I had brought out into the yard. Recently I had become obsessed with the idea of becoming an aviator. I was thirteen years old, and while other boys my age were beginning to plan realistic futures for themselves, I was still locked in a childhood fantasy of airborne adventure. I dreamed of soaring over snow-capped Alpine heights or the steaming jungles of the Amazon, the wings of my plane banking left and right in the brilliant silver air. In 1934 Elena sent me a copy of Antoine de Saint-Exupéry's *Night Flight* with a little note inside: "We should always remember, William, the obsessions of our youth."

"I'm going over to visit Elizabeth right now," Elena declared. "She invited me."

"Go ahead," I said as I continued to toy with the goggles.

"But you should come, too," Elena said. "You should meet her. She's really nice."

I placed the goggles on my head and pulled them down over my eyes.

"I don't need to meet her right this second," I said. What, after all, could a little girl know about the complexities of that infant science, aerodynamics. "I don't need to talk to her. She's just a little girl."

Elena gave me an accusing glare. "You don't even know her."

"So what?"

"Please, William," she said, grasping my arm.

I eased out of her grip. "Go yourself. You don't need me."

"But I want you to meet her."

Finally I relented, pulling the goggles from my eyes. "All right, but I don't want to stay very long."

And so in the spring of 1919, I met Elizabeth Brennan for the first time. She was sitting in her yard with a notebook in her lap, sketching the trees across the way, though not very clearly — a haze of gray smudges over a few jagged black lines.

"This is my brother, William," Elena said.

I nodded but said nothing.

Elizabeth did not look up immediately. First she scratched a few more lines onto the pad, then tilted her head back to get a broad view of her drawing. Her lips curled down. Then she glanced at me.

"You're tall," she said.

I smiled manfully. "Yes, I am."

Elizabeth eyed the goggles. "What are those for?"

"Aviator goggles. For a pilot."

Elizabeth shook her head. "No they're not. Those are welders' goggles. Mechanics use them when they're welding."

I could have kicked her. "Pilots use them too," I declared.

Elizabeth shook her head again. "No they don't. They use a special kind. Those are just for welders, people like that." She turned away from me, patted the grass beside her, and spoke directly — and exclusively — to Elena.

"Sit down," she said.

Elena quickly dropped to the ground beside Elizabeth.

I remained standing, mortified.

"Aren't you going to sit down?" Elizabeth asked.

"I can't stay long," I said stiffly.

"Sit down, William," Elena said. "You don't have to go *right now.*"

I lowered myself to the ground opposite them and looked at Elizabeth. Just to make conversation I said, "Is your mother home?"

"My mother's dead," Elizabeth replied in a voice as featureless as if she had told me nothing at all of consequence.

"Oh," I sputtered. "I'm sorry."

"She's been dead for about a year," Elizabeth said.

"Well, I . . ."

She turned briskly to my sister. "That's a pretty blouse."

"Thank you," Elena said, beaming.

"What's it made of?"

Elena shrugged. "I don't know."

Elizabeth touched the upper sleeve of Elena's blouse, rubbing a portion of it between her fingers.

"Do you know how to sew?" she asked.

Elena shook her head, her eyes downcast. "No."

Elizabeth nodded. "I didn't think so. Want me to teach you?"

Elena's eyes brightened. "Would you?"

"Sure," Elizabeth said easily. "Do you have a sewing machine?"

"My mother has one."

Elizabeth smiled, then slowly brought her hand up to Elena's cheek. "You're very pretty," she said. "You have such a pretty face."

In her short story "Desire," Elena described this moment in her life, using the voice of an old woman remembering: "She leaned forward and I could see her hand rising. The fingers stretched out toward my face, tips raised, and pressed against my cheek delicately, as one might touch the canvas of a painting one has grown to love, the fingers sliding tenderly over the brush strokes, seeking the small rills and valleys within the structure of the whole." Later the old woman walks out into the fields behind her estate and sees the face of the girl in the clouds: "As children, we could find figures in the sky by making the clouds roll and press inward to the shape that we desired. But the face I saw now was not fashioned by a cloud, did not merely occupy some small corner of the sky. It was an elemental force which drew the clouds into itself, shifting light and shadow until the portrait was fully drawn. And it was as if the face had taken the sky as but a canvas upon which to display itself, carving its own wild features with the brush strokes of the wind."

When, after a moment, Elizabeth withdrew her touch, it was as if a line had been cut between them, a current shut off, and Elena seemed almost physically to slump backward.

I stood up immediately. "We'd better go," I said to Elena.

Elena's eyes remained fixed on Elizabeth.

"You go ahead," she said.

"You should come, too," I insisted.

"No, you go on. I'll come later," Elena said, still staring into Elizabeth's face.

Elizabeth stood up slowly, brushing bits of grass from her skirt.

"You'd better go with your brother," she said to Elena. "I have to begin dinner, anyway."

"But I can stay a little longer," Elena said.

"Come back tomorrow," Elizabeth said gently. She looked at me. "You can come back, too, if you want."

She was not in the least contemptuous of me, but I felt contemptible
in her eyes. The power she had over Elena was drawn from a strength
that seemed mysterious, and therefore terrifying, something that had
the force and authority of an older world. Suddenly the absurd goggles
dangling from my hand struck me as being wholly infantile, as repulsive
as a soiled diaper.

Elizabeth glanced at Mr. Brennan, slumped in his chair on the
porch. He had fallen asleep and the brown mug had tipped in his
hand, spilling whiskey across his thighs.

"I'd better go in now," Elizabeth said.

Elena stood up. "I'll see you in school tomorrow, okay?"

"Okay," Elizabeth said. Then she walked toward the house.

Elena's eyes followed Elizabeth's retreating figure. Watching her
as she watched Elizabeth, I felt as if something of great value was
seeping from my life. I bent down quickly and took Elena's hand.
She turned toward me, surprised.

"Let's go home now," I said.

Elena nodded. "All right.'

We walked together for a time, neither of us saying anything,
Elena entirely absorbed in her newfound friend. Then suddenly, she
skipped away from me, and I was left shuffling along behind her,
preoccupied now with a new sensation, that of being utterly alone.

Adolescent loneliness is difficult for an adult to remember or imagine. I do recall, however, that for a time I had not the slightest
notion of who I was, or what, in the end, I might become. There
was only a sense of aimless floating to which was added an intense
and bottomless desire, which, for all its feverishness, had no specific
object, person or idea. It was just desire, naked and dimensionless, a
need that coiled in the pit of my stomach and pulsed there like a
second heart.

In this painful state I frequently took long walks, perhaps believing
that I might finally pass through the border of my desire, leave it

behind me like a road sign. Almost invariably, these treks ended at the gates of Whitman House, a mental institution where vast numbers of insane people were said to reside.

From the outside, Whitman House appeared tame enough. It was a graceful structure with a large portico supported by four high Doric columns. The road beyond the dark wrought iron gate was bordered with azaleas, and huge oak trees rose above it, shading the drive and lending it a peaceful, gentle aspect. Many years later I was reminded of Whitman House by the movie *Gone with the Wind*, when the camera rises above a rounded hill revealing Tara in the distance, cradled in a grove of trees. Elena was sitting beside me in the theater. She turned to face me, neither smiling nor frowning. "That's where Mother died," she said.

There was a small park across from Whitman House, and at the end of my walks I used to sit down on one of the benches there and watch the people come and go. During visiting hours, the imposing gate was swung open and a steady stream of traffic moved in and out. Beyond the gate, visitors sometimes strolled casually with an inmate friend or relative, who always appeared vaguely baffled, as if still trying to discover that open window through which derangement had entered, soiling the carpet and leaving the carefully appointed room in disarray.

I still don't know what drew me to Whitman House, or why, of all the places in and around Standhope, I invariably retreated there. Certainly there was a morbid quality to my interest, the craven curiosity one feels outside the door of a brothel and which only fear or prudence can control. Perhaps I have always been attracted to the freakish and disordered because it is so powerful a counterpoint to my own life, rooted as it is, so utterly predictable. And yet I also feared Whitman House as a place where all the sturdy rules by which men live had somehow been set aside, that one abode on earth where, in Cowper's phrase, "Bacchanalian Madness has its charms."

Consequently my dismay when one afternoon I saw Elena and Elizabeth making their way toward the open gate of the asylum.

I leaped up and bounded across the street, calling to them, my arm raised in frantic warning.

"Elena! Elizabeth! Where are you going?"

They looked at me without the slightest sense of anything unusual.

"We're going inside," Elizabeth said matter-of-factly.

"You can't go in there," I told them, "that's a nuthouse."

Elena shot me a vicious look. "Elizabeth knows somebody in there," she said hotly.

"My grandmother lives in that . . . what did you call it . . . nuthouse?" Elizabeth said.

My mouth dropped open. "Oh, sorry, Elizabeth."

"That is why we moved to Standhope," she added. "So we can visit her."

"So, your grandmother, she's . . ."

"Old," Elizabeth declared. "Very old. She can't look after herself. Once she set her house on fire in Boston. After that, we brought her down here."

"She's just old, William," Elena said. "That's the only thing that's the matter with her. Her mind is old."

I was unaware of the varieties of madness. To me insanity simply meant explosive moods and terrible violence. I knew about mental retardation. Standhope even had one such person, the thirty-year-old son of Luther Coggins, whose nocturnal wanderings had been the subject of more than one town meeting. On one occasion, Dr. Houston, using the medical language of his time, had referred to him as "the Coggins imbecile." I also knew that old people went "soft in the head." But that they might also wind up in Whitman House was news to me. The "nursing home," of course, had not been invented.

"She's senile," Elizabeth said flatly. "But she's very nice and she doesn't hurt anybody."

Listening to Elizabeth's quick defense of her grandmother made me feel like one of those irate and benighted villagers who, torch and rope in hand, demanded the gentle creature of Dr. Frankenstein's.

"I'm sure she is," I said immediately.

"I come here once a week," Elizabeth went on. "My grandmother likes to see me. I usually bring her something." She lifted a beribboned box. "Chocolates."

"Very nice," I said.

"You want to come with us?" Elena asked.

"What? Me?"

"She likes to see new faces," Elizabeth explained. "Elena's coming with me."

I shook my head. "I'll wait for you out here."

"What are you doing here, anyway, William?" Elena asked.

"I just sit around here sometimes," I said.

"Why?"

"I don't know."

"To watch the insane people," Elizabeth said.

"Like animals in a zoo," Elena added in an accusatory tone.

"It's a nice little park, that's all," I said.

Elizabeth's eyes bore into me. "If you're so interested in insane people, why don't you come in with us?"

It was an outright challenge, and with Elena standing there I had no choice but to take it up.

"All right," I said boldly.

"You don't have to be afraid," Elizabeth added.

"I said all right, didn't I?"

I stepped in front of them, gallantly leading the way. Whitman House loomed ahead but I kept a steady pace. There was, of course, nothing at all to fear, but I did not know that at the time and in my mind I saw the interior of Whitman House as a dark labyrinth of seamy hallways down which inhuman cries echoed continually, a world where muscular orderlies brutally wrestled murderous, popeyed lunatics to the floor.

"I guess your grandmother has her own room," I said hesitantly.

"Yes," Elizabeth said. She was walking jauntily beside me, the box of chocolates nestled in her arms.

"Is her room near the front door?"

"No. Second floor."

I could feel my skin tightening around my bones. What in the name of God had I gotten myself into?

At the entrance I stepped back, opened the door, and allowed Elizabeth and Elena to pass in front of me. They strode briskly into the building and trooped directly up to the receptionist's desk.

"Hello, Elizabeth," the receptionist said. She appeared to be a nurse, dressed all in white, with a little peaked cap emblazoned with a red cross.

"Hello," Elizabeth said. "I brought something for my grandmother."

The woman behind the desk smiled benignly. "Well, you may go on up and give it to her, then." She looked at Elena. "Who's your friend?"

"Elena Franklin. She lives down the block."

The woman's eyes lifted toward me. "And the gentleman?"

"That's Elena's brother, William," Elizabeth said.

I brought a stiff smile to my lips.

"Well, your grandmother is waiting," the woman said. "I'm sure she'll enjoy seeing you."

Elizabeth led Elena and me up a wide spiral staircase to the second floor, then down the hall, mercifully empty and silent, to her grandmother's room.

"Hello, Grandma," Elizabeth said as she opened the door.

Elena and I followed in behind her and watched as she stepped up to her grandmother's bed.

The old woman was sitting upright, propped against two enormous pillows. Her eyes twinkled when she saw Elizabeth.

"Did Mama take you to the castle?" she asked.

Elizabeth nodded. "I brought you something." She pulled the ribbon from the box and held it out. "Chocolates."

Her grandmother took the box, lowered it to her lap, and stared at it a moment. The box was pale yellow and trails of small red rosebuds adorned the four sides. I still see chocolates adorned this way from time to time, part of the grace we have not lost.

"You can open it, if you want to," Elizabeth said quietly.

The old woman wiped her mouth with her hand and glanced out the window.

"You can have a piece of candy now," Elizabeth said.

A look of alarm suddenly passed over her grandmother's face. "Dogs'll get you if you don't watch out," she said.

Elizabeth's eyes closed briefly, then opened. "I brought some people to see you," she said, forcing a smile.

Suddenly her grandmother snatched the ribbon from Elizabeth's hand. "Gimme that," she snapped. "I want it!"

"Yes, take it," Elizabeth said quickly.

I felt Elena draw back toward me.

The old woman peered back down at the box of chocolates.

Elizabeth took a small white cloth from the table next to the bed and pressed it tenderly at the side of her grandmother's mouth.

Instantly she slapped Elizabeth's hand away. "Lily took it," she said. "I don't have none."

Elizabeth replaced the cloth on the table and looked at us.

"Sometimes she's better than this," she said.

"It's all right," I told her.

Then Elena stepped toward the bed. "I'm Elena," she said.

The old woman glared at her irritably. "Lily took it, not you."

"Lily was her younger sister," Elizabeth told Elena in a whisper.

Elena's hand swept out in my direction. "This is my brother, William."

I stepped forward haltingly. "Glad to meet you."

She did not look at me. Her gaze fell back down toward the box.

"Want me to open it for you, Grandma?" Elizabeth asked. "It's chocolates. You like chocolates."

"Teddy," her grandmother muttered. She was still looking at the box, her fingers moving shakily along the line of rosebuds. "Teddy died. Daddy doesn't know." She moved her hands over the edges of the box, then stopped, her eyes dwelling on her fingers. "Lily took the whole thing. I seen it."

Elizabeth gently tugged the box from her grandmother's hands and opened it.

"Look, Grandma," she said, lowering the box back into the old woman's lap. "Chocolates."

Her grandmother stared aimlessly at the small, rounded candies. Her head slumped forward slightly.

Elena stepped back to my side and smiled sadly.

Elizabeth took one of the chocolates and delicately placed it near her grandmother's lips. The mouth opened and Elizabeth slid the candy in.

"It's good, Grandma," she said.

The old woman munched slowly, her eyes still fixed on the box.

Elizabeth raised her hand and began gently stroking her grandmother's hair, her fingers gliding slowly up and down the long, wiry strands.

I glanced down at Elena, and something in her face held my gaze. She was watching Elizabeth and her grandmother intently, but it seemed to me that she was also watching the room — the texture of the drapery, the picture of a seascape that hung slightly askew above the bed, the iron railing of the bed itself, the quality of the light as it flowed through the window, silvering the air — all those small, almost invisible details that, as she would later write in *Quality*, "render unto some imagined space the wry and subtle poignancy of earth."

When it was over, they called it, rather romantically, "The Plague of the Spanish Lady." It was the great influenza epidemic of 1918–19. It killed a half-million Americans, and various places responded to it in various ways. They closed the schools in New York, held court in the open air in San Francisco, distributed medicated masks to the entire population in Seattle.

In Standhope, however, we only waited, though with surprisingly little dread. I can remember Elena and myself standing in the school yard listening to a group of children singing the verses to a song that everyone thought extremely funny:

> "I had a little bird and his name was Enza.
> I opened the window and
> In-flu-enza."

For quite some time, the flu epidemic was something that only existed in the newspapers. The slumber of Standhope continued undisturbed. In the small schoolhouse only a few blocks from Wilmot Street, Elena worked at her multiplication tables or relentlessly practiced her penmanship, monotonously drawing the interlacing circles and parallel lines required by the Palmer method, while only a few doors away I struggled through *Poor Richard's Almanac* or marveled at the stately prose of the *Leather-Stocking Tales*.

Then, rather suddenly, Jeremy Blake died. The effect of his death on Standhope was surprisingly severe. The war had ended only a short time before, and some people in Standhope were still wearing "To H–ll with the Kaiser" buttons when the Spanish flu struck. It seemed an unbearable affront, as if from now on we were destined to endure one mortal trial after another. I remember that Mrs. Farrington, the first-grade teacher, wept openly when she announced Jeremy's death to the class, and that even the mayor, surely one of the last men in Standhope to sport a handlebar mustache, looked broken and desolate at his funeral.

Once begun, the plague was a long time passing, and during that period, the single line that connected the various shuttered households of our town was the peripatetic Dr. Houston.

He treated the symptoms of the disease in a hit-or-miss fashion: senna as a purgative, ammonium carbonate to clear the bronchial tubes, phenacetin for fever, nux vomica for the nervous system, digitalis for the heart. He lived in a cloud of medicinal odors, from camphor to cardamom, and each day he seemed to rise with a renewed energy, as if this battle were truly his own. "In one corner, Death," as Elena later said, "and in the other, at one hundred ninety pounds, Standhope's favorite son, Dr. Winston Barrett Houston."

The epidemic was the medical emergency for which Dr. Houston had been waiting all his life, a chance to be the central figure in a great drama of life and death. He took to his role like a seasoned stage performer, moving from house to house with tireless energy, shouting orders at the top of his voice, sending everyone within earshot scurrying about for wet clothes or iodine or baking soda or anything else his chaotic treatment required. "He never seemed more alive," Elena wrote in *New England Maid*, "than in this lethal season."

All my life I have expected to die young. I am over eighty now, and I still expect it. But I have been close to death only once. It started with a cough. I had been sitting in the living room reading *Great Expectations* as if it were no more than a British "penny dreadful." Elena sat across from me, poring over *A Christmas Carol*, though far less intently. Then, suddenly, I coughed, and Elena jerked her head up from her book.

"Do you feel hot, William?" she asked.

"I feel fine," I said, a little annoyed at being pulled away from the woes of poor Pip. Then I saw it: the concern in her face. The dreaded plague. I felt a wave of heat shoot up from the soles of my feet. "Elena," I said softly, "do you think . . . ?"

"I don't know," Elena said quickly.

A breeze rustled the blue curtains at the living room window. I could have sworn it was the wing of death.

"It's just a cough, maybe," Elena said. The somber tone of her voice was not reassuring.

"Maybe I'd better tell Mother," I whispered.

"I'll tell her," Elena said. She bounded out of the room, and within a few seconds my mother was staring down at me with her wondering, confused eyes.

"How do you feel, William?" my mother asked.

"Fine," I said weakly.

Elena watched me, worried. I coughed again and she shrank away, staring at me as if I were already dead.

"Do you feel tired?" she asked.

"That's enough, Elena," my mother blurted. However vaguely, she could sense the terror in my mind.

"Have I got it?" I asked softly.

"Do you have a headache?" Elena asked.

"Quiet, Elena," my mother whispered. "You're scaring William to death." My mother was not one to search for the best choice of words.

"How about breathing?" Elena asked frantically. "Are you breathing okay?"

I still do not know where Elena learned the symptoms of the Spanish flu, but she certainly knew them.

My mother stamped her foot. "Go out and play, Elena."

"It's raining."

"Then go into your room!"

Elena walked slowly down the short hallway to her room. She did not close the door, and I knew that she was listening.

"Now, William," my mother said, then she stopped, thinking, trying to get her disordered mind around this strange new circumstance. "Well, now, William . . . uh . . . um . . . let me know if you get worse."

"What if I've got it?" I asked shakily.

"Well, uh, just don't worry it, don't worry it," my mother sputtered. "It'll go away, that's what it'll do. It'll go away."

And with that she disappeared into the kitchen, leaving me alone in the room, my mind wildly calculating all the things I would miss in life by dying at such a tender age.

Elena came back into the living room a few seconds later and sat down across from me. She pulled her legs up under her and observed me carefully.

"I think I've got it," I told her mournfully.

"You'll know soon, one way or the other," Elena said.

She was right. I did. Within a few hours the coughing became more severe and I began to develop a dull, throbbing pain, which began behind my eyes then swept out across my head and down throughout the lumbar region. A heaviness fell upon me, parts of my body became numb, and my consciousness began to swim in and out as if I were being pulled under water and then raised up again.

The next morning I awoke to hear Elena pleading with my mother to summon Dr. Houston. My mother was having a good deal of trouble deciding what to do, and I could hear her broken, half-finished sentences jerking along as she tried to respond to Elena's insistence.

"You've just got to," Elena said in a high, lean voice. "You've just got to, right now!"

"Well now, Elena, you've, uh, you've . . . listen, I, uh, maybe some juice would be good for him."

"*No!*" Elena shouted. I heard her feet scurrying across the living room floor and then the hard, almost brutal slam of the front door. The unseasonable warmth of the day before had given way, as it often does in New England, to a frigid morning, and as I glanced out the window I saw a few snowflakes drift down and imagined that this would certainly be the last snowfall I would ever see. Then I felt the darkness sweep down upon me and I was asleep.

When I woke up, Dr. Houston was standing over me. Elena had stationed herself directly beside him, shivering in a thick red cloth coat, her hair wet and stringy from the melted snow.

Dr. Houston watched me for a moment, then sat down on the bed and took my temperature. It was a dangerous 104 degrees, and he made no attempt to conceal the state of things. He glanced at my mother, who had edged herself into the doorway, and nodded solemnly. She stiffened and fled the room, her way of bearing the unbearable.

"Has he got it?" Elena asked.

"Yes," Dr. Houston said. He turned to me. "You're going to have to fight, William," he said. He hoisted his medical bag onto the bed. "I've got all the tools in here, but you're going to have to help me. It's a war, young man. Like our boys went to in France. They put up a fight and won, and now you must, too."

"William wants to be a soldier," Elena said. I wanted to be no such thing, and she knew it, but I think that in her child's mind she understood that this might encourage Dr. Houston to do his utmost for my life.

"Good for him," Dr. Houston said. He kept his eyes on me. "We need soldiers."

I nodded.

Dr. Houston turned to Elena. "Would you be a good little girl and go get me a spoon, honey?"

Elena did as she was told, and when she returned Dr. Houston administered a host of foul-tasting elixirs. Then he stood up.

"I'll be going, now," he said, "but I'll be back to look in on you."

Elena's eyes shot around to him. "Maybe you should just stay here," she said.

Dr. Houston laughed. "Stay here? Why, I can't do that, honey. There are other sick people who may die without my assistance."

"William's going to be a soldier," Elena lied. "Soldiers are more important."

"I'm sure they are," Dr. Houston said. "But there are still other sick people I have to see. There's no one else in Standhope who can help them, you see?"

"No," Elena said flatly.

Dr. Houston's face suddenly turned sour. "Well, you will in time," he said, with an unmistakable edge in his voice.

"You stay here," Elena insisted. "You stay here in case William gets worse."

"Yes, well," Dr. Houston said, and then he started to move toward the door.

To my astonishment, Elena blocked his path.

"You stay here," she said. "You've got to."

Dr. Houston's face hardened. "Now look here, young lady," he said coldly, "I don't have time to waste on this sort of behavior. Now please, get out of my way."

Elena stepped into the doorway, lifted her arms, and pressed her hands against the door jamb.

"He's going to be a soldier," she said, "and you've got to stay until he's better."

Dr. Houston took a deep, angry breath, stepped forward, and with one sweep of his powerful arm pushed Elena out the door, sending her sprawling in the hallway.

Through the haze of my illness I saw Elena leap to her feet, then disappear down the hall, following Dr. Houston.

"Mrs. Franklin, please!" Dr. Houston shouted, but I could not make out much else of what he said. I could hear my mother sputtering for Elena to leave the doctor alone. "Now, Elena, uh, you, well, the doctor, you've got, listen, I've . . ." Then I heard more scuffling about in the living room, and Elena's peeling voice. "You've got to stay here, you've just got to!" The front door slammed, and after that, silence, except for Elena's low whimpering as she cried softly by the window. For me the entire scene was more or less unreal, coming to me, as it did, through the fog of my illness. But later I learned that Elena had actually made a frenzied leap and struck Dr. Houston in the face, then followed him to the door and flung her shoe at his head as he dashed down the walkway to his car.

In *New England Maid*, Elena wrote: "During the influenza epidemic of 1918–19, Standhope became a world in which every infirmity, even the slightest, most inconsequential cough, held the possibility of unparalleled ruin, in which life betrayed itself in death, leaving in its wake the shocked and helpless anger of unanticipated grief. Surely within the history of disease there is an unexplored human terrain that is made up almost entirely of rage."

During the next forty-eight hours, I moved in and out of the world with each beat of my heart. I can remember feeling that my body was being pressed down by huge weights, my lungs aching with each breath. "My brother drew life in with each inhalation," Elena wrote, "and with each exhalation tried to drive it out again."

On the third morning of my illness, I awoke in a bed literally soaked with my own sweat. There was a terrific pounding behind my eyes and my head felt as if it were about to blow apart. I looked up and saw Elena sitting quietly beside my bed, her hands curled into her lap.

"Hello, William," she said. Her face was drawn, pale, terribly weakened, as if she had gone through the same illness I had.

I lifted my hand to wave to her, and as I did so, a spurt of blood suddenly shot out of my nose, spilling across my bedclothes.

Elena jumped to her feet and ran for my mother.

Seconds later my mother dashed into the room, stared at the blood as if transfixed by it, and then shouted, "Clean it up, Elena! Clean it up!"

Elena pulled the nightshirt from my body, and wiped my face with a wet cloth.

"You're going to be all right," she said softly.

I looked at her languidly, then dropped my head back on the pillow. In my half sleep, I could feel her stroking my face and hair, squeezing my fingers one by one, murmuring softly, "You'll be all right, William. You will. You just have to."

None of us could have known it then, but that sudden burst of blood was the signal that my fever had finally broken and that I would surely live.

I awoke again a few hours later. Elena was still sitting beside the bed.

"Where's Father?" I asked.

"He's not here," Elena said. "We tried to reach him, but he wasn't in the hotel he said he was going to be at."

I nodded and closed my eyes.

In the final paragraph of the chapter of *New England Maid* that deals with the epidemic, Elena wrote: "My father could not be located during the critical illness of my brother. Because of that, an important experience was lost to him, the special joy of caring for a beloved person who is deathly ill, of soothing him with your voice, cooling him with water, loving him more now, at the edge of loss, than you have ever loved."

I have often wondered what my father must have felt when he read that.

Within a week I was perfectly fit again, although still weak. Often I would sit on the front steps and watch the people pass. Elena usually joined me. She seemed preoccupied with having nearly lost me, forever going over how things would have changed if I had died.

"Your room would be all empty," she said on one occasion. "And I'd have to give the boat away." She meant the Yankee Clipper I had laboriously constructed and which sat like a trophy on my bureau. "And your clothes, your ice skates — no one to use those." She looked at me quizzically. "There's only one of everybody. Only one."

I laughed. "Boy, that's hot news, Elena."

She was only nine years old, and for her, I think, it was.

Where does art begin? We do not know. For its first fruits are nearer to the end than the beginning:

> I go to places in the night,
> Full of terrors dark and bright,

Into forests black and deep
Through which I wander, stumble, creep.
At last I wait until the light
Reveals my courage or my fright.
And then I toss and leap and whirl
Till I return, a little girl.

Elena wrote this poem when she was ten. Nothing she wrote after that more fully revealed her. "In the prologue," as Elena wrote to Martha Farrell not long before she died, "is the coda."

And so I gave this poem to Martha after she first posed the inevitable question. We were sitting in the house on the Cape. To the right we could see the first buds in the flower garden Elena and Jason had planted together many years before. Martha was having a cooler, something made of white wine and seltzer. She was dressed in summery yellow pants and a white blouse, but her mood was deadly earnest.

"I'm after that first spark of creativity," she said, "that very first spark. Was she two or five or twelve? When?"

"You mean when did she actually produce something?"

"Yes."

"She was ten."

"And what was it?"

"A poem."

"A poem. Really? Go on."

Elena was ten, and when I first read that strange poem about a threatening wood, I could not imagine that its author was my sister. She had handed it in to Mrs. Nichols, her fifth-grade teacher, and something in it so alarmed her that she came to visit my mother.

I answered the door. Mrs. Nichols was wearing a dark blue dress which reached to her ankles. There was a thin line of white piping at the hem and collar, but otherwise the dress was quite plain. I remember how homely Mrs. Nichols appeared to me, even at this time in my life, when the humblest female form was beginning to inspire more than a little interest on my part.

"I'm Mrs. Robert Nichols," she said, "Elena's teacher. You're William, aren't you?" She was speaking very rapidly. "I wonder if I might speak with your mother."

"Sure," I said. "Come in."

I walked into the kitchen and brought my mother out into the living room. She was wearing a loose-fitting house dress, and I remember feeling somewhat ashamed of her appearance.

"This is Mrs. Nichols," I told my mother.

She said nothing; nor did she offer her hand. It had been perhaps a year since anyone had been to our house.

Mrs. Nichols cleared her throat. "Pleased to meet you, Mrs. Franklin," she said.

"Pleased, too," my mother said, almost in a whisper.

"She's Elena's teacher," I explained.

Mother glanced about the room. "Where is she? Where's Elena? Is she lost?"

"Mrs. Nichols just wants to talk to you," I said.

"That's right," Mrs. Nichols said quickly. I could tell by the apprehensive expression on her face that she already understood that poor Mrs. Franklin was one of nature's oddities.

"Why don't you ask Mrs. Nichols to sit down," I told my mother in a gentle coaxing voice.

She responded by doing nothing at all. She simply continued to stare mutely at Mrs. Nichols. It had been so long since she had received a guest that she had no idea what to do with one.

"Sit down, Mrs. Nichols," I said. I pointed to a chair. "Over there."

"You sit there, Mother," I said, again pointing to a chair.

Both women took their seats.

"Mrs. Nichols came to talk to you about Elena," I reminded my mother.

"Yes," Mrs. Nichols said, "I did. It's about a poem Elena wrote for a class assignment." She pulled a piece of lined white paper from her purse and handed it to my mother. "This is the poem."

My mother took the paper from Mrs. Nichols and read it, her lips moving as she did so, a crude, ignorant gesture which Mrs. Nichols did not miss.

When my mother had finished, she handed the poem back. "That's nice," she said happily.

"Nice?" Mrs. Nichols asked, astonished.

"It rhymes," my mother explained. "It all rhymes."

Mrs. Nichols leaned forward, raising the pitch of her voice a bit, as if talking to a small child. "Mrs. Franklin, this poem disturbs me."

My mother stared at her dumbly.

Mrs. Nichols rubbed her palms together. "Disturbs me," she repeated emphatically. "The violence, I mean, the underlying violence."

My mother nodded, but it was clear that she had not the slightest idea what the woman was talking about.

Mrs. Nichols edged forward in her chair. "The poem is, well, it's so full of violent things, dreadful things. And Elena is of such a tender age, as you know."

My mother blinked hard. "You think Elena feels bad, is that it?"

"Yes, that's it," Mrs. Nichols said, relieved.

"She's sick?" my mother asked.

Mrs. Nichols glanced at me helplessly, then looked at my mother. "Not exactly sick. It's not like a stomachache. It's something deep inside Elena, something that is disturbing her." She tapped her forehead with her index finger. "Something in her mind."

"Mrs. Nichols means that Elena might be upset about something," I explained.

"Upset?" my mother asked. "What about?"

"I don't know," Mrs. Nichols said, "but I have to tell you that Elena acts oddly sometimes. She daydreams quite a bit. She often stares out the window during class. She looks sullen. I've tried to break through to her, but I've not had much success."

I had often noticed Elena staring out the window, too, but her expression had never struck me as sullen. If anything, she looked thoughtful, contemplative.

"Are you saying that Elena's not normal, someway?" my mother asked.

"I don't know, Mrs. Franklin," Mrs. Nichols said, growing more exasperated. "But that's part of the problem, you see. Elena is very hard to know." She shifted in her seat, and then went on. "I do think — I don't want you to take this the wrong way; but I do think that Elizabeth Brennan is not the best influence on Elena right now."

"Why not?" I asked.

Mrs. Nichols shot me a withering look. "I'm speaking to your mother, William."

I drew back in my chair.

Mrs. Nichols turned back to my mother. "All the other children write about pleasant things," she went on. "They write about swimming or ice-skating. Pleasant things. Do you see the difference between that and what Elena writes about?"

My mother tilted her head to the left and said nothing.

Mrs. Nichols looked at her sternly, unable to keep the severity from her face.

"I don't want to pry into your personal affairs, Mrs. Franklin," she said, "but as a teacher, I thought it my duty to discuss these matters with you."

"Is Elena misbehaving someway?" my mother asked.

Mrs. Nichols sighed. "No, Mrs. Franklin," she said, "not in any particular way." She stood up. "I'm sorry to have bothered you."

My mother got to her feet and smiled brightly. "Thanks for coming," she said. "And if Elena starts misbehaving, you let me know."

"Of course," Mrs. Nichols said dully. She looked at me. "Will you see me to the door, William?"

I stood up and followed Mrs. Nichols out onto the porch. My mother was still standing in the living room looking puzzled when I closed the front door.

Mrs. Nichols turned to me. A small breeze lifted the collar of her dress and she patted it down firmly.

"I'm worried about your sister, William," she said, "and I don't think I made that clear to your mother. The nature of the problem, I mean."

"My mother has a hard time understanding things," I told her.

"And your father?"

"He's away a lot."

"I see," Mrs. Nichols said dolefully. "I suppose it's up to you, then."

"What?"

"To speak with Elena," Mrs. Nichols explained. She handed me the poem. "Read this, William, and talk to her."

I glanced down at the lines written in Elena's tiny, strangely broken script. I could not imagine what all the fuss was about.

"I leave it to you, William," Mrs. Nichols said. "I'm sure you can explain things to Elena."

"Yes, I will," I assured her.

She smiled thinly, then walked quickly away.

I looked down at the poem again and tried to discover what had so distressed Mrs. Nichols. I was still poring over it a few minutes later when Elena came walking up the street. She lifted her hand as she came up to me.

I held the paper out to her. "Mrs. Nichols brought your poem back."

Elena did not seem in the least concerned. "Why?"

"She didn't like it," I told her. "She didn't like it at all."

"She likes Longfellow," Elena said casually. " 'The Song of Hiawatha.' That's what she reads to us in class." She lowered her voice, imitating Mrs. Nichols's stentorian style of recitation. "Forth upon the Gitche Gumee. On the shining Big-Sea-Water. With his fishing . . ."

"It's not funny, Elena," I said sternly. "She came over here to speak with mother."

"About the poem?"

"Yes."

"Why?"

"She said it was bad, disturbing," I told her. "She said there were a lot of strange things in it."

Elena looked entirely puzzled. "Strange? She said strange?"

"That's right. It was so bad she came all the way over here to talk to mother. She looked pretty upset, too. Mrs. Nichols, I mean."

Elena watched me quizzically but said nothing.

"You'd better be careful what you write, Elena," I said. "Mrs. Nichols has her eye on you."

"But it's just a poem," Elena said.

"Mrs. Nichols doesn't think so," I said emphatically. "She thinks you shouldn't write — about black forests, creepy things like that."

For a moment, Elena seemed unsure of what to do. She took the poem from me and read it. Then she looked up. "All right," she said wearily. "I'll write something else next time." Then she walked into the house.

I went for one of my long walks, then returned home around sundown. Elena was still in her room. I knocked on her door.

"Come in," she called.

Elena was sitting on her bed, a pad in her lap, a pencil in her hand. She held out the pad to me. "Maybe this is better."

There was a poem written on it:

I like vacations very much.
I like to feel and smell and touch
The flowers that grow straight and still
At the top of some old hill.
I think that they are best in spring.
That's when vacations are the thing.

"Do you like it?" Elena asked.

"It's fine."

Elena snatched the paper from me, crushed it in her hands, and threw it violently across the room.

"It's stupid!" she blurted vehemently.

I shrugged. "It's just a poem. What difference does it make?"

Elena shook her head. "Go away, William," she said. Then she pointed to the door. "Go away."

Martha nodded appreciatively after I had finished my story.

"Ah, so Elena was suppressed," she said.

"Suppressed?"

"Her creativity. It was suppressed," Martha explained. She took a sip from her glass. "That's the trouble with bureaucratic education. It's incapable of dealing with exceptional children, so it suppresses them.

I nodded. "Perhaps."

"Have you read Katz's critique of nineteenth-century school reform?"

"No."

Martha shook her head. "Terrible what that system was designed to do. Not to educate at all." She smiled. "I can deal with that in Elena's biography. The school she attended was based on a nineteenth-century model."

"I see."

"A school system like that simply can't deal with a gifted child."

"What system can, Martha?" I asked quietly.

She tried to answer, tried conscientiously to answer, calling forth a wealth of learning I could not help but admire. But in the end I was left with Elena, the image of a piece of paper crushed in her hand, of her arm flinging it through space, and it seemed to me that Mrs. Nichols mattered no more to Elena than the school system

Martha was excoriating; that there exists a kind of person who cannot be stopped so easily in his course, the sort for whom passion is not so much an energy as a fate.

I suppose Elena felt betrayed in what we later referred to as "the affair of the poem." I had joined the other camp, that chorus of voices cheering for a scrubbed and polished world. She was left with only one ally: Elizabeth.

They spent almost all their time together now, the two of them shrinking from my approach. I often heard their voices in the shed out back, or behind the bedroom door, which Elena now kept closed to me.

Of course, I was not the only victim of their exclusiveness. Poor Mrs. Nichols suffered far more than I. Elena and Elizabeth launched a conspicuous campaign of silence against her. They sat at the back of her classroom, arms folded over their chests, eyes staring straight to the front of the room, never speaking unless called upon directly. They did the standard exercises well enough and always read what was assigned them. But when asked to produce a poem or a short story or an essay — something, that is, of their own creation — the two of them would conspire to produce works of frightening banality, singsong verses about bluebirds, for example, which went on for page after ludicrous page. Sitting morosely in the front room, I would hear them giggling uncontrollably over their latest creation, and often, when they finally emerged from Elena's room, they would quickly pass out into the yard without so much as a glance in my direction. I was fifteen years old and should have had a life of my own. But I didn't, and so their scorn stung me. Tall, lanky, inhumanly shy, I was plagued by an awkwardness that accompanied me everywhere, an invisible demon forever tripping me in public places or turning over water glasses.

All of this — the loneliness, the sense of being hopelessly awkward and unattractive, the unmistakable scorn of my sister and Elizabeth — produced in me a self-loathing I could not escape except in fantasy.

And so I dreamed of friendship and communion, of some wild boy from a distant land. I imagined him as having a dark complexion and fiery black eyes, telling tales of Krishnapur in a voice accented with that exotic place. Together we would discover a world of dark, vaguely sensual adventure. He would summon forth my self-confidence, dismiss my self-hatred, laugh all my pain away.

This wild boy never came for me, but from time to time I can still see him, dancing at the edge of McCarthy Pond or swinging from the limbs of the enormous elm that shaded our front lawn. He was the piece still missing, as Elena once described it, from the puzzle of my life.

Which is not to say, of course, that my childhood offered no adventures. The first one, I suppose, the very first, was a trip to New York.

I was sitting on the front steps when my father pulled into our driveway in a new car. Elena instantly came out of the house, with that look of eagerness she always had when she saw him in those days.

The car was a Wills Sainte Claire, a long, sleek convertible with a silver eagle hood ornament. I had never seen anything so beautiful in my life, and it seemed to me that my father had somehow found the secret to happiness: a life of high-class vagabondage.

I quickly got to my feet and raced toward him. Elena leaped off the porch behind. My father's arms spread out to her.

"How ya doing, Princess?" he said happily as he swept her up. "Missed you." He kissed her, then returned her to the ground.

"It's a great-looking car," I said excitedly.

My father smiled. "You bet it is, Billy," he said. He shifted his straw boater to the right. "Damn thing's got sixty-eight horse in the engine." He stepped proudly to the front of the car and slapped the hood. "It's got a two-hundred-sixty-seven-cubic-inch displacement. Spitting to go, every inch of her. Salesman said it was modeled after a Spanish power plant."

My mother walked out onto the porch and eyed us warily. The very sight of her seemed to dampen my father's mood.

"Wanna come out and give her a look?" he asked lamely.

My mother massaged her hands under her wet dishcloth, then walked back into the house.

My father smiled at Elena. "What do you think of her, Princess?"

"It's wonderful," Elena said. "It's so shiny."

"I'll tell you what's wonderful," my father said, "New York is wonderful. And that's where we're going. This car and you, Elena, and you, too, Billy, and me to do the fancy driving."

Elena and I stared at each other, stupefied.

"Well, you want to go, don't you?" my father asked grandly.

"Sure!" I said excitedly.

"Good," my father said. "I'll just step inside and clear things with your mother."

He dashed into the house and emerged a few minutes later with a single overnight bag.

"Got all your stuff in here," he said. "Okay, let's go."

"What about Mother?" Elena asked.

My father tossed the bag into the rumble seat, then looked at her. "You coming or not, Princess?"

Without the least hesitation, Elena leaped into the car. I walked around to the other side and took a seat in the front next to my father.

"Ain't this buggy swell?" he crooned. He glanced toward the house. My mother stood at the window, her fingers tugging gently at her lower lip. He frowned slightly, then glanced back at Elena. "You got to give a little something to life," he muttered, "if you wanna get something back."

Once on the road, my father grew extraordinarily expansive. He prattled on about trips he had made in the past, and it was quite a few years before Elena and I realized how much of what he told us was untrue. He spoke of Paris, London, Rome, compared their food and traffic. His descriptive information came from the travel brochures we often found nestled among the clothes in his open travel bag. Thus London was "a foggy town." Paris was "a city of lights." Rome had seven hills, which, he said, made the traffic problem there "a real bottleneck." Amsterdam was aglow with tulips, but you had to watch yourself walking around Venice, because the streets were filled with water, and who would want to tumble in. "A work of the imagination," Elena would later write in *Quality*, "first requires the discipline of fancy." My father never learned that discipline.

We reached New York in about two hours, approaching it from the Connecticut shore, old U.S. 1, the back door of the city, winding first through Yonkers and the Bronx, then finally across the Harlem River to Manhattan.

"We'll take the Broadway route downtown," my father said a bit boastfully, demonstrating how well he knew what was to us a mythic city. Elena, sitting wide-eyed and awestruck in the back seat, took it all in, and she described it later in *New England Maid*: "We entered Manhattan by way of the old settlement the Dutch called Haarlem, but which, by 1920, when I first saw it, was a sprawling Negro reservation, a sweeping grid of dense, noisy streets, which to white eyes must have looked very gay indeed, gay and eccentric with its conk parlors and skin-bleaching emporiums, the blinking lights of the Apollo and the Savoy, the knot of Negro children 'street fishing' with pole and string, trying to retrieve a lost coin from the sewer." Such startling juxtaposition of the frivolous and grim runs throughout Elena's description of our journey through Manhattan that morning. But none of this darker appreciation was visible in her face then. She simply looked like a child whose mind was fiercely engaged in assimilating a rush of foreign data.

"And that's Columbia," my father announced, pointing to the left as we cruised down Broadway. I looked up and saw the rounded dome of Low Library.

"Maybe we should stop around here, have a highball, something like that," my father said.

We parked near a small soda shop only a few yards from the bustle of the Broadway trolleys. My father ordered three egg creams, a drink he said we must try, and we found seats at a table near the front window. I remember that the place was very cramped, that an advertisement for Alois Swoboda's conscious evolution system was taped to the wall, and that at a nearby table two earnest Columbia students were discussing the regatta with Cornell, which was soon to be run on Lake Cayuga.

"Ain't this a helluva town?" my father asked with an enormous smile.

Elena nodded and sipped her egg cream. "I like it here," she said. To the very end she would insist that her decision to leave Standhope and move to New York had been the single greatest one of her life. "Otherwise I might have remained — and in more ways than geographical — exactly where I was put down," she wrote in a letter to Martha Farrell, "another coin resting at the bottom of the pool."

After our brief refreshment, we continued on our way. My father drove us past St. John the Divine, which was still under construction, then swung west to Riverside Drive and took a short detour past

Grant's Tomb, and below it, in the river, Fulton's ship, the *Clermont*, which served as a fashionable tavern in those days.

"He shot himself, didn't he?" my father asked me tentatively. "In the jaw? President Grant, I mean."

I shook my head. "No, Father."

My father fixed his eyes on the road. "Facts aren't everything, Billy," he muttered, somewhat irritably.

We moved southward along the western edge of Manhattan until, at Fifty-ninth Street, my father turned left and we headed across town. Elena, still in the back seat, gazed about hypnotically. In *New England Maid*, she wrote: "The effect was kaleidoscopic, beautiful and amazing, especially to a mind as untutored and isolated as mine. For if all of this existed but two hours from Standhope, then what wonders lay four hours from it, ten, sixteen, twenty? If this wonder were New York, then what sights might strike us blind in Istanbul, how much gold on its towering spires, how long the lines around its public wards?"

At the southeastern corner of Central Park, my father grandly wheeled the Wills Sainte Claire up to the entrance of the Plaza Hotel.

"We'll stay here tonight," he said. Then he smiled and nodded to an enormous mansion just across the street. "You know, next door to old Connie Vanderbilt."

I looked over at the mansion, so very beautiful and remote behind the great iron gate and the circular drive.

"You mean people live there?" Elena asked. "That's a house?"

"Sure is," my father said. "And we're staying right next door."

Within a few minutes, my father had completed all the business of registering us. Elena and I had waited near the tea garden, too stunned to speak, watching the elegant men and women drift in and out of the lobby, carried, as they seemed, on air.

"Well, how about a walk," my father said as he came up from behind. He dropped his arm onto Elena's shoulder. "Feel up to it, Princess?"

"Sure."

"Well, let's give the legs a little work, then. And maybe after dinner we'll give them a rest, maybe take a victoria through the park like all the newlyweds do."

We walked out onto the street. It was late in the afternoon but people were everywhere, strolling along the sidewalk or sitting idly along the rim of the Pulitzer fountain.

"Let's head downtown," my father said. "Maybe find a restaurant, have an early dinner." He glanced at his watch. "I want to get back early, you know?"

"And so it was the good fortune of my brother and myself," Elena later wrote, "to stroll down a Fifth Avenue that would disappear within a decade, an avenue of stately, doomed mansions: Vanderbilt's Renaissance château, the Florentine palazzo of Collis Huntington, and last of all, that curious reproduction of Fontainebleau, whose wrought iron palisade was ordered sunk into the sea and thus preserved from man's vulgar desecration, though not from that of the sea snake and the shark."

We walked all the way to the library at Forty-second Street that afternoon, passed the great churches, St. Patrick's and the Collegiate, the few fashionable men's clubs that still dotted the avenue in those days, and that enormous array of expensive shops, one of which, I recall, was offering a rather risqué item, an "overnight case" for women.

Still, for all the elegance of the avenue, as Elena later wrote, it was the people who most fascinated, for they were unlike anything my sister or I had ever seen. Especially the women, who were entirely different from those in Standhope, their hair cut short and tucked under those tight-fitting toque hats so popular at the time, their eyebrows plucked into sleek thin lines, then penciled in for even more striking effect, their shoulders draped in mink or silver fox, their bodies made straight by dresses designed specifically to conceal their waists. "They did not, in 1920, appear precisely as those flappers on Easter Eve painted by John Sloan," Elena wrote in *New England Maid*, "but the spirit of that later rebellion was already rising as surely as the hemline of their skirts."

My father looked rather tired by the time we made it to Forty-second Street. Evening was falling over the city by then, though the frantic activity along the avenue had not in the least diminished.

"You know, that little snack uptown didn't quite do the trick," my father said, patting his belly. "Why don't we get a bite between here and the hotel."

As it turned out, we "got a bite" at a small but rather elegant restaurant a block or so from the Plaza. The atmosphere was very gracious: round tables with white tablecloths, cut flowers in crystal vases, a pianist at the back of the room gracefully offering selections from his lightly classical repertoire.

I suppose we looked rather odd, seated around that table. My father's stud pin, winking under the chandelier, must have been a disquieting touch for the waiter, as was Elena's wrinkled blue dress and my scruffy shoes. Still, he treated us with great politeness, conveniently looking away as my father poured a bit of whiskey from his hip flask into the teacup.

My father ordered a steak. I followed his lead. Elena asked about trout amandine, however, and after the waiter had explained it to her, she ordered it.

My father smiled. "That'll be a new experience for you, won't it," he said to her. "Fish with nuts." She said that it would. And then something very somber swam into his face, and he leaned toward her, and he said, "I love you, Elena. I always have." He did not look at me, did not give me the slightest glance.

We finished dinner quickly. My father was never one to linger in a place. He offered dessert, but we could tell that he really didn't want to be taken up on it. He wanted to leave, to get back to the hotel.

Our room was at the front on the third floor, facing the esplanade. There were only two beds, but a cot had been wheeled in for Elena.

"Well, I'm bushed," my father said as he slumped down on one of the beds, still entirely dressed, even down to his shoes.

"You're going to sleep now?" I asked.

"You got an objection to that, Billy?"

I shrugged. "I guess not."

"Good," he said. Then he closed his eyes.

For the next hour or so, Elena and I sat and talked about the day. She talked about street signs and shop windows. She was astonished by how many accents she'd heard on Fifth Avenue. We could hardly imagine the deep foreignness that must preside in those more exotic quarters our father had described, Little Italy and Chinatown and the Lower East Side.

Finally, at around nine, we were both exhausted. Elena took to the cot and I pulled myself into the bed across from my father. He was still lying on his back, snoozing peacefully, the hip flask resting on his chest.

I don't know exactly how long I slept, perhaps an hour, perhaps four or five. I remember hearing my father as he walked out of the adjoining bathroom, slapping cologne onto his face and neck. Then he put his jacket on and quietly walked out of the room, gently closing the door behind him.

For a while I continued to lie on the bed, my eyes closed, my mind once more going through the adventure of the day. But my father's cologne gave the room a cloying, musty smell, so after a moment I got up, walked to the window, and opened it. It was then that I saw him. He was standing beside the fountain, his hands thrust deeply into his trouser pockets, as if searching for a coin. From time to time he would weave right or left, then lean back on his heel. He was in constant motion, either tugging at the cuffs of his jacket, glancing down to check the shine of his shoes, fiddling with his tie, or checking his watch. He looked like a man who was waiting for something important. I could not imagine what it was.

She was wearing one of those fur-trimmed coat-dresses so fashionable at the time, and a felt hat. She was tall and walked very gracefully, with her head tilted upward. She approached him from behind, and when she reached him, she gathered her arms around his waist and threw her head back, laughing. He turned around, surprised, then threw his arms about her and lifted her off the ground. For an instant they only stared at each other. Then he kissed her.

I turned away, stricken, and then I realized that Elena was standing beside me, her eyes locked on the same unbelievable scene.

"Go back to bed," I told her sternly.

She shook her head. "No." She stepped closer to the window and stared down at the street. My father had drawn the woman under his arm and the two of them were walking away from the hotel.

"Where are they going?" Elena asked.

"I don't know."

We continued to watch them from the window. They were walking very slowly, arm in arm. Then, suddenly, my father spun around to face the fountain and tossed a coin into it. The two of them laughed and walked on, finally turning onto Fifth Avenue, where they disappeared around a corner.

In Elena's short story "The Tryst," two teenage girls hide a pornographic magazine, and as the story progresses, this sordid act and their mutual involvement in it corrodes and finally destroys their friendship. In "The Keepers of the Flame," two hunters stumble upon the body of a woman both have known and of whose murder both might be accused. Together they burn the body, bury the ashes, and leave the woods. But from that time onward, they speak to each other only in dark corners, only in whispers. "No novelist of her generation," one critic wrote of Elena in 1975, "has so intensely explored the corrosive quality of a single lie."

On the trip back to Standhope, Elena and I sat together in the back seat, locked in silent collusion. My father must have been mystified by the dark mood that had come over his two children, a fifteen-year-old boy who watched him sourly and refused to join him in the front seat, and his daughter, only ten, who stared at him silently but with neither anger nor resentment. For Martha, the incident at the Plaza became the central thread by which she traced Elena's psychological development. She found the secret of my sister's character in that moment by the window: "It can perhaps be stated that Elena Franklin's intellectual honesty flowed from this first experience of moral corruption, her directness from an early experience of extreme deviousness." Thus does a saint sire a prodigal and a prodigal a saint.

But I remember that Elena's response to what she must have known about our father, though perhaps a bit more vaguely than Martha suggests, was very muted. For a time, she took her cues from me and remained chilly toward him. Certainly she knew that something was amiss, but perhaps she also sensed a more general disarray. In her short story "A Summer Trail," a young woman blithely strolls through a pastoral wood until she begins to feel something dreadful around her, a rustling in the brush, which "was not made by wind or falling twigs but which came from the core of the forest. I gazed down at a tangle of vines, which seemed to have lain there through the millennia, silent victims of some early shiftlessness and disorder. And it seemed to me that along this summer trail I had found my way to the center from which all else goes out and then goes wrong, this first garden, our unkempt Eden."

Part of that "unkempt Eden" was my father's infidelity. But to Elena it was only a small part. She forgave him almost immediately, and never took her forgiveness back. For all the criticism of him in *New England Maid*, this particular incident is left out. Martha explained this by praising Elena's reserve. But I think she left it out because it meant so little to her, and because by then she understood that her needs were not much different from her father's. "He didn't need a woman," she said to me once, "he needed passion, and the only place he found it was in bed." She was living in Paris by then, writing *Inwardness*, and passion must have been at the forefront of her mind, since at that time she was trying so passionately to exclude it from her life.

For my part, however, I never forgave him. My father's shadow pursued me everywhere: to the town square where we had sometimes gone with Elena to listen to the band; to Thompson's Drugstore, where he had bought us ice cream and told us riddles; to McCarthy Pond where, at least occasionally, he had taken us to swim. Standhope became the stage upon which my father had acted out the parody of his familial love. I despised it.

There is little to be done with such tumultuous feelings. And although in time their extremity declined, a little ache of unforgiven insult remained in me, one that did not leave entirely until my father died.

Still, there was a positive element as well. For since I hated Standhope, I also became determined to leave it. The only question was how this might be done. For me, the only answer was college. Since I was anxious to prove myself, I thought of Yale, in New Haven, which was not too far away, and of Columbia, in New York, which I had at least glimpsed from my father's car. I could vaguely recall the look of the campus, its sense of a walled-in city, a configuration that, in my insecure state, powerfully appealed to me. And so, in the fall of 1923, nearly a year before I could actually have entered the college, I wrote to Columbia. Within a week or two, I received a letter politely instructing me in the correct procedures for application. I showed it to my sister immediately.

She was sitting in the little shed in the back yard, her feet drawn up under her, a book in her lap.

"I got a letter from Columbia College," I said excitedly as I stepped up to the door.

Elena glanced up from her book. She was thirteen years old but already looked more like a woman than a child. She was wearing a burgundy skirt and white pullover sweater, and I remember thinking that in only a little time she would no longer be the object of purely innocent attention.

"Let me see the letter," she said.

I handed it to her and leaned against the door while she read it.

"I guess you'll be going soon, then," she said matter-of-factly as she handed me back the letter.

"I guess so," I said, playing down my elation.

Elena smiled slightly. "You want to leave very much, don't you?"

"Maybe," I said. I stepped into the shed and sat down beside her. "It's probably a good idea to go away to college. You want to leave Standhope?"

"I don't know, William," Elena said. She closed the book and wrapped both her hands around it. "I don't know about me, about leaving Standhope. But I know about you. You'll go as soon as you can." She scanned my face as if, in some premature way, she was guessing at my destiny.

"I wish you could come with me," I said, though not truthfully. I was ready to strike out on my own now, tired of everything that reminded me of the last few years, even my sister.

Elena glanced down at the book. Her hair was longer than it would ever be again, the strands falling almost to her breasts. "In books things are always moving, people and time," she said, "but really, things are stuck sometimes, completely stuck."

I shrugged. "You can get stuck anywhere, even at Columbia College." I draped my arm over her shoulder and began to draw her close. But she pulled away, almost sharply, and walked back into the house. She never told me the cause of that sudden brittleness, and so I didn't understand until she wrote about it in *New England Maid:* "My brother had taken the first steps out of a life that had so long engulfed us both in its timelessness and tedium. He was leaving all that was flat and pale, moving into a multitude of colors, into a city where the sky lit up at night and the earth trembled beneath your feet as if on the edge of a new creation. So good-by to the elm and the willow, the stream and the pond, the peace that is like death. Good-by to a desert outpost on the New Haven line, to blowing dust and crackling leaves, to monotones and monochromes and me."

I think Elena must have hated me at that instant when she jerked herself from my embrace. I hope it was the only time she did.

In the late spring of 1924, I was accepted by Columbia College and told to present myself on Morningside Heights in September. I expected things to go smoothly from then on. I would drift through the summer in Standhope, then head for New York in the fall. But in June, my mother experienced an emotional crisis from which she never fully recovered. She had always been jittery, living as if she were standing on a high ledge, staring down at the traffic below, sometimes leaning toward it, but always drawing herself back in time. Elena described her in *New England Maid:* "She was a tall, thin woman, high-waisted and erect, her hair pulled tightly behind her head and bound in a bun. She favored long print dresses, hemlines to the ankle, and never in her life wore a petticoat of either silk or crêpe de Chine. She had the body of a farm woman, tawny about the face and arms, thick necked and heavy footed, graceless but not plodding. For there was a contradictory quickness in her, one which spoke to other energies held deep within. Her eyes flashed within the oval of her slack and weary face, and her head sometimes jerked about, birdlike and anxious, distrustful of the crumbs held out to her."

Beyond all this, there was a certain sensuousness about her, which I never noticed until Elena graphically described it in what became a celebrated passage of her memoir:

> In the heat of summer it became visible; never in the winter or the fall. It rose to the surface of her face like a layer of warm, moist air. Suddenly the brown, weathered face took on a kind of tropical intensity, a lushness about the mouth and eyes. She would stretch out beneath the grape arbor upon a sheet she had taken from the line, kick off her shoes, and lie back, her arms spread out from her body as if floating on the grass, her eyes closed, her lips slightly parted. This was the only luxury she knew — the shade beneath the arbor, the sweetness of the grapes, the coolness of the grass, the crispness of the sheet beneath her. She would rest in this dreamy state for hours, languidly accepting a gift her husband had refused, the sense not of passion building but of passion spent.

Predictably, this passage came under close scrutiny when *New England Maid* was published in 1933. That a daughter could think of her mother in such overtly sexual terms was distressing to more than a few provincial critics: "Miss Franklin has in one particular passage of unprecedented tastelessness transformed her mother from the hardworking and thrifty lady she no doubt was into the lolling figure of a sultan's concubine," was one response. "*New England Maid* should only be read behind the green shades of the pornographer's shop," declared another. Still another was somewhat more temperate: "It is one thing for Mr. Freud to deal with intimate matters as a matter of science, and even for Mr. Lawrence and Miss Radclyffe Hall to deal with them in literature. But surely to allow such unwholesome preoccupations to besmirch the noble tradition of the memoir tests the limits of our liberal age." In this, of course, the critic recalled the reticence of Montaigne but conveniently forgot the candor of Augustine.

For my own part, I was somewhat disturbed by the passage when I first read it in 1932. I had always seen my mother as something of a drudge, helplessly tied to a wandering husband and two children whose characters and ambitions were entirely different from her own. As she declined further and further, I saw her madness as inevitable. After all, my grandmother had ended her days more or less locked in the back room of a New Hampshire farmhouse. Madness was something to which the Mayhews had always been disposed. Even so, I could not have predicted that my mother's long-standing nervousness and befuddlement would reach such severity.

It began rather subtly. Sometimes, for example, my mother would suddenly stop her stitching, glance toward the window, and absently allow her embroidery to slip to the floor. At other times she would stand at the sink, her fingers poised above the water, and watch the back yard as if it were about to move. By early summer, her daydreaming had worsened into what Martha calls "acute withdrawal." In the middle of the afternoon, my mother would unexpectedly walk to her room, close the door, and remain there until the next morning. Left to ourselves, Elena and I would fix dinner, and Elena would leave a plate for my mother in her room. Normally the food would be eaten by the next morning, when Mother would emerge casually from the bedroom with the empty plate in her hand.

By summer's end, however, even the most routine elements of life no longer existed for her. She neglected all her household duties. She would not wash herself and sometimes wore the same filthy dress for days. She began to mutter to herself, though never loudly enough for either Elena or me to understand a word of it. She was clearly edgy, irritable, but for the most part she remained silent, spending her days in her dark bedroom, where she felt, I imagine, some sense of peace and safety.

The question, of course, was what to do about all this. Elena and I discussed it quite often during those early days of our mother's illness. No solution emerged, however. At least, not until our father returned home in the middle of June. He had been gone for almost six weeks, our only contact with him those checks which were always in the mailbox each Wednesday, "the little love notes from Father," as Elena once called them.

It was a sweltering day, that Tuesday in June, when he pulled into the driveway. He bounced out of the car, then wiped his neck with a dark blue silk handkerchief.

"How you kids doing?" he asked brightly as Elena and I walked out onto the front porch to greet him. "Hot enough for ya?" He dug his fists into his sides and pivoted slowly, belly thrust out — a little potentate surveying his tiny estate. "Place looks good. Keep the lawn mowed real good, Billy."

I nodded. "I'm surprised you noticed."

He knew very well this was a dig, but he never allowed me the satisfaction of acknowledging it. "Let me tell you something, Billy," he said loudly, "these old eyes see all."

Well, those old eyes had not seen one thing: our mother prostrate on her bed in the middle of the afternoon. Elena, however, intended for him to see, and she got to the point immediately.

"Mother has a problem," she told him as he sauntered up the porch steps.

He stopped and looked at her. "Problem? What kind of problem?"

"She's gone off her head," I said flatly.

My father continued to look at Elena. "Where is she?"

"In her bedroom," Elena said.

"Sleeping?"

"More or less."

My father nodded. "Same way with all those goddamn Mayhews, a nest of loons, all of them." He scratched his chin. "How long's she been like this?"

"Almost a month," Elena said.

My father continued up the stairs. "Well, let's have a look."

He followed us into the bedroom, stared down at my mother's rigid body for a minute, then walked back into the living room and flopped down in the chair by the window.

"You got any ice water, Billy?" he asked, swabbing his neck again with his handkerchief. "Get me a glass, will you?" He looked at Elena. "Sit down, Princess, we're all going to have to talk about this."

From the kitchen, I could hear the two of them talking quietly. It was mostly Elena's voice, describing the onset of our mother's illness very matter-of-factly and in great detail.

My father was lighting up a cigar when I brought him the water. He took it quickly and gulped it down. "Look at this, Billy," he said, handing me back the glass.

"What?"

"This right here," my father said, fumbling inside his jacket pocket. He pulled out a piece of paper.

"Sit down and look at that," he said. He turned back to Elena. "Now, tell me, Princess, what do you make of your mother? Think she'll get better, or what?"

While Elena attempted to answer my father's question, I looked at the paper he had given me. It was some sort of advertisement for land in Florida, a place called Davis Islands.

"What's this?" I asked.

My father turned to me. "Did you read it?"

"Yes."

"And?"

"Well, it says they've sold eighteen million dollars worth of land in thirty-one hours."

My father nodded sagely. "That's right. Land around Tampa Bay. Davis Islands. And what does it say at the top, Billy?"

I glanced down at the ad. "It says, 'Sold out.' "

My father smiled. "That's right, Billy-boy. Sold out. And guess who got a piece of it before that happened?"

"You?"

"Damn right," he said with a wink. "That's what'll be putting you through Columbia, kid." He leaned forward and gave me a lethal stare. "Money don't grow on trees, Billy. You need to know where it comes from."

"Well . . . I . . . ."

Before I could finish, he'd turned back to Elena.

"It seems to me your mother has about had it, as far as the real world is concerned," he said.

"What do you mean?" I asked.

"I mean living out here with the rest of us," my father said. "You know what happened to your grandmother Mayhew? Had to lock her up in the back of the house." He shook his head. "We can't do that here. That's why we got Whitman House."

I stood up slowly. "Are you thinking about Whitman House for Mother?"

"Unless you want to tie her to a tree in the front yard," my father said.

I glanced at Elena. She was sitting quite calmly on the piano stool at the end of the room. She said nothing.

"Well, don't you think that's sort of a quick decision?" I asked, turning my attention once again to my father.

He shook his head. "Why should I? Christ, Billy, those Mayhews don't get better, they just get older. Instead of a middle-aged crazy woman, you get an old crazy woman." He looked at Elena. "You know how old your grandmother Mayhew was when they locked her up? Thirty-seven." He turned back to me. "Your mother is forty-two. It's surprising she lasted as long as she did."

For a moment no one spoke. My father sat back in the chair and puffed on his cigar. Then he crushed it into the ashtray by the window. "Of course, we'll have to make some other plans, too."

Elena looked at him. "What plans?"

"Well, the way I see it, Billy can go ahead to New York," my father said. "But what about you, Elena? What would you do?"

"I'd live here, at least for a while," Elena said. "Someone would need to check in on Mother."

My father shook his head. "A young girl like you, living alone in this town? You're only fourteen, Elena. It's one thing you being here with Billy. It's another story when it comes to living here by yourself."

"It would not be a problem for me," Elena said firmly.

"Well, for me it would," my father said. "No, we have to make other arrangements. You'll probably need to go live with my sister in Pawtucket."

Elena said nothing, but I could see that a great deal was going on in her mind.

"Hattie would love to have you, Elena," my father went on. "Got that big house with nobody to live in it with her, just poor old Hattie and all those pictures of her dead husband." He smiled. "Why, she'd treat you like a queen, Elena."

Elena turned away from him, her eyes riveted on the elm in the front yard.

"And I get up to that part of Rhode Island all the time," my father continued. "We could go into Providence once in a while. Maybe even into Boston. You've never been to Boston."

Elena leaned forward slowly and dropped her hands into her lap. "I don't want Mother put in Whitman House," she said.

"What?" my father asked. "Why not?"

"I can live with her here," Elena said evenly. "William can go on to Columbia. Nothing should stand in his way. But I don't want Mother put in Whitman House."

"Elena," I said hesitantly, "maybe you should just think about it, putting her in Whitman House, I mean. Look, she may never get any better, she might —"

"I don't care if she doesn't get any better," Elena said. There was an edge of anger in her voice. "I will not go along with putting her in the asylum. We can live here together."

"Well, what if you had trouble?" my father asked. "I mean real trouble of some kind. Something you couldn't handle."

"I have Elizabeth to help me," Elena said. "And Mr. Brennan."

My father nodded, then looked very pointedly at me. He knew what I should have done at that moment: at least volunteer to delay my entrance into Columbia. And he knew that I would not do it.

"What do you think, Billy?" he asked.

"I don't know."

"Think Elena can handle her?"

"Maybe."

He looked at Elena. "Are you sure, Princess?"

"Yes."

My father left the next morning, dragging his big black traveling cases behind him. Elena and I watched from the window.

I remained in Standhope for another two months. During that time, Elena and I carried on all the work of the household. Mother began to improve, though only slightly. She never became truly sane again, though from time to time she was able to care for most of her needs, feed and dress and bathe herself. "The relationship of a wedge of lemon to a cup of tea, a slice of cheese to a soda cracker," Elena wrote in *New England Maid*, "these were the connections of which my mother was aware. She had the simple view that the visible is real and the real visible. That her own fate might have been connected to that of millions in their turn, to vast structures into which she had not inquired, secular and religious authorities in whose enormous web she dully slept — that such complexity might touch the texture of her life, this was beyond my mother's will to learn and understand."

I left for New York in September of 1924. Elena waited for the train with me.

"You're doing the right thing, William," she said.

The whistle of the incoming train blew loudly some distance away. "It's funny, I've been looking forward to this for I don't know how long," I said, "but now, now that the time has come . . . well, I'm frightened, Elena."

Elena squeezed my arm. "You're going to do just fine. That's what Father says."

"He does?"

"That's what he told me. He said, 'Billy'll do just fine.' "

I know now that he'd said no such thing. Elena had made it up.

"I'll do my best," I told her.

The train pulled in a few seconds later, part of the old New Haven line, a real wheezer. I hoisted myself onto the first step, then turned to Elena.

"Well, any last words?"

She smiled, but very delicately, and her eyes seemed to look directly into the center of everything I feared and wanted, everything that had been denied and that now offered itself as a promise.

"Whatever you do, William," she said, "stay away from large black traveling cases."

I knew it then, and I've never entirely forgotten it. I looked down at her, at the sober care in her face, and I knew that that strange boy I had dreamed of for so long, the one who would know me well and love me for myself alone, was my sister.

In the photograph there are five of us. We are posing with mock seriousness before the doors of St. Paul's Chapel. In the background, down a slight incline, a few anonymous students can be seen strolling Columbia Walk. We had just come from some sort of senior gathering at Earl Hall. There had been quite a few of us milling about that august parlor, and a platoon of professors' wives had diligently served us hot tea in small bone-white cups. I remember that it was a formal occasion and that the women were dressed in their best Episcopalian attire. It was 1928. Sacco and Vanzetti had been executed a full six months before, but I heard their names mentioned more than once that afternoon, mostly by a knot of earnest young radicals who positioned themselves in one corner of the hall and eyed the rest of us with unmistakable contempt.

Still, despite the sober clothes, the china cups, and the aura of disgruntled politics, the afternoon had been a rather light affair. There was a good deal of talk about O'Neill's *Strange Interlude*. It had opened in January of that year, the curtain rising at 5:30, then coming down for dinner at 7:00, then rising again to a full-bellied audience at 8:20. Everyone wondered how Lynn Fontanne did it and whether the spiritual message was worth the physical ordeal.

After an hour or two, the gathering was over and most of the students began to filter out of Earl Hall. I wandered out with the people who had become my closest friends during the last four years.

And so there are five of us in the photograph. We do not look very formal. There is an impishness in our eyes, a casualness in our stance, an attitude of gentle mockery. We look as idle youth has always looked, hopelessly adrift, careless of ideas, cheerfully ignorant of the fate that will overwhelm us.

Harry Morton looks the least frivolous. He is standing at the far left, back straight, eyes aimed directly ahead, his shirt collar buttoned primly at his throat. Sam Waterman is next, leaning his crooked elbow on Harry's shoulder, a briefcase dangling from his other hand. Tom Cameron stands beside him, one hand curling around the lapel of his blazer, the other pressed deep into the pocket of his Oxford pants. Mary Longford has her arm in Tom's. She is wearing a long dark dress and cloche hat. I am standing next to her at the far right of the photograph. The picture was taken by a Columbia grounds keeper, who tried very hard not to shake the camera. Harry rewarded him with a ten-cent piece of pure gold.

It is odd now to think of it, but at the time I did not feel in the least privileged. If anything, I felt like an intruder in the temple, a peddler's son from rural Connecticut who had bluffed his way into an elite institution. For the first year, I had the uneasiness of the impostor. I half expected to get a letter from the administrators informing me that my acceptance at Columbia had been the result of a clerical error and that arrangements had been made for me to continue my education at some other institution more suitable to my gifts, a cow college in California, perhaps. The letter never came, of course, and as the months passed I began to relax. Still, the sense of inferiority remained, one of the more subtle injuries of my class background. I overcompensated by working furiously at my studies. "You worked at learning like a sweaty shipping clerk who dreams of owning his own line," Sam Waterman once told me. He was right. I dreamed of excelling in everything, of besting all the rich boys who had come to Columbia with their pockets full of their fathers' money. And yet at the same time, I felt that no matter what I did, I would always be beneath them, always lack what had come to them unasked for and undeserved. "You always wanted to have been born to something, William," Elena said one evening in 1936. "You could never be proud of making it on your own. You always thought there was something grubby about that. You inverted the American dream."

Certainly in those early years, I did precisely that. Consequently, when Harry Morton, the scion of an old moneyed family if there ever was one, approached me after an English class and complimented me on some now-forgotten remark I had made about Edmund Spenser, I fairly swooned with joy.

Harry Morton was the first friend I made at Columbia. He was a tall young man, very erect in stature. His face was angular, with strong, resolute features. He looked as though he had been carved from Puritan stone. "I would have gone to Harvard," he told me not long after we met, "but my family broke with that institution over some theological matter in 1804." He was careful in his speech, a stickler for grammar. His dress was equally proper. "He knows what an aristocrat should look like," Sam Waterman once said, "and so he makes it his business to look like one."

But that was not the whole of it. For academically ambitious though

I was, and very insecure, I was not a fool. And if Harry Morton had been nothing more than some witless dandy out of a Ronald Firbank novel, I would have had no use for him. But there was a good deal more to Harry than his exaggerated courtliness. There was a grace and selflessness that money alone could not buy. Elena once said that he lived within the comfort of a few great ideas, and I think that this was true. He was the kind of doleful Platonist who believes that ideas are far too noble to win the day with man. In this, he was hopelessly old-fashioned, and I suppose that his characteristic abstraction, his wealth, and his basic gentleness and charity would be perceived in certain quarters and with a certain justification as a vacuous paternalism. It would be very easy to see Harry's dropping that gold dime into the grounds keeper's hand as a monstrous gesture, utterly blind to the social relationship that produced it. This is how Sam Waterman saw it, and he told the story more than once during his brief flirtation with communism in the thirties. He always ended it with the same aphorism. I heard it first at a rally for the unemployed at Sheridan Square in 1932. Sam was standing at the top of the pedestal, practically swinging from the good general's stone sword: "And so, gentlemen, don't listen to those damned apologists who tell you that capitalism makes charity possible. Just remember, it also makes it necessary."

Of course, Sam did not see Harry Morton in the Burmese jungles ten years later, when he gave his small rations to the weakest men under his command after their plane had gone down miles from where Stilwell's troops were hacking out the Ledo Road. He did not see him stagger forward hour after hour, refusing to let his men give up, walking point himself, dropping only after he could hear the hatchets of Stilwell's coolies in the distance and knew that his men were safe.

That I met other people during my early years in New York is largely due to the dinners Harry gave from time to time and to which he invited a small number of acquaintances. The Morton family had owned a brownstone in Greenwich Village for years, and after Mr. Morton retired and moved back to Massachusetts, he turned it over to Harry, along with two steadfast servants and an Irish setter of extremely limited intelligence.

Harry lived as I might have imagined, in quietly elegant rooms, which he thought rather modest compared to the palatial Massachusetts estate. Sam said that you could live forever in that Village brownstone and never smell the anthracite or see the gutted earth or feel the heat of the Bessemer furnaces that had made it possible. And of course, he was right.

A paunchy man opened the door at Harry's brownstone on that night in October. I gave my name, and he escorted me into a large living room, where Harry and a few others were already sitting around an enormous marble hearth.

That evening I met two of the other people who were to pose with me in the photograph the grounds keeper took almost four years later. Tom Cameron was sitting across from Harry in an identical leather chair. They both stood up when I was brought into the room. Harry made the introductions. Then we all took our seats.

"Tom wants to be a poet," Harry said, and let the matter drop.

And yet, that word, "poet," was so powerful to me at the time that it seemed to alter the very atmosphere surrounding a person. In the present era, when the most vacuous expressions are said to be poetic, the word has lost its fullness, its sense of arcane and special understanding, the awe that inevitably surrounds a work of supreme and private force.

Tom came from the latest generation of a long line of well-heeled New York merchants. Like Harry Morton, he had gone to the best schools. Unlike Harry, he had applied to Harvard but had been rejected on the basis, as he always liked to say, of ideological incompatibility. He drank a bit too much, part of the signature of the time, the image of the world-weary alcoholic being for the twenties what the depressed suburbanite was for a later generation. Predictably, he also pretended to be able to play the violin, though he remained at best a mildly proficient amateur. His hero was Christopher Marlowe. "He would like to have been Faustus," Mary once said, "but learning never meant that much to him, although he might have sold his soul for a good review."

Unlike many aspiring poets of his time, "people who say nothing in verse better than they say nothing in prose," as Mary called them, Tom was a very hard worker. Or at least he gave that appearance, diligently writing through the night, his wastebasket filled with reams of discarded poetry. In the morning, he would emerge looking weary and bedraggled, as if his muse were a wrestler. Mary, of course, saw all of this as an intolerable affectation. "Tom has a gift for the expected appurtenance," she said. "It's the substance that gives him trouble."

No doubt Tom did have his affectations. He would often allow his eyes to wander soulfully during a conversation, as if he were deep in concentration. At other times, he assumed a rather stooped posture, as if the world's weight were entirely upon his shoulders. Once Sam remarked that he would have made a good actor. Mary replied that he already was one.

I saw Tom for the last time in 1948. By then he had been published enough by small presses or in obscure poetry journals to have gained a coterie of admirers. I had heard that he had gone to California with a group of such people to found some sort of poetry collective.

And so I was a bit surprised when I caught a glimpse of him striding across Washington Square late one August afternoon when the fountain was in full glory. He was in his middle forties, and his belly drooped over his wrinkled khaki pants, but it was unmistakably Tom. I followed him for a time, somewhat cautious about calling out to him. So much time had passed; I was not sure how he would receive me. So I simply trailed behind him, until he ambled over to Eighth Street, turned right, and walked into a small tavern. It was the sort that had a sawdust floor and rickety tables. There were pictures of deceased writers hanging all about, a rather ecumenical group, stretching from Jane Austen to James Joyce. Tom seemed very much at home. He smiled and shook hands with the young people who gathered around him, probably undergraduates from nearby NYU. He was wearing a T-shirt and a corduroy vest, upon which he had pinned a "Henry Wallace for President" button.

After a few introductory remarks, Tom began to read his verses. They sounded almost identical to those he had written while still an undergraduate at Columbia. They were in the same singsong, Burnsian style, far too musical for the current taste, which preferred the starkness of Eliot, the murkiness of Jeffers, the vast complexity of Pound.

I remember feeling that I should perhaps go over and say hello to Tom. There was a great deal of news about our old comrades: Harry had died on the Ledo Road; Sam was now richer than all his tribe, Mary was going through husbands like canapés; and Elena was working on her third book. There was news to report, certainly, but it struck me that Tom might not want to hear it. He had constructed his own world, and it was very frail, based upon the uncritical appreciation that only his new friends could genuinely offer. And here I was, the somber Iceman standing by the door, full of tidings that, at this point in his life, could only strike Tom as vaguely noisome. And so I simply slunk out the door, leaving him comfortably within the atmosphere his battered but resourceful vanity had created to hold the line against defeat.

Mary Longford sat on one of those outsize floral sofas so fashionable at the time but which now appear to resemble nothing so much as the living room version of an aircraft carrier. She was wearing a long black dress. Her hair was short, but not bobbed, and she was puffing a cigarette entirely without the sense of barely concealed furtiveness with which women often smoked in those days.

"Pleased to meet you," she said after Harry had introduced her to me. There was something far too chilly in her manner to generate any real attraction, even though she was a relatively pretty woman. Sam once referred to her as "a rather handsome man," but the masculine quality we sensed in her was probably related to our own idea of what masculinity meant: strength, determination, the capacity to hold forceful opinions and express them unhesitatingly. Mary certainly possessed all these qualities, but she added to them the most firmly antiromantic turn of mind I had ever encountered. She believed that all things turned sour in their time, that the world was a web of self-deception, that virtue was not only fleeting but barely present to begin with. Her favorite author, predictably, was La Rochefoucauld, and I think that she admired him for the sardonic intelligence that she herself possessed, an unflinching belief in widespread human delinquency. And although this attitude was in vogue at the time, Mary probably would have possessed it just as forcefully in Ionia or Rome. Predictably, she often appeared insufferably smug. "You could destroy a world with your attitude, Mary," Sam once said angrily, "but you couldn't build a goddamn outhouse with it." To which Mary replied: "In that case, Sam, I'll leave the goddamn outhouses to you."

By the time I met her, Mary had already hardened into a devout suspiciousness toward almost everything, an attitude basic to what she eventually became — a drifter through countless lives, who never made a real life of her own.

In 1968 she returned to New York with the body of her last husband, Martin Farrell, a cardiologist. We were all standing outside St. Patrick's, Mary wrapped in one of her full-length furs, the collar turned up against the blustery wind that was sweeping down Fifth Avenue that day. Her daughter, Martha, was standing beside her, the very image of sixties' chic, dressed in a long black coat with brass buttons and epaulettes which looked as if it might have been designed by a Marxist Coco Chanel. Elena urged them both to stay at her apartment rather than return immediately to California. Mary was adamant, however. She insisted upon going back to the West Coast that night. And so a few hours later, Elena and I watched mother and daughter trudge down the ramp at La Guardia, Mary dragging Martha behind her, slinging quips and insults, the two of them returning to a Berkeley that was practically in flames. I never saw Mary again.

So there were four of us that night in Harry Morton's brownstone. But in the photograph at St. Paul's Chapel, there are five.

Sam Waterman had not been invited, though Harry knew him well. Sam always believed that Harry was anti-Semitic, a Brahmin who saw Jews as grubby peddlers, even when they peddled art. Elena thought differently. "It was a conflict in styles between those two," she once told me. "Harry just couldn't abide Sam's general sloppiness, his huggability, that frenetic pace." For Elena, that was a kind way of saying that Harry thought Sam vulgar, which he undoubtedly did. "You simply can't imagine Waterman sitting down and reading a poem," Harry told me, "unless somewhere in the background a phone is ringing off the hook."

True enough, and all of us marveled at Sam's incredible energy, at the almost destroying force with which he went at everything. "The only way to get a better literature," he said in 1926, "is to find someone to publish a better literature." And with that he set about becoming a publisher himself, a feat he accomplished only four years later.

He dedicated his publishing house to what he called "the modern novel," a phrase that was already out of date, and then began issuing works that he thought experimental but that were for the most part little more than pale imitations of Fitzgerald and Hemingway, whose works themselves already looked rather conservative compared to the wild innovations of Faulkner and Joyce.

Elena once introduced Sam to a distinguished gathering as "the only successful publisher in America who has never read a book." Sam grinned impishly at that, knowing that it was true, but also confident that no one would believe it.

In her essay on Sinclair Lewis's most famous novel, Elena wrote:

"For all his bourgeois shallowness, Babbitt never says that his wealth is the rightful product of his virtue or, conversely, that he wishes to be rich in order to be good. In this, there is at least a denial of that cant which propped up an older world, and perhaps even, for better or worse, a slight innovation in the moral philosophy of the West." In a sense, I think, Elena was also talking about Sam Waterman, his openness and lack of pretense. For her, Sam was always the member of a class that began and ended with himself. "He was like the medieval definition of God," she wrote in her obituary of him, "pure act." It was his energy she loved, his ceaseless activity, his yearning for achievement, all of which flowed, as she said, "not from his thought but from his central nervous system."

Sam retired in 1971, turning over his publishing house to Christina. During the next two years, she made editorial decisions that so inflamed him that he tried to regain control of the house. A court battle ensued, one so vitriolic that even the tabloid press began to follow it. Then suddenly, in the midst of the fray, Sam died. Had Mary been alive, she would no doubt have attributed the cause of death to excessive litigation.

In her remembrance of Sam Waterman, which appeared in the *Saturday Review*, Elena wrote: "Sam Waterman died of retirement, of too many strolls in the afternoon, too many aimless games of chess in the park, of too much idle chatter, too many dead companions. He died of forgone power and wasted zeal, of a lethargy of bone and eye and muscle, of feeling dead before one dies, worthless after a history of worth."

But in the photograph he is still alive, along with the rest of us. It is 1928, and Elena has not yet come to New York. But the web is nonetheless in place, the system of connections that makes so much of life hinge on mere fortuity. Sam Waterman, desperate for his new publishing house to publish something, will read the manuscript of *New England Maid* and decide to issue it as his premier volume. Mary's daughter, Martha, will write the first biography of my sister. Elena will fully cooperate in the writing of it, because of what Martha's mother meant to her. These are the bonds by which ability becomes achievement, and they are, as Elena called them, "ambrosia to the fortunate, but to the luckless, bitter herbs." Certainly no one has ever argued that they are fair, only that they powerfully exist.

Elena spoke only once of the four years she lived alone with my mother in Standhope while I lived at Columbia. We were walking on the beach near her home in Brewster, on Cape Cod. She was using a cane by then, though only for occasional support, and she had wrapped a long gray shawl around her shoulders. I remember thinking how beautiful she remained, even though her body was growing lean and frail, the understudy of a ghost.

I had driven down to the Cape from Cambridge, where I had been living for the last few years. She had written me a month before, telling me that she intended to reside on Cape Cod "from now on" and that she would not be returning to New York. My grandson, David, had helped her with the arrangements. She had gotten rid of everything she owned other than a few books, her letters, and her phonograph and record collection.

I arrived at Elena's house in the middle of the morning and found her sitting alone on her glass-enclosed side porch, the shawl wrapped around her, a vision of Dickensian gravity, with the gray sea behind her and the white light of the morning sun slanting across the wooden floor in front.

She seemed very pleased to see me. She rose slowly as I came through the door and then walked over and embraced me with what seemed at the time an unusual strenuousness.

"How are you, William?" she asked as she stepped back, releasing me.

"Fine. And you?"

"Good. Are you hungry?"

I shook my head. "No, not at all. I ate something on the road. It breaks the long drive from Boston."

"Would you rather go inside?"

"No. Let's stay out here."

We both seated ourselves with a slow, elderly caution, which both of us found rather funny.

"We're turning to glass, William," Elena said.

I nodded. "Of high quality, though. Crystal."

We chatted about the details of her move. She asked if I would stay the night, but I told her I was taking a plane to New York for a visit with my grandson.

"David's a wonderful boy," she said.

"Yes."

"Very helpful with the move."

"So you're not going back? You're going to live on the Cape permanently?"

"Yes."

"Don't you think you should have waited for summer? Moving in November like this, just in time for the winter — it could get very bleak out here."

"No," Elena said, "it'll be fine." The old firmness was in her voice, the gavel going down.

I talked on for a while, mostly suggesting that I might pay her another visit, perhaps for New Year's, or even sooner, perhaps when I returned to Hyannis from New York. I was roaming through the logistics of all that, the way old people do, aimlessly chewing at the possibilities, when Elena interrupted me in mid-sentence.

"Let's go for a walk on the beach, William," she said.

"It's a little chilly for that, isn't it?"

"Just a short one."

"But what if we should fall down, old girl? We might not be discovered for weeks."

She stretched out her hand. "We'll help each other down the stairs."

I was moving to take her hand when she stood up, the light suddenly catching her at an exquisite angle, turning her hair into a silver corona.

"Elena," I said, "would you mind if I took a picture?"

"God, William," Elena said, "still that old obsession with photographs."

"Only one," I told her. "It's just the angle of the light. Very beautiful. Only one. If it doesn't come out, well, my loss."

"All right, but I really don't want this to turn into a modeling session."

"Agreed," I said quickly.

I went to my car, retrieved my camera, and a few seconds later it was done. When, only a day later, I saw the picture swim into view under the red light of my darkroom, I thought my heart would stop. She is standing very straight, her body halved by the horizon, her hands folded around the mahogany cane, the great shawl falling from her shoulders, descending almost to the floor, her eyes staring at the camera with an odd intensity, yet almost humbly, as if offering it something, alms.

Elena and I were both sufficiently agile to make it down the stairs, and it was only at the bottom one, the last wooden step rising above the beach, that Elena offered her hand.

"There now, we've made it," I said jokingly.

Elena poked her cane into the sand and leaned on it, her face turned toward the sea.

"Have you ever noticed," she said, "how sometimes the sea seems famished? The waves come in with this craven appetite for the shore, gobbling it up. And then, at other times, they seem completely satisfied, small, halfhearted, sort of playing with their food."

I assumed a mock-oratorical stance. "Yet winds to seas are reconciled at length, and sea to shore."

Elena smiled. "What's that from?"

"Samson Agonistes."

She tucked her hand under my arm. "You always were a good quoter, William. Always had a very retentive mind. Would you believe it, I couldn't quote a single sustained piece of verse."

"Not even your own?"

"Possibly a few of my own," Elena admitted. "But you know, Martha wrote me a letter a few days ago. She was asking about some interpretation of a line I had written. I couldn't remember what the line was from. I had to look it up. It took me almost an hour to find it."

"Do you hear from Martha often?"

"When she hits a snag."

"Are there many of those?"

"A few."

"Perhaps she'll make an enigma of you."

Elena said nothing. Instead she looked out toward the sea again, then left and right down the beach.

"Which way should we walk?" she asked.

"Whatever suits you."

She lifted the cane to the right.

"Let's go that way, then. Toward the jetty."

We moved closer to the edge of the water, where the sand was more tightly packed and easier to walk on.

It was one of those curious coastal days when the sky, though clear, seems faintly overcast, the usual blue giving way to a strange light gray which somewhat darkens the air without detracting from its clarity. It was windless, and the bay was a sheet of smoked glass.

I held Elena gently by her arm as we walked. She seemed thinner than I remembered. Her shawl had given her a bulk she no longer possessed.

"How far along is Martha on the biography?" I asked casually.

"She's at work on that period when you were off at college and I was home with Mother," Elena said. She tugged her arm from my hand. "I need it free," she said. "For balance."

"When does she think she'll finish it?"

"I don't know. Perhaps another two years or so," Elena said. She stopped and gazed out toward the bay. The monument at Provincetown could be seen very hazily across the water. She seemed entranced by the look of it, the lean gray tower rising out of the sea.

"That time when I was away at college," I said. "Does Martha think it important?"

"I don't know," Elena said.

We began walking again. Far ahead, the stone jetty stretched out into the water, then disappeared. It looked like the remains of some once-exalted dream, to ring the world with one rocky band.

"I remember the way you looked when the train pulled away from the station in Standhope," I said.

"And how did I look then?"

"Forlorn, my dear, terribly forlorn. But you looked even worse six months later when I came back."

"It had been rather difficult, those first months alone with Mother," Elena said.

"You looked very tired."

"I probably was," Elena admitted. "But you, William, when you got off that train, you looked like a new man."

"In a way, that's what I was," I said. Which was true enough. Meeting Harry, Sam, and the rest of them had changed me quite a bit in a remarkably short time. I had gotten roaring drunk with Sam, criticized one of Tom's poems, talked until dawn with Harry about the place of the patron in the arts, and given Mary a long, lingering kiss in a darkened movie theater.

Elena was looking out across the bay again. "It's very beautiful when it's calm. It could be anywhere in the world, some inlet off the China Sea."

"Yes, very beautiful," I said, but my mind was still on the day I returned to Standhope. "You met me at the station when I came back, remember? You brought me flowers, dandelions and daisies."

"A little girl's offering," Elena said dully.

"I wouldn't say so," I told her. "I was very touched."

Elena waved her hand. "Well, it seemed the least I could do, given Mother's condition."

She had declined rather alarmingly during the last six months. I had left her on the porch, nibbling ice. She had been able to understand that I was going away and had even wished me luck, though she did not know exactly in what regard.

"She had that vacant look when I came back," I said as we continued walking toward the jetty. "A very vacant look. No information going in, no information coming out. It was like someone had pulled a plug."

"By then," Elena said, pulling her shawl around her shoulders more tightly, "she had begun to sink into herself completely. She never came out again."

I shook my head. "I think she should have run away, Elena, taken some wild Italian lover."

"Perhaps she might have, if we had not been born," Elena said. "She might have run off with someone like that, gone with him to an island in the Aegean Sea. Grown old there." She looked at me. "Grown old like us, and walked by the sea and dreamed of all she could have had if she'd just settled down in a small New England town and not madly run away with an Italian lover."

I stopped and looked at her closely. "You could have chosen Whitman House for her."

"I did, eventually."

"I mean at first," I said. "That's what Father wanted from the beginning."

"But not me, William," Elena said. "I might have gone along with him, but then he started that business of moving me in with Aunt Hattie, moving to Pawtucket." Her eyes narrowed. "I knew one thing: mother might end up in Whitman, but her only daughter was not going to end up in Pawtucket."

"You still did your duty, Elena," I told her. "You stayed with her those four years."

Elena moved away from me. The tide was coming in. She dipped her cane into the water as she walked along.

"Martha wants to know a great deal about mother's insanity," she said.

"Yes, I suppose she does."

"I feel very remote from all that, as if it were a part of someone else's life."

"That's what youth is, Elena," I told her, "the part that feels unreal."

Elena looked at me pointedly. "But it was real, her madness. You weren't so detached the day you came home."

"I was furious," I said. Even at that moment, on so subdued a day, I could still feel the anger that had risen in me when I saw my mother. "She was so helpless by then, completely helpless. And he hadn't even been back to see her more than once or twice. Just that check in the mail every Wednesday, with those notes, the ones you showed me. 'Keep Smiling. Dad.' "

Elena said nothing.

"Of course, I hadn't come back either, had I?"

"No."

"But you hadn't let me know how bad off she was, how much of a burden to you," I said emphatically. "He'd been back. He'd seen her. He'd seen you. He was a husband, and a father. He had responsibilities."

"And so you went to see him in New York," Elena said, "to discuss his responsibilities, to have it out with him, once and for all."

"Yes, once and for all," I said. "I was going to tell that bastard that he had to help you, and his wife." I kicked at a broken shell, sending it skipping across the sand. "We met in his room when I got back to New York. He was dressed — can you believe this, Elena — he was dressed in a smoking jacket. Lord of all he surveyed, that little room with the plaid curtains, the mock-colonial bed and desk, the chest of drawers with the rollers under each leg."

"He was given that room by mistake, William," Elena said.

I stopped. "He told you about it? About that meeting we had?"

"Yes," Elena said. "He said that the two of you had a talk in this dingy little room he'd been assigned by mistake."

We began moving down the beach again. Elena allowed the tip of her cane to dance along the flattened sand.

"Well, he poured us both a little drink," I said. "Then he sat down on the edge of the bed and asked me how I was doing in school. I told him I was doing fine."

"Which was true enough," Elena said.

"Yes. And so we began to talk about life at the university and all that," I said. And I began to fall in love again with the life I had at college, with all my new friends, with the world that the university was opening up for me, and as I talked to him, it became very clear to me that I would do nothing whatsoever to endanger that life.

"And he enjoyed hearing about it, William," Elena said. "He told me he did."

"Yes, well, the problem is that I had not gone to discuss the life of the undergraduate in America," I said. "I had gone to talk to him about our mother, and about you, about the whole intolerable situation back in Standhope."

"Of course," Elena said lightly.

I glanced away for a moment, allowing my eyes to scan the bay. Then I looked at Elena.

"But of course, I never mentioned our mother once, or you, except in passing, or Standhope, other than that I had had a pleasant trip home. That's what I called it, Elena, pleasant trip."

Elena said nothing. She continued to walk steadily, her eyes latched to the jetty up ahead.

"And since you seem to know everything else," I said, "you probably know why I kept my mouth shut about the real reason for my coming to see him."

Elena was silent. Her cane tripped along beside her like a third, stiffened leg.

"Well, it became obvious that those little checks that arrived at Standhope every week were not the only ones he was writing. There were those other ones, too, the ones coming to me at Columbia, the ones that were making my current happiness possible."

Elena still said nothing. She kept her eyes straight ahead.

I stopped. "Well, do you want this to be a full confession?" I asked. "A real *mea culpa,* from my heart?"

Elena poked the tip of her cane at the water's edge. "No need for such dramatics. I've always known what happened between you and Father."

"In every detail, evidently," I said. "Look, Elena, I know it wasn't easy for you, cooped up with Mother. I knew it wasn't easy, believe me. But to tell you the truth, I'm just too old for another bout of self-loathing. It would turn my bones all soggy."

Elena placed her open hand against my cheek. "You're like the narrator of *The Good Soldier*, William, always telling sad stories, made all the sadder by your naiveté."

I stepped back. "What do you mean?"

"You think being alone with Mother was a terrible burden for me?" Elena asked. "It wasn't. It was a great release. Mother's insanity gave me all the freedom I could have wished for in Standhope."

"You're joking."

Elena shook her head. "No."

"But all the work, all that daily drudgery. What about that?"

"The freedom was worth it," Elena said firmly.

Suddenly I remembered that in one of Elena's poems, "Nocturne," a young owl realizes with infinite delight that it is released, rather than constricted, by the night.

"But all the work fell to you," I insisted. "Just living in that house all the time, it must have been dreadful."

"I didn't live there all the time."

"You didn't?"

"No."

"Where on earth did you live?" I asked, astonished.

"I went traveling."

My mouth dropped open. "Traveling? With whom?"

"With Father."

"Traveling with Father? And what, if I may ask, did you two muske-teers do with Our Lady of the Blank Stare during this time?"

Elena turned and began walking down the beach again. To her left a horseshoe crab glided along in the shallow water, looking like nothing so much as a discarded implement of medieval war.

"What did you do with Mother?" I repeated.

"Father knew a man named Bishop," Elena said quietly. "Bishop stayed with her. Never for more than a few days at a time of course, but I think he brightened her life a little."

"And so you and Father went on the road together."

Elena nodded. "Yes, for a few days at a time."

"And stayed at all the best places, I suppose?"

Elena shook her head. "We stayed in pretty seedy places, William. He had to save all his money. Columbia wasn't cheap, for you or me. He paid for us both. It wasn't easy."

"Don't try to make him out a saint."

"I never would," Elena said determinedly. "But we're both too near the end to keep up any sort of charade. You've always believed that I had an awful time of it while you were at Columbia. I just wanted you to know that quite the opposite was the case."

"You were the Isadora Duncan of the toiletries trade, aye?" I asked with a laugh.

Elena's face remained very serious, as did her voice. "I saw a little of the world, more than you thought I'd seen by the time I left Standhope," she said. "A great deal goes on in those little roadside cafés and honky-tonks, William. People drink and dance and gamble. They take what they can out of life."

I looked at her knowingly. "He was a gambler, wasn't he. That's where those sudden bursts of money came from."

Elena nodded. "Yes," she said. "And when we were on the road together, I'd sit at the table with him. I was his Lady Luck."

"A tinhorn Gatsby, my father. The mystery man."

"He lived in a free state, William."

"And you were out there, taking it all in," I said.

"He never put pink ribbons in my hair," Elena said. "He was a good father to me because he treated me like a son." In her short story "Stigmata," a daughter is mysteriously aware of each time her father bleeds.

I laughed, though a bit self-consciously. "And what about you, Elena, were you a roadside tart?"

Elena laughed too, finally, and shook her head. "Hardly." Then, very suddenly, her face grew almost wistful. "There was a young man named Fletcher. He had slick hair and was a terrific mimic. He could even do Father. You know, the way he throws his head back after he tells one of those salesman jokes. Fletcher could mimic that perfectly. He made me laugh. He was very kind. He told me that he knew he'd never do for me, that there'd be someone else in the end, someone very different from himself, that he was just an escapade."

"Which is what he was?"

"Yes, I suppose," Elena said. "But I can still remember him very well, just as I can remember the sound of roadsters skidding along and beef patties hitting an open grill, that sort of thing."

We walked on for several yards, neither of us speaking.

"The really good part," Elena said finally, "was that after a few days on the road, I'd be back in Standhope with Mother. I would have this solitude after the road. I could just think about all that had happened, relive it, but a step removed."

We walked the rest of the way to the jetty in silence. Then Elena climbed up on the first stone.

"Surely you're not going to walk out on this thing," I protested.

"Yes, I am," Elena said. She took a few more steps, the great shawl blowing slightly.

"Be careful, Elena," I said. "I don't want to lose you to the tide."

Elena eased herself around to face me. "When are you leaving for New York?"

"Very soon," I said. "We barely have time to walk back to your house."

"Give my regards to David."

"I will."

"Good," she said softly.

"You could come with me, if you like," I said.

Elena shook her head. "No. I'll stay here for now." She raised her arms, cradling herself with them, looking rather young despite the shimmering white hair. "I hear there's snow coming up the coast," she said, turning toward the bay.

She remained a moment with her back to me, then eased herself around once again. "Do you remember that line in Jason's autobiography? The last one, I think."

"No."

"I've always liked it. It's so honest." Then she quoted it: "Death completes no circle save the most banal."

I left her about an hour later, flew to New York, and by afternoon I was at Columbia, making my way toward Earl Hall, where David was to meet me. It was snowing quite hard by then and the wind was tossing it about in a powdery extravagance. I stopped for a moment, looked about, and it struck me with curious urgency that I was old now, that most of it was over, and that to be old was to feel that you, yourself, were disappearing, becoming mist, shadowy and insubstantial, that with but a little effort you could pass through walls. I glanced up at the dome of Low Library, then down to the right at Butler, which had long ago replaced it, at all those names carved across that building's face, Sophocles and Cicero and the rest, and I thought, This much we have saved in our passing. And I was overcome by so intense a joy that the modern age would no doubt call it sexual, but which was only the deepest gravity and care.

A few minutes later, I entered Earl Hall and found David sitting in the corner, sipping tea from one of those china cups. He asked if I had had a pleasant flight and I told him that I had. Then he asked how Elena was, and suddenly all of it came together, the embrace on her porch, the way she had held it a beat longer than in the past, the long walk by the bay, that last reference to Jason's memoir. "She's dying," I said, and David's eyes fell toward his cup, while mine fled toward the window and the snow.

NEW ENGLAND
MAID

Elena came to New York in September of 1928. I sat beside her on the train from Standhope. She was elegantly dressed in clothes my father had bought her, a lovely black dress with a velvet collar. She spoke very little during the journey in, and only rarely glanced up from the story she was reading, "Bartleby the Scrivener."

I didn't try to engage her in idle chitchat. I knew she was subdued. I also knew why. Only a week before, she had finally agreed to have our mother installed in Whitman House.

It took almost the entire morning to get Mother ready for the short ride to the asylum. The task had fallen entirely to Elena, and in *New England Maid* she called it "the woman's work of my mother's commitment."

For our part, my father and I stood staunchly outside these female labors. My father smoked absently as he slouched in the chair by the living room window. I watched him coldly from the swing on the front porch.

Just before we left, and with Father already calling impatiently from the front porch, I walked to Mother's room and opened the door.

"Are you nearly ready, Elena?" I asked.

Elena was standing behind our mother, both of them facing the mirror that hung from the door of the armoire.

"Almost ready," Elena said. She was combing my mother's hair, her face nearly expressionless, except for the gentleness in her eyes. "Look at her," she said. "She's still beautiful isn't she, William?" I nodded my head and looked away, then walked distractedly down the hallway. But Elena must have remained for a time, must have turned back to the mirror. For in *New England Maid* she wrote: "As we were about to leave, I sat down beside my mother, both our faces held in the oval womb of her looking glass. We were two women, one older, one younger, one declining toward a final nakedness, stripped of everything but a pulse and the small, unconscious will that commands it; and the other, with all her life before her, and yet made strangely old by this scene of helpless and belated care, made aware, as if by symbol sprung to life, of that most wintry of all human themes: that all our goodness comes to us too late."

We drove to Whitman House in my father's sedan, the autumn leaves rushing before the car while he whistled the Marine Hymn, his arm flung jauntily out the window, as if he were doing no more than dropping off a package at the post office. "Your mother'll have a nice room here," he said. That was his first and last word on the subject of my mother's welfare. From then on, he paid the bills involved with her commitment, but he never really spoke of her again.

Elena sat in the back seat, her hands enfolding my mother's, as if they were the only remaining part of her to which she could still offer a kind of mute protection.

The actual business of my mother's commitment was over in only a few minutes. My father completed that task by writing a check and handing it to the nurse at the front desk. "That'll do until next month, right?" he asked. The nurse nodded slowly, and my father briskly pranced out of the building. Elena always believed that that quick exit was something in him finally breaking, a little wave of remembered love washing him out the front door before anyone could see it but himself.

Elena and I lingered in the building for a while after my father had left. We stood like two helpless bystanders as a rather stout orderly gently guided our mother down the hallway. "She went passively," Elena wrote in *New England Maid*. "Dressed in a dark skirt and a neat gray jacket, the orderly's hand politely clasping her elbow, she looked like a sturdy professional woman who had come to inspect the madhouse for the Ladies' Aid Society."

But she was more than that to my sister, and in the final passage on her in *New England Maid,* Elena attempted a summation, however fumbling, of our mother's life: "She was one whose mind had become the shadow play of all that she had lost, her womanhood so hollowed out that not even the sense of nurturing remained, only a wifery that was no more than habit turned to stone. Wounded early, and never quite restored, she lived as one made luckless by her sex, her station, and her blood. In this, she rose beyond all easy designations to plead the wider passion of her case."

Elena could always love you more, as Jason Findley said, once she loved what you stood for in her mind.

Only a week after our mother's commitment, Elena and I stood in the railway station in Standhope, waiting for the New York train. She was wearing a long blue coat, and her hands were tucked into a fur muffler.

"Sort of dingy in here, isn't it," I said.

Elena glanced about the station. There was dust on the windows and some of them were cracked. A large gray cat, bloated with unborn kittens, twisted about on a soiled cloth near the charred but empty hearth. It was early fall, and the colors of the leaves beyond the station house were extravagantly bright, so that Elena's face, as she stood by the window, was framed by a brilliant canvas, fiery as the reds of Delacroix.

"New York will seem very gay indeed, compared to this," I added.

Elena said nothing.

"Remember how frightened I was, Elena, the day I left?" I asked cheerfully.

"I'm not frightened," Elena said quite firmly.

At the time, I thought her all bravado, saw her only as a timid country girl on her way to the big city. I did not know that she had already watched the world knock back more than a few in steamy roadside bars.

Elizabeth came into the station house a few minutes later. She seemed very excited for Elena.

"I wish I could go with you," she said.

Perhaps she might have, had not Mr. Brennan been in such ill health. I know that for a time Elena and Elizabeth talked of going to New York together, but that Elizabeth had finally declined.

"Maybe when Papa gets better," she said. "Maybe I'll come to New York then." She embraced Elena. "I'll miss you. Please write."

"I will," Elena promised.

"I have to get back to the house," Elizabeth said. "He had a very bad night, coughing a lot, you know. I can't stay away too long. But I just had to say good-by, Elena."

They embraced again, then Elizabeth disappeared behind the station house doors.

"Too bad about Mr. Brennan," I said casually.

"She wouldn't have come anyway," Elena replied.

It seemed an odd remark, but Elena did not choose to explain it. Instead, she walked a few paces toward the front of the station, then glanced back at me. "Let's go out on the platform, William."

"All right."

My father arrived a minute or so later. He had driven us to the station but had then insisted upon driving back to the house for something he claimed to have forgotten. I suspected that the sight of Elena's departure was too much for him and that, typically, he had decided not to face it.

Yet there he was, striding through the station house doors and onto the platform, his coat unbuttoned and fluttering in the breeze. He had a package with him, rather large and cumbersome.

"This is for you, Elena," he said breathlessly. He hoisted it over to me. "Figure she'll be needing this at Barnard. For God's sake, don't drop it, William."

"What is it?"

He looked at Elena. "Typewriter," he said. He seemed almost to glow. Later in life, strolling proudly about various literary parties, martini in hand, his belly edging over his belt, he would boast of how early he had known of his daughter's gifts. "Lots faster than poor Billy, here," he'd say, slapping me playfully on the back.

Within a few minutes, we were on the train, Elena pressed up against the window, staring down at him. He was smiling very happily. He did not seem sad at all, only confident of her destiny.

We rode together very quietly that day. Elena read her book or watched out the window. I scribbled notes for one of my upcoming papers. I suppose I looked like a student, tall and plain and spindly as a desk lamp. And Elena? She looked like nothing more than an attractive young woman, a small-town girl little different from thousands of others, on her way to meet her destiny in the city.

But this young woman was Elena Franklin, and her life would

wind neither toward a palace nor toward that bleak dead-letter office in which Bartleby came to rest at last. Instead, it would be her own, singularly guided by her mind, each part an episode within what Carlyle called "the thought of thinking souls."

"Well, you're here," I said happily as the train pulled into Pennsylvania Station.

She nodded. "Yes."

I did not know at that time how carefully Elena had planned her steps, how determined she was, as Manfred Owen tells his daughter in Elena's last book, "not to have my life handed to me like my head upon a platter."

Harry Morton met us at the train. He was leaning against one of the wrought iron pillars that supported the arcade, and he looked almost ghostly in his long coat and gray fedora, his faced locked in an attitude of forced reserve, "a fellow who seemed to think of life," as Elena characterized him in her first published work, a short story called "Manhattan," "as one long unanswered prayer."

"So this is Elena," Harry said, bowing slightly as we came up to him. "William, I had no idea your sister was so attractive." He turned to Elena. "Welcome to New York."

"Thank you," Elena said. She neither smiled nor frowned but only regarded him closely, as if determined to sum him up.

"It's almost six," Harry said. "I thought we might all have an early dinner." He smiled politely. "Of course, you may be tired from the train ride." This he said only to Elena.

"I'm not tired," Elena said immediately.

"Good," Harry said brightly. He offered Elena his right arm, and with the other picked up her single suitcase. "May I escort you through this vast and confusing terminal, then?"

Elena glanced at me quickly, as if asking how she should deal with this oddity. Then she took Harry's arm and allowed herself to be ushered through the glass-domed and steel-ribbed pandemonium of Penn Station.

Once outside, Harry stepped up to the curb and opened the door of one of the many taxis that lined the entire block in front of the station in those days. Then he came back for our bags. Elena was staring up at the imposing façade of the station.

"It's patterned on the Caracalla Baths," he said.

Elena gave him a blank look. "What is?"

"The station."

"Oh," Elena said, getting into the cab.

I lumbered in after her, dragging the typewriter with me. The driver slung our suitcases into the trunk, then Harry pulled himself into the back seat.

"The Commodore, please," he said.

The cab cruised up Seventh Avenue, past Macy's and along the line of plain brick buildings that stretched toward Times Square in those days. At Forty-second Street we turned east, and all the glitter of Times Square spread out before us, a whirling dervish of multicolored illuminated signs, which certainly would have looked beautiful, as Chesterton once remarked, to one who could not read.

Mary was already waiting for us in the Palm Room of the Commodore. She was sitting alone at a table near the back, the waiters buzzing about while she puffed languidly at her cigarette.

"I don't know why you chose this place, Harry," she said as the three of us approached her. "It's so dreary."

"Where would you have preferred, my dear?" Harry asked with mock concern.

"The Algonquin."

Harry shook his head disapprovingly. "So passé. The Algonquin is all tourists now," Harry said to Elena. "Everyone coming in from Indiana to see where Dorothy Parker sat. The literary wits aren't there anymore, Mary."

"Well, at least it has the memory of wit," Mary said testily. "Not like this place — palm fronds and curtains. It looks like a mortuary."

Elena smiled thinly.

"Where is everyone?" Harry asked Mary.

"Sam can't make it," she said crisply. "He's got some kind of meeting with backers for that publishing company scheme of his."

Harry sighed. "What an absurd idea," he said. "Poor Sam presumes that the literacy rate in this country is increasing." He smiled at Elena. "That's the first of his many mistakes, I fear."

We were still standing by the table, the waiters edging around us laden with enormous silver trays.

"Mary, I'd like you to meet William's sister, Elena," Harry said at last.

"Oh, I know who she is," Mary said. She forced herself to smile.

"Welcome to New York." She stared impatiently at the three of us. "Well, don't just stand there, for God's sake. Please, sit, sit, sit."

When we had all taken our seats, Mary turned to Harry. "Tom can't make it either," she said. "Working on one of his great poetry projects." She looked at Elena. "Has William told you about Tom?"

"Very little," Elena said.

"Fancies himself a poet," Mary said. "Of course, the stuff he writes, a seed catalogue wouldn't publish."

"I wouldn't be so harsh," Harry said mildly.

Mary's eyes widened. "You wouldn't? Why not?"

"Well, he's just beginning. He has a lot to learn."

Mary turned to Elena. "He doesn't hang around with the rest of us much anymore. That's romantic, don't you think? The lone poet, tormented in his isolation but learning the dark path of inner vision." She laughed. "I don't suppose you have such grand ideas, Elena?"

Elena shook her head. "I don't suppose so."

"Good," Mary said. "With a little luck, you may never be a fool." She took a long draw on her cigarette. "I'd like to get fried in the hat tonight."

"Mary, please," Harry said.

Mary glared at the little teacup that rested by her ashtray. "The hooch hounds are ruining the world," she muttered. She crushed her cigarette into the ashtray and promptly lit another.

"William tells me that you're going to study literature at Barnard," Harry said gently to Elena.

"Yes," Elena said. She continued to watch Mary warily, as if she thought Mary's frenetic display was little more than a parody of the Modern City Woman.

"I'm just drifting, myself," Mary said. "No graduate school for me. I'll leave that for William. No family business to take over, like Harry." She smiled. "No, I'm just a woman on the prowl."

We ordered dinner a few minutes later. Elena ordered trout amandine because, I suppose, it was the only familiar thing on the menu.

"I'm sure you'll do fine at Barnard," Harry told her. "Of course, with William at Columbia, you'll have a little help available."

"Is that why you came here, Elena," Mary asked, "for William's help?"

Elena looked pointedly at Mary. "No, it isn't," she said. "I came to New York when I was a little girl. I always wanted to come back."

Harry stroked his chin and nodded sagely. "You seem to have a serious nature, Elena."

Mary laughed dismissively. "Serious! What is seriousness, anyway?"

It appeared for a moment that Elena might actually try to answer Mary's question: her lips parted briefly, then closed again.

"Tom, for example," Mary went on, "thinks of himself as a serious poet. But he is living in a mist. He's never really faced himself. He thinks he's a tragic figure, but actually he's just a pathetic one."

"Please, Mary," Harry said, "could we talk about something else? Elena doesn't even know Tom."

"Oh, sorry. Yes, you're right. Sorry, Elena. It's very rude."

Elena smiled politely. "Not really. I'm very interested."

In my memory I can see her clearly at that moment in her life, suddenly surrounded by a group of young moderns who know so little of the world they think they know it all, a tiny circle of poseurs, harmless and ineffectual as we surely were, slightly snide but basically generous, the sort who could with a nudge in one direction or the other either enrich the world a bit or draw it more deeply into poverty.

"Interesting? Is that what you're finding all this?" Mary asked with a grin.

Elena nodded. "I really am. I'm like the country mouse in the story."

"But that was the wise one, wasn't it?" Mary asked. She smiled, then looked at me knowingly. "Your sister's all right, William." She glanced back at Elena. "Quite all right, I think." She took out another cigarette and lit it. "So you've come to New York to experience things, is that right, Elena?"

"Yes, I think so."

Mary nodded. "Well, would you like to begin this very night?"

Harry leaned forward. "What are you talking about, Mary?"

"I'm proposing, my dear Harry, that we all go have a drink to celebrate Elena's arrival in New York."

Harry eyed her in disbelief. "I'm not sure it's the best way for Elena to spend her first night in the city."

"Oh, stop being so pompous, Harry," Mary said. She looked at me. "Have you ever noticed the way Harry pours cold water on everything? My God, the minute Harry shows up the whole damn world turns gray. Even Tom, the wild poet, even he gets stuffy around Harry." She frowned impatiently. "Haven't you ever noticed the way we act? Like a bunch of elderly ladies having tea in Cornwall." She looked determinedly at Elena. "I'm off for a drink, Elena, and I would love your company."

"Sit down, Mary," Harry said firmly.

Mary continued to watch Elena. "Stuff it, Harry."

Elena got to her feet. "I'd like to see a speakeasy."

"Perhaps we'd better go with them," I said to Harry.

"Absolutely," Harry said. He glared at Mary. "I presume you have time to permit me to get the check?"

Mary laughed. "Harry loves to get the check. Do you know why? He doesn't want all his friends grappling for it over the table like a gang of hairy Goths."

Harry paid the check and we walked out to find a cab. On the way downtown, Mary suggested we sing together and was good enough to wave her finger back and forth, counting out the rhythm, as if she were directing a disorganized choir through a classical arrangement. Her voice often rose painfully above the others, then broke up in laughter. In a letter fired off to me from the seclusion of her old age, she described herself as "a gray old thing with rouged cheeks and puffy eyes and ostrich legs who sits in the park, barely moving, a vulgar piece of sculpture called *Decrepitude.*" But I have her finger waving in the air that night in 1928, and the sound of her voice belting random lyrics from *The Pirates of Penzance.*

The speakeasy was very much like the one painted by Ben Shahn. It had a short bar with a brass rail along the bottom. There were a few wooden tables with unmatching but comfortable chairs. There was no music, not so much as a lone saxophone player, but couples swayed slowly before the radio that rested on the corner of the bar. It was smoky, and the conversation tended to be rather hushed, although the crowd was young and spiffily dressed.

"What'll you have?" The bartender did not bother to come to the table but simply called to us from behind the bar.

"Gin and tonic for me," Mary said immediately.

I ordered a Scotch and Harry ordered a brandy. Then he turned to Elena. "And the young lady will have a White Rock, please."

"White Rock?" Mary said loudly. "She won't have a White Rock, Harry. She'll have a drink like the rest of us."

Harry glared resentfully at Mary. "Perhaps Elena would not like to get — as you put it, Mary — 'fried in the hat' on her first night in the city."

"Well, why not let her decide," Mary said hotly.

All eyes turned to my sister.

She smiled. "Do they have sherry?"

"Of course," Harry said.

"Then I will have a sherry," Elena said. Then she looked at the bartender. "A sherry, please."

"I've never understood the appeal of these places," Harry said, glancing about. A couple was now dancing slowly a few feet from the radio. "Quite an interesting experience for you, I suppose," he said to Elena.

Elena nodded but she did not look at him. She was watching the couple at the bar, the boredom of their embrace.

"Perhaps you'd like to dance, Elena," Harry said.

Elena shook her head. "I don't dance very well."

It was news to me, of course, that she danced at all.

"Neither do I," Harry said, "but we could give it a try."

"Go ahead, Elena," Mary said. "I've never seen Harry dance, or do anything heedless."

Harry laughed and stretched out his hand. "Shall we?"

Elena took his hand and followed him to the small makeshift dance floor. I took a sip of my drink and watched them out of the corner of my eye.

"She's really quite an interesting girl, William," Mary said. "How well do you know her?"

"She's my sister."

"You might be surprised how little that tells me," Mary said. "I have four brothers, all of them idiots." She looked at me intently. "None of them know the foggiest thing about me."

I leaned back in my chair. "Well, what is it you want to know about Elena?"

Mary shook her head. "Nothing specific. But let me tell you something. I've caught on to this already. Your sister sees through us, William, sees right through us like we were made of glass."

I laughed. "How do you know that?"

"When Harry asked her to dance, did you see her face, just that quick little shadow that passed over her face?"

"No, I didn't."

"You have a brother's blindness, my dear."

"What shadow are you talking about?"

"The one that told me quite plainly, William, that she was going to dance with Harry because she felt sorry for him."

"That's ridiculous, Mary," I said. "Harry's wealthy, and almost debonair. He might even be able to sweep Elena off her feet."

I glanced back toward the front of the room. The melody on the radio was drawing to a close, and as it did, Harry said something to Elena, and she tossed her head backward, her hair turning almost black beneath the light.

In Elena's story "Manhattan," a dour young man tritely muses that every individual should have one delightful year. I am relatively sure that Elena did have hers, and that it took place during the time between her arrival in New York and the beginning of her brief but profoundly important relationship with Dr. Stein.

Since I was very busy in my first year of graduate school at that time, I saw relatively little of my sister. But not long after her death, I found a kind of diary she kept of that first year in the city. It was entitled "What I Saw," and it is the only available record of her life during the period that Martha, at least, thought so important — "the critical plunge," as she called it, "into the literary and geographical landscape that would hold her all her life."

The problem with the observations in "What I Saw," however, is that they are not very critical. Martha herself pronounced the journal trivial and used it very little in her own book. But for me it is evidence of my sister's happiness at this time in her life, and given the rather somber tones that shaded most of what came after, it seems important to relate its spirit, if not its details.

In part, "What I Saw" is the description of Elena's early friendship with Mary Longford. Time after time they meet at Hewett Hall, the tall pink-brick dormitory where Elena lived during her first year at Barnard. From that central point, they move in all directions around the campus, Mary smoking everywhere, even in the old Milbank buildings, as Elena reports, the only place on campus where it was forbidden.

They attend various political rallies, and in the fall of 1928, with the presidential election in full swing, there were plenty of them:

"Mary and I went to meetings of the Democratic, Republican and Socialist clubs," Elena writes in her journal, "and Mary was equally offended by them all." The campus was covered with banners and posters: "At noon in the Jungle, stump speakers come from everywhere and hold forth about everything from Coolidge to Kropotkin." In November, as the election drew near, the women of Barnard staged a huge parade in which various political factions participated: "It was like a sort of toast to the madness and energy of it all," Elena writes, "with everybody laughing and cheering and singing disrespectful songs. Two girls even dressed themselves up as a donkey and wandered the campus braying at the top of their voices."

After the election, political life on campus subsided, and Elena's journal turns to other aspects of her life on Morningside Heights. She writes of her daily routine, of trudging up to the laundry on the top floor of Hewett Hall, of entertaining a male or two in those rooms especially provided for that purpose: "I talked to Harry for a while in one of the manholes on the first floor. He said he thought the ten-dollar-a-point tuition at Barnard was absurdly high. He kept going on about it, figuring up the cost of a twenty-eight-point major with fourteen points in three other areas, which the college requires. When he got the grand total, he shook his head over it and talked as if it were an impossible amount of money. He's always going on about the HCL, as if he could be affected by it."

In December Elena decides to investigate campus clubs. She attends meetings of the Botanical Club, the Wigs and Cues, the Politics Club, and even the Deutscher Kreis, but she does not join any of them, although she does audition for the Glee Club, which rejects her: "They were very nice in the way they told me that I sounded rather like the banging of a pan."

But Elena also leaves the campus quite often, wandering the city with Mary. They take a bus down Fifth Avenue from Central Park to Washington Square, riding on the top of a double-decker. "For this one experience," Elena writes, "I am eternally grateful to the Fifth Avenue Coach Company."

For New Year's Eve, 1928, Elena records the frenzy of Times Square:

We all went in Harry's car and sat in it passing the flask while the pandemonium continued outside. The revelers were everywhere, and even the mounted police were full of spirit. One of them took a swig from a bottle of bonded that someone from the crowd had handed him, laughed, and passed it back. Harry predicted that 1929 would be a good year, "businesswise," as he always says. Mary made a New Year's resolution that if she weren't married within twelve months, she'd hire herself out to Texas Guinan down in the Village and specialize in men "with a college-girl fetish." William looked rather out of sorts, forever mumbling about his Cowper paper, about how much trouble he was having with it. Tom commiserated with him, said he'd like to write a poem about Times Square on New Year's Eve, but since language has structure, it can't portray chaos. Later that night, in a speakeasy downtown, Harry gave the waiter a huge tip. I told him that in light of his conservative politics, such behavior could be called "noblesse oblique," and Mary laughed and leaned over to me and whispered, "You know, Elena, my dear, you're almost smart enough to be a man."

The winter months that follow constrict Elena's movements, and her response is to sink deeply into her studies. She records classes in Roman history, organic chemistry, and eighteenth-century litera- ture. As often as possible, she rejected the so-called instrument courses, hygiene and physical education, in favor of classes in history and literature. She makes reference to the authors she is reading — Austen, the Brontës, Scott, Tennyson. "I am more excited than ever about literature," she writes, "and Mary thinks this preoccupation unnatural. Yesterday she said that she spotted me trotting down Columbia Walk toward the library, and that I looked like a Hottentot heading for a wadi."

It is at this time that she becomes somewhat more aggressive in the classroom: "Dr. H. treated my statement on *Emma* with what seemed to me pure condescension. He kept nodding and muttering, 'Interesting, Miss Franklin, yes, yes, interesting,' but it was clear that he thought me more or less unworthy of his time. He is a Columbia professor, and Ann Dodd told me that they don't like teaching the girls at Barnard, that they consider Barnard a weak stepchild of the great Columbia, a 'little girls' school,' nothing more." Tension builds between Elena and Dr. H. until, in March, there is a confrontation: "I finally stood up and told Dr. H. that I wished to be excused from his class. He seemed a bit nonplused but still tried to keep the upper hand, telling me that although my contributions would be greatly missed he nonetheless expected to be able to conduct his class without them."

But there were victories as well. Later that same month, Elena wrote: "Professor B. asked me to stay after class and talked for a while about my paper on Walter Scott. He said another professor was working in Scottish mythology and might be interested in taking on a student assistant. He asked if he might show the paper to this professor, and I said yes."

I actually saw Elena in class only once during that year. I was on my way to one of my own professor's offices, when I glanced into one of the classrooms and saw her sitting quietly in her seat, her eyes fixed on the instructor, her hand tightly gripping a pencil poised above her note pad. Frozen by the artist's brush, that scene might have been a painting entitled *Young Scholar*. For all the elements were there: the open, receptive expression on her face, the pencil held in suspension like a conductor's baton at that instant before the symphony begins, the sense of thoughtfulness that should precede, I think, the ultimate devotion.

In late April, a dazzling spring swept over New York, and Elena's journal records scores of long walks through the city: "I told Mary that when winter finally ends it seems that New York must be discovered all over again." For sheer entertainment, she joins Mary in a tour of Columbus Circle: "It was a fool's paradise, in a way. Countless people were milling about, listening to the soapbox orators who gather on the Circle. You could get just about any idea you wanted — socialism, anarchism, any form of religion — everything was there. I mentioned a quotation from Samuel Johnson to Mary, the one in which he said that the library was the depository of all the great variety of human hope, and I said that Columbus Circle with all these speakers was like that."

By May summer is upon the city, and Elena describes the sweltering little room she occupies at Hewett Hall. "There is hardly enough room to turn around, unless one wishes to stand upon one's bed. The windows are so small that hardly any air comes through, and since almost all the rooms are singles, there is not even a roommate with whom to share the misery. Thus we fly to the out-of-doors and sit beneath that double row of European linden trees that stretches between Brooks and Barnard halls, the kindly legacy of Dr. Griffin's sweet regime."

Despite the heat, however, Elena continues to work. She submits a short piece to the *Barnacle*, but it is rejected as highbrow. She never sends anything to that publication again.

In June, after classes have ended for the summer, Elena takes a job in the admissions office, which Mary had arranged for her. Entries in her journal taper off, until the final one, recorded on July 22, 1929: "Tom brought over one of his poems. I went out to sit on a bench in the commons to read it. It was an odd poem, the style rather like Tennyson, although the references were terribly modern, shot through with allusions to 'hennaed hair' and 'marcel waves,' which seems very strange since someone is always playing an octavina or a viola da gamba in the background."

Elena's journal ends with this observation. Thus there is no record of that day late in August when we all gathered on Rockaway Beach to escape the heat of Manhattan.

We lounged there under Harry's beach umbrella, looking every bit as dissolute as young people can on such occasions. Harry wiped his brow with a plain white handkerchief. "I hear Tom's completed a new poem," he said to me. "Have you read it?"

I shook my head. "No."

"Neither have I," Harry said. He glanced at Elena, and something seemed to empty out of him. By then his infatuation had become a deep romantic yearning, even though she continually broke luncheon and dinner engagements, a rudeness he could dismiss only with much difficulty, but which, as he told me much later in one of the few poetic usages I ever heard from him, "came from her abundance, William, that overflowing cup she was." One afternoon a year later, he came to my apartment and sat massaging his hat like a dislocated shoulder while he related how deep his love was for my sister. His longing was so great it appeared almost comical. "I want you to play John Alden to my Miles Standish, William," he said in a low, strained voice. "I trust that since Elena is your sister, history will not repeat itself." Harry's love became a topic of solemn conversation within our circle as the months passed. Tom even wrote a poem about it, though so well disguising its ultimate meaning that when Harry read it he thought it was about a cousin of his then living in Brazil. Of all of us, Mary was, not surprisingly, the most generous. "It's all rather sad, William," she once told me. "He loves her for the very things that make it impossible for her to love him."

As the afternoon progressed, it was obvious just what those things were. Harry tended to go off on tangents, wandering through history and art as if they formed a whirling pool beneath his feet. Only when he talked of business matters did his mind assume that analytic order which Elena required in everything. "Get to the point, Harry," she'd insist repeatedly as Harry struggled through the jungle of his thought. Still, she bore a strange affection for him all her life, and at his funeral she leaned over to me as the coffin was wheeled out under the cavernous vault of Riverside Church and whispered, "You know, William, Harry had the great good fortune to have lived his whole life in the age of courtly love."

This was true enough, but it was also true that Harry remained a sort of moderator all his life, the figure who surveys the course but rarely alters it, the sort who, as Elena wrote of a rather weak man in her Depression novel, *Calliope*, "might have had a light to shine, had he been born upon a star."

But at moderating, Harry was quite adept, and after fruitlessly trying to get our group to discuss one of Tom's poems that afternoon, he turned his attention to me.

"How's the Cowper thing coming?" he asked. He was referring to a graduate paper, which I would turn into a doctoral dissertation and which Sam would later publish as a favor, and which, because of that, still languishes with stubborn permanence in the half light of a thousand dusty shelves.

"It's coming along at its own pace," I said.

"A long work?" Harry asked.

"It keeps getting longer and longer."

"A book," Mary said mordantly.

Harry looked at her. "You disapprove?"

"I don't care for the subject," Mary said. She had already read the first chapter and found Cowper's madness and religious mania wholly tedious. Of course, although I hadn't said so, these were the very things that fascinated me. Mary claimed that I was attracted only to what she called the "Great Unstables" — Ruskin and Swift and the like. And later she gave a highly psychological interpretation of my concern for such figures, asserting that Whitman House with all its implications had finally seeped beneath the lining of my brain.

Harry turned to Elena. "And what are you working on?" he asked.

Elena had been looking out at the sea. Her hair was tightly wrapped in a black bathing cap, which, I noticed later, she took off before plunging into the waves.

"Just the usual papers and things," she said indifferently.

Harry arched an eyebrow. "Nothing special?"

Elena shook her head. "No."

But if Elena was not working on anything in particular, she was working at everything tirelessly and with enormous energy. She may not have been the brightest student at Barnard in those days, as I once told Martha, but she was certainly the hungriest. Even Sam was impressed by the ferocity with which she went at her studies. "At first I thought it was just an affectation," he said to me many years later. "You know, just a lot of undergraduate whiz-kidding. Then she came into that little office of mine and handed me this neatly stacked manuscript she called *New England Maid*, and I read it that afternoon, and, William, I cannot tell you what it did to me."

Harry looked worried. "I hope you're not finding it boring up on the hill," he said to Elena.

"Of course not, Harry," Elena said.

"Nothing for a woman without a college education," he added with that strained paternal look.

"Nor *with* one, either," Mary said dryly.

Harry turned back to me. The last thing he wanted to do was get into a discussion with Mary about the poor life chances of womanhood.

"And how are things on your job, William?" he asked.

"Fine," I said. I had recently taken a position with a travel agency in the Village, and for the last few months I had spent a great deal of time acquainting various portly individuals with the exotic possibilities of England, France, and the Greek Isles.

"I don't think you'll be in that job very much longer," Harry said confidently. "As a matter of fact, I was thinking, you might be interested in coming to work for one of my —"

I shook my head immediately. "No, Harry. I have one rule. I don't go to work for a friend."

"Ditto for me, by the way, Harry," Mary said.

Harry looked at Elena. "And of course, you have to complete your education. There'll be nothing but school for you until then."

Elena stood up quickly, dusting the sand from her legs. "I think it's time for a swim," she said. "The water looks just right." Then she darted away.

"She's like a deer," Harry said.

I watched as Elena pulled the cap from her head and dove into the first large wave, her long white legs disappearing into the rush of foam.

"How's she doing in her classes?" Harry asked. "She never talks about them."

"Very well, I understand," I said.

"But nothing extraordinary?"

"Well, evidently Dr. Stein has taken an interest in her," I told him.

Harry was genuinely impressed. "That's wonderful. How did she meet him?"

"He read a paper of hers on Sir Walter Scott," I said. "Another professor showed it to him. Then he contacted Elena about a research position."

"That's quite something," Harry said. "Dr. Stein is a very formidable person."

Elena came bounding up to us a few minutes later. She toweled herself vigorously and shook her hair. Harry watched her, dazzled. But she noticed him so little that he must have thought her a cruel and exquisite temptress. Jack MacNeill would later have a similar opinion. "Elena never teases with her body," he once told me, "just with everything else."

When Elena had finished drying herself off, she sat down and glanced all around. I remember thinking that in this light she looked surprisingly like her father — the set of her jaw, the depth of her eyes.

"I understand you're working for Dr. Stein, Elena," Harry said.

Elena pulled on her blouse and tied it in a knot at her waist. "Yes."

"Have you read any of his books?" Harry asked.

"Only one," Elena said. She stood up and slipped on her shorts. "It's called *The Moors*. It's about the Moors of England as they appear in literature."

Harry nodded. "Oh, I see. How is it?"

"I'm not sure," Elena said. "I think there's something very interesting about it. But I'm not sure what."

Later that afternoon, as we were about to leave, Harry insisted on taking a picture of Elena. He later gave the photograph to me, and it has rested for over fifty years in one of the folders in that large file I have kept almost as long and which is marked simply

"On Elena." She is very erect amid a small city of drooping beach umbrellas. She is wearing her dark shorts, and her blouse has become untied and falls loosely at her waist. Her hair is almost totally covered by a large bandeau. She is waving at the camera with her right hand, while the other casually holds a magazine. In no other picture will she ever appear quite so thoroughly happy. In subsequent photographs she will look more willful and accomplished. But she will never in her life look more free.

I think Martha Farrell had a little trouble dealing with Dr. Stein. During one of our first interviews, before she began writing the biography, we sat on Elena's small porch overlooking the bay. It was summer and the water was dotted with scores of brightly colored sails. Martha was peculiarly relaxed as she leaned back into her deck chair. "One of the things that really struck me in all of my research," she said, "is how many men had an influence on Elena."

"People don't sprout fully made from Zeus's head, Martha," I told her.

"No, of course not. But with regard to Dr. Stein and Jack MacNeill, well, I was surprised at how important their influence was."

"If my sister's life can be thought of as a Künstlerroman," I said, "then yes, you'd have to say that Dr. Stein and Jack MacNeill and Jason Findley were central characters."

Martha took a pad from the small table beside her, then drew a pencil from her blouse pocket. "How would you describe Dr. Stein? Generally, I mean."

"I would say that he came close to realizing the medieval idea of a holy being, Martha."

"Which was?"

"Pure mind."

Martha wrote this down in her notebook. "Sounds rather pedantic."

I shrugged. "He was a very intense German Jew. Such people are not known for their frivolity — only for their achievements."

Martha cleared her throat. "Where did you first meet him?"

"At a little restaurant near Columbia. Elena wanted to introduce me."

"Did she find him attractive?" Martha asked.

"She found him edifying," I said. "He was an old man, Martha. He was already dying when she met him. But he was still a great scholar and, I think, for Elena, a kind of ideal. The way he removed his spectacles and rubbed the lenses with his handkerchief — every gesture was scholarly. He embodied seriousness of mind. And Elena was so very young. How could she not see him as a towering figure?"

Martha nodded that peremptory nod of hers. "How about politics? Was he a reactionary?"

"I'm not sure he thought about politics in the usual sense," I told her.

Martha looked at me as if I were holding something back. "Well, Elena was a sophomore by then, wasn't she? So it had to be late 1929 when you met him."

"It was November of 1929," I said. "We all had dinner together."

"About a month or so after the crash?"

"Yes."

"And you didn't talk politics?"

"Not everyone expected the Depression in November 1929, Martha," I said. "But if they had, I'm not sure Dr. Stein would have discussed it, or its ramifications. He was busy writing about Ossian, this presumed Scottish poet."

"All right," Martha said, "no need to pursue that aspect at this time." She jotted down another note or two, then looked up at me. "Just tell me about that evening."

"Fine," I said, "that evening."

We met in a small café off Broadway at around 110th Street, a sort of chophouse, which students frequented but which the faculty shunned. Still, Elena had picked it herself, and so I expected it to be suitable to Dr. Stein.

They came in at around seven-thirty, Dr. Stein wobbling on his cane. He had white hair, thinning quite a bit, and a silvery goatee. He looked very much like a caricature of himself, an old German schoolmaster.

It took Elena and Dr. Stein some time to maneuver themselves into the sunken dining room of the café, and Dr. Stein appeared rather wearied by the time they reached the table.

"Good evening, William," Dr. Stein said after Elena had introduced us.

"Good evening, sir," I said.

Elena stood behind Dr. Stein's chair until he had seated himself, then she took the chair beside him.

"Your sister is most helpful to me, William," Dr. Stein said. He reached over and patted Elena's hand. "I'm so old, you see. It is difficult for me to run about the library as I once did."

"I'm glad she's helpful," I said.

Dr. Stein wagged his finger at me. "And not just the running about. But the reading and the thinking. She does these things, too, William, not always chasing after Valentino's cape, you understand."

"Yes."

"They think it's easy to know and learn," Dr. Stein went on, "these students here." He shook his head. "They think ignorance will fall before them when their trumpets sound."

"Yes, of course," I said. I glanced at Elena. She was not gazing at him worshipfully, as Martha later portrayed it. She was simply listening to him intensely because she had come to believe not that he was infallibly wise but that he stood for very deep and feeling scholarship, the sort, as she would later write in *Quality*, "that enlightens even when it errs."

Dr. Stein glanced about, taking in the place for the first time.

"I have heard of this place," he said. "Steak and potatoes, American style." He grinned impishly. "It's a little dark, but not a bad place." The grin broke into a wide smile. "For steak and potatoes, I mean."

"My brother is working on William Cowper," Elena said.

Dr. Stein nodded. "William Cowper. Very good. Then you must know his poem 'The Task.'"

"Of course," I said.

"That poem is interesting in many ways, you know, Elena," Dr. Stein said. "For you see it has a meaning in its direction, almost a moral position. The poet begins by wanting not to tax himself, to write something on a humble theme, undemanding. But he can't; and that is where his greatness lies. And so, this little poem about a sofa becomes a profound treatise on education and public corruption." He smiled once again, a curiously inward, almost self-mocking smile, which seemed to warm the atmosphere. "Cowper knew, you see, that a petty theme will insure a petty work, just as Melville knew that a mighty theme will make a mighty one."

"Providing the artist is mighty," I said.

"Which he can never know, William," Dr. Stein said, "until he attempts a work that is larger than his ability."

"So the greatness is in the attempt?" I asked.

"No, in the steady realization of it," Dr. Stein said. "And that is made possible, William, by dissatisfaction with your own mediocrity." He wagged his finger. "It is not made certain, you understand, only possible." He grabbed one of the menus resting on the table and opened it. "So, do you want steak or chicken?"

Elena laughed. "Chicken."

I could see his eyes crinkling just above the menu. "Fried or baked or broiled?"

"Fried," Elena said.

Dr. Stein shook his head disapprovingly. "So it always is with Americans," he said. Then he summoned the waiter and ordered fried chicken for us all. "I am a citizen of this country, so I must do as other citizens, eat what they eat, but not necessarily believe what they believe." He leaned back and folded his hands over his stomach. "Ah, if we could get learning in the brain as easily as food in the belly," he said, "all those subjects that drive us mad would be reduced to a sigh of forgotten urgency." He nodded. "The glory of God and the majesty of the state, to begin with. Foolish notions, William. They beget nothing but public mischief." He chuckled, as though he were casting a wry look at his own grandiosity. "People yearn for a community of light," he said, becoming more serious, "but they search for it in the darkness. Take this notion with you into Cowper. Use it as a torch."

Our dinners came a few minutes later. Dr. Stein talked on about Cowper, then turned to Ossian.

"It is not really Ossian who interests me," he said with a shrug. "It is Macpherson who evidently wrote the verses he ascribed to Ossian."

"It was a forgery," Elena said, looking intently at me. "A great literary forgery."

Dr. Stein nodded. "Yes. Macpherson wrote poetry, then claimed it for someone else, an ancient Gaelic warrior."

"You're going to expose this?" I asked.

Dr. Stein shook his head. "Of course not, William. This forgery has been known for quite some time. Dr. Johnson attacked Macpherson as a charlatan. Wordsworth never believed that Macpherson's Ossianic translations were genuine. No, the exposé was done long before my time."

"So what is your interest, exactly, Doctor?" I asked.

"The chill in Macpherson's soul, William," Dr. Stein replied with a sly look, "the peculiar situation in which he found himself, the author of competent poetry which he claimed to have but translated, poetry which came from him but which he had to defend as the work of someone else in order to keep the fame his falsehood had won for him." He looked at Elena. "Had he been less gifted, he could not have written the poems he ascribed to Ossian. Had he been somewhat more gifted, he may not have needed to ascribe them." He turned back to me. "Macpherson was in the odd position of having an imperfect gift, one which he could neither fully deny, taking himself as nothing more than an amateur, nor fully use, since it was not of the first order."

"I see."

Dr. Stein forked a bit of dinner into his mouth and chewed it slowly. "I don't care a fig for Ossian. Macpherson is the heart of my story."

"It's the moral implications, William," Elena explained.

"Not the implications, Elena," Dr. Stein corrected. "Not the moral implications of Macpherson's dilemma, but the moral terror in which he found himself."

Elena nodded quickly. "Yes, his dilemma, William."

Dr. Stein laughed. "Dilemma, that is a wonderful word. To be caught between two equally unfavorable possibilities."

I looked at Elena quizzically.

"Dr. Stein believes that the moment you are certain of something, you are also bored by it," Elena explained.

"Oh," I said. "Well, I suppose."

"Nothing profound in that observation, of course," Dr. Stein added quickly. "But I also suggest that moral dilemma is the best sort because it cannot ever be resolved; it can only be endlessly pursued." He smiled. "Why, imagine, William, how boring Ahab's life would have become if he had survived the whale." Dr. Stein shook his head. "No, William, the best that a great mind can hope for, a great doubting, uncertain, searching mind can hope for, is a moment here and there when the entire edifice presents itself."

I chuckled, though rather self-consciously. "Does that ever happen?"

"Why yes, it does, William," Dr. Stein replied. "It happened to Matthew Arnold on Dover Beach and I think, perhaps, to Wordsworth at Tintern Abbey. It was a moment, very quickly passing, when the mists coalesced, just for a second, and the whole story swam into view."

"And told them what?" I asked.

"Told them, dear boy, that they were different from the rest," Dr. Stein said. "Told them that there is a small world, a very sparsely populated one, of men and women who, from time to time, see the ecstasy as clearly as the dread in being alive."

"Artists," I said.

Dr. Stein gently shook his head. "Minds, William, deeply thoughtful minds. There is a difference between a grave consciousness and the craft necessary to display it. The former may exist without the latter." He turned to Elena. "Would you like a dessert?"

"No, thank you," Elena said.

He turned to me. "What about you, William? I am certainly willing to pay for it. After all, Barnard raised faculty salaries last year."

"I'm really quite set as is," I told him. "But thank you."

"Very well," Dr. Stein said. "At least my generosity cannot be doubted." He pulled his pocket watch from his vest. "My word, quite late for a dotard like myself." His eyes remained fixed on his watch, but his mind clearly was elsewhere. He seemed, just for an instant, entirely lost in his own thought, and it struck me that he was one who bore within his person — at least symbolically for me and certainly for Elena — the ancient creed of thoughtfulness and concentration, and that surely it had been someone like him who had watched as Odysseus set sail from Calypso's island, or stood on a windy beach, staring out to sea, as the *Pequod* slowly drifted from Nantucket Shore.

Elena leaned toward him after a moment, her hand gently touching his.

"Are you ready to leave, Dr. Stein?" she asked.

"Oh yes," he said, rousing himself. "Sorry, was I daydreaming again?" He looked at me. "My apologies, William. I think my brain misfires from time to time, shoots me into space like a cannonball." He laughed lightly. "Please forgive me."

"I very much enjoyed having dinner with you, sir," I told him.

"Good," Dr. Stein said. "I shall take a quick drink of water, then go." He reached for the glass and took hold of it, but as he did so his hand began to shake with sudden violence, sloshing the water back and forth near the rim of the glass.

Elena quickly stretched her hand out toward him.

"No, no," Dr. Stein said, "I'm fine." Then, with very obvious determination, he let go of the glass and slowly drew his hand back into his lap.

"We'll sit for just a moment, Elena," he said quietly, and with a somewhat embarrassed smile.

"Of course," Elena said. "As long as you like."

Dr. Stein nodded. "Thank you, my dear," he said weakly. "Only a minute."

After a short time, the two of them left. Something in that scene remained forever in Elena's mind. It grew there, reaching beyond her initial sympathy into the world of related meaning, she would later describe in *Quality*, "where all things join, all disconnections finally unite. This is the world of that integrated life which the mind insists upon when it insists upon its greatness, when it reaches toward certain gestures that draw us powerfully into man's estate, into a commiseration deeper than pity, an empathy more vast than love and more fully comprehending — gestures like the trembling, for example, of a great scholar's hand."

I did not see Elena again for several weeks. I assumed that she was immersed in her work with Dr. Stein, and I certainly had my hands full with Cowper. It might have been quite some time before we got together again if Elizabeth had not decided to visit New York.

We had seen her only occasionally since moving to the city, short hurried visits during which we had spent most of our time with Mother in Whitman House. So we were delighted that Elizabeth planned to spend an entire weekend, and Elena was particularly excited as we waited for her train.

She arrived toward late morning, and I saw her instantly. She was dressed in a long wool coat with a high fur collar, and I remember thinking how out of place she looked as she jostled through the crowd. I had known her among the greenery of McCarthy Pond and Wilmot Street, and it was hard to re-imagine her now, very womanly indeed, as she made her way through the haunting maze of light that bathed the arcade in a soft, smoky radiance.

"There she is," I shouted, and Elena rose onto her tiptoes, craning her neck to get a glimpse of her friend.

Then I caught sight of the young man who walked directly beside her, carrying a piece of luggage which I recognized as Elizabeth's. Elena must have seen him at that instant too, because she glanced up at me questioningly.

I shrugged. "Perhaps someone she met on the train?"

But that was not the case, and as soon as the embraces were over, Elizabeth introduced him.

"This is Howard Carlton," she said. "He moved to Standhope about a month ago."

Howard smiled politely. He was quite handsome — tall, lean, with dark curly hair — not at all the frail and scholarly type I had envisioned for Elizabeth.

"It's good to be in New York again," he said. He was dressed in a full-length overcoat that had an expensive look to it, and his hands were sheathed in elegant leather gloves. He looked older than the rest of us, and a great deal more experienced. There was a concentration in his face that lent it an almost feminine loveliness, and I think that because of him Elena would come somewhat to distrust men of too much beauty. In her novels, for example, she would choose to make her great men those of the least imposing physical presence, men like Raymond Finch in *Calliope*, "sent down to earth in a gunny sack of skin."

"I know New York quite well," Howard said, smiling tentatively, "but I would find it difficult to live here now."

We were still standing amid the bustle on the platform, bumping about as the crowds shifted by us, but Howard seemed oblivious to this. His voice was calmly modulated and soft, as if he were speaking to us in the serenity of a Victorian parlor.

"Elizabeth wanted to see it, of course," Howard said. "And I think that everyone should." He glanced at Elena and me, then shifted his weight uneasily from one foot to another, an early sign, as Elena would later point out, of the basic fears within him, the sense that the earth was not firm beneath his feet.

I glanced at my watch. "Well, why don't we get out of this smelly place and have a nice lunch."

Howard nodded, as if I were addressing him alone. "Yes, that would be good," he said quietly. "Someplace nearby, perhaps."

We ambled out into a glittering wintry brilliance, Howard and I in front together, Elena and Elizabeth lagging behind.

"You said you knew the city?" I asked.

"Yes, I lived here for quite some time," Howard said. He tugged one of his gloves on more firmly. "With my father. Before he died." He looked over toward me. "I wanted to go someplace small. I tried a few places outside the cities. Quincy, outside Boston, for a time." He shook his head. "But even that was a bit too much for me." He smiled delicately. "You might as well know, I have a nervous condition."

"I see."

Howard lifted his collar against the cold. "Nothing serious, I hope, only a sort of . . . well, a sort of confusion." He looked at me then with the saddest eyes I had ever seen. "A rather helpless confusion." He glanced away. "There's Schrafft's," he said. "We could have lunch there."

We steered our way across the avenue to the restaurant.

When we were all seated, Elizabeth pulled the small hat from her head and laughed. "Well, what do you think?"

She had cut her hair, reduced that wall of flame to a small mound of embers, in the interest, I suppose, of modernity.

"What do you think?" she repeated.

Elena and I exchanged glances.

"Well, just fine, I suppose," Elena said. "But why did you do it?"

"At my suggestion," Howard said as he absently opened the menu. "Something I read about long hair being a symbol for enslavement." He looked at Elena. "You wear your hair long, I see."

"Yes."

"Black hair," Howard said. "Coal black."

"It always has been," Elena said, looking at him oddly, as if, at last, she had met a creature far too strange for immediate evaluation.

Howard's eyes fell back down toward the menu. "Mine is thinning just a bit now," he said. He shook his head. "How silly, to talk about one's hair." He chuckled then, but at something known only to himself.

"I'll have soup and a sandwich," Elizabeth said excitedly. "My God, Elena, it's wonderful being in New York with you."

"Yes, wonderful," Howard muttered.

"How did you happen to get to Standhope?" I asked him.

"Well, when my father died, I left New York, as I said." He smiled. "I inherited a good sum of money, you see, so I could live anywhere I wanted to."

"And you chose Standhope?" I asked unbelievingly.

"You find that odd, don't you?"

I laughed lightly. "Well, yes, I do."

"Elizabeth says that both you and your sister were anxious to get away."

"Yes, we were."

Howard picked up the salt shaker and twirled it about in his hands. "Well, I had the same feeling, only I wanted to get away from New York." He smiled again. "I was looking for a restful place, like a sanitarium, you might say."

"And you found that in Standhope?"

"That, and Elizabeth," Howard said quietly. His eyes shifted over to her, and it could not have been more clear how much he loved her.

We ordered a few minutes later. We all had our fill, and the check could hardly have been more than three or four dollars.

Back on the street again, Elizabeth stood glancing east and west as we stood under the Schrafft's awning, as much in awe of the city as Elena had once been.

"What would like to do, Elizabeth?" Howard asked. "I told you, anything you like."

Elizabeth looked at Elena. "You know the city. Make a suggestion."

"The entire day is on me, by the way," Howard added quickly. "So please, do whatever you like."

"Well, we could go to the theater," Elena said.

And that is what we did. We went to the Hammerstein Theater to hear Helen Morgan belt out the songs from *Sweet Adeline* — a rather superior form of drivel, as Mary once said, definitely preferable to the zoo. After the theater, we found a small, darkly illuminated lounge. It seemed to put Howard in more animated spirits. He draped his arm over Elizabeth's shoulder as they sat across from us in a booth.

"I like places like this," he said, "dark and cozy."

"Why is that, Howard?" Elena asked him.

He seemed to appreciate the question. "It is enclosed," he said. "I have a very small house in Standhope, very small, just two rooms and a little kitchen." He glanced quickly at Elizabeth, then back to Elena. "I've always been this way, since I was a little boy. I've always felt somehow, well, unborn." He laughed slightly. "How silly, I'm thirty-one."

Elizabeth nuzzled Howard's cheek. "It's the money, don't you think, Elena?" she asked. "He's never had to get out in the world."

Elena did not answer, but I could see how carefully she kept her eyes upon them, as if trying to unearth the secret of their relationship.

"I behave like an invalid," Howard said, "and I'm never sick." He shook his head. "I'm a mystery to myself." He looked at Elizabeth. "Can you love a mystery?"

Elizabeth kissed him very gently. "Yes," she said.

"How did you two meet?" I asked.

"At the library," Elizabeth said. "I work there, you know, and Howard came in one afternoon and asked for something." She looked at him. "It was *The Canterbury Tales*, wasn't it?"

Howard nodded. "That, and maybe a volume of sentimental poetry, something like that." He looked at Elena. "I don't like my own taste. I resent my own taste. It's so juvenile."

Elizabeth laughed delightedly. "Well, I had the book, of course. I mean, who in Standhope would ever read *The Canterbury Tales?* It hadn't been checked out in thirty years."

"She thought I was shy," Howard said. "People think I'm shy, but I'm not. I used to approach strangers all the time, when I was a little boy, and ask them questions. But of course, you can't keep doing things like that. Not when you're grown-up. You frighten people if you do. They think you're after something, or just crazy, perhaps." He shrugged. "So I stopped doing that about twenty years ago. I still miss it."

"He came up to me, though," Elizabeth said. "He told me who he was and where he lived and why he'd come to Standhope. He told me all this before he mentioned *The Canterbury Tales.*"

"Because of her face," Howard said in an almost wistful tone of voice, as if relating events so long past that they were already golden with nostalgia. "Her eyes, you know. They were very clear." He laughed. "It helps my confusion, you see, to have clear eyes around."

Elena looked at him skeptically. "Are you serious?"

"Oh yes," Howard said. "No matter how crazy it sounds."

"Howard has a sort of condition," Elizabeth said.

"That's right," Howard said, quite openly. "A condition of being easily thrown off balance." He was looking very closely at Elena. "Have you ever had a day when you just couldn't manage anything?"

"Yes," Elena said.

"Well, I have years like that."

I couldn't help it. I started to laugh, then caught myself. "Sorry, Howard," I said, trying to regain my composure, "I didn't mean to laugh."

"Oh, that's all right," Howard said. "Really, quite all right." He looked at Elena. "I'm not sensitive about it. I don't try to hide it. I know that if I weren't wealthy, I'd probably starve. But there are times when it seems almost a blessing, you know?"

Elena was evidently intensely interested in this person, and she would later write that he had seemed to her like a floating cloud, a sympathetic presence, "precious and unreal, a figure carved from the prose of Walter Pater."

"You say a blessing?" Elena asked.

Howard nodded. "Yes."

"In what way, Howard?"

"Because I feel I'm everywhere at once, sometimes, and so everything lives in me, you see?"

Elena smiled. "Not really."

"Well, I'm many things at once," Howard went on. "Partly an adult, partly a child." He smiled. "Even partly man and partly woman." He turned to me. "It must seem odd to you, William."

"It surely does, Howard," I told him.

He laughed, then put his arm around Elizabeth and squeezed her to him. "She understands as much as anyone can."

"He explained it another way once," Elizabeth said. She looked at Howard. "You don't mind?"

Howard shrugged. "If I said it, you can repeat it."

"He said he sometimes felt that the basic thing had been reversed in him."

"The basic thing?" Elena asked. "What do you mean?"

"Life," Elizabeth said. "He thought it had been reversed in him. The process, I mean. So that he was really a ghost, only born out of turn, before it had a life."

Howard smiled. "So now I'm a ghost who hasn't died."

I shook my head in despair. "Well, it certainly must be an interesting feeling, Howard."

He nodded quickly. "It's a handicap, though, being odd. Not really crazy, or anything like that. Certainly not dangerous. Just odd."

"Yes, I suppose it is," Elena said.

"It's like being scarred or something," Howard explained. "You know that people want to know about how you got cut or burned before they want to know anything else. Then, once it's been explained to them, well, then they lose interest." He took a sip of water, his eyes on Elena's. "That's why I always tell them first, like I did with Elizabeth, before I mentioned *The Canterbury Tales.*"

It seemed an appropriate time to change the subject. "How's your father, Elizabeth?" I asked.

Her mood immediately darkened. "Not very well," she said.

"He sleeps on the porch a lot," Howard added. "I help Elizabeth get him back into the house sometimes."

Elizabeth looked at Elena. "I don't think he has much longer."

"I'm sorry to hear that," Elena said.

"Sometimes he gets a letter from an old war buddy or something," Elizabeth said, "and he'll go out on the porch with his whiskey and read it over and over until he passes out."

"Then we bring him in the house," Howard said. "We never drank in my family. Teetotalers, all of us."

"Well, my father has been known to have a few," I said.

"I was all for Prohibition," Howard told me. "So was my family. I think my father gave some money to help push it." He nodded sternly. "Good cause, I think."

"Perhaps," I said dully.

Howard slapped his hands together. "Have you seen any of Elizabeth's new paintings?"

Elena looked surprised. "I didn't know there were any old ones."

"Well, I've been sketching a few things," Elizabeth said modestly. "Nothing much."

"Actually, they're very good," Howard said. "Especially the ones of the town bandstand and the front of the library."

Elizabeth waved her hand in a dismissive way. "Howard is such a fan," she said.

"Next time you come to New York, you should bring a few with you," I told her. "Elena and I have some friends who might be interested."

Elena looked at me quizzically.

"Harry," I explained. "He's interested in painting." I turned back to Elizabeth. "Are you doing mostly sketches?"

"Anything, really," Elizabeth said casually. And she quietly went on to tell us how Howard had coaxed her into what I believe she thought of as the beginning of a more creative life. She talked about her paintings, first describing them physically — the color and design of each canvas — then describing the mood she hoped to portray. There was a sameness in all of this, not of unoriginality, which in the end devolves into self-parody, but rather of a uniformity of vision, a sense of the world that was her own. Elizabeth saw the life of Standhope as something that shifted continually but remained unchanged, the fickleness of the human mood anchored by the clockwork of the seasons. That vision was more pleasant, perhaps, than mine, and certainly less severe than Elena's became, but it remained distinct and comprehending.

"I guess I've come to love Standhope," she said, as if in conclusion. "That must seem very silly to you, Elena."

"No, it doesn't," Elena said. "It's just a question of what you emphasize."

Elizabeth looked puzzled. "What do you mean?"

I think it was the first time Elena had ever been asked a direct question concerning her own feelings about Standhope. She would answer it in New England Maid, of course, but on this day when such a book was beyond both her intent and her ability, she could only begin to address those matters which would so enflame the prose of her first book, giving to it, as one critic wrote, "a sense of lost amusement which darkens every page."

"You don't like Standhope at all?" Elizabeth asked.

"I feel as if it got in my way, Elizabeth," Elena said. "It's just something I feel. I don't understand the implications of it."

They talked on for a while, both of them reliving, as they had not had a chance to do in some time, the shared pleasures of their childhood. They talked of McCarthy Pond, of diving off the cliff above it, with me always diving last, as they said, "in the role of manly protector." They talked of their schoolroom antics, and poor Mrs. Nichols was once again skewered by their wit. They seemed to delight in each other, and Howard and I sat enjoying them as well, though Howard repeatedly glanced apprehensively at his watch.

The reason for this was finally made plain, to my disappointment and, yet more pointedly, to Elena's.

"I suppose we should think about getting a train now," Howard said.

"A train?" Elena asked. She looked at Elizabeth. "I thought you were staying for the weekend."

"Howard didn't want to do that," Elizabeth said.

Elena was not satisfied. "Why not, Howard?" she asked him.

"I like to be back in my house," Howard said. "I don't like New York for a whole day anymore." He glanced at me helplessly, then turned back to Elena. "It's one of the inconveniences of knowing me. Quirkiness. I'm working to get rid of it. But I decided on the trip down that I'd better not stay in the city for more than a few hours."

"I see," Elena said. She looked at Elizabeth. "Well, if you have to."

"I do," Elizabeth said.

Within an hour they were on the train headed back for Standhope and Elena and I were walking along together down Seventh Avenue.

"Well, he doesn't seem so bad for all that craziness," I said.

Elena did not look convinced. "You have to know what you'll indulge," she said.

"Of course."

"You have to be able to say, 'All right, I'll do this, but not that.'"

"Yes, you do."

"It's like a voice in your mind," she added.

I laughed. "Careful, you're sounding a little cracked yourself."

"A separate voice," Elena added. "Like Dr. Stein has described Ariadne's, full of guidance."

"Well, maybe Elizabeth has a voice of her own."

Elena nodded. "And maybe it's telling her to stay in Standhope."

"Maybe."

We continued to stroll down Seventh Avenue, the Saturday evening bustle sweeping by us in all directions in carnival chaos.

I laughed. "I mean, when you compare it to this noise and frenzy, small-town life may not be so bad."

"Perhaps," Elena said.

"Especially for a painter," I added. "I mean, Monet preferred Giverny, right? And Cézanne left Paris for Aix-en-Provence."

Elena walked on silently, glancing randomly right and left as if trying to get hold of the city itself. "I couldn't have stayed in Standhope," she said after a minute. Her eyes filled with a sense of determination. "I always thought it was trying to make me disappear."

I shook my head. "I don't think so, Elena."

"I do," she said firmly. "And I was not going to let that happen." She seemed certain that she'd made the right decision. Later, though perhaps only fleetingly, she would question the course that had led her from Standhope for good. "I would not become the shadow my hometown would have made me," Dorothea Moore says in *Inwardness*, "and so, avoiding that, I became a stone."

A few weeks after Elizabeth's visit, Mother died in her sleep at Whitman House. The orderly who found her the next morning said that the bedclothes had been completely smooth. "She couldn't have had pain, Mr. Franklin," he assured my father as he stood in the portico of Whitman House the next afternoon, "because, you see, when they have pain, well, they just twist around and things get all tangled up." Many years later, when an overly romantic essayist wrote that Elena Franklin's mother had "died the death of Keats's fond dream, 'to cease upon the midnight with no pain,' " Elena responded in a terse note that "Keats's fond dream had nothing to do with the death of a woman who had been slowly going mad for twenty years and of whose pain you can know nothing whatsoever."

Miraculously, the director of Whitman House found my father at our house on Wilmot Street when he telephoned there on the morning of my mother's death. Minutes after hearing the news, Father telephoned Elena in New York. Then Elena called me.

"William, I have some bad news," she said, her voice noticeably strained. "Mother died this morning. We need to get back to Stand-hope today."

An hour or so later, Elena and I met at Penn Station and boarded a train. She was very self-contained, completely controlled. From time to time I would attempt to engage her in conversation, but she always resisted, mumbling one-word answers to my questions. In *Inwardness*, when Dorothea's mother asks her how she intends to deal with the grief she feels for her dead son, Dorothea replies, "I intend to think and think and think."

That is probably what Elena did on the train that afternoon, refusing to be drawn into conversation, using a book only as a prop, something upon which she could hold her eyes to keep them from searching ceaselessly about the train. By the time we pulled into the station, she looked exhausted, yet somehow vibrantly alive, as if thought itself refreshed her.

Father met us at the train. He was wearing a trim black suit and black bow tie. He stood very erect, as if a huge weight had been lifted from his shoulders. That weight was, of course, my mother, as Elena was to make plain in *New England Maid:* "At the railway station my father looked as though he had regained his youth, the happy gait that was synonymous with his vitality, a freedom that was but newly his — the carefree consequence of a woman's death." That my father was able to reconcile himself to Elena after he read that line was one of the minor miracles of his small life.

"I'm glad I was here in Standhope when the news came about your mother," he said to us as we stepped off the train. There was a hint of liquor about him, or perhaps cheap perfume.

I shook my father's outstretched hand. "What happened exactly?"

"You mean cause of death, Billy? Well, nobody seems to know. She just died in her sleep, that's all." He moved away from me and embraced Elena. "Just died in her sleep, Princess."

Elena looked at him steadily. "Where is she?"

My father seemed puzzled. "You mean the body?"

"Yes."

"Still at the asylum."

"I want to see her," Elena said firmly.

"The body's not ready yet," my father said. He gave me a helpless look, then turned back to Elena. "It's got to go to the funeral parlor."

"I want to see her before then," Elena said.

"They won't let us do that, will they, Princess?"

Elena smiled thinly. "How can they stop us?"

A few minutes later, we were standing before Whitman House as my father struggled to explain to its director that his daughter wanted to see her mother's body before any further preparations had been done.

The director listened patiently, then spoke to Elena. "This is normally done after embalming, you understand."

"Yes, I do," Elena said.

With that, the director ushered Elena and me into the building and down a flight of stairs to the basement. My father had decided not to accompany us.

"This is not the most graceful way to view a body, I'm afraid," the director said as he switched on the light and pointed to a metal table. "Mrs. Franklin is under that sheet," he said. "I'll leave you alone for a few minutes, of course."

The room was very musty, but it was cool. There was a battered sink in the corner and a jungle of piping overhead. Metal shelves lined the far wall, stacked with assorted supplies — trays and light bulbs, rolls of toilet tissue.

Elena walked quietly to the table and turned back to me. "Do you want to see her?"

I shook my head. "Not really, Elena. Why do you want to?"

Elena did not reply. She drew the sheet from our mother's face and looked at her. In *New England Maid*, she described what she saw: "My mother was resting on her back, her face pointing directly toward the ceiling. Her eyes were closed, but her lower lip drooped slightly downward, so that the tips of her bottom teeth were visible. The light fell across her face from the left, throwing the right side into shadow. There were deep creases beneath her eyes and two vertical ones on either side of her face. Her skin looked parched and leathery, as if already fossilized, but unconsciously enduring, joined at last to earth."

Elena drew the sheet back over our mother's face. "All right," she said, "we can go now."

The two of us walked quickly up the stairs and out of the asylum. My father was standing casually in front of his Whippet 4, looking for all the world like a cab driver waiting for a fare.

Once we had returned to the house on Wilmot Street, he informed

Elena and me of the funeral plans he'd already made. They were spare, to say the least.

"I'm not having any visiting hours at the house, either," he said in conclusion. "I don't want all the neighbors trailing through here staring at me. I know what they think. Believe me, I know."

Determining what my father did or did not know of this world might have occupied the lifetime of more than one researcher. But as the evening progressed and he drew deeper into the whiskey, he hinted of certain disappointments. While Elena read quietly in her chair by the window, he spoke to me of dingy hotel rooms, bad investments, missed chances. It was the litany of a little man, the droning complaint of a tiny soul, and after a time even Elena could stand no more of it.

"Perhaps you should get some sleep," she said, cutting him off. My father glanced up. "What's that?"

"I said you should get some sleep. There's a lot to do tomorrow." Father nodded slowly. "Putting your mother in the ground."

Elena closed her book. "Go to bed, Father."

He struggled to his feet, his head weaving right and left. "Didn't mean to get sloshed, Elena. Not nice, what with the funeral. You'll forgive my bad manners, please."

"Go to bed," Elena repeated.

He obeyed immediately, with a groggy nod to me, and passed down the hall, propping himself against the wall. He closed the door softly behind him.

"He's sleeping in her room," I said. "Been a long time since he's slept in there."

Elena returned to her book.

"I'll never understand the power you have over him," I said, "the way he obeys you."

Elena did not look up. "We understand each other," she said crisply.

The next afternoon, under the weepy auspices of a slight drizzle and to the muttered incantations of a young Congregational minister who had never met her, my mother was buried in Standhope's town cemetery. Elizabeth and Howard were there, standing respectfully at Elena's side, my father and I across from them. The minister was beginning his brief commentary on my mother's life, when Mr. Brennan came trudging up the hill, hat already in his hand, the wind tugging at his enormously baggy pants.

"Sorry I'm late, boy," he hissed into my ear. He seemed thinner than I remembered, but his eyes remained red rimmed and glistening so that he looked, as he always did, either on the verge of a seizure of weeping or as if he had just completed one.

After the funeral, we all made our way down the hillside. At the bottom, Mr. Brennan rushed over to Elena, embraced her, muttered, "Sorry, so sorry," then rushed away.

"He's got to get back to the drink," Elizabeth explained apologetically to my father.

"Oh well, I can certainly understand that," my father replied.

The rest of us went back to Wilmot Street, where we sat gloomily at the dining room table. Elena made coffee and my father produced some sort of cake to go with it. After a while Elizabeth and Howard excused themselves.

"I loved your mother," Elizabeth said as she embraced Elena at the door, "I really did."

Elena smiled faintly. "I'll write when I get back to New York."

Elena disappeared not long after Elizabeth and Howard left our house. She simply eased out and left me sitting in the living room watching father snooze.

At first I thought she had merely gone for a short stroll, but as the hours passed it became clear that she had done a good deal more than that. At a certain point, my imagination got the better of me and I began to construct lurid notions of what might have happened to her.

"I'm going out to look for Elena," I told my father.

He had roused himself just a minute before. "Where?"

"I don't know."

"She just wants to be alone, Billy," my father said. "She's got that in her blood. I've known that since she was a child."

"It'll be night soon."

My father smiled. "She can walk in the dark."

I shook my head. "No. I'm going after her."

Evening had already begun to fall by the time I found her. I had gone to the town square, now so much more brightly lit and bustling than it had been in my boyhood. I peeped in at Thompson's Drugstore and saw old man Thompson himself, ancient as ever behind the counter, shakily moving mortar and pestle. I passed through the park, edging near that bandstand where Wilson had spoken so firmly in his Presbyterian black suit. Then it struck me where she was, and I found her there, sitting on the bench across from Whitman House.

"I thought you might be here," I said as I neared her.

She looked at me. "I'm glad you came, William."

"Really? Father thought you just wanted to be alone."

"I did. But that's lasted long enough." She patted the bench beside her. "Come, sit down. You've walked quite a long ways."

I sat down beside her on the bench. The light rain had stopped hours before and now the clouds were breaking up entirely, silver lines shooting out above the horizon.

"Have you been here a long time?" I asked.

"About an hour," Elena said. "We'll go back home in a little while. I just want to stay here a bit longer." She turned to face the gate of Whitman House. In his memoir of her, Jason wrote that thought moved across Elena's face in a very physical manner, like a cloud passing over a field. I remember very clearly that at this particular moment it did.

"What are you thinking, Elena?" I asked.

She shrugged. "Just things in general." She glanced about the park. "It's very peaceful here."

Elena would take that sense of peace back with her to New York, the sense, perhaps but half-remembered, of the lines of silver after the long grayness of the day, of the tall, firm gate and the little road that curved gently beyond it. She would take these things back with her, and they would lend a curious calm to the final page of *New England Maid*, ending that often angry work with a respectful quiet: "And so I sat in a small park across from the madhouse in which my mother died and thought about those things which are a part of all our thinking, from the most common to the most grand: our own youth, the childhood of our children, the old age of our parents . . . all that lingers but does not abide."

Elena plunged ever more deeply into her studies after her return
to New York. Martha called this a "compensatory act, one involving
the release of cathartic effort, transferable from mourning to labor."
There may, in fact, be some truth in this; but it should also be remembered that, at the same time, Dr. Stein was beginning his final assault
upon Ossian, and that much of the labor involved fell directly on
Elena as his support.

I was attending graduate classes regularly during 1930, and I often
ran into the two of them as they made their way down the steps
of the library, Elena carrying the books, Dr. Stein barely carrying
himself.

Despite evidence of decline, Dr. Stein always appeared quite relaxed
and congenial on those occasions. "So good to see you, William,"
he'd say. Then we would chat awhile, one or the other of us pursuing
some willowy thread through Cowper or Gaelic mythology, while Elena
stood silently on the steps, clutching a stack of books to her chest.
Looking back on those encounters now, I realize that Elena must
have felt somewhat left out as Dr. Stein and I, old professor and
ambitious graduate student, grandly elaborated some literary notion
or plowed through a complex exegesis of doubtful interest to anyone
but ourselves.

At the time, of course, Elena gave no hint of this. But once, years
later, when I was late for an appointment and full of involved apology,
she cut me off quickly with a single cryptic retort: "Never mind,
William, I know how to wait." There was an edge of personal affront
in her voice, and I think it came from all the times she had been
made to feel invisible by Dr. Stein and me and countless others. In
Quality, she finally expressed this sense of what she called "female
waiting" in a passage that deals, at least tangentially, with Kate Cho-
pin's The Awakening:

In those idle moments on the verandah, while the heroine waits amid
the lingering smell of departed cigars, there is all we shall ever need
to know of that part of woman which ceaselessly petitions for a wider
life, which waits through time, from Sappho on the rock of Leucadia,
to Virginia Woolf staring down into the canal, still living in that ghostly
pose she thought her only true and living self. Thus is female life
stranded in the outer chamber, beneath the arched hallway, while
behind the tightly closed, exclusionary door the delegates convene,

the generals confer. And then, beyond the great hall and into the streets and houses of ordinary life, this waiting persists endlessly, until it becomes more than manners, custom, law, becomes more than what one does and forms a part of what one is, a silence at the center of the self, one which can no longer contemplate its own release. Until on a sweltering summer afternoon, while the rest of the party watches the regatta from another shore, the summons comes to wait no more, and later there is found only a parasol rammed into the wet sand, and beyond that, nothing at all but the open sea.

If my sister's resentment was this powerful in 1930, she kept it very much to herself. She did not permit it to spoil the relationship which had grown between herself and Dr. Stein.

This relationship kept our little group buzzing for a time. Tom called it Elena's "May/December thing," and Sam said that the problem between my sister and Dr. Stein was mainly aesthetic. "You don't put a pretty young thing like Elena next to a withered old crone like Stein and come out with a balanced portrait," he said. Mary was not in the least bothered by it, however. The real worrier was Harry.

"You really should do something about this situation, William," he said to me as we sat in my apartment one afternoon. "It's unnatural."

I laughed. "Unnatural? Really, Harry, don't you think that's going a bit far?"

Harry nodded self-consciously. "Well, maybe you're right. But she's just a young woman, and a person like that, innocent, you know, she . . ."

"I think Elena can take care of herself, Harry," I said.

"You don't know that old Agrippa, William," Harry said. "The mind — and he has a powerful one — the mind can do strange things."

I smiled. "Are you suggesting she's been hypnotized, Harry?"

"Of course not. But have you seen her lately?"

"Not for a few weeks."

Harry shook his head. "She looks very bad, William. Sort of frumpy, if you want to know the truth. Old clothes — wrinkled ones, at that. She looks pale, unhealthy, as if she never sees the sun."

"For God's sake, Harry, she's very busy. She has all her own work, then she has this other stuff she has to do for Dr. Stein. She can't run about looking like a debutante all the time."

Harry shifted uncomfortably on his seat, then stared at me pointedly. "Perhaps so, William, but when you get right down to it, do you think it's healthy for a woman her age not to go out, not to be with other people her own age, to stay cooped up with a man old enough to be her grandfather?"

The protective instinct rose in me suddenly. "All right, Harry," I said. "I'll make it my business to check in on Elena."

And that is what I did, the very next day. When she came into the lobby of her residence hall, I could not have been more astonished. She did not look pallid; she looked radiant, her eyes shining, cheerful, her whole manner full of sparkling energy.

I lifted my hand slowly toward her. "You look . . . Elena . . ." I stammered, "you look beautiful."

Elena laughed. "William, please."

"No," I said, "it's amazing. Harry told me you'd grown pale and shriveled with too much reading. What foolishness." I smiled. "Now I know how I am destined to be remembered, Elena."

"How's that?"

"As the man who had the beautiful sister."

Elena laughed again and took my arm. "Let's go out for a while. It's such a lovely day. We'll go for a walk, get an egg cream. Let's just do something outside. Harry's not altogether wrong, you know. I spend too much time indoors."

We walked down to Columbus Avenue and stopped in at one of the dairy stores that were in every neighborhood in those days. I remember that a large man carefully followed Elena's instructions as he cut an enormous slice of cheese from the tub, then wrapped it in wax paper.

We took a bus up Broadway. They were green and white double-deckers then, and we sat on the upper level, munching cheese and talking quietly about whatever street scene passed below us. Elena always drew energy from the city, transformed its currents into her own.

At 125th Street — at Elena's insistence — we took an open-air trolley cross-town to the ferry station. A few minutes later we were chugging across the Hudson, the two of us standing together at the rail, watching Manhattan drift away. Elena pointed upriver to an old tumbledown shack on the New Jersey side.

"That's the Columbia boathouse," she said. "Dr. Stein took me over there once. He has very fond memories of that place." She looked at me. "He used to go over there with his wife, to watch the boys practice."

"I didn't know he was married."

"Oh yes, for many years. She died in the Spanish flu epidemic. The same one that almost killed you."

"He's been a widower that long?"

Elena nodded, then turned back toward the boathouse. "Yes, he has."

I touched her arm. "Elena, has it ever occurred to you that this relationship you have with Dr. Stein . . . that it's unusual?"

Elena continued to watch the boathouse. A breeze from the river lifted a strand of her hair. "No, but I know that others think it is."

"Well, I'm thinking particularly of Harry."

"Why?"

"Because he's been very worried about you."

Elena glanced down at her hands on the rail but said nothing.

"Are you at all aware that Harry is in love with you?" I asked.

"I am," Elena whispered.

"Do you plan to do anything about it?"

Elena turned to me. "Do? Do what? Marry him?"

"I'm reasonably certain that's what he has in mind."

"He hasn't asked me."

"And if he did?"

"I'd say no."

Someone began playing an accordion inside the ferry cabin.

"He loves you, Elena," I said. "He would marry you in a minute. Yet you seem to belong to Dr. Stein."

Elena was listening to the music. "Belong is a bit much, William."

"What is it, then? Enchantment?"

Elena looked back out over the river. A large white ship could be seen far downstream.

"I learn from Dr. Stein," she said crisply.

I shook my head. "That's not enough. For God's sake, you're twenty years old. And he's near — what, eighty?"

Elena nodded. "That's not the point."

"What is?"

Elena straightened herself. "I've decided to leave the residence hall. I'm going to move into Dr. Stein's building."

I was astonished. "You're what? You're going to move in with him?"

Elena shook her head. "Of course not, William. I'm simply going to move down the hall from his apartment. There's a woman, a Mrs. Connolly, a widow whose two sons now have families of their own, she has a room. I'll be able to come and go more or less as I please."

"And be near the good doctor?" I asked sarcastically.

Elena said nothing, but I could see the heat rising in her.

"Remember that night with Howard and Elizabeth?" I reminded her. "Remember Ariadne's voice?"

Elena turned toward me. "I am following Ariadne's voice."

I smiled thinly. "And it's old and has a German accent?"

"Yes, it does," Elena said firmly. "He is teaching me to be wise, and I am going to stay with him, William, until he dies." She waited for me to digest this new set of circumstances, then she smiled tentatively. "I'll be living down the hall from him, but he needs me quite a bit, so I'll be at his apartment much of the time. You may visit me there, if you like."

Two weeks later I did just that. It was early in the evening, and I had first gone to Mrs. Connolly's. As expected, Elena was with Dr. Stein, and so I walked down the corridor and knocked at his door.

Elena answered it.

"Hello, William," she said. Her voice was flat, but her eyes were questioning. She was trying to guess my mood.

"I've just come to pay you that visit," I said softly as I removed my hat.

Her face brightened. "Good," she said. "Come in."

It was a lovely room, lined with mahogany bookshelves, an enormous desk by the window, and in the corner, a cello resting upright in its stand.

"Can't play the cello anymore, William," Dr. Stein said as he came into the room. He thrust out his hand. "Good to see you."

I nodded. "And you, sir."

"Sit down, won't you?"

I took a seat opposite a small sofa. Dr. Stein lowered himself onto the sofa, Elena's arm under his, carefully helping him.

"Now you sit, my dear," Dr. Stein said.

Elena sat down beside him.

"Would you like a drink, my boy?" Dr. Stein asked immediately.

"Yes, perhaps a brandy, if you have it."

"Of course," Dr. Stein said casually. He turned to Elena. "Would you mind?"

Elena went to the kitchen. I could hear her tinkling glasses together.

Dr. Stein seemed to take my measure for a moment, then he spoke. "I understand you disapprove of Elena living down the hall."

"I'm surprised she told you that," I said.

"Why shouldn't she?" Dr. Stein said. "Is it true still, my boy?"

"I have a sister . . ."

"Whose reputation you must protect?"

"Yes."

Dr. Stein laughed and shook his head. "I am dying, William. How could I possibly commit an offense against your sister?"

"It's just that it seems odd, sir," I said cautiously.

"To whom?"

"I'm told that some people talk about it at the university," I said, repeating a rumor whose only source was Harry Morton.

"Idiots," Dr. Stein said emphatically. "You must ignore such foolishness, otherwise your life may be crushed by it." He leaned back into the sofa and smiled. "Let that be an end to it, then."

Elena came out with the glasses of brandy, distributed them, then returned to her place on the sofa.

Dr. Stein lifted his glass in the air. "What shall we toast?"

I shrugged. "I really don't know."

Dr. Stein regarded me pointedly. "To dutifulness, then," he said.

And so we toasted this virtue, then went on to discuss many things. Dr. Stein talked about Calderón and Elena about Pindar. She sometimes took exception to one of Dr. Stein's remarks, and he would listen very carefully to her, though he rarely recanted.

Toward six, Dr. Stein invited me to dinner. I immediately agreed, and for the next hour the three of us worked in his small kitchen, which Dr. Stein had stocked with a copious assortment of Old World spices and delicacies. He was not able to move about with much ease by then, but he could shout orders with terrific energy, while Elena and I worked at the cutting board and the stove.

At eight we dined on the meal we had prepared — lentil soup and beef Stroganoff, with a Riesling that a friend of Dr. Stein's had managed to smuggle into the country a year or so before.

"To all that keeps the heart uplifted, then," Dr. Stein said, his glass raised high. "And to you, Elena," he added, glancing at her with a smile.

After dinner, we talked mostly about the work they had been doing together, a conversation I found somewhat tedious since I knew little of the subject.

Dr. Stein noticed this after a time, and he stood up, walked to his desk, and pulled out a large typed manuscript. "Here, William. Better just to read it."

I took the book from his hand and absently flipped over the title page. He had dedicated it to my sister.

"A university press is set to publish it," he said, returning to the sofa, "so it won't be advertised in *The American Mercury*, if you know what I mean."

I looked up from the manuscript and smiled.

"No tall stacks of them in the window of Scribner's downtown, either," Dr. Stein added with a wink at Elena. "There is only one genuine elite, that of great intelligence." He chuckled. "A snob? Yes, perhaps I am, but only in a small sense. I am pleased that Mr. Brand has given the world *Destry Rides Again* this year." He leaned back in his seat and swept his right arm out, indicating the tall line of bookshelves at the far end of the room. "But I am also pleased that Thomas Hardy did not choose to write about cowboys." He looked at me questioningly. "Is anything deeply wrong with such an attitude?"

"I don't think so, Dr. Stein," I said.

He nodded. "Good."

Then he talked on for a while about those ideas which had meant most to him, his voice turning almost nostalgic. At one point Elena brought him another brandy.

At around ten, I decided that I had stayed long enough. I stood up and shook Dr. Stein's hand.

"Thank you very much for having me," I said.

Dr. Stein did not get up. "Very pleased, William," he said. "I wonder, would you do me a favor?"

"Of course."

"Would you take a picture, William, of Elena and me?"

"Now?"

Dr. Stein nodded. "Yes, now. Just as we are, quite casual, nothing posed, just the two of us on the sofa."

Elena stood up. "I'll get the camera," she said and went into an adjoining room.

Dr. Stein smiled quietly. "I trust your mind is at ease, William?"

"Yes, sir."

"Good."

Elena walked back into the room and handed me the camera. I stepped back, indicating to Elena that she should move closer to Dr. Stein, then snapped the picture.

In the photograph they are seated quite close together on that weathered floral sofa, which later became Elena's and which now rests in the front room of her house on Cape Cod. She is wearing a white blouse and long dark skirt, her "girls' school uniform," as she came to call it. Her hair is long, parted at the middle, the strands of the right side held back from her face by a tortoise shell barrette. Dr. Stein appears rather ponderous beside her, dressed in his black three-piece suit, the gold watch chain dangling from his vest. It is a grainy photograph, taken with a flash in indoor light, but one can sense that patina of dust which forever marred the good doctor's shoes and the flecks of lint which clung to him like tiny flakes of unmelted snow. He has placed one hand beneath his coat, European style, and his head is thrust back, almost cockily, as if captured in a moment of transcendent pride. He seems — how shall I put it? — most deeply pleased to be alive.

Franz Jacob Stein died three weeks later on December 12, 1931. I never spoke to him again after that night with Elena in his apartment. I remember that he walked me to the door, though with some difficulty, and together, standing side by side, he and Elena waved to me as I made my way down the hallway to the stairs. I waved back cheerily.

On the street outside their building, as I waited for a bus to take me downtown, I thought how often prudery triumphs over sense, convention over the innovations of the heart, and thus how easy it is for someone like myself — the "Cold Bill" that Jack MacNeill later called me — to grow passionate about matters of trifling passion, careworn with petty care, dry and bloodless as that soulless critic Pope despised, "bold in the practice of mistaken rules."

For about three months after Dr. Stein's death, Elena kept very much to herself, moving, I think, into the region of quietude and reflection she would later write about in her novel *Inwardness*. Dr. Stein's death had created an empty space, which, as it turned out, she could only fill with some formerly uncreated part of herself. The guidance he had given her never served her better than in the way it directed her through those months of silent mourning. "I think of him often," she told me one evening a few weeks after his death, "and it's strange, William, but I don't feel drained or lonely or anything like that." Then she smiled. "I feel invigorated. Isn't that odd?"

Odd, yes, and a bit too easy. For there is no doubt that Elena was not always able to assume so serene an attitude. From time to time, Mrs. Connolly would call to tell me that Elena had not been out of her room for a day or so and that she was worried about her. I can never know what happened to my sister during those long hours she spent enclosed in her small room at the end of the hall, while Mrs. Connolly tiptoed back and forth to listen at the door. Perhaps she wept like a brokenhearted schoolgirl, or sat by the window like one of those mute, abandoned heroines so beloved by our mother. But if during that time she almost died of pain, she gave absolutely no sign of it, outside those reclusive hours.

Then it ended, her withdrawal, and Elena emerged with what amounted to a happy buoyancy. It was like the break of day after a long, disgruntled night. The phone rang in my apartment late one afternoon almost three months after Dr. Stein's death. It was Elena, and her voice sounded more fully commanding and vital than I had heard it in quite some time.

"I've decided to move out of this building, William," she said. "I've found a new place."

"A new place?"

"Yes. Further down Broadway. Do you think you might help me move? It would only be a couple of trunks."

"Of course," I said. "But why this sudden urge to move?"

There was a brief silence, as if she were considering her answer. "I just think it's time," she said at last.

I arrived at Mrs. Connolly's apartment two days later. She pointed to the room at the end of the hall.

"Down there," she said. "And you take care of your sister once she's out of my sight." She shook her head disapprovingly. "She wouldn't go back to Hewett like she should have. Wants a place of her own. You keep watch on her, Mr. Franklin. That's my word to the wise." And with that, she strode out into the kitchen.

When I walked into Elena's room, I found her seated at her desk, her head resting on her arm.

"How are you, Elena?" I asked.

"Well, I think," she said. She stood up and nodded toward two large trunks that rested at the foot of her bed. "I hope we can manage all that."

We managed very well, and within a few minutes Elena and I were in a taxi heading for her new lodgings, a women's residence called Three Arts.

"Mrs. Connolly seemed a bit cranky," I said.

"I would never tell Mrs. Connolly," Elena said as the taxi edged into Broadway, "but, for one thing, I really didn't want to live with her anymore." She looked at me. "I don't intend to submit to that." Later, in *Quality*, she would write with fierce anger about the mother of Emily Dickinson, "that sleepless creature who bestowed on her daughter the dreadful opposite of neglect, that wary maternal care, which, despite its tenderness, remains intrusive, watchful, relentlessly abiding, and from which one evening when it was 'amazin' raw,' Emily fled into the embracing chaos of the snow."

And Elena, on a summer day, fled into the embracing chaos of Broadway traffic.

"I feel good about this, about the move," she said as we drove to her new quarters.

"It's the best thing you could do, Elena," I said lightly.

"Yes, I think so, too."

Her spirits lifted the farther we drove away from Dr. Stein's old building, but I could sense that much of what she had felt in that place was now permanently situated in her mind.

After a moment she spoke again. "How's the work on Cowper coming?"

"Ploddingly, I'm afraid."

"He believed you had a great deal of promise, did you know that?"

"Who?"

"Dr. Stein."

"Oh, did he really?"

"Yes. He often mentioned it to me," Elena said. She shook her head. "I'm going to stop talking about him." She sounded determined.

I smiled delicately. "Why, Elena?"

"I think I have to," Elena said. "Really have to." She turned away, her hands poised above the small typewriter resting on her lap in its battered brown case. Not long ago I received a letter from the Smithsonian asking for it: "Because your sister, Elena Franklin, was an esteemed American author . . ." and so forth. They have it now, no doubt locked away in one of their dark vaults, so that it has its small place in the vast attic of our history.

It must be noted now, in our own more liberal time, that in the late twenties and early thirties young single women very rarely lived alone. Instead, they tended to congregate in large boarding houses known as "clubs." The era of the rogue female was yet to come, and even those women who preferred to have their own apartments, as I suspect Elena did, could do so only with much difficulty.

The Three Arts Club was presided over by a formidable woman named Mrs. Frederick Markloff. It was a large brick building on upper Broadway some distance below Columbia. Once in the lobby, one had the sense of being in an entirely female world. There were about a hundred young women then living at Three Arts. They were mostly aspiring dancers, actresses, writers, and painters. In a letter to Elizabeth a few days later, Elena noted that all the women around her had glorious ambitions, and that they expected them all to be fulfilled. "It's as if the Depression is a play they're watching," she wrote, "not the world they're living in."

This contradiction would finally make its way into Elena's Depression novel, *Calliope*. In that book, the narrator, Raymond Finch, picks up his date at a club very like Three Arts. Growing impatient as he paces in the lobby, Finch muses on the building and its inhabitants:

> It was no more than a few stories high, a stunted little building with a brick façade looking down on the bustle of upper Broadway. Every form of human delusion flourished there, flourished wildly, a hothouse plant of teeming vines. But down by the wharves where the ships were docked and the jute lay out in the rain, down there, in that Hooverville which stretched out forever along the oily Hudson, down

where the wharf rats grew to abnormal size and it was famously told that in the night they sneaked into the tiny hovels of the exhausted poor and took their babies from their cardboard cradles, nothing endured but the will to put something in your mouth and chew it. Compared to that, the Pittman Club was carved out of moonbeams, and the girls giggled in a topsy-turvy world, full of crazy hope, sunk in a vast illogic, casting all their dreams upward as if to hook an anchor on a cloud.

By the time Elena wrote that, she had experienced some of the trauma of Depression America for herself. The isolation of Three Arts was by then a part of her personal history, an early fragment from a longer tale. But in the spring of 1931, still supported by my father's agile maneuvers to ward off the engulfing catastrophe, she remained securely a part of a small and very privileged stratum. It was a part of her good fortune that often rose to haunt her, and she always felt vulnerable because of it. Once during an argument with Jack MacNeill, she asked him to list the elements of human experience she did not comprehend, and when he replied that she had missed only the most universal ones — hunger, cold, and homelessness — she seemed almost physically to shrink away from him, as if, against this, she could make no argument save the most blatantly defensive and absurd.

In her biography, Martha placed much emphasis upon Elena's life at Three Arts. She wrote that Elena "probably found her vocation there, among all those other exuberant young women, artists of one sort or another, who, simply by existing in proximity to Elena, allowed her to recover from Dr. Stein."

And yet, from the first moment we entered the building that afternoon in the spring of 1932, I realized that Elena would never feel altogether at home there. The circle of young women who flooded toward her, laughing lightly, joking, filling the air with their own electric ambitions, were already captured in a mood of unreserved brightness, which seemed utterly different from Elena's mood, from the essential somberness that characterized her from this time onward.

Still, she was smiling quite happily when she came back down the stairs after dropping her bags in her room.

"Do you have time for a walk, William?" she asked.

"I suppose."

"Let's go down by the river, then."

The Hudson was ice blue that day and a small breeze blew up from it, lifting the fledgling leaves of that early spring.

"What do you think of Three Arts?" Elena asked.

"It seems fine. You'll probably prefer it to living with Mrs. Connolly."

Elena nodded. She had drawn her hair into a bun behind her head. From a certain angle, she looked almost matronly. "How's your job in the Village going?" she asked casually.

"Well enough."

She kicked at a small stone as she walked. "I'll be graduating soon." She stopped and looked at me. "What then?"

I shook my head. "I don't know."

"Graduation is like a wall. I don't know what's on the other side."

I smiled. "The rest of your life, Elena."

She took my arm and tugged me forward. "That's a bit glib, don't you think?"

"I suppose so."

"When Dr. Stein was alive, I could always think of working with him, doing books together, that sort of thing."

"And now?"

"I feel cut off," Elena said. She stopped and pulled me toward her. "It's very strange, but sometimes I even resent him for dying."

"You need to find yourself a project," I said, "something to keep you busy." It was pedestrian advice, but all I had.

"I'm busy with school, but there are times when I think I'd like to do something different . . . something of my own, like you have with Cowper."

I moved forward, nudging Elena along with me. Her mention of Cowper reminded me of all the work I had yet to do. It made me impatient with the pace, the talk, even the slowly rolling river. "Well, if there's something you want to do, some project, you just have to roll up the old sleeves and do it, right?"

Elena nodded quickly and released my arm. She had caught my impatience. "You've been taken from your work too long, William. Please, go on home now."

"No, Elena, I — "

"Please, William, you go on. I'd just like a stroll. Really. You go ahead."

I left her there overlooking the river, standing by a small rock wall, staring out toward the Jersey shore. "One learns solitude," Dorothea Moore says in *Inwardness*, "through the open field and the silent room, by knowing that sunset will not bring you home nor sunrise set you on the road again, by seeing well the finite path, by watching as your shadow is erased before a cloud."

When I left Elena standing by the Hudson that afternoon in the spring of 1931, I had no idea what that "something of my own" which she spoke of might be. But six months later, *Scribner's* magazine published a satirical short story called "Manhattan." Its author was Elena Mayhew Franklin.

Other than *New England Maid*, of course, nothing Elena ever wrote was more strictly autobiographical. It was a breezy little story that revolved around a group of Columbia students who spend their time sitting in a speakeasy, discussing themselves and the world, all of them "very cheerful in their cheerlessness." I am there, puffing a pipe, and my sister describes me as "very severe, though given to a grudging smile, thorough and precise. His face would not stop a clock, but it might remind you to wind one." Harry is sitting with us, disguised as an anthropologist forever espousing "doctrines having to do with primitive populations." For passion, Mary sits puffing her cigarette and casting barbs here and there, but most particularly at the tweed-coated anthropologist. Tom Cameron wanders in, recites a lugubrious poem, then bows his head in a seizure of romantic weeping. The entire assembly is served by an irritable young waiter, whose exaggerated solicitousness to these well-heeled undergraduates has "the precise but edgy manner of a ticking bomb." This, of course, is Sam Waterman.

In the 1980 interview, Elena described "Manhattan" as "perhaps not the worst thing I have ever done but certainly the silliest." One critic in a larger study of Elena's work called it "perfectly forgettable and not in the least representative of her later work." For her part, Martha dismissed it as a false start and tactfully dropped the matter.

From all of these dismissive remarks, one could never guess that the publication of "Manhattan" was an occasion of terrific joy for my sister. Certainly the modesty of the story's achievement was entirely overshadowed by the work that was to come. And yet I remember the phone ringing in my apartment late one afternoon, and the wonderful excitement in Elena's voice when she told me about it.

"I'm standing at the hall phone at Three Arts, William," she said breathlessly. "I can't sit down."

"Elena, what are you talking about?"

"I haven't told you that I wrote a little story, have I?"

"Story? No."

"Well, I did. A short story. I called it 'Manhattan,' " Elena said frantically. "And the thing is, William, the thing is, somebody's going to publish it."

I laughed. "Are you serious?"

"Yes. *Scribner's* is going to publish it, William. I just sent it in to them. Sort of on a whim. And they're going to publish it. I wrote it my first year in New York. Set it aside. Found it. Sent it in."

I could hardly believe it. "That's wonderful!"

"I feel silly being this excited."

"You have a perfect right to be excited," I said. "Listen, we're going to have to have a party. It's mandatory on such occasions. Okay with you?"

"Sure."

And so a week later, we all went to celebrate at a Village restaurant. Elena had taken the trouble to type several copies of the story, and for the first few minutes we sat reading it, chuckling delightedly to ourselves. It was as close as some of us would ever come to immortality, Characters in a Story.

"Well, you've certainly got me down correctly," Harry said after a moment. By then he had pretty much given up on Elena and had begun seeing the lovely young socialite he would later marry, but whom he had the good taste not to bring along that night. He had also grown a full mustache, which aged him ten years, frightening us all with its physical suggestion of our own middle age.

"It's supposed to be a satirical portrait, Harry," Mary said, laughing. "You're being made fun of, don't you see that?" She glanced at Elena and smiled.

Sam sat across from me, reading slowly, finishing after everyone else. Then he looked at Elena with a thoughtful, calculating stare. "Tell me, Elena, do you have anything longer than this? A novel, say? Something like that?"

"My God, Elena," Mary howled, "I think you've found yourself a publisher."

Sam looked at Mary scornfully. "Don't be so sure she hasn't. My backers are lining up for the shooting match. We're going to build this house."

Harry ran his index finger across his mustache. "Are you really going to start a publishing concern in these times, Sam?"

"Yep."

"It seems a rather fanciful ambition."

"Well, personal ambition is something you silver-spoon types don't have to worry about, right, Harry?"

I tapped my fork on the rim of my glass. "Now, gentlemen, let's remember this is a festive occasion."

Harry did not seem to hear me. "Tell me, Sam, have you joined the Communist party yet?"

"Just edging in that direction, Harry," Sam said. "Sort of the left-wing version of the old school tie."

"And your backers — are they equally committed to the overthrow of capitalism?"

"They're split on that question," Sam said, turning his eyes wearily toward Elena.

"Split?" Harry said. "Well, shouldn't you apply the thumbscrew of democratic centralism?"

Sam looked back at Harry. "How do you know all that jargon, Harry? Are you a government agent? Do you run off to the local fascist headquarters and report our conversations?"

"One must know one's antagonist, right?" Harry said, arching one eyebrow.

"Well, I'll tell you what, Harry," Sam said. "When I join the Communist party, I'll let you know, okay?"

Sam did join the Communist party, very quietly, the following December. He sent a Christmas card to Harry with a hammer and sickle emblazoned on the front. They never spoke warmly to each other again.

"We're supposed to be celebrating Elena's short story," Mary said emphatically.

Tom had sat glumly during all of the political discussion. Now he came to life. "Sam, are you really going to have a publishing house?" he asked.

"I think so."

"Well, do you mind if I ask you a question? Are you by any chance thinking of publishing poetry?"

Sam stared coldly into Tom's eyes. They had never really cared for each other, and Sam was particularly contemptuous of Tom. "He writes like a deranged schoolgirl, William," he once told me. "All that idiocy about uniting with the forces of the universe. He'd be lucky if he could unite with a paying job."

"The thing is, Sam," Tom went on, heedless of Sam's lethal gaze, "the thing is, I've got some poems that I think are *really good.*"

"I'm sure you do . . . think they're good," Sam said in a very measured tone.

"Well, if you'd like to see . . ."

Sam's eyes slid over to Elena. "About that longer piece, a novel, that sort of thing. What do you say, Elena?"

Elena shrugged. "I don't really have anything, Sam."

"Well, if you think of anything, a story idea, something like that," Sam said casually, "just anything that comes to mind, I'd like to hear about it."

Years later, at a cocktail party launching a new young author, Sam staggered over to me, somehow moved by his own past, his own success, and began a story about Elena. "So Elena's manuscript came in, William," he said, "this book she'd called *New England Maid.* We'd discussed what it was going to be about. Then I started to read it. I read the first paragraph and I thought, Oh, God, this is a disaster, this is not anything like we talked about. But I kept on reading, William, and when I was halfway through the manuscript, I picked it up and waved it in the air and I said to Teddy McNaughton, who was the only other editor we had at Parnassus at that time, I said, "Teddy, this book will be in print for a hundred years." Sam was old by then, gray and full of too many leisurely meals. He lifted his glass in the air. "I knew what she was, William. I knew it from that first moment." He touched his glass to mine. There were tears in his eyes.

Harry flipped through "Manhattan" once again, then dropped the pages on the table. "When is *Scribner's* going to publish it, Elena?"

"Next month."

Harry nodded quietly. When he looked at Elena, the romantic longing in his eyes seemed a relic from an older time, like the shield of Lancelot. "Well, I'm sure we all wish you the very best," he said.

"Thank you, Harry."

"I've been submitting a few poems here and there," Tom said, "but so far I haven't gotten any responses." He looked at Elena as if she were suddenly the expert on such matters. "Do you think that means they're being read carefully, that they're under consideration?"

"I really don't know," Elena said. Several years later, when Tom's first poem was published in an obscure journal, Elena wrote him a congratulatory letter, which he probably took as the height of saintly condescension and to which he never made reply.

"We're planning to publish a wide range of fiction," Sam said to Elena. "Keep that in mind. Serious stuff, but also quality satire, humor, that sort of thing." He lifted his copy of the story. "Like this, Elena. Longer, and with a plot, but more or less like this in tone."

"I see," Elena said.

"Would that interest you?"

"It might."

Sam glanced down at the story, then back up at Elena. "Well, like I said, just something to keep in mind."

"I will, Sam," Elena said.

Sam proceeded to launch into a tedious explanation of the business of publishing. As he spoke, I could not help noticing something in Elena's eyes, and I think it was, as Chesterton says, "in the deep sense of a dishonored word," ambition. Jack MacNeill always believed that there was a bit of the hustler in Elena, that a bit of her heart was devoted to what he called "that charnel house ideal — making it in America." But there is something called the ambition of the soul, and if it cannot be detected, say, in the canvases of Watteau, it is everywhere visible in the apocalyptic swirl of van Gogh. I believe that although Elena was never seized with the kind of feverish compulsion that drove van Gogh to paint his *Starry Night* or drove Gauguin to Tahiti, there remained within her always a deep longing to express the vision that had been rising in her for so long, and which she defined in *Quality* as "the sayable truth within a work of art, that moment when the statement and the artifice are one."

So if that calculating expression which overtook her face as she

watched Sam wander through the labyrinth of literary entrepreneur-
ship meant anything at all, I suspect it was something far less than
the lighting of some flame, and far more than the meticulous accounting of one's main chance. Perhaps it was simply the recognition that
a sudden happy accident had occurred, that if literature were to be
her ambition, then the agent of her success might well be sitting
next to her, boring the rest of us with tales of financial connivance.
There is no doubt that something happened at that table, and that
Elena's long silence was more than a gesture of politeness. The look
in her face told everything. After a time even Sam felt drawn toward
it, and his sentences trailed off into the air.

"Are you all right, Elena?" he asked.

"Yes, of course," Elena said. "Why?"

"You looked a little out of sorts, in a daze, something like that."

Elena stared about, amazed by the sudden attention. "Absolutely
nothing. What do you mean?"

We could not answer that. Nor, at the time, I think, could she.
But in a 1957 interview, she spoke of that moment in her life: "There
may be a time in every artist's life when he suddenly glimpses his
possibilities. It's all just a dream before that time. But then you sell
your first painting, or hear your first score played, or see your first
story published, and at that moment, things change, I think. You
feel fear and elation. But more than anything, there is a sense of
being cut loose from all the ties that seemed so very strong before."

Only a few days before she died, I moved Elena out to her study
in the back of the house. She sat propped up in her chair and watched
the sandpipers dodge the surf. I left her there for a long time, silhou-
etted against the tall window, her long white hair spread out over
the back of her chair. When I came back in, carrying her lunch on
a tray, she seemed oddly distant as she stared out toward the sea,
hardly noticing my presence. Then she looked at me and smiled delicately.

"What are you thinking, Elena?" I asked.

"Oh, nothing, William," she said, in a voice that had grown tremulous by then. "Just that . . . well . . . I have no complaints."

On the day "Manhattan" was published, Elena asked me to dinner. We met at a restaurant in the Village, one of those small sidewalk arrangements, desperately imitative of the Parisian Left Bank. It catered primarily to that aging and increasingly desolate clientele who remembered the Village in its prewar incandescence and who muttered grudgingly about all the changes that had taken place since then. For them, the Village was a city of ghosts, haunted by the shadows of John Reed and Emma Goldman and dwarfish Randolph Bourne. I am struck now, remembering their outmoded clothes and low, complaining voices, by how much tenderness we must retain for all those who reside, however uncomfortably, at the very edge of living memory.

It was early evening when Elena and I met, and the air had the peculiar passive blueness that will always be the color of New York in my youth. Elena was sitting at a small wrought iron table. She was wearing a white dress with red piping along the shoulders, open at the neck. She waved when she saw me, jostling the glass of lemonade in her other hand.

"How are you, Elena?" I said as I sat down.

"Fine," she said. She drew a magazine from the bag beside her chair. "Here it is."

It was *Scribner's*. I picked it up and flipped quickly to the story. There was an illustration portraying a group of well-dressed young people at a speakeasy. The faces did not look anything like us, but the mood, a sort of somber biliousness, was well established.

"It's near the center of the magazine," I said. "That's a good position."

Elena looked pleased. "Is it?"

"So they tell me."

I glanced back down at the illustration. "Not a bad rendering. Harry doesn't really look like that, of course, but he would be more in character if he did." I folded the magazine. "May I have it?"

"Of course."

"Will you autograph it for me?"

Elena smiled. "You want me to?"

"I certainly do." I opened the magazine to the story and gave it to her. She drew a pen from her bag, signed her name above the title, and handed it back to me.

"I suppose you already know how pleased I am for you," I said.

"Yes."

"I hope it's the first of many."

Elena took a sip from her glass, and I saw her face take on that strange seriousness.

"In a way, that's what I wanted to talk to you about, William," she said.

"What is that?"

"About doing something else, another piece of writing."

I smiled. "So, Sam's put the spur to you, has he?"

"He really seems to want me to do something, a book."

"Of course he does. Why don't you?"

"I'm thinking about it."

The waiter stepped up, and since liquor was still not available in public restaurants, I ordered lemonade.

"Well, do you have any book ideas?" I asked after the waiter had left.

"Only one, really," Elena said. She put her glass down firmly on the table and leaned forward. "William, do you ever think about Standhope?"

"Sometimes. In what way?"

"About our life. Doesn't it seem a little eccentric to you? Father away all the time, and mother in her own world. It's peculiar, don't you think?"

"Not a typical childhood, certainly. Why?"

"I've been thinking about writing something along those lines. Something about Standhope, our life — the whole thing there in that small town."

"You intend this as a novel?"

Elena nodded. "Oh yes, absolutely. I'm sure that's what Sam wants. They have a few nonfiction books already. Sam says they want to — he calls it 'fill out the list.' "

I smiled. "What are you doing, Elena, asking my permission?"

"In a way, yes," Elena said. "I wouldn't want to write about all that went on in Standhope if you didn't want me to."

I shrugged. "You'll make a novel out of it. That's fine with me." I, of course, had no idea whether Elena could actually write a novel.

"Good," Elena said. She seemed satisfied.

"What sort of novel are you thinking about?" I asked. "The material, how do you plan to handle it?"

Elena thought about it for a moment. "Well, rather lightly, I think. Sort of like the story."

"That's what Sam wants?"

"More or less. He's pretty open about it. But I think the style of the story is what he's looking for."

"Whimsical. Breezy."

"That's right," Elena said, "that's what he's looking for."

The events of our lives in Standhope did not seem to lend themselves readily to such a treatment, but I didn't think I needed to point that out.

"I already have the first paragraph of the book," Elena said brightly.

"My God, Sam really has lit a fire under you."

"The fire was already there. I really enjoy writing, William."

"Perhaps it's your destiny," I said with a flourish of the hand.

"Don't you like it, too?" Elena asked. "The Cowper book, aren't you enjoying it?"

"Like protracted surgery, yes."

"Really? That bad?"

"Only at times," I said. "The unusual insight, the sudden turn of phrase — I like those moments. But the rest is very tedious, grueling. I don't care for it that much." I smiled and changed the subject. "But what about that first line of yours?"

"It's more like a first paragraph."

"Want to read it to me?"

"Sure," Elena said. She took a piece of paper from the pocket of her blouse and unfolded it on the table. "This sets the mood for the whole story. As you said, whimsical."

"Go ahead. No preface necessary."

Then, hesitantly, Elena read what she conceived at that time to be the opening paragraph of *New England Maid:* "I was born to a father who, though not a Christian parson, had his trials, and a mother who, though not a noble lady of the stage, had her quirks and crinolines. To their duo, I made a trio, and with Brother, a curious quartet." She looked up slowly. "What do you think?"

"Well, it's breezy."

Elena folded the paper. "You don't like it?"

"I read Cowper, remember?" I said, smiling to allay Elena's fears. "I really am sort of dour, Elena. Whimsical writing is for a different audience. But I'll tell you this, Sam will love it, and so will many other people. I mean it. Go ahead and finish the book in just that style."

Elena placed the paper back in her pocket. I could tell that I had spoken hastily, unmindful of the sensitivity with which Elena regarded her work at that time, of the extraordinary need she must have felt that evening for my unconditional approval. Later in her life, having been wounded so much, she could no longer be wounded so easily. "There was a point in Elena's life," Jason wrote in his memoir, "when it became almost impossible to touch her. By then I think her soul must have resembled Rodin's statue of Balzac, towering, monumental, as impregnable as a fortress on the Rhine. I am not sure, however, whether this invulnerability could be accounted loss or gain." Nor, I might add, am I.

But that evening in the Village, while the air grew dark around us and the first streetlights began to glow, Elena sat silently, no doubt wondering if she had gotten everything wrong — the whole tone of the story, the characters, the rhythm of the sentence, everything from the smallest detail to the overall structure of the novel, which, at that time, existed only in her mind.

Finally she looked up. "I don't know what's right, William."

"The story's fine, Elena. I didn't mean to criticize it."

"It's not just the story."

"What then?"

"Maybe the way I'm thinking about it. Maybe that's all wrong."

I touched her hand. "Elena, you shouldn't let anything I said interfere with what you intended. You and Sam have obviously worked it out. It looks like he'll be your publisher. It's between the two of you. And that's the way it should be."

Elena did not seem convinced.

"It's the narrowness of my taste, Elena," I insisted, "it's not what you wrote. Believe me."

Elena shook her head. "William, if you don't mind, I'd just like to talk about something else."

"All right," I said weakly.

We ordered dinner and ate almost without speaking. Then I walked Elena to her bus stop and waited with her. She seemed intensely preoccupied, as if her mind were taking stock of itself, figuring the credits and debits of its own ability and measuring them against an ambition that could only be glimpsed at the time. When the bus came she stepped on quickly, took her seat, and waved to me with a faint, halfhearted movement as it pulled away.

A year later, at this same bus stop, Elena would rush out, plunge a manuscript into my hands, then rush back onto the bus, saying only, "This is it, William, the best that I can do."

The year during which Elena wrote *New England Maid* was probably the single most solitary of her life. Still supported by my father's tottering finances, she had the luxury of spending her days holed up in her room at Three Arts. "You heard that little typewriter of hers going day and night," a former resident of Three Arts is quoted as saying in Martha's biography. "It was a constant clatter on the floor, like the knocking on the pipes when the heat came up, only the typing never stopped." Martha called *New England Maid* an "obsession," but I think that only a lazy, dilatory age would label such deep commitment and determined striving with a word that conjures up pathology.

Sam was elated by Elena's determination. "She's working like a demon, William," he told me over breakfast one morning, "like a demon." But when I asked him if he had seen any of the results of all this labor, he shook his head glumly. "No," he said. "And to tell you the truth, it makes me a little jumpy."

Elena's nervousness about the book increased as the weeks of writing passed. Even Mary, normally so casual in the face of such things, grew concerned. "I would usually dismiss something like this as an affectation," she told me. "You know, like Tom in his garret, nibbling at moldy Swiss cheese. But with Elena, it's different."

It was very different, and at times a little grim. Much would be made of it later — those long days she spent alone, that ceaseless typewriter — all of it would finally enter modern literary folklore, another of those tiresome tales which place the artist in a separate realm.

Still, the reality was curious enough. Elena really did go through something very intense during the writing of her book. Jason said that the work "blasted her out of Eden," but this has always seemed to me grotesquely overstated. The physical evidence of her intensity, however, was perfectly obvious during the late winter and spring of 1932. She neglected herself to an alarming degree, grew thinner and more pale. She often looked as if she never slept, her eyes sometimes tired and watery, at other times almost glazed, as if a thin, diaphanous cover had been placed over them, shielding her from anything but her own inner lights.

During those months, meeting Elena for dinner was a disquieting experience. She would pick at her food while I rambled on about the topics of the day. It was difficult to draw her into anything remotely resembling idle conversation. At times, I found it insufferably self-indulgent, and perhaps even pretentious, given that I thought she was writing nothing more significant than a whimsical treatment of a bizarre New England family.

"Elena, you really should snap out of this," I told her one evening at my apartment.

She looked up from a magazine she had been scanning. "Out of what?"

"This damned silly mood you're in."

She closed the magazine and gave me an absolutely withering stare.

"It's really sort of boring, Elena," I added irritably. "You're not much fun anymore."

Elena said nothing. She simply held her eyes on mine for a moment. Then she stood up. "I'm tired, William. I'm going home now."

"Well, it was a splendid evening," I said.

Elena placed the magazine neatly on the table beside her chair and quietly left the room. I did not see her again for a month.

But Mary did. She became far more devoted to Elena during this period. The poet Horace once said that certain people are "privileged to dare what flights they please," and Mary understood, as none of the rest of us did at that time, that Elena was one of these. During all of that long spring, she was amazingly solicitous toward Elena. She later explained it rather simply to her daughter. "People have said that Elena was near a breakdown during the time she wrote New England Maid. She never was. Elena had sadness, that's all. A very bad case of sadness."

This "case of sadness" grew less severe later in the spring. Perhaps by then Elena had decided that she would, in fact, write the book that was in her. By May the pall that had darkened fall, winter, and early spring lifted entirely, and Elena finished up her classes in a final burst of vigor. She was able to graduate right on time, in June of 1932.

My father came to New York for the graduation ceremonies, and we sat together in the auditorium and watched the long line of graduating seniors as they marched across the stage. When Elena's name was called, I saw his eyes lift toward the front of the room with a sudden energy, all his weariness and boredom dropping from him like crusted earth.

Outside the hall I took a photograph of the two of them together. Elena stood beside him in her cap and gown. She smiled reservedly, while he beamed proudly at the camera.

After Elena changed clothes at Three Arts, the three of us wandered down Broadway, casually chatting about matters of limited scope. Elena talked about a job she had applied for at the New York Public Library, about Elizabeth's letters, which were hinting at a move to the city, and about the general run of her college life. My father smiled appreciatively at everything she said.

Later that evening, he took us to dinner at a restaurant a good deal less fashionable than was usual for him. There were small wooden tables with checkered tablecloths, and toward the back a myna bird squawked the president's name from a large cage shaped like a pagoda. Nor did my father look as much the dandy as he once had. There was no silk handkerchief peeping up from his breast pocket, and the stud pin that adorned his tie was lusterless and vulgar. He had probably left the gold one sitting on a hotel nightstand or had pressed it into the hand of some woman who had asked for nothing more. He lifted his water glass high above the table. "Here's to Elena's graduation."

We touched our three glasses together gently. My father drank the water as if it were a fine red wine, rolling it over his tongue in a mocking gesture which he ended with a large, brave smile. "The Democrats will get the booze back again," he said. Then he folded his hands together and looked soberly at each of us. "I know this is a celebration," he began, "but since I've got to be in Hartford early tomorrow morning, there's something I have to tell you tonight. There's just no other time to do it." He looked at Elena. "I hate to spoil the evening, though."

"What is it?" Elena asked immediately.

My father shifted uncomfortably in his seat. He was dressed in a plain brown double-breasted suit which added a note of unaccustomed shabbiness to his appearance. In *Calliope*, Raymond Finch describes a down-and-out hustler as being "plain as a wood shaving, a dapper little man with oily hair who'd gone to seed at the betting tables and had ended up in a shiny suit and cracked calfskin shoes, which he tapped incessantly to some tune playing in his mind." Except for the betting tables, it could have been our father that evening in the restaurant, his rubber soles beating a muffled cadence under the table as he spoke to us.

"You know how times are now," he began. "Well, they've finally hit home. I've tried to stay afloat. But what with all the trouble these days, it's been hard."

I suppose my face must have looked like a blank desert landscape to him. I was, after all, so inexperienced with the world he knew, with the battle for territorial dominance he waged up and down New England, the jungle warfare of the general store.

He glanced from my face to Elena's then back to mine again. "I managed to put you through school, Billy, right?"

I nodded.

He looked at Elena. "And now I've done it for you."

Elena's eyes softened as he spoke to her, and she lifted her face to him, offering it up, like a prayer on his behalf.

He leaned back in his chair and lit a cigarette. "I made quite a few shrewd investments early on," he explained, leaving out the details, I suppose, because he suspected that we would never be able to understand them. "Mostly land deals in Florida. I did some selling down there, too. And just at the right time. Before the bust." He blew a stream of white smoke out of the side of his mouth. "You've been living off those investments for quite some time. They paid for your college." He crushed the cigarette into the ashtray. "Well, to make a long story short, the money's about gone. And that's what I've come to tell you."

Elena and I looked at each other. We had no idea what to say to him or what he was asking of us. Did he want pity, gratitude, respect? I suspect he already had them all, in some degree.

Elena leaned forward and touched his hand. "You know I'm already looking for work. You don't have to worry about me."

My father smiled. "I've never worried about you, Elena, not for one moment." He looked at me. "And you've been on your own for quite some time, Billy. Having any trouble?"

"I'm getting by."

My father shook his head. "No, you kids'll do fine. The only reason I'm talking about all this is because the place in Standhope is getting to be a burden for me."

He was talking about our home, the "place in Standhope" he used like a hotel room — though, I am sure, with less pleasure.

"The fact is, I can't afford to keep it anymore," he added. He picked up his glass and twirled it in his hands. "It's as simple as that. It just sits vacant most of the time. I hardly ever get back there. When I see you kids, it's in New York, not Standhope."

"So you want to sell it?" Elena asked.

"That's about it."

I looked at him questioningly. "And live where?"

He smiled. "Here and there, Billy. There are hotels everywhere." His face was luminous. That was what he wanted: a life lived entirely on the road, the apotheosis of a nomad. For the rest of his life, he would live in a world of small kingdoms, rooms ten feet square with the toilet down the hall. "Of course, I might be able to rent the house," he went on. "Keep it that way. Sort of for sentimental reasons, if you kids would prefer it."

I shook my head. "No need."

He glanced at Elena for unanimous approval.

"William's right," she said. "Sell it."

"Well, I wish I didn't have to spoil things with bad news. I'm really sorry for having to bring it up on your graduation day, Elena."

I forced a chuckle. "Actually, I'd always wondered how you managed everything, where the money came from."

My father smiled radiantly. "I'll tell you where it came from, Billy." He tapped his index finger against his skull. "Brains, that's where. But I'll tell you something else. After a while, they're not enough." He looked at Elena. "You just get swallowed up by the wave, like those little razor clams you used to pick up on the beach. Remember?"

Elena nodded.

"Just a little thing, a razor clam," my father continued, "but for a long time it can hold its own. Then one day its luck runs out. Same thing happened to me."

He went on for quite some time in a kind of monologue on his life. It was an artless account, delivered with slowly dissipating energy as he neared the bad news of the present. I could almost hear the little engine in him running down. In a sense it made me wistful for those earlier days of his lustrous dandyism — the hop in his walk, the way he bounded down the walkway to his car, the swaggering tip of his hat. And yet there was a certain resilience in him even now. He was no doubt pleased that his idea for selling the house on Wilmot Street had met with so little resistance from Elena and me. But there was a more telling buoyance, which was inseparable from him. I felt somehow delicate and frail in his presence, incapable of weathering the storms he had already weathered, and I think, although I learned it very late, that my father was, all his life, a curiously happy man.

"But one thing I want both of you to know," he said, drawing his commentary to a close. "I don't want you to think that I made great sacrifices to keep you in college. I didn't. I had money at the time. Now I don't. It's as simple as that." He took a sip from his glass. "Which finally gets us back to the beginning, I guess, with this whole business of the house in Standhope, the fact that I need to sell it."

Through all of my father's tale, Elena had sat watching him warily, as if trying to maintain her own necessary detachment. I think now, that as he spoke she must have been thinking of all the painful things she had already written about him and that one day he would read. When he did read them two years later, he drove down to New York from New London, picked up Elena at her apartment, and took her to dinner. When it was over, Elena told me, he pulled out his copy of *New England Maid* from his briefcase and handed it to her with his best salesman smile. "Would you sign it for me, please?" he asked.

My father leaned back in his chair and looked at us intently. "Now, just one last time, I want to make sure we're in agreement about the house."

"Sell it," Elena said without the slightest hesitation.

He sold it two months later, then telephoned Elena to tell her the news and suggested that she might want to tour the house a final time. "There might be some of your mother's things you'd like to keep," he said.

We rode on the train together, Elena sitting beside me, writing in her notebook.

"That the whimsical novel?" I asked jokingly.

"Yes, it is," Elena said flatly, without looking up from the page.

We took a cab from the railway station and found our father drinking from a flask on the steps of the house. He waved as the cab pulled up, darted down the walkway, then swept us both into the house. I had never seen him look more unencumbered. "Whatever may be said of my father," Elena wrote in a letter to Martha Farrell, "he never attempted to give his feelings a more noble face. He could not counterfeit guilt or love or mourning. In his own strange way, he was as guileless as a child, though never would I say he was as innocent."

"The place is empty," my father said as he halted at the front door. "I sold the furniture. Didn't think there'd be anything you'd want." He pulled a handkerchief from his back pocket and wiped his mouth. "As for your mother's stuff, I put it in a few boxes and stacked them up in one corner of her old room."

While my father spread out leisurely on the front steps, Elena and I quietly wandered through the house, our voices echoing softly down the long hallway and out into the yard. In my mother's room, we went through the boxes my father had stacked so precariously. All her jewelry was in one of them — brooches of imitation emerald, rhinestone pins, an elegant cameo which her own mother had given her and which I offered to Elena. She shook her head. "No," she said, "you take it." I took nothing else, and Elena, after meticulously sorting through all the boxes, even flipping through a recipe book my mother had made of clippings from the *Standhope Gazette*, took only one of my mother's old romantic novels.

At the time it seemed a baffling choice. I did not really understand it until, years later, I read a passage in *Quality:* "It is one of the powers of symbolic thought to free an object from its native and inherent qualities, granting to the mundane and unexalted a special dispensation of the imagination. By this process a leaf crushed between the pages of an old picture album, a necklace rescued from the darkness of an ancient portmanteau, a book of crusty yellowed pages — these humble curios, valueless to those uninformed of the secret meaning with which they have been invested, are for the symbolic imagination articles of the most profound resonance, slowly shaped by memory and experience to form the kind of rich, instantaneous recognition to which the best in art aspires. This is that high achievement of thought whose general result we call, in an uninspired phrase, 'sentimental value.' "

My father left shortly after Elena and I had finished going through our mother's things. "Just close the door behind you," he said. "Nothing in there to steal." Then he walked jauntily to his car and drove away.

For a few minutes Elena and I walked the house again, glancing at the curtainless windows and the bare wooden floors.

"What do you think we're supposed to feel, William?" she asked me after a few minutes.

I opened the front door and looked back at her. She was standing near the center of the small living room, one hand thrust deeply into the pocket of her sweater, the other holding Mother's book tightly to her side.

I stepped out onto the front porch. "We need to catch our train," I said.

Elena walked passed me, stopping at the first step. She seemed reluctant to move farther.

I closed the front door and turned toward her. "Well, I'll say this much," I told her, "it'll be hard to treat this part of our story whimsically."

Elena looked back at me, smiled very faintly, then walked slowly down the stairs and out into the yard.

Four months later, in a cold autumn rain, I waited at the bus stop, drenched and irritable, for Elena to arrive from downtown. Seconds later she had come and gone again, and I trudged back to my library cubicle, her manuscript held securely under my coat to protect it from the damp. That same evening, warming my soaking feet by the radiator, I opened the envelope and withdrew a sheaf of neatly stacked typing paper. I remembered the first line Elena had recited to me almost a year before — all that business of duos and trios and quartets — and I sighed wearily, expecting her book to be far from my personal taste but willing to do my editorial duty as a brother. Then I turned over the title page and read the first lines of *New England Maid*: "Memory is the iron that sears but from which we cannot draw away. I was born to a wandering father and a mother who stayed at home, into the autumn hope of an optimistic age, into a town grown cold as if by wintry destiny, into a family fumbling for its pride."

It was almost midnight by the time I finished, but that didn't matter. I called Three Arts immediately, rousing a weary dancer from her sleep no doubt, and demanded to speak, absolutely demanded to speak, with Elena Franklin.

She came to the phone a few minutes later. "Yes?"

"Elena," I said, "it's beautiful. Very, very beautiful."

Her voice sounded weary, strained. "Good, William, thank you."

"I mean it. This is not just brotherly pride. I tried to be objective."

"I'm pleased, William," Elena said, "I really am." Her voice was low, almost tremulous. I felt all that I revered sweep out to her, to all the thought and strength and labor that had gone into the making of that book, and all the somber decency and justice, too, the penalties she exacted and the pardons she dispensed, all the terrible clarity with which she had seen our lives, and then that final act of will, to write it down. And I suppose that I wanted to tell her all these things, to let go of my restraint and speak in sheer and edifying rhetoric to the greatness of my sister's book.

"You must be tired, Elena," I said. "I'm sorry to wake you. It was just my . . . my enthusiasm, you see."

"Thank you for calling," Elena said. And then there was only silence on the line.

I saw Elena the next day. We met at one of the ponds in Central Park, the small one near the Plaza. Elena seemed almost as weary as the night before.

"What's the matter?" I asked. "Surely you don't have any doubts about the book."

"No, I don't," Elena said. She watched as a gangly swan made its awkward way to the water.

"What is it, then?"

Elena shrugged. "Oh, only that I feel as if I treated everyone very unfairly — you and Father and all the people in Standhope — that I nailed them to a public cross."

I lifted the manuscript from my lap. "Elena, there is nothing false in this book."

Elena looked at me and shook her head. "Truth is not the only value, William. It may not even be the highest one."

For a long time I sat silently beside her. Any defense of the book I might make seemed at the time superfluous.

After a few minutes, Elena's mood lightened somewhat. She watched a very old man as he walked shakily beside the pond, his cane dipping rhythmically into the water, his figure bowed, all his days behind him.

"Well, whatever happens now," Elena said, "it must be sweeter to be like us, to look forward to life rather than back on it. Don't you think, William?"

I could not answer her then. Now I can. No, Elena, the sweetness is at the end.

CALLIOPE

When I think of that paneled meeting room in which Martha's biography was launched, I am amazed at the miracle Sam Waterman wrought. In the very trough of the Depression, he established a publishing company dedicated, at least in relative terms, to quality, controversy, and the social ideals he held at the time, an amalgam of Jewish compassion and Marxist dialectics. As Jack MacNeill never tired of pointing out, this resulted in the publication of some of the most mystical proletarian literature ever written, novels of revelatory class consciousness, along with a few tough detective stories in which the vaguely left-wing private eye saves both a principle and a pretty girl.

Sam opened the offices of Parnassus Press during the winter of 1932. He rented three rooms in a rundown, nearly empty building in Hell's Kitchen. The lobby door was left open at night, and the homeless swept in at sunset, stretched themselves out across the floor, and slept until morning. Then they struggled out onto the street again, leaving behind nothing but the rolled newspapers they had used as pillows. Each morning Sam cleaned up after them, trudging down the littered staircase with mop and pail in tow, his freshly shined shoes and carefully pressed pants safely tucked into a pair of enormous black galoshes. "I could keep the stiffs out," he once told me with a smile, "but the Party frowns on that sort of thing." When I asked him if he did not fear theft, he assured me that the upper floors of the building were sealed off. "I'm a philanthropist, William," he said, "not a fool."

In fact, there would not have been much to steal, since the actual offices of Parnassus Press were quite Spartan. They consisted of three drafty rooms, each containing one lamp, one desk, and one typewriter. The floor was covered with a speckled gray linoleum which buckled up at the corners. There were no curtains, sofas, or potted plants, and there was only one picture on the wall, a kind of sampler which hung behind Sam's desk, with Horace's advice to writers quilted in red over a blue canvas: "Take this, leave that, and fitly time it all."

"Well, how do you like it?" Sam asked expectantly after he had given me the tour. "A humble beginning, wouldn't you say? But what the hell, William, that's the story of my life." He sat down in the swivel chair behind his desk and pulled a large manuscript from a drawer. It was the original typescript of *New England Maid*. "I suppose you've read this?"

"Yes."

"And?"

"I think it's a very remarkable book."

Sam grinned. "Normally a brother's ideas about his sister's manuscript wouldn't be worth all that much, William. But in this case, I think you're right."

"Have you told Elena that?"

"Yes, I have," Sam said. "By phone, this morning. We even settled on the advance. One hundred dollars. Of course, that's not much." He waved his arm out, indicating the barrenness of the room. "But then, we're not much, either." He lifted the manuscript from the desk. "But this? This is something rare, William. We're going to depend on it. It'll be the premier volume of the house. The way I see it, we'll either sink with this book or sail to heaven."

I was skeptical. "That seems a little imprudent, Sam, putting everything on one book."

"Depends on the book," Sam said. He looked at me dolefully. "To tell you the truth, the stuff we had to pick from was pretty weak." He waved Elena's manuscript in the air. "But this is the real thing, William, the sort of book that could get the bluenoses in a terrible dither. And that, my boy, means sales, sales, sales." He placed the book gently down on his desk. "But the main thing, William, is that Elena has written a very fine book, and we're going to put all our resources behind it."

Sam elaborated at some length on the campaign he envisioned

for *New England Maid.* "The goal," he concluded finally, "is to establish Elena with one book, to get that name out there in capital letters."

Teddy McNaughton came into the front office just in time to stop Sam from launching into another lengthy discussion of the publishing business. He was a short, thin man, and I suppose he was no more than twenty-five at the time. Sam had always described him as a whiz kid, a boy who was so smart he had even had the good sense to drop out of Harvard. But to me, he always seemed shy and insecure, already suffering from the strain and nervousness which would make New York unbearable for him only five years later.

There was a young woman with Teddy that morning. She was slender and dark, with strangely languid eyes. She was wearing a belted tweed overcoat, which she took off and folded over her arm. The two of them moved toward Sam's office, then glimpsed me and held back.

"Oh, come on in," Sam said loudly. "This is William Franklin, Elena Franklin's brother. You know Teddy," he said to me, "and this is Miriam Gold."

She nodded to me as she stepped into Sam's office. "Your sister wrote a very fine book," she said.

"We snatched Miriam from the offices of *New Masses,*" Sam told me. "I got her by making promises I don't expect to keep."

For perhaps the first time in my life, I made a directly flirtatious remark. "Well now, Sam," I said, "Miriam doesn't look like the sort of person you could dupe that easily."

Miriam watched me expressionlessly. "I was surprised when I heard that Elena was in her twenties," she said in one of those husky voices which were coming into vogue at the time. "It is a very mature work for someone so young."

"Well, Elena is a very mature person," I said. Then I spread my cape before her once again. "As I suspect you are, as well, Miss Gold."

I have sometimes wondered why, of all people on earth, I chose to pursue Miriam Gold. I was twenty-seven years old, and by that time I had had a few inconsequential romances. But I was also old enough to have grown tired of mirthless, solitary meals, of the silence that swept over me when I turned out the light above my bed, the same one that greeted me next morning.

I took one look at Miriam's lambent eyes and instantly sensed as if it were a revelation that the oldest commandments were perhaps the best ones, closest to our most basic needs, and that the first mandate of an ancient creed had long ago declared that a man should not live alone.

"I'm sure Sam's delighted to have you at the press," I added lamely, feeling, under her stringent gaze, witless as a toad.

"Well, it was nice to have met you, Mr. Franklin," she said. "And please tell your sister that I look forward to meeting her very soon."

And with that Miriam walked quickly out of Sam's office and took her seat in the adjoining room. I could hear her typewriter clattering away as Sam began another summation of his plan for Elena's book, and the sound of it, of those long brown fingers dallying upon the keys, was curiously thrilling.

I did not see Miriam again for several months. By that time, Elena's book was, as they say, between the boards, and Sam had arranged a press party to introduce it to the New York literary world. Harry had offered to provide a hall at the New York Athletic Club, but Sam had refused. "Jesus," he told me irritably, "up there on Central Park South with that cold, formal exterior and God knows what kind of stuffiness inside. Hell, William, that place is an island of anti-Semitism surrounded by a sea of anti-Semitism."

And so the New York Athletic Club lost the distinction of having Elena Franklin's first book introduced there. Instead, Sam chose the somewhat less imposing atmosphere of the Columbia Club, and it was there, on an afternoon in the fall of 1933, that Elena, her friends, and a varied assortment of "book people" gathered for the occasion.

Typically, Elena herself arrived early. She was dressed plainly, as always, in a dark skirt and white blouse. She had had her hair trimmed, however, and there was a hint of rouge on her cheeks.

"I have no idea how to behave today," she said.

"Just be charming," I told her. "That's what's expected, isn't it? Charm and wit and intelligence."

Sam quickly shuttled her away from me, and from across the room I watched as he instructed her for a few minutes, drilling his advice into her with many nervous gestures. Then he escorted her to a sofa near the back of the room, one so large she looked lost as she sat upon it, her hands folded neatly in lap, as if she were posing for a photograph much too formal for her nature. Still, she did not seem entirely ill at ease, and I think that her apprehension that day may have come from a feeling that she had to appear more unsophisticated than in fact she was. It was a pose that she maintained a good deal longer than I expected and did not entirely abandon until she returned from France with the idea for *Quality* already in her mind, not completely realized but powerfully imagined.

The guests soon began to filter in, and Elena nodded to each of them. Everyone received a copy of *New England Maid* upon arriving. Thus, at the age of twenty-three, Elena was treated to the sight of her own eight-year-old face — for one of her childhood photographs adorned the cover — staring back at her from beneath the arms of countless, gossipy strangers.

Mary came rushing in not long after the hall was half-filled. She was carrying a copy of the *World*.

"Look at this," she said excitedly as she thrust the paper in front of me.

I glanced down at the photograph of a group of baggy-pantsed farmers dumping milk on the highway outside Sioux City, Iowa, while their fiery leader, Milo Reno, looked on approvingly.

Mary tapped her finger beside the photograph. "That's my uncle Bill," she said with delight. "Never would have figured him for a Red." At that time, Mary still retained her satirical edge; but during the coming months, as the lines around soup kitchens steadily lengthened and small, brooding cities grew up along the wharves or out from under the bridges, she fell victim to a crazy panic, avoiding shadowy streets, slinking away from yawning alleyways, talking in mordant tones of what she called "uncontrolled events." And of course it was not long after this that she sought out and married her first doctor, a man named Philip Newman.

But on this happy day, Mary was spritely as ever. "Tom's not coming to the party," she said. "To tell you the truth, William, I think Elena's success has got his goat a little." She smiled at me impishly. "Are you sure you don't understand his feeling?"

"Not enough to resent Elena's success, Mary," I said. "If I were as good a writer, it would be my book being launched today. But I'm not. How can I blame Elena for that?"

Mary looked at me seriously, then reached over and squeezed my arm. "I think Elena has a very good brother," she said softly. "I think I'll go over and tell her so."

Then she released my arm and I watched as she walked over and joined Elena on her voluminous couch. Elena listened quietly a moment as Mary talked to her. Then she looked up at me and nodded very delicately.

Harry came in a few minutes later, his fiancée on his arm. Her name was Felice, and she was as flighty a child as I had ever had occasion to meet. Harry nonetheless seemed very proud of her, making a great show of what was, without doubt, her very considerable beauty. Still, her conversation was entirely vapid, and I remember thinking of her later as the most singularly trivial being I had ever met. Thus it was with profound surprise that I learned, years later, that she had taken charge of Harry's daunting empire after his death in the war and had run that disparate kingdom with what was said to be both a firm hand and a foul mouth. Until then, it seemed to me, I had never guessed the depths of woman's masquerade. When I related this to Elena, however, thinking it a rather cunning insight, she merely laughed and said she suspected there were plenty of beautiful young socialites who were every bit as empty as they seemed.

Harry was still sweeping Felice gracefully about the hall when Miriam came through the door. Teddy was with her, looking ghostly, but Sam quickly tugged him away, leaving Miriam standing alone near the center of the room.

"Remember me?" I said as I came up behind her.

"Oh, yes," she said dryly. "Hello."

I glanced about at the elaborate festivities. "I always thought that a book might sell merely on the basis of its quality. I suppose that's naive?"

"Yes, I think it is," Miriam said. "Very naive."

I was about to serve another ball into her court when a large and very handsome man stepped up beside her.

"Hello, Miriam," he said.

Miriam smiled. "Oh, hello, Jack. Are you enjoying the party?"

He nodded almost shyly and withdrew a copy of New England Maid from under his arm. "I already had a copy of this, but someone shoved it at me as I came through the door."

"Have you read it?" Miriam asked.

"Yes."

"What did you think?"

"That it was very interesting. I'll write a favorable review."

"Good," Miriam said. "I'm sure Elena will be pleased." She seemed suddenly to remember that I was standing beside her. "By the way, this is Elena's brother, ah . . ."

"William," I said and thrust out my hand.

"Happy to meet you, William," Jack said.

"This is Jack MacNeill," Miriam told me. "He's a freelance journalist. I met him when I was working at *New Masses.*"

"Yes, *New Masses,*" Jack said. "Funny how that already seems like the good old days." He was wearing a brown suit, with a light blue open-collared shirt and no tie. His shoes were scruffy brown brogans, and his belt looked as if it had survived several near-fatal encounters. He was about thirty years old, with an angular face and tangled, rust-colored hair. In that elegantly appointed room, he looked shockingly out of place, like a jagged piece of metal sculpture set down by mistake in a gallery of Dutch masters.

Elena was still seated across the room, and I noticed that Jack's eyes often drifted toward her as he spoke. "Your sister is really very gifted," he said. His voice was low, almost gentle, and it seemed curiously contradictory to his roughhewn façade. Of course, at that time I did not know Jack MacNeill, did not know that native tenderness which was deep within him but which he himself felt inconsistent with the tough, two-fisted reportage he was laboring to construct. It would be quite some time before he would abandon that tiresome duplicity and become the simple, kindly man he always was. But it was also one of his glories that in the end he did abandon it, so that, by the fifties, when he was hounded from the university and finally driven to England, he had embraced the gentler qualities of his own nature. And I remember that on the way up the gangway of the ship that would take him into exile, with reporters shouting baiting questions and flash bulbs popping all around him, he was able to turn toward them, pull the rose Elena had given him from his lapel, and toss it to that mean and gloating crowd. "This is for America," he said. "It needs all the beauty it can bear."

But in the fall of 1933, Jack was cultivating a somewhat more brawny image, one which his every gesture enhanced, even down to the way he gripped his wine glass in a tight, white-knuckled fist.

"I suppose I could find only one real fault with the book," he said, glancing first at Miriam, then at me. "It seemed a bit interior to me."

"Well, it *is* an autobiography, of sorts," I said.

Jack nodded. "Oh, of course. But something beyond that. There is an interior quality, a distance, as if the whole story wasn't really told by a person, but by a ghost." He looked at Miriam. "I mean, the larger world is shut outside — never intrudes upon the book, as if it didn't really exist. You have the town and the family, and that's all. You hardly know the war happened, except for that boy who comes back to Standhope and shoots himself."

"Well, she wasn't writing a history book, Jack," Miriam said.

"And I wouldn't want her to," Jack said. He looked at me. "It's the graphic element that's missing, the sense that the life she talks about was lived, not just thought about."

I nodded toward Elena, who was still seated on her sofa, looking rather stiff and wearied as one person after another joined her there briefly, then departed. "Perhaps you should talk this over with the author herself," I said.

"I think that's an excellent idea," Miriam said. She took Jack's arm and tugged him forward. "Come on, let me introduce you."

The seat beside Elena had just been abandoned by a pudgy reporter from the *Times*, so that she was sitting alone as we approached her.

"Elena," Miriam said, "I'd like you to meet Jack MacNeill. He's a freelance journalist, and he has some interesting opinions about your book."

Jack did not wait for Elena to respond. He immediately sat down beside her. "First off," he said, "I should tell you that I liked your book quite a lot."

"Thank you," Elena said demurely.

"But I had some reservations, too," he added cautiously. "I thought the book was a little too internal, as if everything in it only happened in your mind, not in the real world."

Elena smiled slightly but said nothing.

"America is missing from the book, I think," Jack added.

He meant, of course, the America he had seen and documented in report after report as he wandered from his birthplace in Seattle, after his mother's death when he was fifteen, to his present flat in Greenwich Village. He had worked as a migrant, lived as a migrant, and, as he said, thought as a migrant. "I don't have a vision, you see," he said, "just a fair amount of experience."

And so when Elena asked him what America he meant, he was able to tell her, speaking softly, his steady voice almost inflectionless, his eyes burrowing into hers.

"Well," he said, "have you ever seen a room with maybe fifteen living in it, and nothing on the windows to keep out the wind but ripped-up corn flake boxes?"

Elena admitted, somewhat stiffly, I think, that she had not.

And so he presented to her, in brief, America as he had come to know it.

". . . And in South Carolina they work from what they call 'can see,' meaning dawn, to 'can't see,' meaning dead of night. And down in Oklahoma, when the dust storm comes, people die because they swallow so much dirt, even with masks on. I know a family — interviewed them — that walked from Arkansas to the Rio Grande because they heard that cotton was grown by the river's edge. Have you ever heard of that?"

Elena shook her head, her eyes fixed upon his.

"I've seen shacks made out of soup cans and Kotex boxes, and a good many other things. That's part of the American story, don't you think?"

"But Elena wasn't writing what you call 'the American story,'" I protested.

Jack looked up at me. "I know that. I'm just trying to suggest what grit is, the little detail that makes you feel something instead of just think about it." He turned to Elena. "I don't mean to offend you, and I don't think it's my place to tell you how to write. It was just an opinion. You can take it or leave it."

Elena looked at him pointedly. "Too internal, you said?"

"Yes," Jack replied. He nodded toward the windows at the front of the room. "There's a lot going on out there." He tapped the side of his head with his finger. "And there's a lot going on up here. The hard thing is to get those two worlds together."

Elena continued to watch him, but said nothing.

"You have a lot of talent, Miss Franklin," Jack said. "That internal world of yours, it's electric. A kind of steady charge runs through your whole book. But the fire keeps dying away." He stood up. "It was nice meeting you, Miss Franklin," he said.

And with that, he sauntered away, edging gently through the well-heeled crowd.

Elena's gaze followed him, a very intense look in her eyes. I saw that same look years later, when she and I were walking in the wildly disordered garden surrounding her house on Cape Cod. She had been talking about Jack with immeasurable fondness and affection, her

white hair dancing in a small breeze from off the sea. Then that
look came in her eyes. "I was growing a eunuch's soul, William,"
she said. "Then Jack came along for me."

And she might have added that same afternoon, just as she turned
to watch a line of surf break along the shore — the foam very much,
as I remember quite vividly now, the color of her hair — she might
have added, "Just as Miriam came along for you."

I suppose a less lonely man might have given up after Miriam's
casual, but repeated, rebuffs. He might have found a less demanding
and independent woman, "selfless," as Raymond Finch says of his
working-class girlfriend in *Calliope*, "because she has no self."

Miriam Gold, on the other hand, had a pronounced self. Her early
childhood had been spent in those crowded tenements on the Lower
East Side which Mike Gold (no relation) had already immortalized
in his novel *Jews without Money*. By the time she was ten, however,
Miriam's father had moved to the upper reaches of Manhattan, settling
his family into a spacious Harlem apartment and beginning the life
of reasonable comfort that had been his waking dream for forty years.
Thus Miriam's early poverty had been transformed into miraculous
prosperity by the time she came of age. But it had not been forgotten.
She would often talk of the smells that had wafted up into her bedroom
from the open store windows, of peddlers' carts below, of the incessant
noise that had poured into her room from the hawking and bickering
of that vast open bazaar which was once Orchard Street. On those
same streets, she had listened to tales of an older world, of pogroms
and forced migrations, and from these she had gained a sense that
for the generation that preceded hers, America had offered itself as
a dream of unprecedented dimension, one whose bounty she could
not deny and wished, I think, only to extend.

To all of this, Miriam added the experience of moving from an
earlier density into the world bought for her by her father's good
fortune, so that she could sit in that grotesque parlor he had designed
in imitation of David Belasco — all swooping oriental drapes and

Middle Eastern water pipes — and dream of the junk markets of Houston Street, its swarming crowds and myriad dialects. From her ornate and luxurious bedroom, she looked back purposefully to those earlier days, to a world of direct and simple toil, presided over by the dictates that had come down from Sinai rather than by the labyrinthine contortions of the New York Civil Code. Her father's good fortune had set her both morally and ethically adrift. It was a complex condition, one which Elena tried to capture in the section of *Quality* that deals with the Jewish novel of immigration. The great accomplishment of that genre, she wrote, "was to give our literature the profound sense of a beached moral order, of reluctant but inescapable abandonment, of the ransom the old exacts from the new, of that deep nostalgia which is unmistakable in the closing passages of *The Rise of David Levinsky*, and which is essentially a form of ethical wistfulness. It is the voice of the cantor heard above the roar of urban traffic, the call of the shofar over the hum of the shirtwaist machines."

Certainly Miriam felt this wistfulness. As her father's finances became more and more entangled with those of the barons so excoriated by her fellow workers at *New Masses*, she sensed not only the oddity of her circumstances but their cruelty as well. She believed that her father was a victim of his own ambition, that he had forfeited the more intense life of the ghetto for the cold and charmless one of the Jewish middle class, and that this was a betrayal of his heritage far more serious, as she said, than grabbing a hot dog at Yankee Stadium.

For Jack MacNeill, of course, all this was nothing more than a privileged person's romanticization of early poverty, and he told Miriam so more than once during the years we lived so closely together. But I have always thought that there was more to Miriam's conviction than that. Once she told Jack that America was the sort of country in which when you win, you lose, and when you lose, you lose. Jack had laughed quite a lot at that. But I believe that Miriam was talking about the losses that accrue to success in a very subtle way, moral losses of the most delicate sort, as well as about the grace and struggle of communal life, the wealth and strain of tradition, the charm of ancient things.

Thus when Jack called her the most conservative radical he ever knew, he was probably right. To this day, when I think of her, I see her not as a fiery instrument of revolutionary revenge — a popular image in those days, one which numerous female Russian revolutionaries were said to embody — but as a peculiarly willful and competent person, one whose life was ennobled by a memory rather than a dream of justice.

It is surprising to me now how little I actually know of the life she lived before we met. I know about her time on the Lower East Side, but once her father whisked her up to Harlem, things grow vague. I know that for a long time she was on the outs with her family and that the questions in dispute were mainly political. Perhaps on some morning she had marched into breakfast, hurled a few epithets at her father while he sat stunned above his wheat toast, then stormed out onto the street, slamming the door behind her. I know for sure only that there was a break, a series of hapless jobs, during which Miriam attempted, perhaps, to fuse her experience with that of the working class, and then a retreat. For she went back to her family after a time, gave an accounting of her life since she had left them, and asked if they might help her do the thing she had by then decided upon: go to college. Her father said yes immediately, and all of them alternately laughed and cried throughout the entire afternoon, until, as Miriam always said, the carved mahogany elephant on the mantel looked as if it would die of all this unexpected sweetness.

The following year Miriam went to Smith, and she would remember her time there almost as fondly as her childhood in lower Manhattan. Perhaps, in the end, it was simply that for her the past was a sacred thing, that nothing could ever seem wholly ugly through the prism of remembrance, that remembering well, as she once said, is a kind of art. All her life she loved the sort of object that soaked up time — old letters and photographs, discarded magazines and yellowing newspapers. Perhaps it was finally this reverence for things remembered that drew her to *New England Maid*, then to Elena, and, at long last, to me.

She finally agreed to have dinner with me during Christmas week. By then *New England Maid* had been out for almost three months. Reviews poured into Sam's tiny office from all over the country, most of them either very favorable or very hostile. Miriam was coordinating everything for the book — directing the advertising, setting up all the interviews, whisking Elena from one reception to another. The two of them were so exhausted at day's end that Elena would often collapse back in Miriam's room and spend the night on the short, worn sofa by the window.

"Surely Elena's enjoying all this," I said. "The attention, I mean."

Miriam took a sip of wine. "She does it well, but I'm not sure she enjoys it."

"But it must be dazzling," I insisted.

Miriam shrugged, then glanced away. She was wearing a gray wool suit with notched lapels, and I remember thinking how professional she looked, how completely in control of everything around her. It seemed a kind of miracle that she had consented to this dinner, and in a way it was. Not long before Alexander was born, we sat in the living room of our small apartment and talked about that first night while I pressed my hand to her stomach, searching for some movement, thrilled when it came. "It's all such an accident, William," she said, smiling quietly. "I was so damned tired that afternoon that I couldn't face the prospect of going home and cooking. Then the phone rang and it was you offering a free meal, and I just thought, Oh, what the hell."

And so we had ended up in the dining room of the Hotel Lafayette, small and very French though it was only a block or so from the drab façade of New York University.

Miriam turned back toward me. "Elena says you're writing a book."

"Sort of."

"On Cowper?"

"I've been plowing through it for quite some time. Since graduate school. I think of it as my doctoral dissertation, not really a book."

Miriam nodded but said nothing. She seemed preoccupied.

"I suppose you meet a great many dashing men in your profession," I said.

Miriam closed her eyes wearily. "Dash is not all it's cracked up to be."

I looked at her intently. "You know, of course, Miriam, that I've been trying to make an impression on you."

Her face softened a bit. "Yes, I suppose I do."

"Wit didn't work. I suppose now I'm trying . . . what, humility?"

Miriam kept her silence. She was watching me with those calculating eyes. She had been "gone over" by the best of them, had batted away the most refined pitches. But not without some loss to herself, for there was something in her that had already been scraped to the bone.

"I don't think I'm a weak man," I said. "I can live without you. I can live, I think, without anyone. But I don't want to."

Miriam sipped her wine, her eyes evaluating me over the rim of the glass.

"You don't have to be clairvoyant to see that I'm sort of lonely, sort of tired of being lonely." I shook my head. "I don't know how to court you, Miriam," I said feebly. "I wouldn't know where to begin."

Miriam lowered her glass slowly to the table, her eyes still watching me with either the deepest seriousness or the most blasé indifference.

"I think Elena loves me," I added. "Might I offer her as a reference?"

Miriam smiled. "Elena says you have the heart of a little boy trapped in a man's body. She says that's your great gift, William."

"I want you to agree to have dinner with me again, agree right now. No matter how this evening turns out, I want to know that there will be another one."

She thought about it for a moment. "All right," she said at last.

As it turned out, the rest of the evening was very nice indeed. Miriam grew increasingly relaxed, talking almost exclusively about herself. She recalled her days at Smith, of long walks about the campus, of the girls gathering in their rooms to smoke with delicious malice while the matronly house mother patrolled the hallway outside with warlike rectitude.

"She was very, very proper," Miriam said, laughing, "the sort whose parents came to America a few months behind the *Mayflower*, and who never really felt quite right about herself because of that." She took a sip of wine. "I suppose your family's old New England stock?"

"Perhaps," I said. "I really don't know."

"You're indifferent to your family history, then?"

"Yes, indifferent."

Miriam looked at me strangely. "That's very American, isn't it? The notion that everyone starts his own life when he's born."

"I suppose it is. It doesn't seem such a bad thing."

"No one uplifted or brought down by their family's past," Miriam said. "It's a myth, though, one of our illusions."

"Except that no one really believes it," I said. "Certainly the rich know better, and the poor know better still."

This launched us into a political discussion, which was mercifully ended after several minutes when the waiter stepped up with the check.

A few minutes later, Miriam and I walked out onto Ninth Street. We drifted toward Fifth Avenue, then down toward Washington Square.

Miriam drew her scarf more tightly around her throat as we walked. A steady rain had been falling, soaking the densely packed leaves, which gathered at our feet so thickly you could imagine yourself walking through a drenched New Hampshire wood.

"Well, tell me, Miriam," I said, quickly avoiding any return to politics, "is it true that editors are all failed novelists?"

"Maybe not all," she said, "but I am."

"Really?"

"Oh yes," Miriam said. She glanced up at the spires of the Church of the Ascension, then back at me. "I've probably a thousand manuscript pages in boxes around my apartment. Terrible stuff. Really terrible. It's the rage and self-pity that get you."

"Has Sam seen any of it?"

Miriam laughed. "Sam? My God, no. If he saw that junk, he'd fire me."

"Oh, it can't be that bad."

Miriam stopped and gave me a serious look. "It's terrible. It really is." Years later she let me read a little of it, a page or two, no more. She was right; it was terrible. A kind of awful moan rose from every page, then disappeared into a little hiss of bitterness and resentment. I could hardly imagine that she had written it, that so much anger and disappointment rolled about within her, like the floating uterus posited by ancient medicine as the final locus of all female woe.

"Now, Elena — she's a different story," Miriam said, walking on once again.

"In what way?"

"Talented, William. I think that the words must flow directly from her mind into the typewriter. There doesn't seem to be a jerk anywhere, just that amazing fluidity. A natural writer."

"Very little work for an editor, then," I said lightly.

"Fortunately, yes."

We stopped to watch a group of young people struggling to maneuver a large canvas up the stairs of the Salmagundi Club. I started forward to offer my help, but Miriam caught my arm. "They're artists," she said. "They know how to move a painting."

Within a few minutes we were walking on MacDougal Street, not far from Miriam's apartment. The street was alive with tearooms and nightclubs in those days, and there was a constant flow of taxis and private cars. But just around the corner, at the entrance to Miriam's building, the welter suddenly subsided and we were once again on one of those New York streets which, in its serenity, resembles nothing so much as a country lane.

"Well, just to make us even," I said as Miriam turned to say good night, "I'm no novelist either. I'd probably be embarrassed if I were."

"Why?"

"Well, because my book would probably be so old-fashioned, full of medieval virtue and romantic fire."

"The cloister and the hearth."

"Exactly."

Then, just at that moment, the year's first snow began to fall lightly, each flake silver in the glow of the streetlight. Now, a symbol may be, as Elena wrote in *Quality*, "as blatant as a trumpet or as maudlin as a tear of dew trembling at the leafy edge," but I will always insist that the snow began to fall just as we parted, that the light did, in fact, turn each flake to silver.

"I enjoyed the evening very much, William," Miriam said.

"So did I."

She put out her hand, and as I reached out and took it, she pulled herself forward and kissed me, drawing her arms around me tightly.

She has been gone now for over thirty years. But there are times, particularly late at night, when the rain is heavy or the snow rests in waist-high drifts beside the wall, when I wrap my own arms around my body and pretend that they are hers.

Mr. Brennan died in January of 1934, delivering Elizabeth from her long vigil at last. Two months later, Howard married her in a quiet ceremony in the Congregational church. Elena acted as bridesmaid and I was the best man.

They planned to go to Europe on their honeymoon, a decision that surprised me, given Howard's agoraphobic tendencies. And yet that April, Elena and I found ourselves on a bus heading down to the west-side piers to see them off.

A taxi strike had been going on for quite a while by then, and the previous evening a small riot had taken place near the docks. As Elena and I rode toward the towering stacks of the *Rochambeau*, we passed a disturbing array of cars turned over on their sides, some of them little more than burned-out husks, a black smoke still rising from their charred interiors.

"Sign of the times," I said.

Elena glanced out the window as the bus moved down Eleventh Avenue. There were scores of mounted police still patroling the littered streets, eyeing the line of strikers picketing the garages of the Parmelee, Radio, and Terminal cab companies. At Twenty-third Street, the avenue turned almost blue with police uniforms, while across from the Parmelee garage, silent, disgruntled cabbies broke slats to feed a huge bonfire.

"It's getting worse, you know," I said. It had been getting worse for at least two years, but the rich had maintained their taste for travel and I had managed to hang on to my job at the travel agency. Still, the times intruded even upon my modest security, and I remember the dread that always washed over me as I passed a soup kitchen or a stack of men sleeping in a doorway. There was a tone of rising tension in the atmosphere more tangible than the sight of hurling bricks or the sound of scattered gunfire, a disquieting concern, as Evelyn Waugh once put it, that the train from the capital might never arrive.

Elena continued to watch the streets. She had remained rather remote and preoccupied since Mr. Brennan's death, and even Miriam had noticed a flagging of energy, a drawn quality in her face.

"I suppose you'll miss Elizabeth," I said.

"I suppose," Elena said. She glanced to the right at a group of shabby vagrants sprawled along a stretch of hurricane fence not far from the river.

"Times are out of joint, aren't they?" I said.

Elena turned back toward the front of the bus and stared straight down the avenue. Later, in *Calliope*, using the hard, almost mordant voice of Raymond Finch, she would describe what she saw:

Some of us had decided to head down to the pier and see Harvey off on the *Normandie*, so we motored down the west side by the river. The whole avenue was littered with smoking cabs, some overturned and smoldering, huge metal insects helpless on their backs. Davey said it had been "great fun" the night before, the mounted cops galloping down the street while the cabbies dove out of the way of the horses, scattering, he said, like ants across an anthill. That was the way he thought about them, the way he'd been taught to think about them, the way we'd all been taught, all of us in that sleek black car, which cost plenty and which, we all thought, could never be turned over and set on fire by a bunch of crazy hacks. But I looked up ahead and got a little twinge of, well, anxiety, I suppose, because of the Hooverville stretching out into the water like the raft of the *Medusa*, and then down below that, the international piers where the great luxury liners sat heavily in the water, their gangplanks pulled up like the drawbridges of besieged medieval fortresses, and below them a line of striking seamen filing about, muttering to themselves, while a heavy breeze from off the river slapped at the placards they juggled above their heads. And I guess, just for a moment, all the sorry dislocations of the time swept in on me from that long, gray avenue, as if everything about the current troubles had become concentrated on either side of the street, that one desolate stretch of protest and ruin which lined the avenue from Times Square to the squat little boathouses of the Cunard line.

We got off the bus a few minutes later and began walking southward toward the huge fleet of ocean liners we could see in the distance.

"You should be on top of the world, Elena," I said cheerfully. "The book is a raging success. And you certainly have your youth."

She continued to walk silently beside me.

I shrugged playfully. "Of course, you know that line of Samuel Butler's, that youth is like spring — an overpraised season."

Elena glanced away from me. She looked curiously baffled, as if her recent success had only served to increase the vague distress which, it seemed to me, had dogged her almost all her life. I guessed that my sister was one of those about whom the Buddha wrote, the sort who seeks only fulfillment, and finding that, seeks only the renewal of desire.

For a time we continued to walk silently together, both of us looking needlessly forlorn, I suppose, to the army of striking dock workers and longshoremen who lined the wharves. To them we must have seemed impossibly self-absorbed.

"I feel *enclosed,* William," Elena said after a moment.

"What do you mean?"

"Captured. Locked up."

"I still don't understand what you're talking about."

Elena nodded apprehensively to one of the strikers as he passed. "Morning, ma'am," he said softly.

"You're in a kind of postpartum depression, Elena," I said. "Miriam says that most writers feel that way in between books. They think they've poured everything into the last book, that they have nothing left to say."

Elena looked at me, almost coming to a halt as she did so. "But I really don't have anything else to say."

I laughed. "You'll think of something. You're only twenty-four years old." I pulled her gently over to a street vendor and bought two ears of roasted corn. "Here, take this," I said. "This'll give you a bit of energy. You shouldn't look so run down when you see Elizabeth."

Elena took the corn and we walked on toward the pier. I decided to change the subject.

"It's too bad Howard and Elizabeth couldn't have stayed in New York before leaving," I said.

"Howard wanted to leave right away," Elena said without the slightest interest.

I let her keep her own counsel after that. She was never one to be lightly extracted from a mood.

We found Howard and Elizabeth only a few minutes later, both of them looking quite elegant as they waited near the gangplank of their ship. Elizabeth was dressed in a fashionable velvet coat with a fur collar. Howard held to his characteristically conservative attire: tan cashmere coat and Homburg.

"Well, I'm awfully glad you two could make it to see us off," he said cheerfully as we approached.

There was a round of handshakes and embraces, and then Howard, as usual, anticipated the question he no doubt thought foremost in every human mind. "I suppose you think it odd that I can run off to Europe now," he said with a laugh. "Poor Howard Carlton, who couldn't stay a single night in New York."

When no one ventured to remark upon this, he began again, monotonously going over the nature of his disorder. He reminded me of that character in Stendhal, the one who greatly loves music, but only three songs.

"The fact is, I'm doing it for Elizabeth's career," he said. "Her painting, you know."

Elizabeth smiled happily. "Howard thinks that all painters should live in Paris for a while."

Howard patted her hand. "Yes, that's right. And so, despite my condition, I've decided to take her there."

"For the good of my career," Elizabeth repeated. She looked affectionately at Elena. "Speaking of careers, I read *New England Maid*, Elena. I'm Jennifer, aren't I?"

Elena nodded. "Of course."

"And Dr. Houston's in it, and Mrs. Nichols," Elizabeth said excitedly. "I think I knew most everyone in it."

Elena smiled. "Well, you probably did. Most of them still lived in Standhope when you moved there." For a moment the darker tones of Elena's mood, that film of worried preoccupation, seemed to vanish in her delight at seeing Elizabeth on the eve of a great adventure. "I've never been on one of these liners," she said.

"They're quite wonderful," Howard told her, "but, you might as well know, quite expensive, too."

"They have restaurants and libraries — just like a small town," Elizabeth added. She giggled. "Just like a floating Standhope."

"Well, let's hope it's better than that," I said.

"It's going to be a splendid trip," Howard assured us. He sounded as if he were trying to convince himself. "And it will be such a treat for Elizabeth, such an education."

Not far from us, a woman in a fur coat flung a spray of confetti into the air and sullenly watched as it floated down. The man beside her quickly drained the last of his champagne, and then the two of them hurried into their waiting car. Across the street, one of the striking seamen hurled a can at their departing limousine, and the men around him laughed and slapped him on the back as he returned to the line.

"Sometimes I think we're getting out of this country just in time," Howard said.

"You won't find it any better in Europe," I told him.

Howard laughed, but a bit nervously. "Perhaps we should disguise ourselves, then. As peasants, maybe." He looked at Elena. "What do you think?"

"I think you look just fine, Howard," Elena replied dully. She looked at Elizabeth. "How long's the honeymoon?"

"We don't know," Howard said. He swept Elizabeth under his arm. She nuzzled him delightedly. "We've not decided."

"How . . . romantic," I said.

"You'd probably rather tour the United States, William?" Howard asked.

I shook my head. "Not in these times."

Howard turned to Elena. "We'll live like kings for a while, you know, live the high life. Then we'll come back and Elizabeth will get on with her work."

Elena said nothing. She simply turned to the array of passenger ships that lined the harbor, dwarfing the small wooden boathouses along the shore.

"Oh, Elena, I forgot to tell you," Elizabeth said. "Standhope has a bookstore now. Just a small one, right in the center of the square."

Elena nodded. She was watching the line of seamen on strike, clearly preoccupied with them, as if the real focus of the day's drama was on them, on the flapping of their placards, their resentful, muttering voices.

"We're going to stay outside Paris for quite a while," Howard said. "The light in the provinces is supposed to be perfect for painters. I want Elizabeth to try it." He glanced at his gold watch. "Well, Elizabeth, we'd better be boarding, don't you think?"

Elizabeth drew Elena into her arms. "I hope everything goes well with the book," she said. She kissed Elena's cheek. "I don't know when I'll be back in the States."

Elena stepped slowly out of Elizabeth's embrace, then pulled herself back into it again, hugging her fiercely. "I want to hear all about your adventures," she said. "Promise to write me."

We both shook hands with Howard, then watched as the two of them made their way up the gangplank, Howard steering Elizabeth from behind, as if she were a pushcart. At the passenger deck they turned and waved to us. Then, very slowly, with a kind of massive deliberation, the ship backed out into the river then made its way southward toward the bay.

I took Elena's arm and we began to move out of the crowd. "Do you want to go home now?" I asked.

She shook her head. "No, not yet."

And so we walked to a small coffee shop not far from the docks and took a table in the back corner. Elena was preoccupied again.

I regarded her closely. "What's bothering you? You should be very happy these days. The book's doing better than anyone could have expected. You have enough money to sit back and relax for a while."

For a long time, Elena simply sat silently in her chair, her eyes moving from one object to another, focusing on nothing.

The waiter came up and I ordered coffee for us both. Outside, a wet snow had begun to fall, turning the edges of the sidewalk slate gray. I dreaded the slippery walk back to my Village cubicle, to its bad lighting and its sudden drafts and the wooden crate littered with books about a poet who had been dead for over a hundred years.

Elena continued to stare silently about the room until our coffee arrived. Then she took a hesitant sip, the steam rising into her hair. "I'm sorry to have gotten so out of sorts," she said.

"You're like that, Elena," I said. "You're moody."

Elena placed the cup back down on the table. "Am I, really? I've never thought of myself as a moody person."

I smiled coolly, "Take it from me, you're moody."

We talked of inconsequential things after that, both of us rather tired of each other's company. When we'd finished our coffee, I walked Elena to her bus.

Later that day, I ended up at Miriam's apartment off MacDougal Street. She greeted me cheerfully and ushered me into her tiny, plant-strewn living room.

"Elena's in one of her bad moods," I said. "What do you suppose it is?"

She shrugged. "General dissatisfaction, maybe. Don't you ever feel that?"

I shook my head. "No, I always know exactly what's bothering me."

Miriam sat down beside me. "Well, some people aren't so lucky."

The phone rang as I was about to add something else. Miriam answered it. She listened for a moment, staring at me pointedly the whole time.

"Yes, I have it," she said into the receiver. Then she recited a telephone number and hung up. "That was Elena," she said.

"What did she want?"

"Jack MacNeill's phone number."

I suppose she must have rung him up that very night, because the next morning Jack called Miriam at Parnassus and told her that he had had a very interesting conversation with Elena, that she had asked for what he called "a guided tour of the other world," and that he had agreed to give it.

In her biography, Martha called the period during which Elena and Jack were so closely associated her "social period," the time during which she seemed to confront, in Martha's words, "the full contradictory thesis of Depression America."

Of course, for those of us who lived through the thirties, the notion that the Depression had to be "confronted" seems a bit odd. It was simply *there,* a constant presence in our lives, "like living on a fault line," as Raymond Finch says in *Calliope,* "when the earth begins to tremble."

I suppose that some people could have avoided the surrounding misery. One did not have to seek it out, as Elena did, with Jack's help, on that Saturday morning when the two of them began what Martha melodramatically refers to as their "odyssey." Elena did not need to feel her own dissatisfaction so deeply, or to have listened to Jack so attentively when he spoke to her at the Columbia Club, or to have called him up a few weeks later with her peculiar request.

In my mind I have heard Jack's phone ringing a hundred times, the sound of it rattling through his disheveled flat, disturbing that old yellow cat who slept, more or less continuously, in the open suitcase beneath his bed. Now, as I think of it, it seems quite romantic. But in fact, the phone must have been jarring, the disordered room dank and smelly, and Jack's voice when he answered somewhat cold and irritable, since he liked to nap in the afternoon and was probably sound asleep when the phone rang beside his bed.

The miracle, as I once told Martha, was that he picked it up at all, and then, having done so, that he listened to what must have seemed to him the innocent and naive voice of my sister. But he did.

And so it was Jack MacNeill who introduced Elena to that larger world she thought it necessary to explore, who tempered, as he would always claim, her learning with experience, playing Virgil to her Dante. And when there was no more hardship to soak up, Elena turned to the work before her, thinking it would be *The Forty-eight Stars* of Jack's vision. But it became *Calliope*, a curiously medieval book, which begins in a ballroom anointed with champagne and ends in a dream of crucifixion.

She met Jack in the lobby of Three Arts the next Saturday morning. She had telephoned me the day before to break our lunch date.

"You remember Jack MacNeill?" she asked, almost hesitantly.

"Yes, the fellow who had some suggestions about *New England Maid.*"

"That's right," Elena said. "Well, we're going to sort of tour the city tomorrow, so I don't know if I can make it for lunch."

"You mean you can't."

"I can't, yes."

"Dinner, then?"

She thought about it for a moment. "All right, about seven. Meet me at Three Arts."

Through most of the next day, I worked on the final draft of my Cowper book. Sam had by then read enough of it to offer a contract. "We need some highbrow stuff," he explained. "I mean, something for the serious egghead, you know?" Despite his obvious lack of enthusiasm, I leaped at the chance to publish and hauled myself into the heavy labor of rescuing from all those piles of notes one small book about a poet.

Thus as I was going about the last stages of my editorial work, Elena was beginning a relationship that would, for better or worse, last for forty years.

Jack had borrowed a car that morning, a Graham Prosperity Six which a friend of his had bought three years before and which Jack loved because of the irony of the name. He picked Elena up at Three Arts and they set out, driving south down Broadway. Later, over time, Elena would relate her experience to me bit by bit, stitching small anecdotes together, until finally, years later, I had a vivid image of the entire journey.

When they started out, Elena told me, Jack began to talk again about the provincial air of *New England Maid*, reiterating the objections he had voiced before. Then he moved into a more general discussion of the American literary community, which he held in some contempt, calling the literary life "one-half wind and one-half breeze." At the same time, however, he confessed to a few literary ambitions of his own. He had already published one novel, about a strike in Detroit. It was a bad novel, he said, too narrow in its scope, completely ineffectual in rendering what Jack grandly called "the whole life of the workplace." He suspected that he lacked the particular talents of the novelist: the ability to make a fictional circumstance genuinely real, the flair for the brilliant image or the galvanizing scene, or even the capacity to tell a story.

For Elena this first conversation alone with Jack would always be precious, and throughout her life she would return to it again and again. "He could have come on as completely worldly and self-assured," she said in the 1980 interview, "but instead he modestly displayed his failures, so that he seemed almost to be asking *me* for guidance, just as the day before I had asked him."

He took her directly to the southern tip of Manhattan, where they watched the Staten Island Ferry chug toward them. Jack spoke quietly about what it was like on the immigrant ships, of the terrible shock of Ellis Island, its grueling and pathetic chaos. "I've seen people walk out of that place," Jack said, "and not know what sex they were, or even what their names were — their real names, not the one some Irish cop gave them."

In everything, Elena told Martha Farrell, Jack was kind and generous. And to me she related more than once the almost boyish innocence in the way he spoke to her or touched her arm. "I never felt any effort at what we'd call a seduction," she said to me one night at my apartment, with Alexander in her lap. "Not the slightest hint of anything like that." Then she drew her arms more tightly around my little boy, as if it were not a sleeping child she was protectively embracing but Jack MacNeill's reputation.

After leaving Battery Park, Jack and Elena journeyed north to the Lower East Side, and there they walked the crowded streets of the noisy tenement district, glancing at the unplucked chickens that hung in the shop windows along Hester Street. On Delancey, Jack good-naturedly bargained over the price of a lacy tablecloth, which he finally bought and which covered the small dining room table in Elena's house on Cape Cod the day she died. He told her that Walt Whitman had walked these same streets and had learned more about the city from them than he could have learned from a thousand government statisticians. He then launched into a sermonette on the purposes of poetry, hailing Whitman and Vachel Lindsay and dismissing Eliot peremptorily with Floyd Dell's remark about his "beery, bleary pathos." To this, Elena made feeble objection. "But Jack was really on fire then," she told me later, "and he bluntly insisted that all of Eliot was just prissy poor-mouthing, and he smiled and did a parody, putting his hand on his heart and reciting loudly, 'We are the hollow men, whining together.'"

They went to the Bowery after that and had oxtail stew for fifteen cents a bowl at Blossom's Restaurant. The Bowery was as dreadful then as it is now, its brick streets little more than jagged roadways through a landscape of vagrancy and destitution, an alcoholic purgatory. Jack made sure that Elena saw it all, every bit of it, from Houston Street to Cooper Union. Just how powerfully she was affected became clear in the scene in *Calliope* when Finch, after a night of drinking, is tossed from a cab for throwing up in the back seat and is left helplessly sprawled in the gutter, still lucid despite the alcohol:

He left me, that modern Samaritan, in the inch-deep gutter wash. There was something green floating near my ear, and I tried to get my eyes on it, jerking my head to the right. It swam into view — a crumpled package of Lucky Strikes, and a bunch of soggy cigarettes — but I couldn't get my hand up, and so I just lay back, letting the water seep down the collar of my shirt. As I lay there, everything went very dark, then brightened to a kind of heavy, gray fog. I thought I was going out, but the sounds got to me first, a few voices mumbling over me.

I could smell the stink coming from them, that nickel-flophouse smell of rat poison and watered-down disinfectant. They bent toward me and I could smell them perfectly now, smell the shaving lotion on their breath, and the cloying sweetness from the cheap fruit wine. The sores on their faces smelled like over-ripened grapes, kind of sour in its sweetness. I felt them then, their fingers, stubby, bumbling, shaking with the tremor of too little booze. They were in my pockets and unfastening my watch. They were pulling down my socks and tugging at the gold ring on my finger. After awhile they stopped, and I could feel the breeze on me and knew that they had stripped me clean, left me sprawled and soaking in my underwear, and I thought it was over then.

Time passed, hazy time, while the sweet smell lingered, and then I saw something else, a face, staring down, getting closer. I was clear enough by then to see how haggard it was, a crone's face, with shaggy hair and dark creases that would scare children, and I thought, almost laughing, This person must know about Saint Jude. This person knows there's a saint whose special province is such desperate cases. I heard myself laugh a little, just under my breath, and the face heard it too and stiffened a little and reared back, the eyes narrowing. A shadow passed over my face and then I felt something hot on my cheek and I realized that she had slapped me, had slapped my grinning face with all her drunken might.

After the Bowery, Jack took Elena to the watchman's shack on Coenties Slip, on the East River, and for the next hour or so she listened as Jack and the watchman discussed the life of the waterfront. Then they crossed Manhattan once again, stopping at the enormous Hooverville that stretched out to the river from the west-side wharves. Jack told her that the police were wary of entering such places, that they called the crime there "shanty trouble" and let it go. He said that there were similar places from Maine to California, and that in St. Louis he had seen a row of makeshift houses made from nothing but old barrels and tarpaper, and that it stretched for a full mile along the riverbank.

The rest of the afternoon was a hopscotch tour of various quarters of the city. They went to the municipal incinerators and saw the men sleeping beside them to keep warm. He showed her bread lines and soup kitchens. In the Bronx, he told her how coal was smuggled into New York by unemployed miners from Pennsylvania. On Sixth Avenue in Manhattan, they stood among the sea of unemployed gazing up at the chalkboard displays of the employment agencies lining the avenue from Forty-second to Thirty-fourth Street. Jack marveled at their passivity and the mild hum of their conversation. In the West, he said, things were different. There men set forest fires in order to be hired to put them out. He took her to the sweatshops of the garment district and the near-empty hiring halls of the trade unions. And over everything, as Elena later said, he cast his own peculiar shadow, carefully guiding her away from mere shock, mere pity. "He showed me the underbelly of a great city," she said in the 1980 interview, "and I must tell you that I had lived in New York for quite some time by then, but that much of this had been invisible to me. For Jack, it was important that I see it. He believed that experience was instructive in the making of a life — not an artist's life particularly, but any life. He took me on that trip because I was a person, not, God forbid, because I was a writer."

The trip ended at around seven, when Jack finally dropped Elena off at Three Arts. I was waiting in the lobby when the two of them came in. Jack was walking behind my sister in that ambling gait of his, which Mary was sure he had borrowed from Jack London. He glanced about the room as he trailed behind, taking in everything, the neatness and enforced femininity of the place, its detachment from any of the things he had seen that day.

"Ah, William," Elena said as she came over to me, "I'm glad you're here." She turned toward Jack. "You've met my brother, I think."

Jack nodded, his hands thrust deep into the pockets of his flannel pants. "Yes. You're seeing Miriam Gold quite a lot now. She's a very interesting woman."

"Yes, she is."

An awkward silence followed while the three of us stared mutely at each other.

"Well," I said finally, "I was thinking of taking Elena out to dinner."

Elena glanced quickly at Jack. It was obvious that she had entirely forgotten about our previous arrangement. "Well, actually," she said hesitantly, "Jack and I were thinking of eating in."

"At my apartment," Jack said. He smiled at Elena. "But we don't have to do that. Especially since William's come all this way." He turned to me. "Why don't we all go to this little hole-in-the-wall place I know over on Eighty-ninth?"

I felt a bit awkward at the suggestion. One did not have to be very perceptive to see that a great deal had already transpired between Elena and Jack, that their tour of the city had opened up new wonders, at least for my sister, and that one of them was Jack himself.

"Well, I wouldn't want to interfere," I said halfheartedly.

"With what, William?" Jack asked.

"With whatever you two had already planned."

"Nonsense," Jack said cheerfully. "It'd give me an opportunity to learn more about you. Please, come along with us."

I glanced at Elena, trying to read what she might want, ready to go along with it. She was standing silently beside Jack, and her face gave not the slightest hint of what she wanted me to do. Even in such small matters, she was always careful to let one's choice be truly one's own. Perhaps she later abandoned this attitude, especially after what happened to Elizabeth. In her last novel there is a scene in which Manfred Owen's daughter finds a small deer trapped in the underbrush. When Owen moves to free it, his daughter tries to stop him, portentously declaring that "all things have a fate, and for some deer, it is the bramble." But Owen pulls it free, blurting angrily at his daughter, "You wouldn't accept such a 'fate' for yourself. Why should you accept it for another?"

But that small scene was written years after the one currently transpiring in the busy lobby of Three Arts, and at that time, when Elena was only twenty-four, she was a good deal more quietly rigid than she later became. When I think of her that afternoon, carefully withholding any gesture of guidance, I see the small child that New England and our strained and secretive household had finally bred. Her silence seems to me at one with the stony reserve of those New England oddities about whom she read in her youth, but from whose fatalism she ultimately escaped, so that in her last book Manfred Owen could, at last, set free a deer.

"Oh, come on, William," Jack said. "You don't want to go all the way back down to the Village."

"Well," I said, like a reluctant old gentleman who doesn't wish to be a bother, "if you're sure you don't mind."

The restaurant was small and dingy, with pocked tables and squeaky, unstable wooden chairs. But the food was cheap, and in those days that was everything.

"This place used to be quite a hangout," Jack said after we had taken our seats. "I remember when I got back from Seattle in twenty-nine, it was jumping like a bedbug."

The waiter stepped up immediately and we all ordered sandwiches and beer. Then Jack began to talk in his animated fashion, fingers always plucking at the air, head bobbing and weaving like a fighter under attack.

"I remember I was here one night in March of twenty-nine," he said. "I'd just gotten back from the West Coast. I was working on one of those 'ten-years-after' stories. This one was about going back to Seattle ten years after the general strike of 1919. The editor figured I was the best man to cover it since I'd actually been in Seattle in 1919." He laughed. "I was just a teenager at the time the strike began, and I remember the things Mayor Johnson said about the strikers. My God, he painted them as devils. I thought it was the end of the world."

"You weren't at the barricades in those days?" I asked.

Jack shook his head. "I wasn't anywhere at all. Just a kid on the corner with nothing in his head." He looked at Elena. "I needed experience."

"Yes, I suppose we all need experience," I said lamely.

Jack's eyes darted toward me. "I've been talking to Elena about a book," he said.

"Your book?" I asked.

Jack chuckled and shook his head as his gaze drifted back to Elena. "No. Elena's new book."

"I didn't know she had one."

"I don't," Elena said. "But Jack was telling me that he thought it was about time for someone to attempt an important novel about the Depression."

"Then why doesn't Jack write it?"

"Because I don't have the talent," Jack said bluntly. He looked at Elena. "But you do. That's clear from *New England Maid*." He turned back to me. "If Elena can combine the intensity of *New England Maid* with the scope of, say, Dos Passos's *Nineteen-Nineteen*, then I think she might end up writing *the* great novel about America at this time in its history."

"I told Jack that I've only written one piece of fiction in my life, that short story, 'Manhattan,' " Elena said.

"What she's done before doesn't matter," Jack said. "The point is to release the talent that's already in you. Once you do that, everything falls into place."

It was certainly the oddest theory of artistic creativity I had ever heard, but I let it pass. Try as I might that night, I really could not bring myself to dislike Jack, and I think that it was true, what Mary used to say, that even his enemies adored him. One could almost picture a blindfolded J. P. Morgan standing against a brick wall, a victim of Jack's triumphant revolution, saying, because he simply couldn't help himself, "Ah hell, Jack, no hard feelings. Go ahead and tell the boys to shoot."

"Of course," Jack added, almost as an aside, "you need more experience. Experience is the key to everything." He looked at me. "Don't you think so, William?"

"It depends on the experience," I said cautiously.

"What you need is a great deal of simple, human experience," Jack said. He looked pointedly at Elena. "Why live like a stone?"

Elena was watching Jack as intently as she had ever watched anyone in her life. There was, I noticed then, a palpable yearning in her eyes, along with something that was growing soft and pliant within her. Even the sort of feeble, bantering resistance she sometimes offered to Dr. Stein had been swept away.

"One thing experience can't teach you, though," he said as he continued to gaze at her, "it can't teach you how to be free. That's an act of will."

I cleared my throat loudly, hoping by this crude gesture to break his spell. "Well, that sounds a bit romantic, don't you think, Jack?"

Jack turned slowly toward me. "The world acts like a fist on us, William. Haven't you ever noticed that?"

"Maybe some people just feel the grip more intensely than others."

Jack looked at me doubtfully. "Are you saying you don't feel it?"

Before I could begin my answer, I heard Elena's voice, very soft, but determined. "I do," she said, "I feel it."

Jack smiled at her. "I know you do. Maybe we feel the same things. Like that line from Verlaine: 'You burn, and I catch fire.' " He added nothing else. He did not have to, and he knew it.

The waiter arrived with our long-delayed orders, and we sat munching our sandwiches and sipping our beer while a light rain began to fall outside. The conversation was light as well, and almost immediately after we'd finished eating I excused myself.

"So early?" Jack asked. "I thought we might go for a walk, all of us."

I nodded toward the window. "It's a little damp for that."

Jack waved his hand. "Oh, don't be silly, William. A brisk walk in the rain is good for you."

I glanced at Elena. Her face had changed a bit. It was telling me to leave.

"No," I said, "I think I'll head on back down to the Village. I have some last-minute work to do on my Cowper book."

Jack nodded. "I understand." He stood up and shook my hand. He was a very perceptive man, and each of us knew what the other was thinking, and that the subject of our thoughts — though from very different perspectives — was Elena.

I released Jack's hand and turned to my sister. "Good night, Elena."

At the door, I glanced back at them. Jack had moved his seat closer to my sister, and his hand was very gently covering one of hers. I turned and walked out into the street. The rain had stopped, but the glare of light on the wet pavement gave it an oddly surreal appearance. I crossed the street, waited for the trolley, and climbed onto it quickly when it finally came. Elena and Jack were just coming out of the restaurant as it pulled away. They did not turn south toward Three Arts but walked toward the subway to the Village, where Jack lived in that little disheveled room with the yellow cat snoozing in the open traveling case. I watched them until they became so small that I had to squint in order to see them. Then at last they disappeared.

There are places where I cannot take you, doors that have been closed to me and so now must be closed to you. I know that Elena spent the night with Jack because she told me so, but then she fell silent at precisely that place where I must now fall silent, too.

About a month after my dinner with Elena and Jack, Mary Longford — out of work for almost two months and threatened with a return to her Indiana farm, where, she said, the last thing her family needed was an educated mouth to feed — married Philip Newman, a general practitioner. The ceremony took place at Riverside Church, that monument to Rockefeller's piety, as Jack called it, which had been completed only a few years before.

After the wedding, a reception was held at the Newman home, a spacious estate in the Riverdale section of the Bronx. From the back deck one could see the Hudson River hideaway that had once belonged to Mark Hanna, McKinley's cunning campaign manager, about whom Jack had more than a few unkind words to say that afternoon.

But if Jack could hardly conceal his contempt for the wealthy old New York family into which Mary had just married, Philip Newman, the groom, was the soul of charm. He was a chubby man, with a jowled face and light blue eyes. Even in his youth he had looked just a bit over the hill: in the sepia baby pictures his mother insisted upon showing to us all that afternoon, he looked rather like a bald middle-aged man dressed up to be a baby. Mary claimed that he had contracted gout while still in prep school, and that while on the Grand Tour, in his twenties, a Parisian whore had rejected him on the grounds that he was already too far gone to take the strain. He had, as Mary said, been born in money, swaddled in money, bathed and powdered in money, so that he assumed money came to him as naturally as air to other men. His medical practice had thrived almost immediately. His office was filled with so many New York luminaries that the limousines parked outside his building often obstructed the flow of traffic down Fifth Avenue. According to Mary, he read almost nothing, spoke only in the most vacuous generalities, and disliked argument of any kind. He took a mistress three years after his wedding day, set his paramour up in one of New York's most fashionable hotels, slipped off with her — for his health — to Martinique, and in general behaved in so doggedly flippant a manner that in 1938 Mary was able to get what she called "the best divorce settlement ever handed down by a nonecclesiastical court."

I brought Miriam to the reception and Elena came with Jack. Harry arrived late with his new bride. He had gained some weight, which he contrived to hide beneath the ample folds of a black double-breasted suit. Sam came a bit later with the first of those thin, sharp-nosed, and waspish blondes to whom he seemed ever after addicted, and Tom, cool and scornful, came alone.

We all sat together at one of the large tables that had been brought into the cavernous dining room of the Newman house. There was a nine-piece band at the far end of the hall, and throughout the afternoon the strains of the latest melodies — "Paper Moon" and "Stormy Weather" — wafted lazily over us while we ate lobster Newburg and drank white wine.

"Well," Harry said, "I've been out of the country for a few months. How's *New England Maid* doing?" He addressed this question to Sam rather than Elena.

Sam leaned back in his seat. "Great, Harry. For a book like that, it's a real hit."

Harry nodded. "Of course, you've got some new competition. Reynal and Hitchcock. They've got a hit, too. Hitler's book, *Mein Kampf.*"

Sam's eyes narrowed. "They can publish that schmuck if they want to, Harry. I'll stick with good red-blooded American authors."

"Pink-blooded, you mean," Harry said coldly.

Jack looked up from his plate and started to speak, but Elena stopped him with a glance. Then she turned to Harry. "Why are you behaving this way, Harry?"

Harry looked at her innocently. "What way?"

"Like an ass," Mary blurted out.

Harry stiffened. "What's the matter? We used to joke about everything."

There was a strained silence, then Elena lifted her glass. "Come on," she said quietly, "let's just toast old times."

Rather reluctantly, each of us raised a glass toward the center of the table. The band drifted into "Lazybones," and a few couples got up to dance, but all of that seemed very far away. For it was clear that something had finally gone sour between us, that the old energy had turned into a poisonous tension that gathered around us like a noxious cloud. It was a scene Elena would always remember, rendering it finally in the voice of Raymond Finch in the first chapter of *Calliope:* "Teddy was there, and Ralph, who helped to win the regatta the year we all graduated, and Hugo, who went out west to write and came back with a drinking problem, and Todd, with his new wife and job and car, and together we were the rowing team again — at least, we had been once before; but now, looking at each other, we could not recall the surge of the boat when we all pulled back upon our oars, for we had scattered to little boats now, each still powered by some of our old undergraduate dreams, but growing strained, because for some of us those dreams were fading, and this separated us further from the others, the ones who'd had the dreams, too, only theirs were coming true."

We touched our glasses. Another short silence followed while we shifted uncomfortably in our seats, each trying, I suppose, to find some common ground upon which we could all stand casually once again.

Tom cleared his throat. "So, Sam, you say Elena's book is doing fine?"

"That's what I said," Sam said dully.

"I guess the public wants that kind of thing, then."

Sam looked at him. "What do you mean?"

"You know, small-town stories."

Jack's eyes flashed. "Is that what you think *New England Maid* is?"

Tom glanced around uneasily. "Well, sort of. Don't you?"

Mary laughed. "For God's sake, Tom, have you read it?"

"Sure I have," Tom said. He stared about plaintively from one face to the next.

"I'm working on something a lot different now," Elena said. "It's about the times, the Depression."

"I'm writing a lot of new poetry about that," Tom blurted out, but when no one asked him to comment further, he sank back into his chair and nervously folded his arms over his chest.

"Go on, Elena," Harry said.

"I don't have much more to say," Elena said. "Jack has been very helpful in trying to bring some structure to the idea."

"Yes, of course," Harry said. "But what is the idea?"

"To do a great novel about the Depression," Jack said, "a panoramic novel about the entire country as it is right now."

Sam smiled happily. It was the kind of idea he loved, a huge canvas of teeming characters and incidents. All his life Sam was a dupe of great display. "Sort of the *War and Peace* of the American Depression," he said eagerly.

Elena flinched at the comparison, but, to my amazement, Jack suggested that it might be apt.

"No novel has really caught the complexity of this whole period," he said. "We've got a lot of novels about poverty and strikes and that sort of thing, but no great book about the whole life of the nation."

Sam nodded energetically. "That's right. No one has really caught the whole thing." He smiled at Elena. "But you will. I know it. You've got the eye for it, and the pen."

Elena smiled faintly in response, then let her hands drop softly into her lap, fully accepting the way Sam and Jack discussed her work, with what appeared to me then as an alarming passivity.

"A doorstop is what the literary world needs right now," Sam said determinedly. "A big son-of-a-bitch, maybe a thousand pages long, with a thick binding — a *volume*, by God. He glanced at the blonde who sat beside him, staring up at him with vapid but adoring eyes. "You can't get this New York crowd's attention with some limping little book. They're like the farmer's mule: you've got to get their attention by whacking a hefty tome right between their eyes. Otherwise, the critics just glance at it, sniff the binding, sneeze, and throw it in the garbage."

Tom shook his head despairingly, a gesture Sam caught. "What's the matter, Tom?" he asked.

"You can't write a thousand pages of poetry," Tom answered. "You can't get the critics' attention that way."

"Who said anything about poetry?"

"Well, I've got this poem that deals with the way things are in California — the Pacific swell forever sweeping the people in and out, you know? Rolling them in the foam, making them newly born each day. That's what I mean."

Sam and Jack exchanged glances, then both of them stared at Tom.

"Have you ever been to California?" Jack asked.

Tom shook his head. "No."

For a moment, Jack looked as though he were about to say something. I suppose that some image of California's distress must have passed through his mind. All his life Jack had the great gift, and perhaps the curse, of being able to call up scenes of the most devastating misfortune as if they were personal memories. In *Calliope*, Elena has Finch describe Markham, a journalist of his acquaintance, in words that could refer only to Jack: "In his mind he staged a continual horror show. Mention Johnstown, and he would describe the flood; Chicago, and he would bring the fire to life. And in these and a thousand other ways, he reviewed the old despair of man, the failure and venality and misfortune that was his lot. He knew the deeds of the Duke of Padua, could recite the daily course of the Children's Crusade, and over a light dinner he might recount the slaughter at Drogheda or the rape of the Highlands that followed the disaster at Culloden. None of this was ever done for effect, it was simply the globe that revolved in his mind's eye. Before this horror, everything appeared as little more than cruel irony: all laughter was heard beneath a symphony of screams, all warmth felt below the chill of frozen bodies, all happiness seen against a panoply of ancient misery and misery to come." This was surely a portrait of Jack *in extremis*. It might have been more aptly said that while eating lobster Newburg, Jack could smell the beans cooking in some hobo jungle he had flopped down in years before.

I leaned forward to get the attention of my sister. "Is that what you're planning, Elena, a big book?"

"Perhaps," she said quietly.

"You object to that, William?" Jack asked.

I shook my head. "No, not that in itself."

"What then?"

"I'm just curious as to what Elena actually has in mind."

All eyes turned toward her, and even Philip stopped munching at his dessert long enough to look up at my sister. Her hands were still folded in her lap, her food still untouched on the white china plate. She was only twenty-four years old, but she no longer looked entirely young. The first shadows were, however lightly, already upon her face, the first creases already finding their way into the corners of her eyes. It was a pentimento effect, the older Elena glimpsed almost as a vision beneath the younger one.

"I don't know how to experience the times," she said, glancing first at Miriam, then at Jack. "I have to find out how to experience them before I can have any idea about how to write about them."

Jack's brows drew together. "Experience the times? Well, Elena, the times are what they are. You only have to walk out into the streets to experience them." He looked at Sam, who nodded approvingly.

Elena sat back and lowered her arms to the table. Jack watched her, almost warily, as if he had just discovered some part of her that had been concealed before, some artistic overelaboration, a tendency toward endless tenuity in the manner of Henry James.

He laughed. "The times are kicking you in the face, Elena."

Elena regarded him steadily. "Maybe they are, but I don't know how to think about them."

Jack looked quizzical. "You don't? Well, you just sink into them. You drop down on your hands and knees and press your cheek against the pavement and watch the shoeless feet march by." There was already a kind of anger in his voice, a frustrated edge. For him, personal experience was absolutely everything, and at the drop of a hat he would give you the details of his own.

Which, at that moment, was exactly what he did, ticking off all the possibilities, artistic and otherwise, that the beleaguered times offered to the artist, the revolutionary, the man of conscience, or anyone else ready to seize the times by the throat, as, he said, they must be seized. In this mood, Jack was wondrous to behold, a real Roman candle of a man, as Miriam once called him.

For Jack was a fountain of passionate needs and sympathies, as he would later prove in Spain and during the fifties. He believed, as Elena once said in an interview, that there could be no distinction between "what the mind thought and the hand attempted." But, as she added, he also held unswervingly to the notion that whatever he believed was absolutely true. It was this fanatical aspect of his character that Elena drew upon in her portrait of Markham in *Calliope*, to whom Finch intends to turn over his father's financial papers, a record of corruption for which the zealous reporter so single-mindedly yearns: "Markham was standing under a streetlight on Montague Street, with his tweed overcoat and rumpled hat, looking like the sword of justice he imagined himself to be, gnawing at his cigarette as if it were the bent, rusty spoon he'd been fed with as a child. Looking at him under that waterfall of foggy light, that holy cloud of mist and vapor, I thought of Godric, crouched and bleeding by the river Wear, his skin torn open by self-flagellation. I could feel Markham's rage. It was his whip and pincer. The smoke from his cigarette smelled of a thousand immolations. I felt the envelope of papers like a greased torch beneath my arm and saw my father strapped to the post with faggots piled beneath his feet, and then Markham, hooded in his monkish zeal, waiting for me to pass him the torch. I turned before he saw me and sank back into the darkness, saving, as I supposed, my father from the flame and Markham from the fatal presumption of his holiness."

When Jack finished what amounted to a speech, the rest of us glanced at each other in silent surprise that such a peroration could be carried off amid the trivialities of a wedding reception. Jack instantly sensed the disparity and looked as if he were afraid that he had made a fool of himself.

"As you can see," he said, laughing self-consciously, "Elena's book is a passionate subject for me."

"Well, I'll say this much," Harry said, "I think that you, Jack, would be a perfect editor for Parnassus Press." He smiled. "And I don't mean that statement to be a red flag."

For a moment the atmosphere lightened. Philip talked about the rigors of medical school, Harry, some of his business dealings, Sam, his upcoming titles, and Tom, when anyone would give him the least opening, his poetry.

By late afternoon, all of us had grown tired, from both too much eating and, I think, too much time together. The old affection of our circle had dwindled, and we all knew that this was the last time we were likely to be together.

As we lingered on the front porch of the Newman house, I suggested that I take a picture.

"Picture?" Harry said, "I didn't know you were interested in taking pictures, William."

"It's a new interest of mine," I told him. "Stay right there, everybody. I'll be right back."

I trotted to the car Miriam had borrowed from Teddy McNaughton and retrieved my camera. Then I carefully posed my oldest and dearest acquaintances as I wished most to remember them, huddled closely together, as if against the cold.

W/hen did she tell you?" Martha asked.

It was only the second time Martha had interviewed me, and we were still awkward with one another, Martha cautious in her questions, while I remained cautious in my answers.

"About a month after your mother's wedding," I said. "We'd spent the evening with my father. He'd taken us to dinner, as he always did when he came to New York. But he no longer wanted to stay overnight in the city, so Elena and I had accompanied him to Port Authority, where he got a bus to Bridgeport."

"And that's where she told you, at Port Authority?"

"Yes," I said. "I was about to leave. But Elena took my arm and pushed me toward the front of the terminal."

We had stood near the western curve of the building, where a display urged New Yorkers to tour Wisconsin. There was a large board cut in the shape of the state, and Elena's eyes lingered on it while she continued to hold my arm. I knew she was stalling for time.

"What is it?" I asked.

She looked at me. "I've decided to leave New York for a while," she said.

"And go where?"

"Everywhere."

"You mean, all over the world?"

"No, just America."

"I see," I said.

"I'm going with Jack," she added quickly.

"With Jack?"

"Yes," Elena said. "He believes it would help me write my new novel. The title is *The Forty-eight Stars*, and Jack thinks I should see a few of those places the stars represent, the stars in the flag."

"I know what stars you're talking about, Elena."

"I've already told Father. While you were in the bathroom, during dinner."

"And of course he gave his approval."

There was a hard edge in her voice. "I wasn't asking for his approval, William, and I'm not asking for yours."

"You want an opinion?"

She drew in her breath slowly, then let it out. "I expected you to have one."

"Well, I certainly do," I said firmly.

"What is it, then?"

"That you're making a mistake."

"I expected you to feel that way," my sister said.

"Elena, listen to me, I like Jack. He's an intelligent man. But —"

"But not my type?"

"I'm not that stupid, Elena. I have no idea what your 'type' is."

"Then what's your objection?"

"I think you should find your own book. You don't need Jack to help you."

Elena said nothing. I remember thinking that she had been given the world and didn't know it, that she was gifted and financially independent — at least for a while — and that she was now throwing it all away to trail after Jack MacNeill, like the dust behind his battered old sedan.

"Well," I said after a moment, "what is it that you two plan to do on this little tour of the forty-eight stars?"

"Work. Jack has several assignments. I'll research my book and probably write a few articles."

"Articles? About what?"

"The state of the country."

I shook my head, exasperated. "Oh, for God's sake, Elena, every hack in the country is out doing that."

A bus lumbered into the driveway near us and stalled, the motor rattling feebly while the driver tried to get it going again.

"What does Sam think about this," I asked. "Does he want his prize scribbler out in the hinterlands when she could be promoting herself and Parnassus all over New York?"

"Sam thinks the trip's a fine idea."

"To give you the sweep and panorama for your *War and Peace* of the Depression?" I asked sarcastically.

"New York is not America, William," Elena said.

"You don't have to tell me that. I'm from Connecticut."

Elena smiled and looked out toward the street.

"It's a pattern with you, Elena," I told her. "First Dr. Stein, now Jack."

Elena turned to me, her face rigid with anger. "What are you talking about?"

"You . . . and men."

"Dr. Stein was my teacher," Elena said stiffly. "Jack is something else."

"I know quite well what Jack is, and I know that you may be following certain . . . what would you call them — urges; following them instead of your brain."

Elena was so angry now she was almost trembling, but I didn't care. I thought I was fighting for her life.

"When you get right down to it, William," Elena said in a measured voice, "what I do is none of your business."

"No? Well, there's the little matter of your being my sister, Elena," I said hotly.

Elena's eyes flashed left and right, as if looking for some door through which she could escape. "I am sick and tired of being treated as if I'm still a little girl from Connecticut with a big pink ribbon in my hair." She glared fiercely. "My life belongs to me!"

I held firm. "Really? Are you sure? I was thinking that perhaps it belonged to Jack."

Elena stepped back slightly, amazed, I think, by my ferocity, as if the one thing she had not anticipated in my response was its passion.

"I once read a book called *New England Maid*," I said. "It was written by an artist. I wish the author well. I really do. But I have my fears."

And with that, I walked away.

I refused to go to the little farewell party the staff of *New Masses* threw for Jack and Elena when they left on their American tour. Nor did I help them pack the car the morning they left. But Miriam did, and she told me that Elena took her hand and squeezed it very hard as she got into the car, and smiled sadly and said, "Tell William that I love him." As the car pulled away, Jack threw his gray rumpled hat out the window into the air.

She was gone a year and a half, relentlessly touring the low spots of the era, until, from the portrait of wretchedness her letters detailed, it sometimes appeared that she had fallen in love with the nation's misery. Week after week she wrote of almost nothing else, and eventually I came to dread her letters as one fears a phone call in the dead of night.

But Elena's letters were not the only bad tidings of that time. All Europe seemed to be sinking toward a frightening abyss. The belabored businessmen and their snarling wives who were the travel agency's best customers increasingly decided to stay in the United States. As a consequence, I lost my job.

For a while, I had no idea what to do. The prospect of hunger and homelessness became far more real than the sort described in Elena's letters. I had no savings, having squandered my weekly pay on books or on eating out when I should have been cooking at home. Of course, I knew I could always go somewhere, to someone, if I really hit bottom. Harry, at the very least, could find me some kind of job. Because of that, the bottom for me was far above the bottom for a great many other people.

Still, without a job I felt helpless. I wandered the streets, joining that gray army which stood staring at the chalkboards on Sixth Avenue, hoping for something to come my way — a job, any job. I applied for everything from short-order cook to president of a small women's college in the South. But the weeks passed, and my landlord began to eye me warily each time we met in the lobby. I grew more and more depressed. Even the prospect of publishing my Cowper book, which Sam had scheduled for September, could not lift the pall that had come over me. No one knew better than I did that something had to give.

Finally something did: a suggestion from Sam that I apply to the newly created Federal Writers Project in New York. "You can say you're a writer, William," Sam urged me. "Hell, your book's been bought."

So I trudged down to the enormous armory at Lexington and Twenty-sixth, where a horde of "writers" gathered each day, chewing their nails and yapping irritably at each other, all hoping to snatch a federal job from the stale, smoky air.

To my astonishment, I was hired as an editor, at a salary of a little over twenty-three dollars a week. And so, on a cold, rainy Monday morning I appeared at the offices of the New York Project. They were located at the Port Authority on Eighth Avenue and were accessible only by freight elevator, which had been designed to lift ten-ton trucks rather than this motley, griping, and insistently political assembly of writers, or people who, on the flimsiest evidence, claimed to be writers.

Once on our floor in the Port Authority building, I discovered that layers of disorganization had been built into both the project and the personnel. The hierarchy of administration was always shifting, the writers almost always moody, sometimes bitter, and often divided in their loyalties, some primarily committed to the project, some to their particular political persuasion. Yet despite the factionalism, the strikes and sit-ins and slowdowns, the drunkenness and sloth and endless political wrangling, especially between the Trotskyites and the Stalinists — despite all of this, a great deal was accomplished during my short tenure there, and I came away after six months with a curiously tender feeling of camaraderie with that intransigent and interminably bickering lot of scribblers who finally turned out a decidedly odd list of publications, everything from the wonderful *New York Guide* to *Who's Who at the Zoo*. Years later, when Elena was working on the section of *Quality* that deals with the radical literary atmosphere of the thirties, she asked me what I had thought of the New York Project. I told her that I had come to think of it as being much like a zebra Marianne Moore had described in one of her poems, "supreme in its abnormality."

Three months after I'd starting working at the Project, my Cowper book was published. I had delivered the manuscript to Sam several months before, under the title *The Poetry of William Cowper: A New Study*. Sam, sitting at his desk, looked up from the manuscript and asked me if I expected anyone to buy a book with a title as dull as that. I stared at him helplessly. He thought a moment, then scratched out my title and penciled in his own: *Method in Madness: A Study of the Bizarre in William Cowper.* And with that lurid title, the book was published in November of 1935, "to share the highbrow Christmas trade," Sam said to me with a wink.

The Cowper book — I would always call it simply that — limped along for a few months, selling primarily, as Sam pointed out, "in the sort of shop that sits between an opera house and a museum specializing in medieval artifacts." Then it disappeared entirely, inhabiting now only the most remote corners of university libraries and brought out only by desperate graduate students in search of an aged thesis for their bright new scholarship to annihilate.

When the book appeared, Sam, indicating the difficulty of the times, said that Parnassus could not afford either a publishing party or a single penny of advertising. Thus it fell to some of my colleagues at the Project to throw me a small party. Miriam provided her cramped apartment, and Harry provided the booze. As a celebration, it was certainly subdued. Sam couldn't make it, nor could Tom, who was busy on a poem he described quickly over the telephone as being a cross between Milton and Whitman. Hearing this, Miriam simply shook her head and walked away, while Harry poured himself another drink.

The party droned on for several hours, though the mirth drained away quickly. There was hardly cause for any to begin with. I was broke; the book was a dud. It was being published as a personal favor, perhaps to me, perhaps to my sister. I never learned Sam's thinking on that matter, but I did discover that Parnassus could not possibly have published my book had not *New England Maid* been such a towering success. This bit of information, which Sam confided rather offhandedly a few days before my book was published, further darkened for me what would have been under any circumstances a drab occasion.

Finally, toward midnight, the last of my weary guests left Miriam's apartment and it was just the two of us, picking up the disordered cups and saucers, snatching floating cigarette butts from glasses before pouring the now-tepid whiskey down the drain.

"I suppose I should have tried to be a better sport about things," I said.

Miriam smiled and pulled me into her arms. We were standing

by the kitchen sink, not the most romantic of settings; yet it was somehow extraordinarily romantic at that moment, suggesting the gentle domesticity we had finally reached.

"Perhaps it's time we got married," I said.

Miriam looked at me skeptically. "Really?"

"Or maybe we should just hop in a station wagon and head to parts unknown, like Jack and Elena."

Miriam shook her head. "No, you're not that type, William."

Half joking, I said, "Bring a cushion from the living room, and I'll get on my knees."

"Not necessary."

"Well, will you, Miriam, marry me?"

She said yes, but that she did not want to do it immediately, and that is how we left it.

A month later, Teddy McNaughton's nerves got the best of him. He promptly left New York, and Sam offered his job to me. We were sitting in a bar on lower Broadway. It was snowing heavily outside, and the trolleys were pushing waves of white fluff before them like plows.

"So," Sam said, "with Teddy gone, the job's open. The money's not great, but it's better than you're getting with the government." He lowered his voice conspiratorially. "And you know as well as I do that your salary amounts to a handout. That whole Project business is just a form of being on the dole."

I rankled a bit at that. "We work quite a lot over there, Sam."

Sam shook his head. "I don't want to get into that. You have a job offer; not much money, but a lot of opportunity. You can take it or leave it." Years later, testifying before the House Un-American Activities Committee, Sam would claim that in his heart he had been so opposed to what he then called "the Lefty programs of the New Deal" that he had actually offered jobs to Project writers "in order to allow the private sector to generate honest labor for these struggling artists." One of the names he offered the committee as evidence of this activity was mine.

Sam continued to stare at me. "William, I have a hundred guys would take this job in a minute. You want it or not?"

I took it, gladly. On Monday of the following week, I took my seat behind Teddy's old desk, emptied its drawers of his random notes and curious sketches, and in doing so, I suppose, chased his lingering spirit from the room.

For the next month I worked on whatever book Sam assigned me. It was generally agreed that I would not be asked to do any editorial work on anything written, now or in the future, by Elena Franklin.

Accordingly, when the first few pages of Elena's new novel arrived at Parnassus, they went directly to Miriam's desk. She read the pages immediately, her eyes fastened on the manuscript as if it were a holy text. Then for a long time she was silent. Finally, unable to bear the suspense, I marched up to her desk.

"That manuscript you were reading," I said, "it was from Elena, right?"

Miriam looked up at me. "Yes."

"Well, is it any good?"

Miriam hesitated. "It's different."

"What does that mean, 'different'?"

"Different from her usual work."

"May I see it?"

"I thought you and Sam had agreed that you'd keep away from Elena's work."

"I don't want to edit it, Miriam, I just want to read it. Surely I have that right."

Miriam considered this for a moment, then she handed me the manuscript. It was no more than twenty pages long. "It's what she proposes as the opening chapter," she said.

I nodded. "Thanks. Do you want to know my opinion of it, once I've read it?"

"Not really, William," she said.

I took the manuscript back to my desk and began reading the introductory chapter of *The Forty-eight Stars*.

I was, to say the least, astonished by what I found. Structurally, it was pure chaos, a maelstrom of randomly selected images: disgorged eyes falling down blackened mine shafts; fingers digging beneath prison walls; trees tumbling through space with nooses swinging from their limbs. It was as if Elena had taken the most hideous scenes from her letters, cut them out, and thrown them into the air. The writing seemed to have been blown out of a blast furnace, wild and overheated.

After about five pages, however, this lurid whirlwind began to slow. A parade of caskets passes by, each draped with a flag — red and blue stripes with a single white star — the slow-motion funeral march to the grave of America. Somewhere in the distance a bugle is heard, and suddenly the caskets pop open and a series of American types haul themselves out of their coffins. There is the soldier, the sturdy yeoman, the teacher, the businessman, the politician, the liberal re-former, the cowboy . . . the list is long. It is also exact: there are forty-eight types. These ghostly personages proceed to engage in a good old American hoe-down, dancing and prancing and grouping themselves in various combinations probably meant to convey natural alliances, the farmer with the urban worker, for example, the politician with the rich industrialist. As time passes, the dance becomes more frantic, the spinning and whirling more desperate, until we are once again in the maelstrom with which the book began. And it is there, spinning madly, that Elena leaves us on page twenty: America as a wildly whirling top.

When I had finished reading it, I took the manuscript back to Miriam and dropped it softly on her desk. I lingered, waiting for her to ask me what I thought. She never did.

For the next few weeks, scattered sections of *The Forty-eight Stars* drifted into the office. Miriam always read them first, while I waited in the adjoining office, staring intently at her, trying, always in vain, to determine what she thought about this book, which seemed to me, as I read one section after another, increasingly strident and disordered.

Finally, after what appeared to be approximately half the novel had come to us, I asked Miriam bluntly what she intended to do about it. She told me that she intended to do nothing at all until Elena returned home.

Elena came back to New York in February of 1936. I was walking along the sidewalk toward my apartment when they pulled up in that same old battered Model A, Elena on the passenger side, Jack, smiling brightly, at the wheel. She bounded out of the car the instant Jack brought it up to the curb, and I swept her into my arms, relishing the feeling of having my sister back.

"I missed you very much."

"Oh, William," Elena said excitedly, "it was a wonderful trip. I've never learned so much in my life."

"Good," I said, carefully avoiding any mention of her book. "I'm glad it was a good experience for you."

Jack sauntered up and shook my hand. "Well, Bill, why don't you ask us up for a drink? We're what they call road tired."

"Of course. Please, come on up."

In my apartment, I made coffee for the three of us, spiking Jack's with a touch of whiskey.

"I'm sorry I wasn't here for the party, William," Elena said.

"What party?"

"For your book."

"Oh, that was nothing. Just a little get-together at Miriam's. Even Sam didn't make it. Just mostly some of the people from the Project."

"How is the Project?" Jack asked.

"Interesting," I said. "But I prefer working at Parnassus."

"I guess you know I've been sending in parts of my new novel," Elena said.

"Yes, Miriam told me."

Elena smiled brightly. "Have you read it?"

I shook my head. "No. Miriam likes to keep things like that to herself."

"Do you have any idea what she thinks about it?"

"No, I don't, Elena," I said, which in a way, at least, was true.

Jack slapped his leg. "Wait until you read it, Bill. It's amazingly imaginative. Not that old Socialist realism stuff at all. It's like a painting by Hieronymous Bosch, a word painting, you might say." He took a quick sip from his cup. "Oh, and by the way, congratulations."

"For what?"

"Engagement to Miriam," Jack said. "You're a lucky man."

"I think so," I said. I turned to Elena. "So, now you're back for a while?"

"Yes," Elena said. "More or less indefinitely."

"Not me, though," Jack said. "I've got a piece to write for *New Masses*, then I'm going down South. Got a hell of a lot going on down there."

I looked at Elena. "You're not going with him?"

Jack shook his head. "No, she needs to finish the book. That's the most important thing. And you can't write the Great American Novel from the back of a Model A."

"No," I said quietly, "I suppose not."

"I guess you've been following the events in Spain?" Jack asked.

"I read the papers," I said, "that's about all. There's a lot of talk about it around the city."

"Really?" Jack seemed surprised. "Who's talking, the liberals?"

"Communists, mostly," I told him. "A lot of my old colleagues at the Project."

Jack nodded. Then, without being asked, he launched into a lengthy discussion of the issues involved, predicting the civil war that would break out only a few months later. When he had finished, the conversation turned to subjects closer to home. Elena mentioned that she had managed to keep in touch with Elizabeth while on the road and that all seemed well with her in France. She had also gotten several letters from our father, mostly having to do with his itinerary.

All of this clearly bored Jack to death. He fiddled impatiently with the little doily on his chair or allowed his hands to flop about randomly, never suspecting that this might prove a distraction to anyone but himself.

Finally the conversation wound its way back to Parnassus Press and the fate of my Cowper book. Elena was sorry to hear about the poor sales but argued that the book was not yet dead.

"Oh, yes it is," I said. "As a doornail."

"I think the trouble may be Cowper himself," Jack said, unsuccessfully concealing a yawn. "He's not modern enough to attract attention."

"He attracted William's," Elena said, defending me.

Jack laughed. "Well, you must admit that William is a special case."

I smiled. "Jack's right. Cowper is slow going, even for the most plodding scholar. I've been thinking about another book though, about Coleridge."

"That's better," Jack said. He stood up, stretched, walked to the window, and stared out idly.

"I've been thinking about a full-scale biography," I told Elena.

"Yes, William, that might be —"

"Used to be a soup kitchen down on the corner," Jack said, still gazing out the window. He turned to me. "Did that dry up?"

"It moved over to Twenty-third Street," I told him. "Every Thursday."

Jack nodded dully, then turned back toward the window.

"Anyway," I said to Elena, "the Coleridge book would have more natural interest if only because Coleridge is so much more famous than our dear friend Mr. Cowper."

Jack abruptly left the window and took a seat across from me. "Coleridge sounds fine to me, Bill." He glanced back at the window, drowsily watching as the curtains drifted back together, leaving only a slant of light on the living room floor. "I'm working on a migrant-labor piece." Jack smiled at me knowingly. "I guess that sounds terribly topical to you."

"The world is wide, Jack," I said. "There's room in it for both my Coleridge and your migrants."

"Certainly is, Bill." Jack looked at Elena. "And by God, there's sure going to be room for Elena's book."

"I'm sure there will be," I said. But I concealed my steadily growing fear that my sister would prove to be only a flash in the literary pan, the sort about whom she herself later wrote in a passage on Delmore Schwartz in *Quality*, mourning "that early incandescence which precedes nothing but the slow and steady dying of the light."

Jack left for the South only a few weeks after he and Elena returned to New York. *New Masses* was interested in knowing the latest on the class struggle in rural America and dispatched Jack to the most intransigently reactionary region of the country. Even Jack failed to romanticize it in the reports he later wrote, essays as austere as James Agee's *Let Us Now Praise Famous Men* would later prove grandiloquent. But in Jack, as Elena once said, Twain was always at war with Howells. It was a contradiction that even found its way into his dress, and I remember thinking, as Elena and I said good-by to him at the bus station the afternoon he left for North Carolina, that Jack's floppy hat was all gallant vagabond, while the leather briefcase he carried and the carefully arranged notes spoke of a perfectly ordered bourgeois professionalism.

"Take care of yourself, Jack," I said, offering my hand.

Jack slapped it away and embraced me instead. "You'll never change, Bill," he said. "Don't you know that I don't shake hands with friends?"

Elena smiled as she watched us. In a letter to Elizabeth, which Martha published, she wrote that "William sometimes seems to think that an embrace impinges upon his rectitude."

If this was true of me at that time, it certainly was not true of

Elena. She almost dove into Jack's arms as the bus drew up beside the ramp. They held each other for a long time, Elena clinging to him with a desperate physical urgency.

"I'll miss you, Elena," Jack said as he drew himself from her arms.

He turned to me and held out a stack of papers he had been carrying. It was loosely bundled in brown paper and ragged twine. "Sam said I should give you this. My novel, for what it's worth. You're to be my editor."

I glanced down at the bundle. "I see."

"Sort of puts you on the spot, I guess," Jack said. He placed his large hand on my shoulder. "But remember this, William, whatever you think about the book, I won't hold it against you."

"I'll do the best I can on it, Jack."

"Good," Jack said. Then he turned and pulled Elena into his arms again.

"Take care of yourself," he said. "And don't run off with any sweet-talking medicine man. I've hired a private eye to keep tabs on you, so you'd better keep straight with me."

Elena smiled weakly.

Jack bent forward and kissed her. Then he disappeared into the bus, purposefully sitting on the side away from us so that Elena could not see him.

Elena and I lingered for a time after the bus had pulled away. Elena was preoccupied with Jack's departure, no doubt meditating upon all the particular joys that had departed with him. Finally we made our way slowly down Thirty-fourth Street.

I lifted the bundle of papers. "Have you read this?"

"No," Elena said. "Jack prefers to keep his work to himself before it's finished, then he likes an editor's opinion before any other."

I shook my head. "I'm not sure I'll be a very good editor for Jack. I'm not very political."

"You're worse than that, William," Elena said, "you're a little smug about politics in general."

This assessment was not news. "Maybe I am," I said casually.

"But does it ever bother you, this business of not being really committed to anything?"

"I'm committed to a great many things, Elena," I said. "I'm committed to you and to Miriam. I'm committed to Jack, I suppose, at least as far as doing a good job on his book is concerned."

"But do you think you can be fair to a book like his?" Elena asked. "Do you think you can judge it properly?"

"Yes, I do," I said. Elena's questions were beginning to annoy me, simply because they hinted at something else, something that did not concern Jack, or even politics.

Finally it came out. Elena stopped and turned toward me. "You've read *The Forty-eight Stars*, haven't you?"

"No," I said immediately.

Elena stared at me steadily.

"Don't lie to me, William," she said. "Don't do it to protect me. And, by the way, don't do it to protect yourself."

Once again I denied knowing anything about *The Forty-eight Stars*. I even added a little laugh for effect. "What makes you think I've read it?"

"I know you've read it," Elena said. "I knew you had the moment you told me you hadn't that day I got back to the city. You said you hadn't read it, but your eyes got sort of distant, and the little finger on your left hand twitched, and you tried to turn away from me but caught yourself in time." In her short story "Jordan," Elena would write of a man "whose body kept telling me the truth even though his voice was lying."

"I don't like being lied to, William," Elena said firmly.

I cleared my throat. "All right, Elena. I have read it."

"And hated it?"

I took a deep breath. "Yes."

For a moment the two of us seemed suspended, as if in water. Then Elena simply put her arm in mine and tugged me forward. We continued slowly up the street, the heavy traffic whizzing by us, until finally, under the canopy of Macy's, we stopped.

"I'm going to take a taxi back home," Elena said. She smiled, but rather wanly. "It's Bargain Monday for the cabs, you know, one-third off."

I nodded but said nothing. Once again we simply stared at each other.

"Elena, I . . . I . . ."

Elena put her finger to my lips, silencing me, then turned and walked to the street, hailed a cab, and disappeared into it.

I did not hear from her for almost a month. I worked steadily on Jack's novel, trying to divest the story, about a strike in the Midwest, of those elements which debased it. Jack was fine on physical detail, deftly rendering the look of corn silk in the air, the playfulness of children as they built a small mud dam outside the factory gates, the chatter of women as they hoisted food into the factory, using broom handles and baskets tied with apron strings. But in describing human beings and the relations between them, Jack often foundered, romanticizing in fiction what he would never have romanticized in his straight reportage, and thus saddling his novel with what Elena later called, in connection with the proletarian fiction of the time, "the unreality of Socialist realism."

As for Elena, I assumed that she was once again moving into that seclusion she had previously insisted on while writing *New England Maid.* Thus when I found out that in fact she was whirling about the city, primarily with some of Jack's cronies from *New Masses* and the John Reed Club, I was surprised and more than a little dismayed. It was a feeling I could not suppress when she finally called me at my office one dreary Friday afternoon. I was still busy with Jack's book when the phone rang, my red pencil flying over his manuscript like an angry witch.

"William," she said, "I've decided to move from Three Arts."

"I see."

"I need a little help."

"Like you did when you left Hewett Hall?" I said, unable to keep my sense of being poorly used from my voice.

There was a moment of silence while Elena tried to figure out what she could say to soothe my wounded pride.

"I've not been avoiding you, William," she said finally. "It's just that I've been very busy."

"Really? I think it's something else. I think that if you hadn't really wanted to hear what I thought about your book, then you shouldn't have asked me."

Elena said nothing, so I continued. "Maybe we should just come to an understanding about things like that, about your work. I think that I should not read anything you write, perhaps until after it's published, perhaps never."

"That would not be a solution, William," Elena said.

"Why not?"

"Because I will always want your advice."

"I don't want to be flattered, Elena."

"Look, William, I want you always to give me your frank opinion. How I deal with that opinion is my business. I've been busy gathering more notes for my book, the one you don't care for. I listen to you William, but I don't follow you blindly."

"Of course not."

"Then let's just leave it at that. You tell me what you think is the truth. I will listen with an open mind."

"And not avoid me for a month?" I asked.

"Not avoid you at all."

It seemed almost like a contract, but it was the sort of thing upon which Elena tended to insist — clear understandings, the rules stated and agreed upon. It was, perhaps, one of her failures that she could not endure prolonged ambiguity or irresolution. When I said as much to Martha, she looked up from her notebook, her eyes wide with sudden understanding. "So that's what she did that night with Elizabeth," she said. "She laid down the law." And all that I could do in response was lower my eyes and mutter my answer. "Yes."

At Three Arts the day after Elena called me, I waited while a troop of young women helped her move her accumulated possessions down the stairs into the lobby, where, and only where, a man's assistance was allowed. Then we laboriously hauled boxes of books and papers and clothes out onto the street. Several cabs passed us by, but finally one pulled over and agreed to transport the whole works to Brooklyn Heights, where Elena had taken a new apartment.

Once we were in the cab and moving down Broadway, I asked her why she felt the need to move.

She shrugged. "Just something about the atmosphere," she said. She added nothing else, but in *Calliope* Raymond Finch adds a great deal as he delivers his assessment of a women's residence very similar to Three Arts, where he has just dropped off his date for the evening:

I knew Sherry was heading back into a dream world. I had shown her where the people slept under the bridges, but she'd had other ideas about what constituted a great date. She'd expected the works from a wealthy young plutocrat like myself, the whole works — wine and steak and dancing with the big bands. She wanted the dream, but I'd done my crazy routine and taken her to the sewer. She was pretty huffy after that, and had wasted no time in telling me to take her right back to this little fantasy world on upper Broadway. Here you bought dreams by leaning back on your bed and closing your eyes. It was as simple as that. You buffed your nails and listened to the radio, waiting for the phone to ring in the hall, the call from some producer or publisher, the one with that big break.

But the real world was where I'd taken her, down on the wharves, where men guard their shacks against the rats and throw bricks at the herds of cats howling and scratching and screwing in the alleyway, where they think of the places they left as if those places no longer existed, as if the wind had blown them away, like the harvest. And they lean back in their shacks and wait for a job or a meal or a word that will set them on a new direction, they puff on stubby cigarettes and blow the smoke toward the hole in the roof, and they wait, I suppose the whole damn country waits . . . for the phone to ring in the hallway with the big break.

By moving into an apartment of her own, Elena had finally broken from an atmosphere that had never agreed with certain aspects of her character, that New England wintriness which is so suspicious of easy enthusiasm. To Elena, too much hope always seemed as deadly as too little, and as the Depression deepened and her commitment to its exploration in *The Forty-eight Stars* continued, Three Arts must have represented the epitome of all that was callow and mindless and self-absorbed in American life.

Her new apartment was on Columbia Heights, not far from Plymouth Church, where, some seventy years before, Henry Ward Beecher had enthralled a packed throng with tales of moral uplift. The church itself was magnificently understated, and Elena often went there during the years that followed. There was something in the irony of its physical somberness — the small windows and dark-hued pews combined with the shuddering rhetoric Beecher had hurled across it — that attracted Elena's attention.

Her apartment, on the other hand, was rather spare. It had a small kitchen, a long, narrow bedroom, and a somewhat larger living room, complete with a modest marble fireplace.

"Well, it looks quite cozy," I said as I walked in.

Elena nodded, her eyes moving from one window to the next, then over to the hearth. "I should be able to work here."

Within an hour we were staggering up the stairs to the third floor with the last of Elena's boxes.

"I'd like to offer you something to drink," Elena said, "but I haven't done any shopping yet." She smiled. "The cupboard's bare, I'm afraid."

She walked to the window and glanced out. From the back of the apartment, she could see all of lower Manhattan and, beyond that, Ellis Island and the Statue of Liberty.

"Quite a nice view," I said as I stepped up beside her. "Windows at the back and front, lots of natural light."

Elena nodded, her eyes randomly scanning the gray waters of the East River and the equally gray skyline that rose above it.

"I'm having a little trouble with the book," she said.

She was approaching me almost warily, cautiously making a vague inquiry but unwilling to go further than that.

"Well," I said offhandedly, "it's a difficult thing, writing a novel. You can expect trouble, especially with something as complex as the whole nation at a particular moment." I smiled. "You are after greatness, aren't you?"

She faced me slowly. "It has a sour sound, doesn't it? To be 'after' something. It's so predatory."

I shrugged. "Only a work endures, Elena, not the reason for making it."

"You make it sound as if all I've seen, all the poverty and misery, are just grist for the mill of my ambition."

I shook my head. "You're not that callous."

"No, I'm not. But I can't feel the distress of the times the way Jack does. With him it's all an open wound."

"It's a simple thing to explain, Elena. You're not Jack."

"But I believe, honestly believe, William, that his way is superior to mine. I mean, the feeling he has for suffering, that intense feeling — I don't have it."

"And if you try to fake it, Elena, in your work, I mean, everything about it, every word, will ring false."

Elena left the window and made her way pensively to the center of the room. "We were outside Seattle once, in a shantytown, a small one, just a tiny village of shacks with a few homeless men in it. They were freezing. The wind was blowing right through those little hovels, and Jack was feeling something terrible for those men, feeling, actually feeling, how cold they were. I could see that in his eyes, I could see *their* pain in *his* eyes." She looked at me very intently. "I understood intellectually what they were going through, those men. I could understand the cold and their helplessness and their anger, all those things. But to feel the way Jack felt . . . I couldn't do that." She smiled sardonically. "You know what I noticed? I noticed how the whole landscape seemed to have been bled of color, so that everything, even the trees, looked like frozen bodies, pale or grayish blue, like cadavers."

"And that makes you feel what, Elena? As a writer, I mean. Inadequate?"

Elena said nothing. She seemed to be thinking about my question. I repeated it. "You feel inadequate as a writer?"

She shook her head. "No. As a person."

"That's ridiculous," I said. "You're just suffering from that old dichotomy — you know, thinking and feeling."

Elena nodded. "There is a difference between them, isn't there? It's not just a sophomoric notion. There is a difference."

All her life, Elena would observe the various implications of this difference. In *Inwardness* she sided with the mind, and in *To Define a Word*, the heart. In *Quality* she would choose *Billy Budd* over *Moby-Dick* because, as she wrote, "In this work alone, Melville walks with perfect balance, and for an extended time — not for the short stroll of a sonnet, but for a breathtakingly intense length of time — on that line which does not so much divide thought from feeling as define the place where they merge."

But that day, standing in her new apartment, Elena seemed adrift among questions a good deal larger than her experience, and too young to take control of the wheel. Certainly she was not then, as Martha later described her, a woman moving through "passages" but ever in control, steady at the helm, beyond the false steps and misspoken words that, one later learns, give to life a kind of baffled heroism. According to Martha, Elena moved to Brooklyn Heights with the certain knowledge that a great book was in her. Perhaps she did know that; but even if she did, she was still very far from knowing that such a book could actually be written. On the day she moved into her new apartment, I believe that Elena was very close to abandoning not only *The Forty-eight Stars* — that misbegotten work she did, in fact, abandon — but her own sense that there were depths within her, thoughts and sentiments, which were fine and authentic and deserving of expression. A writer, as Jason once told her, can lose a hundred books and be freer for it; but he cannot lose the sense that what he knows is real. Elena, I think, was on the verge of just that sort of loss.

"Your book, the one on Coleridge," she asked just before I left her. "You're still working on it?"

"Yes."

"It must be hard, since you have a full-time job."

"Yes, it's hard."

Elena simply watched me for a moment, saying nothing.

"Do you want to know why I keep at it?" I asked her.

"Yes, I do."

"Because there are things about Coleridge that are important. These things, they won't take one man out of that Seattle shantytown of yours. But they are important nonetheless, because there are people who may be warm and full and living in nice places but who are poor because they lack knowledge of these things that are in Coleridge and Marlowe and Shakespeare."

Elena nodded.

"And so I do this book on Coleridge," I continued, my voice almost quaking suddenly — so passionately did Cold Bill believe these things. "Maybe it's futile; I don't know. But I have found a value in his work that I know is real, and when I'm exploring that, I feel I am exploring something essential in life."

Elena stood quietly, facing me. Her body was framed by the large windows at the rear of the house.

"I don't know what else I can tell you about it," I said. My own words were still echoing grandly in my mind. It seemed to me that I had sounded quite touchingly Ciceronian. I smiled. "Jack would no doubt laugh at such obscure motives."

I could not tell from Elena's face whether she took me for a wise man or a fool.

"Thanks for helping me move again, William," she said finally.

I let myself out and walked down the stairs. On the street, I looked back up to Elena's apartment. The windows were curtainless, and at that moment they seemed forlorn in their nakedness. In the fading light, I could see my sister setting her papers in order, shelving her books, ordering those piles of notes from which she was drawing her extravagant novel. I envied her the courage of her purpose, and in doing that, I suppose, I envied my own — all those scattered sheets cluttering my desk at home, from which I intended to bring forth Coleridge. And it struck me suddenly that I had entered upon a new way of thinking about him. I had broken through the stately academic portrait that might have made my book no different from the one I had written about Cowper. In my sister's struggles I had

recognized something true of others like herself: a relentless preoccupation with that which cannot be defined. She and Coleridge and a
host of others great and small were involved in exploring, not the
heights of experience, nor its depths, but only that which it is reasonable for one to desire. In that recognition, my work and Elena's and
even Jack's came together in a true fraternity. This thought rather
grandly lifted my spirits, and as I walked down Columbia Heights I
actually smiled to all who passed my way.

Elena worked continually while Jack was away. At times she was
quite full of energy, and at other times exhausted. Her mood became
the steady gauge of her work, bright and exuberant when it was going
well, tired and dejected when it was not.

According to Miriam, Elena was unable to find a satisfactory way
to reshape the raw material she had collected. She tried repeatedly
to forge a tale out of the heartbreaking data she had gathered on
the road, but each time the material stubbornly resisted. She tried
an epistolary structure, then a documentary one, then one of small
vignettes told by different characters. Nothing worked.

Jack, of course, continued to encourage her. His letters, several of
which Martha published in her biography, came at the rate of two
or three a week. But although they were written with the best inten-
tions, they were very stern indeed in what they required of my sister.
They reminded her that the main purpose of her book was the portrayal
of the "Big Picture." "Anyone can write a sad little book about the
widow who's forced out into the snow by the mean old landlord,"
he wrote, "but you are one of the very few who can write a book
that deals with the whole story." They encouraged her to rely on
her notes: "Forget about the idea of a central story. The notes are
the story. Start with hunger, the hunger we saw across the country.
Just start with that and see if maybe the whole nation can be portrayed
by this metaphor of starvation."

Elena's replies to these letters, some of which Martha also published,
reveal a young woman who is trying to come to terms with another
person's vision of what her work should be. She asks for advice as
to proposed story lines and narrative techniques. She introduces characters who might serve as the voice of the novel: a reporter, a labor
organizer, a Communist party functionary, a derelict, even a "bourgeois politician." Each letter grows more desperate than the last, and

in the final one, written only two weeks before Jack's return to New York, there is an obvious exasperation with the material itself, all those thousands of gloomy notes, "which keep watching me from every corner of the room."

Jack came home just in time to make it to my wedding. It was held in the courthouse, a very simple affair, with Miriam in a plain blue dress and me in one of my two black suits. We had decided upon a completely secular ceremony, conducted by a magistrate who was paid a set fee, and who read the official words rather quickly before hurrying on to more pressing business.

We had a small reception in Miriam's apartment. Mr. Gold had insisted upon hiring a catering service, which set out an elaborate spread on Miriam's small kitchen table. There were even two waiters in bolero jackets, who found it rather difficult to maneuver in the space of Miriam's living room and spent the afternoon muscling through the crowd and bumping their large silver trays against the walls.

It was altogether a happy occasion. Sam was there with another blonde, and Harry came with Felice, his new bride. Mary strolled about, smoking a cigarette, eyeing every man as if already on the lookout for another husband. Philip did not come at all, nor Tom, with whom all of us had more or less lost contact by then.

The somber note, however, was Elena. She stood alone by a small table in front of one of Miriam's many mismatched bookshelves. She looked perplexed, which was the way she had looked almost continually during Jack's absence. I had expected this attitude to change upon his return, but it hadn't. Perhaps it had even deepened, so that her face now suggested the profound bafflement that no doubt plagued her. Watching Jack as he and Sam laughed and joked and talked politics a few feet away, she seemed almost like the Elena of years before, the little girl reading in the broken-down shack which creaked and moaned with every breeze that swept through our back yard.

I walked across the room, a glass of champagne in my hand, and stood beside her.

"You're looking rather at odds with things, Elena," I said.

She smiled slightly. "You know me, William, full of moods."

I took a sip from the glass. Across the room, my father was talking animatedly to Mr. Gold.

"The old man seems to be having a good time."

"I suppose," Elena said. "He came over to my apartment last night.

Jack was there. We all talked for a while. Jack was going on about the situation in the South, about how he expected the Negroes and the whites down there to make an alliance and overthrow the plantation owners."

I smiled. "That must have been inspiring for Father."

"Actually, he listened quite carefully," Elena said. "He asked Jack a few questions. Jack answered them. Then, after a while, Jack had to leave." She stopped and watched our father for a moment. "After Jack left, he said to me, 'Elena, I've always let you go your own way. But just one word of caution from an old toiletries salesman: Your boyfriend is a fool.'"

I shook my head. "Oh, for God's sake, Elena, you shouldn't let that bother you. He's just an ignorant old man."

Elena's face was very grim, and she spoke slowly. "Sometimes your mind just thinks something, William, thinks it independently, before you have a chance to stop it." She looked back at our father. "The moment he finished that sentence about Jack, the next second, I heard my own mind as if it were a separate voice, and it said, 'Yes, Jack *is* a fool.'"

I stepped around in front of her, blocking my father from her view, trying, by this gesture, to capture her complete attention.

"Now you listen to me," I said. "I've been married about three hours, so I know everything there is to know about romance. And I know that couples have their ups and downs. Right now, you and Jack are in a down. That's all, Elena. Nothing to go crazy about."

Elena shook her head. "No, it's more than that. It's more than a difference of opinions or attitudes or anything like that. It's a difference in the way we think, and not about any particular thing, William. It's a difference in the *process.*"

"Are you talking about your book?" I asked pointedly.

"Only in part," Elena said. "What I'm really talking about is sort of hazy to me." She glanced randomly about the room, then she looked at me. "I love Jack, but that has very little to do with the way I think about him." She shook her head, exasperated. "I know it's a strange distinction," she said.

It was, as Elena said, a strange distinction. But in its early suggestion of the mind as a kind of separate entity, a willful creature struggling to be free of the complex sentiments which deflect its power, it was extraordinarily characteristic of my sister in the last years of her life, when it was just herself and the beach and the bay, living, as she said, "with that other person, the one who thinks."

By late afternoon most of the guests had left, and Elena, Jack, and I sat down on the sofa by the window while a few other people continued to stand about, idly drinking the last of the champagne. Jack stretched himself out comfortably, his long legs almost spanning Miriam's small living room.

"Well, Bill," he said, "I think the time has come for you to tell me what you think of my novel."

"Well, I think it needs a little work," I told him, keeping as much jollity in my voice as possible.

"You want me to make it more highbrow, right?"

"Not exactly," I said. "But you know as well as I do that the audience for this book is not the working class. Middle-class leftists will read it, maybe some students, most of the past and present members of the John Reed Club."

Jack smiled. "I can go along with that, Bill, I really can. But I'm mostly a naturalist, you know. Strictly out of Stephen Crane." He glanced at Elena. "I'm not like Elena, I can't pull off something sweeping. Hell, she's writing an epic, an American classic." He swept his arm over her shoulder. She seemed to stiffen at his touch. "The way I see it," Jack added, "*The Forty-eight Stars* is practically an American *Aeneid.*" Jack's eye, of course, was anything but clear when it came to Elena or his own ambitions for her. "*The Strike* is a book for the average, intelligent, maybe sympathetic reader," he said. "I'm shooting for that person. But Elena, she can get the real elite." He grinned. "So, Bill, you should save the highbrow editing for Elena and just let me muddle through with a few split infinitives and not a single reference to Shakespeare or Dante or any of the big boys."

I was about to give Jack some details of how I expected him to improve his novel, when one of the waiters stumbled forward from across the room, balancing his tray precariously for an instant, then losing control altogether, so that it slid from his hand and crashed to the floor, spewing out a spray of broken glass and champagne.

"Oh, Jesus," Jack cried. He leaped up and began helping the waiter clean up the mess. Miriam started helping too, then Mary and Sam and the rest of us pitched in with bathroom towels and toilet paper.

It was, I suppose, a rather comic scene, certainly not a momentous one. Jack never mentioned it again, and Elena wrote no notes on it. And yet it was with a scene very much like this one that she finally chose to open *Calliope:*

> In the beginning was the Word. That's what they say. That's what they were all saying at Tim's wedding: "Did you get the word? Have you got the word?" They meant tips on Consolidated Oil. The "word" was, it was going up, way up, a ticker tape cathedral. In the corner, holding my glass, smiling at Patricia in her gown and Tim in his tuxedo, I thought the word would come to me, come dressed in purple robes, pointing a jagged finger at a single dot on a line of dots strung out on an endless scroll. "There, there you are, that dot, that is you on the Chain of Being." Then I would know, then I would have the word. I was grinning, a little feebly, very pleased with my meditations, though Father was scowling at me, his white eyebrows inching together, almost speaking, like two furry lips: "For God's sake, Raymond, act your age. I have interests to protect." And so I wiped the smile from my mouth like a residue of heavy cream and turned and saw it, like a vision. The waiter, dressed in a little red jacket with winking gold buttons, had begun to lose his footing. He was trying to get it back, but his legs were crossed and he was sinking toward the floor. The tray, huge and filled with champagne glasses, was slanting downward, then moving, sweeping, hurling itself from his hand until it crashed nose down across the polished floor, and a terrible noise of shattering glass filled the hall, while we jerked around frantically to avoid the wave of spilled champagne, flipping and flopping about as a snake coils and uncoils after the shovel has taken off its head.

When I reread that passage now, I am struck by how certain the voice is, how true to the story it will tell, and how far my sister was from it on my wedding day, and yet not far at all.

She never learned his name, that young man in the black tuxedo who did so much to shape the final structure of *Calliope.* Perhaps if she had learned it during their short conversation across from Woolworth's that afternoon, she might have dedicated the book to him, rather than to Jack MacNeill. But she didn't, and so he remains a nameless figure in her life, buried so deeply now that not even the tireless excavations of Martha Farrell could unearth him. Thus he lives only as "the pale, blue-eyed young man" Martha describes in her biography, who came along at precisely the right time in Elena's life.

It was the early fall of 1936, only a few weeks after Miriam and I were married. Elena was still at work on *The Forty-eight Stars*, reworking yet another draft. Her relationship with Jack had been continually cooling since his return, and she was making very little effort to rekindle it.

"I have stopped talking to him about my book," she told Miriam and me one afternoon not long after our wedding, "and soon I will stop talking to him about my life."

And yet she could still be persuaded by him, coaxed into doing things that no longer really appealed to her. One of them, I am sure, was the suggestion he made that rainy afternoon when we were all together, to go down to the Fourteenth Street Woolworth's, where the shop girls had taken over the store.

"Who knows," Jack said to her as he stood by the window, watching the rain flatten against the pane, "you might use something about it in your book."

Elena glanced at me, then at Miriam.

"Not me, Jack," Miriam said. "I've got my own work to do."

"Okay," Jack said. "How about it, William?"

"All right," I said. "I'll go down with you."

"Good," Jack said. "It should be quite interesting. All the workers are women, you know." He turned to Elena. "You should come with us, too."

Elena looked up from the magazine though which she had been idly flipping. "Why?" she asked.

"More material for your book, Elena," Jack said. "Why else?"

Elena nodded wearily. "I doubt it," she said. "But I don't have anything else to do."

"Hang around here, then," Miriam said. "You can help me with the novel I'm working on."

Elena shook her head and smiled. "I don't think I could be much help to you, Miriam." She walked to the door and pulled her raincoat from the rack beside it. "All right, let's go."

And so the three of us made our way over to West Fourteenth Street, silently pushing through the rain. Elena walked determinedly between Jack and me, her face expressionless, as Jack rambled on about the implications of what he now called "the battle of Woolworth's."

It was completely calm at the store. A single policeman stood guard outside the door, for reasons which, when Jack asked him, he could not explain. "Maybe they just don't want the girls stealing no panties," he said.

Jack presented his press card and we were immediately allowed inside. The women were milling around, randomly examining the counters of dry goods and cosmetics, as if they were shoppers. A few of them had gathered in the back of the store, and their occasional laughter rang over us as Jack began his interviews.

"We want a union here," one woman told Jack bluntly. "We want a forty-hour week, and we want a minimum wage of twenty dollars a week." She grinned at the other women who gathered around her. "When we get that, then F. W. Woolworth can have his store back." She glanced at Elena. "You a reporter, too?"

"In a way," Elena said.

"Good," the woman said. "This is mostly a female thing, here. That's the way it is in all of old F.W.'s stores. He thinks he can get away with paying women less than men, you know?"

Elena nodded, and the other women murmured their agreement.

"Who you with, the *Times?*" one woman asked from the circle that had gathered around.

"*New Masses,*" Jack said.

"That a New Jersey paper?" the woman asked.

Jack shook his head. "Listen, who's been passing all this food and bedding in here?" He tipped the eraser of his pencil toward the heaps of sheets, pillows, and blankets that had been carefully folded and stacked on the top of the counters. "All this stuff, where'd you get it?" He grinned. "None of this belongs to old F.W., does it?"

The women laughed. "Husbands mostly," one of them said. "They're behind us all the way."

Jack continued his interview, playfully joking with the women, jotting down their comments, putting a star by any he thought especially quotable. He was a master at eliciting the printable remark, and Elena once said of an interview he conducted with a farm woman in Idaho that when he left her, she looked as if she had been made love to by an expert.

After a time, Elena and I eased our way out of the steadily thickening circle of women who had gathered around Jack. We wandered over to the back corner of the store, where a few sleepy parakeets stood rigidly on their spindly wooden perches.

"Jack's thinking about going to Spain," Elena said passionlessly.

"Spain?"

She tapped her finger idly against one of the cages. "The situation there. To help the Loyalists."

"Do you think he'll go?"

"Probably," Elena said.

The subject seemed closed, so I let the matter drop. I glanced about the store, feeling rather awkward, a reluctant wheel on Jack's bandwagon.

"Well, we're here," I said. "Now what?"

"Jack will work them himself," Elena said dryly.

I laughed. "You make him sound like a carnival huckster."

Elena did not take her eyes from the bird. "I don't mean to." She turned away from the cage and began walking up the aisles, occasionally fingering whatever rested on the counters.

When we reached the front of the store, she stopped, facing the windows that looked out on the street. The patrolman tipped his cap to her and smiled.

"It's very dark outside," she said offhandedly. "Like night."

"Just a stormy day in old New York."

She nodded and started to turn away, but just then a Pierce-Arrow limousine slowly pulled up to the curb across the street. It was driven by a chauffeur in a black cap, and there was a young man in the back seat. When the car stopped, he rolled down his window and peered out, looking directly into the store, his eyes scanning left and right.

"Pretty expensive car for a company spy," Elena said.

"Maybe it's old F.W.'s son."

Elena continued to watch the car as the chauffeur got out, walked to the back door, opened it, and waited as the young man stepped out onto the street. He was in full evening dress — black tuxedo, complete with rosebud boutonniere — as if he were headed for the opera. He could not have looked more out of place among the squat brown shops of Fourteenth Street.

Elena glanced at the women who surrounded Jack, their dresses rumpled from the day's wear, their shoes dull and unpolished. Then she looked at the young man across the street.

"What's he trying to do," she asked, "start a riot?"

The young man leaned casually against the side of the limousine, withdrew a gold cigarette case from his breast pocket, and lit a cigarette.

"What an odd looking man," Elena said, her eyes now intently fixed upon him. "What's he up to, William?"

He continued to lean against his car, smoking his cigarette with affected grace. He carried a black cape in the crook of his left elbow, and from time to time he would wipe a crease from its folds. Then he would look up again, staring steadily into the drab interior of the store, as if it were a question to which he expected, after a bit more study, to find a pure and simple answer.

"I'm going to go talk to him," Elena said finally.

I followed her outside and together we walked slowly across the street toward the young man. He did not move. But his chauffeur, watching us warily, stepped forward to block our path.

"Now, now, Randall," the young man said quietly, "let the people pass."

Randall stepped away.

The young man smiled thinly. "My father has hired someone to protect me."

Elena and I were standing in the middle of the street, neither of us really sure what we were doing. Being blocked by a bodyguard was a new experience. Neither of us knew exactly how to react.

The young man motioned us forward. "Come, if that's what you had in mind."

Randall followed behind us as we walked up.

"You are employees of Woolworth's?" he asked when we reached him.

"No," Elena said.

"Friends and supporters? Comrades?"

"We came with a friend," Elena said. "He's doing a story on the strike."

"That fellow with the girls around him?"

"Yes."

The young man nodded, took a puff from his cigarette, then dropped it to the ground and crushed it with the tip of his freshly shined black shoe. "It's been a rather nasty day," he said, his eyes still fixed on the store. "But then, it's been a nasty age."

"Where are you from?" Elena asked, moving right into the interrogation, as Jack had no doubt taught her.

"New York, of course."

"You have a special connection with Woolworth's?"

He smiled. "Do you mean, am I the son and heir?"

"Something like that."

He shook his head. "No connection at all, except, of course, that my father no doubt owns stock in the company. But he owns stock in everything. He's one of the pillars of capitalism." He laughed lightly. "No, I'm just down here because it interests me."

"Strikes interest you?" Elena asked.

"Distress interests me, and contradiction," he said. "I've lost my taste for other things, theater and literature." He smiled at her. "And women."

It was then, I think, that Elena saw it for the first time, his monkish loneliness and intensity. Years later, when she and I were at Mont Saint-Michel, in the solemn monks' dining room there, she said that his soul must have been like this, chill and sober and full of grayish air.

The young man looked back toward the store. It had gotten dark enough for the lights to have been put on, and inside the women were beginning to put down their bedding for the night.

"I come here every evening at this time," he said. He looked at Elena. "Do you know how they sleep? They huddle together in one aisle near the back of the store, packed tight, like hamsters." Through the window we could see Jack walking down one of the aisles, his arms loaded with sheets and blankets.

"Your friend," the young man said, "— I suppose he is sympathetic?"

"I suppose he is," Elena said.

He took his cigarette case out again and opened it. "Care for a cigarette?"

"No, thank you," Elena said.

He lifted the open case in my direction. I shook my head. He lit one for himself.

"My father made a speech to one of his boards yesterday," he said. "In the speech he said, 'As you all know, I have the deepest

sympathy for the lower classes, but . . .' " He smiled. "That 'but'
— it divides the world, don't you think? Just as surely as it divides
a sentence."

"What side of it are you on?" Elena asked bluntly.

He ran his fingers slowly through his dark hair. "Do you know
the line from Ennodius, the one about how difficult it must be to
be a saint and yet not have a saintly reputation?"

Elena shook her head.

"You should know more about medieval texts," he said, with only
a touch of condescension. "They define this age, this catastrophe."
He looked at Elena warily. "Of course, someone like yourself, a modern
woman, you want new answers. You wouldn't define the present situation as a theological dilemma." His whole face suddenly darkened,
as if lighted with a candle from below. "But I will tell you, our guilt
is very old."

"What guilt is that?" Elena asked.

"Mine. Yours." He nodded toward the people in the store. "Theirs."
He looked at Elena closely. "You think that's facile, don't you? You
think I'm just concocting some romantic notion of myself as dissolute
rich boy touring the slums."

"I've seen a lot of places like this, strikes and sit-ins," Elena said.
"I've never seen anyone who looks like you at one."

He nodded, glanced at me, then back at Elena. "You know the
warning Oscar Wilde gave to Lord Douglas? That he should not
fall in love with the things of the gutter. That's good advice, don't
you think?"

Elena kept her eyes locked on him, but she said nothing.

"A few weeks ago I saw a group of policemen evict a large family
on the Lower East Side," the young man went on. "An old lady
was screaming at them while they dragged her down the concrete
steps. The whole neighborhood was screaming, and people were throwing garbage and rotten vegetables down on the cops from the other
tenements." He laughed. "It was quite a sight. A real circus. I watched
the policemen and it struck me that they hate the poor. Do you
know why? Because they are troublesome, and the police are too
simple-minded to understand the philosophical dimensions of trouble,
how it acts on our moral sensibility. For them, all the terrors of
earth are nothing more than a 'police problem,' trouble for *them*,
aggravation and paperwork. The greater horror would elude them,
because their minds cannot engage it."

Elena studied the young man's face. "Engage it, how?" she asked.

"Clearly, relentlessly," the young man said, "as if searching for the center of it — that kernel which the Hindus believe generates everything else — and with the absolute certainty that this central thing does not exist."

Elena's eyes narrowed. "But if it doesn't exist, then why look for it?"

He smiled. "Because looking for something very intensely gives the mind a powerful focus, and the exercise of looking for something it cannot find gives it a sense of humility, so that it must recognize its own processes, and their limitations."

Elena's voice was soft. "So that by looking outward powerfully, the mind must look inward."

Behind her eyes, I could see her mind working, as if the young man had lit a hundred fires in her brain. Years later, she would say in an interview that she could not remember any statement of his that had made any particular sense, only that, "in the chaos I was going through with the structure of *The Forty-eight Stars,* his remarks about focusing the mind and about doubting the ability of a panoramic view to yield anything of importance — this spoke to me, and I finally incorporated it in the writing of *Calliope.*"

The young man looked back toward Woolworth's, his eyes following Jack as he moved through the aisles, pad and pencil in hand, questions at the ready.

"What does your friend want from those women?" he asked Elena.

"He's a reporter," Elena said matter-of-factly.

The young man shook his head. "No, he's more than that. He is their comrade in arms."

"Is there something wrong with that?" Elena asked.

"Nothing at all," he said. "That's one side of the story, certainly."

Elena continued to watch him. "What is?"

"Injustice," the young man said. "And the struggle against it." He scanned Elena's face. "That's one story. That's your friend's story." He laughed gently, and much of his smug exterior seemed to dissolve. "And then there's another story, of course."

"Which is?" Elena demanded.

"Mine."

Elena was not buying it. "There are plenty of stories about the rich," she said bluntly.

The young man nodded. "Oh, of course there are." He opened the door of his limousine and got in.

Elena stepped around to his open window. "You're a fake," she said, but with a curious gentleness.

He regarded her steadily. "And you are not as intelligent as you think you are, my dear."

"It's the rosebud that gives you away," Elena said, "and that quote from Ennodius."

He turned toward the driver. "Perhaps we should leave now, Randall."

"And that slithering speech," Elena said, this time in a voice that was not gentle at all.

The young man's eyes narrowed. "Step away from the car."

"The man you pretend to be would be interesting," Elena said evenly. "But you are a fake."

Then she stepped back and allowed the car to pull away. She watched it, standing in the middle of the street, until it turned the corner and disappeared. Then she looked at me, her face very thoughtful, as if her mind were reworking everything all at once, setting all her many notes in order, discovering the character who could relate the tale — this young man with the rosebud boutonniere, only thoroughly remolded by the fire in her mind, transformed into Raymond Finch, that "sensibility hanging from a hook," the voice, at last, of *Calliope*.

In the winter of 1936, Jack MacNeill left for Spain. The day before his departure, Elena and Miriam and I joined him on what he called, with a wry smile, his "farewell tour of New York." We took the el down to South Ferry, then made that lovely eastward loop near City Hall, the cars swinging to the left, then curling back so that all of Manhattan came into view. We could see the old circular aquarium resting at the water's edge, and the tower of the Woolworth building, its topmost spire hidden in the clouds. Elena sat quietly between

Jack and me, her body rocking left and right as the train made its slow turn.

We got off in lower Manhattan, walked to Battery Park, then turned northward and trudged the long distance to Times Square. Through it all, Jack could hardly have been more boyishly excited. He talked about the adventure before him, the needs of the Loyalist cause, and the vision of unity embodied, he said, in the very idea of the International Brigades. He joked with Elena about that first trip of theirs around Manhattan, and their trek across the country, and about his hopes for *The Forty-eight Stars*. "You'll have it finished by the time I get back," he said brightly. "I expect you'll be a famous woman by then."

Miriam and I left them at Times Square, with Elena under his arm. It seemed as though he did not at all suspect how far she had drawn away from him during the last few weeks. Years later, when Elena and Alexander were in the midst of one of their periodic sparring matches, she told him that one of the peculiar burdens of being a woman was having to deal with the obliviousness of men. I have always believed that she was thinking of Jack when she said that.

She saw him off later that evening. He had signed on with one of the ships of the Fabre line. He would work on the ship until it docked in Marseilles, then take another boat to Barcelona.

Elena took a cab to my apartment from the pier. Miriam was safely ensconced in the tiny cubicle beyond the kitchen that had become her inner sanctum, where she intended to write her novel. She spent long hours there, her typewriter clattering away, sometimes almost until dawn.

It was, in fact, clattering when I opened the door to Elena. She was wearing a dark raincoat, and her hair was tightly bound up in a large white scarf.

"He's on his way," she said.

"To your slight relief?"

"More than slight."

I stepped out of the doorway and waved her in. "Coffee?"

"Yes, thank you, William," Elena said. She walked into the living room and took off her scarf and raincoat.

I made the coffee, served her a cup, then sat down opposite her on the little sofa by the window. I could hear the rain patting softly against the glass. It sounded curiously like the muffled tat-tat-tat of Miriam's typewriter.

"Well, I hope Jack gets back safely," I said.

"So do I," Elena said. She nodded toward the back room. "Working on her novel?"

"Yes."

Elena cradled her cup in her hands. "I'm going to be working on mine, soon."

"I thought you'd already been working at it for quite some time," I said.

She shook her head. "Not that one. Something new, I think."

"Not *The Forty-eight Stars?*"

"No." She took a sip of coffee. "It's still about the Depression, at least in a way. But not like *The Forty-eight Stars.*" She smiled quietly. "I'm going to write this book in the way it seems best for me to write it, William."

"I'm glad to hear it," I told her.

"That young man we met," Elena said, "— the one at Woolworth's that day. Remember him?"

"Very well."

"He gave me an idea." Elena set her cup down. "I think that maybe to study a catastrophe like the Depression, you have to know about other catastrophes in history."

"Why is that?"

"I'm not sure," Elena said. "Perhaps just to give it dimension. In the mind, I mean, a dimension in the mind. Otherwise it's just suffering and injustice, all those things Jack says it is."

"Well, it is certainly those things," I told her.

"But more, too." Elena was staring at me very intently. "I don't think I can do the 'Big Picture,' William. It's not the way my mind works. It's like asking a miniaturist to do a mural."

She finished her coffee and stood up.

"Leaving already?" I asked.

"I think so," she said. "I don't want this to sound melodramatic, but I have a lot of work to do."

She began her research immediately. Some days she would work at a small carrel at the Columbia library. Or she would sit hour after hour in the reading room of the New York Public Library, her head bent forward beneath one of those green-shaded lamps which, in row upon row of subdued light, lend to that vast hall a strangely intimate atmosphere.

I was still working at Parnassus, only a few blocks away from the library at that time, and I saw Elena often, usually for lunch. As the months passed, she grew increasingly enthusiastic about her book. Over a hot dog in Bryant Park, she would talk about her latest findings, the terrible etiology of the Black Death, for example, or the exact dimensions of the Iron Virgin. Interspersed with these remarks she offered random news from Elizabeth or Jack. Elizabeth, Elena said, seemed entirely unaware that Europe was on the brink of war. Jack, on the other hand, was already in the thick of it, reporting in one letter after another on the progress of the republic's dreadful collapse. But it was clear that the only thing upon which Elena's mind was powerfully focused was her book.

By the fall of 1937, she had decided to get rid of the old title. We were sitting in a small coffee shop not far from the library, and she had just finished a long exposition on the writings of Gregory of Tours. "I've decided to call the book *Calliope.*"

It seemed a very odd choice. "You mean for that musical contraption they have at the circus?"

"No," Elena said, "from mythology. The last of the nine sisters, according to Hesiod."

"Oh yes," I said, "the muse of epic poetry."

"That's right," Elena said. "But I think of her a little differently — as the god, you might say, of empty rhetoric."

I had not read a word of the manuscript, and so I had no idea to what extent she had transformed her material from the chaotic jumble of *The Forty-eight Stars.* "I'm looking forward to reading it," I said politely.

Elena smiled, put some money on the table, and stood up. "I've got to get back to work."

It was finished by the summer of 1938. Miriam found it lying on her desk when she arrived at work one morning. Elena had gotten to Parnassus long before the rest of us so that she would not be asked any questions about the manuscript.

Miriam stared at it for a moment, then she turned to me. "Well, this is Elena's book," she said. "God, I hope it's good. What can I tell her if it isn't?"

"The truth, Miriam," I said.

Miriam nodded, took the manuscript into a small room that had been set aside for undisturbed reading, and closed the door behind her.

Almost four hours passed before she came out again. She walked into the outer office where I sat drowsily reviewing yet another unsolicited abomination.

"Step in here, please, William," she said, retreating back into the reading room.

She was seated behind the desk when I came in.

"Close the door," she said.

"That bad?" I asked.

"Just close the door," Miriam said, "and sit down."

I did as I was told. I could feel the tension building, the terrible feeling that you must now deliver to an unprotected mortal the worst imaginable news.

Miriam drew a single page of the manuscript from the pile. "All right," she said, "listen to this." Then she began to read what turned out to be the final paragraph of *Calliope*, an internal monologue in the mind of the narrator, Raymond Finch:

> Ah, Markham, what am I to do with such stranded zeal? Betray my father? To what use should I put my moral bafflement? Feed the hungry? Clothe the naked? Inspire the faithless? But with what faith? Where do we stand, those like me — silent, full of doubt, bannerless, beyond all anthems — what can we do but choke on our anger? And after anger, what? You must know that to free the moth suspended in the web I would suffer the lash; to save the deer from a crippling leap, I would bear the weight; to save the infant blistered in the sun, the bushman wounded by a spear, the Bedouin poisoned at the well, I would lie down across the wood, stretch out my arms; to end all this, I would open up my hand, receive the nail.

Miriam looked up. "It's all like this," she said, "the whole book."

"Is that bad or good?" I asked.

Miriam reinserted the page. "I'm not quite sure," she said, "but it is different." She lifted the manuscript toward me. "Your turn."

I read it in one sitting, just as Miriam had, though in the comfort of my apartment. I sat in the front room, while Miriam struggled at her typewriter a few yards away, and read the book word by careful word, and with a steadily rising sense of Elena's achievement. For she had managed to take the notes she had brought back with her from the road, those painful details of hunger and distress, and then to strip them almost entirely of their topicality, so that in the end they stood far beyond the scope of anything social or economic theory could embrace. The smug young man whom we had met outside Woolworth's that day had been transformed into Raymond Finch, a man of almost theological grandeur, full of the deepest moral insight and complexity, a character of constantly shifting lights, part infidel, part Jesuit, a man who moves continually between the poles of what love and rage have made him, a medievalist drifting through the modern plague of the Depression, a modernist staring back at the undeniable horrors of the medieval world, at times a Christ who has lost his faith, at times a pagan who has found it.

It was still fairly early when I finished it. For a long time I sat in the living room, rethinking it. It was the voice of the novel, rather than the very simple plot, that remained most powerfully with me, so full as it was of chants and litanies, so different from my sister's. And yet it was quite deeply hers — thoughtful, measured, softly resonant, almost Gregorian; a low, monkish hum.

I was still sitting by the window, the book in my lap, when Miriam came out of her room, wearily rubbing her eyes.

"How's the novel coming?" I asked.

She shrugged, then nodded toward the manuscript in my lap. "What do you think?"

"I think it's remarkable, Miriam," I said. "I think everyone will like it."

Miriam gave me a doubtful look. "Not everyone, William," she said. "Believe me, not everyone."

I knew instantly whom she meant, but at that moment he seemed so far away.

Madrid fell in late March of 1939. Jack was there, caught in the dead center of a resistance that had been collapsing for two years. Later, in his autobiography, he wrote of his own panic, of his madness in "trying to book passage on a ship while living in a city that was not only besieged by a large armed force but which could hardly have been more thoroughly landlocked." He did get out, however, trudging southward for no apparent reason, "except that that appeared to be where other foreign refugees were headed." He finally reached the southern coast of Cádiz, booked passage to Tangiers, and from there at last managed to sail to New York on a creaky steamer "that listed continually to the right no matter what the wind direction, giving you the distinct impression that the earth was limping."

He arrived in New York on a steamy July day with nothing but a duffel bag and a few books to his name. He looked wizened, graying at the temples, and much thinner than I had ever seen him. He told me he had contracted pneumonia while crossing the Montes de Toledo. A gypsy family had treated him by making him sleep on mounds of dried peppers. "Didn't do much for the pneumonia," he said with a wry smile, "but it sure did wonders for my headache."

He still had an ambling gait, but it was slower now, as if his experience in Spain had used up his youth. And as he stood slumped against Miriam's desk with Sam and me gathered around him, he looked almost old, a body trimmed in white.

"Thanks for sending me a book once in a while, Sam," he said.

Sam nodded. "Like any of them?"

"Oh, sure," Jack said. "I thought Carla Weatherwax's novel was pretty good." He looked at me. "Sorry about *The Strike*." He was referring to the poor reception of his own novel. Sales had sagged badly. The reviews had not been enthusiastic.

"We can't always have a hit, Jack," I said.

Jack shook his head. "Aw, hell, I'm no novelist. I'm barely a journalist. Christ, it was hard covering that war." He looked at Sam. "Man, if you think we've got factional problems over here, you should have seen the situation in Barcelona when they expelled the POUM." He turned back to me and smiled.

"Did Elena publish her book yet?" he asked.

"Yes. It's called *Calliope*. Haven't you seen her?"

"It's my vanity, William. I look like a tramp. Worse. A sick tramp."

"I'm sure she wouldn't mind."

"No, but I would," he said. "When did the book come out?"

"Last month."

"Doing well?"

"It's a little early to tell."

Jack scratched at his face. Even clean-shaven now, he looked somehow scraggly. "You got a copy of it?"

"Of course."

"Could I borrow it?"

I walked over to the bookshelf behind my desk and pulled one down. "I'm sure she'll autograph it for you."

"Do me a favor, William. Don't tell her I'm in town, yet."

I agreed, and he walked out, waving to Sam, then to Miriam and me.

"This is not a vanishing act," he said, trying, I think, with all his will, to bring some lightness to his voice. "I just need a little rest."

Then he was gone, leaving Miriam and me standing in the foyer outside Sam's office.

Three weeks later a review of *Calliope* appeared in *New Masses*. It was facetiously entitled "Oh Woe Is Me," and it had been written by Jack MacNeill:

Let's get this much down from the start: this is a book that has us look at the terrible reality of our times through the eyes of a tipsy upper-class Augustine, the sort who wants to be saved from his iniquity, but not, O Lord, quite yet.

We are supposed to believe that this plutocrat can actually comprehend the misery around him better than the poor fellows who have to live in it, which is a little like saying that the housewife who lays the trap knows it better than the mouse.

The book begins at a wedding. It doesn't matter who is getting married, it only matters that they're rich. All looks well. But then a waiter stumbles. This is enough to change the life of the book's hero, Raymond Finch. He discovers that some people don't have it so good in These United States and decides to investigate. If this were all that was needed to bring a sense of justice to the wealthy classes, then I'd say let's hire stumbling waiters by the thousands.

So off Raymond trots. He pops in at the local labor hall and muses about the nature of labor. Then it's off to the docks, where he muses about the soiled world of international trade. He takes chow at a tumbledown greasy spoon, and here he muses about the way people eat.

By now Raymond is *moved*. Only one problem: he can't seem to get off the dime, and he doesn't know why. But I do. For all his thundering avowals, Raymond's conscience is as thin as a pancake.

Raymond keeps on sniffing around the slum side of life wondering what he can do about all this. Then it happens. Raymond discovers that his father the capitalist is rottenly corrupt.

But what to do? Raymond doesn't know. I can tell him. Turn the money-grubbing bastard in! But Raymond is more subtle. He needs to think. A nasty investigative reporter tries to persuade him to turn over the papers that will destroy his father. But all he can do is more of what he's good at. He thinks.

Then, at last, the vision comes, the ultimate death wish. Raymond wishes to be crucified, dreams that he is crucified — one or the other. It's hard to tell. The prose is unclear. Anyway, Raymond is crucified. Or maybe he isn't. Maybe only Raymond knows. He's more subtle.

My phone rang early on the Sunday morning that Jack's review appeared. It was Elena. Her voice was flat.

"Did you know that Jack was back in New York?"

"Yes," I said drowsily, rubbing the sleep from my eyes. "He looked pretty bad. He wanted to get fixed up before he saw you. He said he'd let me know when he was ready to contact you."

"Have you seen the latest issue of *New Masses?*"

"No."

"Go down and get it. I think Jack has made contact."

I went out immediately, bought the issue, brought it back up to my apartment, and with Miriam staring wide-eyed over my shoulder read Jack's review with ever-deepening consternation.

When I had finished, I looked up at Miriam. She looked thunderstruck.

"I can't believe he'd do that," she said.

I folded the paper and let it slide to the floor. "I didn't think he'd agree with all of it, but I'm surprised that he would be so vitriolic, that he'd be so blind to the merit in it."

"It must have been agonizing for Elena," Miriam said.

But as Elena wrote in *Calliope*, "After anger, what?"

As the days passed, it became clear that Jack's review had sounded a trumpet. Before its publication, *Calliope* had been treated with respectful interest as the second, and long-awaited, book by the controversial author of *New England Maid*. Sam had been discouraged. He stormed about the office, declaring that there was nothing worse for a book than respect. "Respect is boring, boring," he shouted. "What gets people going is love or hate. Those critics out there are respecting *Calliope* right into the literary bone yard."

But after Jack's bitter attack, the forces arrayed themselves, and

Elena once again found herself in the middle of a raging controversy. The left-wing press, given the screaming go-ahead by one of its most honored journalists, bared its teeth and leaped for the jugular. In city after city, they hauled *Calliope* through the streets, burned it in effigy, hung it from the neck till dead. Sam was jubilant. "Jesus Christ, William, did you see this?" he'd thunder, waving another attack in the air. "God damn, William, Elena's great. She can't put pen to paper without pissing off half the country. Wait until the reactionaries catch on to it. They'll come to her defense like the Seventh Cavalry. Just you wait and see."

And indeed they did. For every attack in something like *New Masses*, there was a spirited defense in the right-wing press.

But how, in the end, did all of this affect Elena? It drove her into silence. She remained secluded in her apartment, refusing interviews with an absoluteness that enraged Sam Waterman.

"People don't get famous in this country," he told her one tropical day in late August, "by running from the press."

But Elena was adamant. Standing by her window, wiping the sweat from her neck with a wet cloth, she told Sam exactly what she thought.

"If you think that all these attacks on me by many old friends don't hurt, Sam, you're crazy."

"I know it does. Fight back."

"How?"

"Use the method they use. Let the reporters in here. Give them a Scotch and soda. Sit down by the fan. Then, when they're nice and comfortable, let them have it. Draw as much blood as you like."

Elena shook her head. "No."

Sam looked at me helplessly. "Tell her, please, William."

I said nothing, and Sam walked over to the window.

"Look, Elena," he said, "I stood up for you once. Remember all the trouble with *New England Maid?* Parnassus didn't take one step back, right?"

Elena nodded silently.

"Well, this time you've got to stand up for yourself. And I don't mean just for publicity. I mean they're lying about you. All of them. The people following Jack's lead, and the stuffed-shirts who are defending you. But when the smoke clears, there's only *Calliope* left, and that book belongs to you. Don't you think you have a duty to defend it?"

Elena looked Sam straight in the eye. "No, I don't," she said.

She resolutely maintained this position, and after only one more attempt Sam gave up entirely and trudged out of the room, exasperated.

"I hope he can forgive me," Elena said after he had left.

"You should do what you think is right, Elena," I told her.

Miriam nodded. "Yes. A writer should think like a writer, not like a publisher."

"Speaking of writers," I said, "I thought you might like to waste some time looking over my new manuscript." I pulled it from my briefcase and handed it to her. It was hefty, to say the least: over seven hundred pages on William Blake.

"I'll read it right away," Elena promised.

"No rush," I said with a slight smile. "It won't change the world."

She had finished it a week later, and on an overcast Saturday morning I returned to her apartment to get her response. I had expected only a few words, mostly of encouragement, perhaps some advice about this idea or that. But instead Elena delivered what amounted to a learned address on the subject before her. And as she spoke, it became clear to me how well my sister had used her time, all those many hours of solitude in Standhope, then in her room at Hewett Hall, and after that at Three Arts, and finally in this apartment in Brooklyn Heights, with its sober, book-lined walls and undistracting potted plants. During all those years, she had gathered that harvest of unelaborated fact which any mind may gather, but had then reshaped it in miraculous configurations, as only a great one can.

Certainly there were scores of scholars who knew more about Blake than Elena. But I suspect that few of them could have spoken of that poet with greater feeling or more passionately expanded upon what I had written. She made Blake's dream of an English Jerusalem rise like a revolutionary force, portraying this vision of a Broad Street hosier's son as the human miracle it surely was.

"It is odd, isn't it, William," she concluded, "that beside someone like Blake, most ordinary striving looks not only petty but willfully mischievous?"

I did not have the opportunity to comment, for just as I was about to speak, Miriam came into the room with a letter for Elena, which had been sent in care of Parnassus Press. It was from Joe Tully, that affable man who was one of the leading lights of New York left-wing society.

Elena opened it, read it, then handed it to me. It was an invitation for her to "confront your critics in a lively give-and-take, sponsored by contributions from our membership. There will be no admission charge, and I presume, Elena, that you will not require a fee?"

I handed the letter back to Elena. "They'll butcher you. It's a setup."

"Joe's not like that," Elena said.

"He won't be the only one there," I told her. "They mean to sink you. There won't be one person with guts enough to take your side. They'll all be coming for the express purpose of carving you up and serving you to the membership like little bits of flank steak."

Elena winced. "For God's sake, William, you don't have to be so lurid."

"It's true. There is nothing ecumenical in their mood. They're going to burn you alive."

Elena raised her hand. "Enough." Then she looked at Miriam. "What do you think?"

"I think William's right, but I also think that you can hold your own against them, if that's what you want to do."

Elena smiled slightly. "Sam would love it, wouldn't he?"

"Sam wouldn't be the one on the spot," I told her. "And frankly, I don't see why you should."

Elena looked at me as if I were a small child who knew nothing of the world. "Because I wrote the book."

"Yes, you did," I said. "But if you want to defend it, then why not do it the way Sam suggested a long time ago. Write a defense. You wouldn't have any trouble finding someone to publish it."

Elena sat down in her chair by the window, the little blue envelope still in her hand. She stared at it several moments, holding it perfectly still. Then she looked up at me. "I'm going to do it," she said.

The arrangements were made quickly, and so, as Martha Farrell matter-of-factly records it, "on September 15, 1939, a mere two weeks before the Nazi invasion of Poland would plunge the world into a devastating war, Elena Franklin drove with her brother and sister-in-law to 112 East Twelfth Street and walked up three flights of stairs to a large loft owned by Michael Joseph Tully, a local official of the Communist party."

Joe was waiting for us. He was dressed in flannel work clothes, the sleeves rolled up to the elbow.

"Good to see you, Elena," he said cheerfully. "We're going to have quite a turnout tonight." He laughed. "The name Elena Franklin draws a crowd these days." He nodded toward several reporters slumped together in a corner, idly smoking cigarettes. "Press, too."

It was then that I heard Sam lumbering up the stairs behind us, pulling his substantial frame up the last steps, already breathless from the climb.

He nodded to us, then turned to Joe.

"Expecting a noisy crowd?" he asked.

Joe smiled knowingly. "I wouldn't be surprised."

"I didn't know you were coming, Sam," I said to him.

He looked amazed by what I'd said. "Listen, William, a good publisher publishes good books; a great one stands behind his authors." Then he turned back to Joe. "Now, I know a lot of the people who'll be here tonight, Joe," he said, "but I don't know them all. So you spread the word that Sam Waterman, Elena's publisher, is here, and that if anybody tries to lay one finger on her, I'll kick their ass down every one of these goddamn stairs. You spread that around the room, you understand?"

Sam was like a blowfish: When he wanted to, he could look extremely imposing, and it was clear from the expression on Joe's face that Sam had left no doubt that he meant exactly what he said. Some thirteen years later, when I sat, stunned, reading the wheedling testimony Sam had given before the House Un-American Activities Committee, I felt so insulted that I actually threw the paper across the room. I was still fuming silently when, two days later, a telegram arrived from Elena, who had read a similar account in Paris. The telegram read: RE WATERMAN STOP MEN OF PROVEN GREATNESS NEED NOT ALWAYS CLEAN THEIR TIES STOP. When I showed it to Sam, he sat down behind his desk and cried.

But on that September evening, he still had the courage of his youth, and no man ever looked more commanding as he swept Elena along beside him to the small waiting room that had been set up behind a makeshift stage.

People began showing up almost immediately. They filed in singly or in groups, muttering and shaking their heads, some of them looking glum and others staring toward the empty lectern with almost fiendish anticipation. They were dressed informally, of course, and some of them had brought umbrellas, since rain was predicted for later in the evening. A few came by to chat with Miriam and me, but for the most part they carefully avoided us. Of course, neither Miriam nor I looked very amiable, worried as we were about what might lie ahead for Elena. Sam, on the other hand, swept into the crowd, shaking hands and slapping backs. It would not have been hard to mistake him for a ward politician.

Within a few minutes, the loft was filled, all the chairs completely occupied and the space behind them and along the outer aisles crowded with people forced to stand. Cigarette smoke clouded the lights overhead and gave the entire room an eerie gray radiance. A few placards had been hoisted, most of them detailing coming events of note. Only one of them referred to Elena. It said, ELENA FRANKLIN SOARS ABOVE PARTY STRIFE, and beneath the words was a crude drawing of Elena seated on a cloud obliviously typing at her desk, while beneath her a huge urban mass writhed in agony. There was some laughter when it was first brought in, but for the most part it was ignored. A few people milled around handing out leaflets announcing upcoming unemployment rallies or promoting Party officials who were candidates for local office. One man wandered about with a small wooden box, requesting money for what he called "our efforts in the South." After a while, Joe Tully asked him to explain who he was and with whom he was affiliated. When he could not, he was escorted to the door, and the crowd booed loudly as he left. "We got to be careful with these guys," Joe shouted. "These bunko creeps are everywhere. Before you give any money to anybody, be sure they have the proper authority to receive it."

"Probably collecting for the FBI," someone called, and everyone laughed.

Joe elbowed his way through to the small stage, stepped up, and lifted his arms to request quiet. "Listen up, please. We're already getting a late start, and some of us have to get up early for a meeting in Washington tomorrow. So listen up, and let's get the meeting under way."

Almost grudgingly, the crowd straightened itself and grew silent. In the back, the reporters chatted with each other, bored with everyone but themselves.

"Now, you all know we have Elena Franklin here tonight," Joe said.

The comment was greeted with a restless murmer.

"Look here, now," Joe said, "we don't want a riot. Elena has come to talk to us. As you know, there's been some debate over her book, over its treatment of the Depression. She's going to talk about that for a few minutes, I guess, and then maybe she'll take some questions." He signalled to Elena, who was sitting quietly in the front row.

The crowd seemed to growl as she walked onto the platform. She was wearing a pair of dark blue slacks, with a white blouse and brown duffel coat. She kept her hands in the pockets of the coat as she stepped forward, firmly staring straight ahead. When she reached her position, she drew her hands up and held tightly to the lectern.

There was no applause, only the uneasy shuffling of bodies, but Elena waited until even this muffled noise subsided before beginning. Then in a clear, strong voice, she spoke. Dismissing preliminaries or a formal greeting, she got right to the point, reading from a statement she had been preparing for almost two weeks.

"Man is unique," she said, "not simply because he is intelligent but also because he can imagine a destiny for himself. I have not come here to defend one book. Even if it were worthy of defense, it would remain only a small thing. But when it comes to the right of an individual to imagine the human destiny in any way he chooses, then that is a very important matter, and it deserves to be defended."

There was some rustling, and a few people moaned wearily, but Elena continued as if she had not heard it, or was afraid to, keeping her eyes locked on the paper before her.

"It seems to me that political aims are, by their very nature, immediate and narrow. Their goal is a victory that can appear almost ready to hand: the next election, for example, or the winning of the sort of war that was lately lost in Spain. The aims of literature are, by their very different nature, not at all immediate, except in the sense that a single person may be immediately moved. This singularity of response is the sole 'narrowness' to which literature aspires. It is narrow only in the sense that it can 'win the world' only one person at a time."

"Or lose it," someone shouted, and there was a smattering of laughter and applause.

Elena continued to stare unflinchingly at her text, as she waited for the room to quiet down.

"Soar above party strife, Elena," someone shouted near the back of the room. I looked back and saw it was the man holding the poster of Elena seated on a cloud. He waved it up and down and right and left while the crowd laughed and cheered.

Elena straightened herself, dropping her hands from the lectern and placing them at her sides. She raised her voice to be heard above the growing tumult.

"To expect literature to share the immediate goals of politics, no matter how worthy those goals might be, would be to expect it to rebel against its own nature."

A woman jumped up from her seat and raised her hand in the air. "You talk about literature as if it were a living thing. It's not."

The crowd burst into applause, and I noticed that the reporters were no longer slumped against the back wall but were listening attentively, their notebooks ready. One of them was loading a camera, while another began to move slowly toward the front.

"Raymond Finch is false," someone shouted loudly, and the audience applauded once again.

"I'm not here to talk about Raymond Finch," Elena said.

"You're not talking about anything," someone cried, and derisive laughter swept the room.

As Elena began to speak, a news photographer darted down the center aisle, dropped to his knees, and shot a picture. The flash swept over Elena, slamming a black shadow against the wall behind her and briefly freezing her body in a silver light. For a moment she seemed to stagger, like a bull after it has received the first lance. I instantly leaned forward, but Miriam caught my arm. "Leave her alone," she said.

I sat back. Elena had begun to read again, but this time more loudly, raising her voice over the noisy, shifting audience. "Each generation reimagines the possibilities of mankind, and in doing so, it contributes to the making of a destiny that the narrowness of political theory cannot begin to understand."

The crowd roared its disapproval, but Elena continued, her voice still raised. "It is the task of art to sound the depths of our need, and it is the task of politics to teach the justice of a cause. They are related only in this: that it is from our need that the cry for justice comes."

The audience hooted and jeered and a group of people near the back began stamping their feet. Elena realized that she could not be heard above the uproar and glanced helplessly at Joe Tully, who then joined her at the front of the room, raising his hands above his head to silence the crowd.

"Now listen, people," he shouted, "listen up. This is not some goddamn Brown Shirt speaking here. This is Elena Franklin. She's been around for a long time, and I, for one, think we owe her a little more simple respect than she's gotten so far."

"Tell 'em, Joe," someone shouted.

There was a smattering of applause, and then Sam was on his feet, batting the smoke from his face and pointing toward the back of the room.

"You schmucks in the back, shut the hell up," he shouted. Then he turned back to Joe. "Let's get on with it, now."

"All right," Joe said loudly, "now let's keep it respectful from here on out. Down South's where they have the lynchings." He turned to Elena, who stood quietly behind him. "Go ahead, Elena." he said.

Elena stepped back up to the lectern. Her voice was much lower as she began, but it could be heard without difficulty throughout the room. "All mankind could be fed and clothed and housed, made well in all their physical needs, and there would still remain those needs of the heart or soul or whatever you choose to call it, needs that it is the right of art to confront." She looked up from her notes. "I don't deny the right of any writer to deal with nothing but politics, if he so chooses. But I also believe that other writers also have rights, and that they may exercise them in all conscience and without being guilty of either political or moral irresponsibility."

She looked back down at her notes and began reading once again. "I do not believe that once we have provided for the physical needs of man, we will also have ended his distress, that once he has been fed and clothed, he will know no further poverty. I do not believe that the riddle of life is nothing more than the riddle of production. Nor do I believe that equality and justice are the same. The former may be addressed by the pettiest of bureaucrats, but the latter is a subject that would tax a god." Her eyes ranged about the crowd. "But since there are no gods, it is up to art."

She looked down again at her notes. "We may allow ourselves to be wrong about a thousand technical things, but we cannot allow ourselves to conceive of mankind as less demanding than it is. We may fool ourselves in a thousand ways, but about one thing we cannot permit ourselves to be deluded: we cannot think of man as more simple than he is, full when only his stomach is full, clothed when only his back is clothed, warm when only his house is warm. For an animal, perhaps, this is enough. But it is only the beginning for a man."

There was actually a smattering of applause as Elena folded her speech and stepped down, joining Miriam and me at our seats at the front of the room. Miriam took her hand and squeezed it. "Good job, Elena," she said.

Elena nodded quickly, her eyes darting around nervously. "I was scared to death," she said.

"Didn't show," Sam said as he patted her gently on the back.

On the small stage before us, Joe Tully was busily thanking my sister for her attendance, when someone shouted from the back of the room, "What about the goddamn questions?" Joe craned his neck to see the speaker. It was the man with the poster of Elena on a cloud. "I thought you said she'd take some questions," he shouted.

I glanced at Elena. She had lowered her head, as if preparing to receive a blow.

Joe looked down at her. "What about it, Elena?"

Elena looked up at him and nodded. Then she stepped back up onto the stage. A few people applauded her, but mostly there was only shifting and mumbling.

"What you just said," the same man shouted from the back of the room. "All that high-class stuff about art. It all just sounded like a bass drum to me."

Elena said nothing. She merely stared back at him, her eyes directly upon his.

"I mean, what the hell is all this stuff about the needs of the soul, anyway?"

Elena cleared her throat slightly. Her voice was very soft as she replied, but there was great agitation in her face. She looked, as Miriam later said, like someone on trial for her life.

"I'm sorry we don't have low-class ways of talking about art and literature and things like that," she said, "but I suppose we don't. So when you talk about these things, you sound very grand. Maybe that's because these things are in themselves so grand, that when we talk about them, we take on some of that grandeur, or at least our language does."

She stopped and took a step forward, peering out toward the man who had called to her, squinting to bring his face into focus. "When I talk about the needs of the soul, I'm not talking about anything religious, about a soul that floats on a cloud, like you have me floating on that poster. I mean that part of our life which requires a special warmth or understanding or consciousness, something like that. I mean all the things that we would still need after we'd been fed and clothed and housed and all that. Surely you don't for one minute suggest that you don't have such needs." She looked him up and down. "You look pretty well fed and clothed. You must have made that poster somewhere. Was it in your own apartment? Was the heat on in that place? Was there a roof to keep the rain out? I think there probably was."

"Of course there was," the man called to her. Then he laughed. "I don't live under a goddamn bridge."

"So you have food and clothing and a warm place to live," Elena said. "All your immediate needs fulfilled. So why are you here?"

"Because there's plenty of people in this country who don't have those things, Miss Franklin," the man shouted back at her.

"Yes, that's right," Elena said. "And you are here to help them get those things. You have a need for them to have those things. And that need is not in your belly. It is in your heart. One of those needs of the soul I spoke about." She turned her attention to the entire audience before her. "The last thing I expected was that my book would offend anyone in this room. I still don't know why it did." She stopped, waiting for the next question. There wasn't one, and after a moment she stepped off the stage, walked to her seat next to Miriam, and sat down.

Joe Tully stepped onto the stage to thank her briefly once again and then went on to other matters, coming rallies and drives and marches. She was watching Joe quite closely, as if interested in what he was saying, in all the day-to-day details, quite honorable and necessary, with which the political consciousness must engage itself. But she also seemed somehow completely aloof, and as I watched her, I thought that somewhere long ago, while the earth was still reeling from the first blast of creation, a human being had squatted at the entrance of a cave, and while the others had gnawed bits of meat and bone by their humble fire, he had gone outside to watch the shifting veils of the Northern Lights and had experienced, for the first time, those precosities of the heart about which my sister had just spoken. And I thought that more than I was like her, I was like those others squatting in the cave, staring out with inexpressible admiration at that graver being who watched the world from his lone post, the one he accepted now as home.

INWARDNESS

In an interview with *Publishers Weekly* which appeared a month or so before her biography, Martha said that she would never forget an afternoon she spent with me at Elena's house on Cape Cod. It was in early December, and she drank tea and I drank brandy while a severe northeastern storm tore at the bay, churning the waters so violently that they looked not just battered but maliciously tormented.

I was living in Elena's house by then, having given up my Cambridge residence entirely. Martha had come out for the day, looking rather predatory, since it had already been established that this interview would be about what she had already half-jokingly dubbed "the dark night of Elena's soul."

We sat down in the back room of the house, the one with the large window facing the ocean. It had always been Elena's favorite, as it would probably have been anyone's, the view from it was so magnificent, particularly in the fall when the sea grass turned golden. Elena had once referred to the scene that presented itself from that room — the sea and shore, gulls and sailboats — as her favorite cliché.

"From everything I've been able to gather," Martha began, "Elena had a pretty rough time of it from around 1940 until, say, 1954?"

I shook my head. "That's too long a stretch."

Martha flipped open her notebook and grabbed her pen. "Well, there were some distressing events in her life during that time."

"Of course," I said, "but most of them were over, the events themselves, I mean, by the mid-1940s."

"So her time in Paris was not distressing?" Martha asked.

"I don't think so."

Martha glanced at her notebook. "Elena came back to the United States in 1954." She looked at me. "Because your wife died?"

"That's one of the reasons." I was about to elaborate on this, give at least a suggestion of that spectral presence who stood across from me the day we buried Miriam, but Martha, wanting to keep things in chronological perspective, lifted her hand to stop me.

"Let's go back to 1939," she said quickly. "Now, after the speech, what happened?"

"Happened? Nothing very dramatic. Miriam and I took Elena home. Miriam was already pregnant by then, about four months gone, and she tired easily. So, we just drove Elena to her apartment and then went back to ours."

"Did Elena look shaken?"

"No."

"How did she look?"

"In control," I said. Then I smiled. "Jack MacNeill once told somebody that Elena had always lived like a middle-class woman who was slightly suspicious of middle-class life, and that what she wanted most was passion and control. That night, at least, she had control."

Martha jotted it down. In her biography, she would refer to it as the central contradiction of my sister's life, this war between her need both to release and to control herself. But since Martha's book was not exactly made of a mingled yarn, this contradiction had to be locked up in the straightjacket of a larger one: Elena's fear of being deserted and her need to control that fear. Thus does the quest for the prime mover triumph over an intolerably scattered heaven; the mind, as Elena once said, avoids chaos only by embracing error.

"So Elena wasn't terribly upset when she left you?" Martha asked.

"No. Like I said, she looked completely in control. She had handled herself very well that evening. Even Joe Tully came over to congratulate her." And I remembered that as I looked over Joe's shoulder, I had seen Jack slink back out the front door and down the stairs.

Martha tapped her pencil lightly against her ear. "When did you see her again?" she asked.

"A week or two later, but it was uneventful. She was the darling of the liberal press by then, practically the patron saint of the anti-Stalinists. The reactionaries loved her, too, and even some of the decidedly Socialist papers had now altered their course a bit, granting her at least the benefit of the doubt." I took a sip of my brandy. "Of course, the real hard core kept up the attack. The fools simply called her a traitor. The more learned ones said she was sadly mistaken, and that *Calliope* belonged with the worst of *feuilleton* writing — subjective vignettes — and that her book was an imitation of Schnitzler and von Hofmannsthal, that Viennese bunch who, like Freud, had fallen in love with neurosis."

"How did Elena react to that?"

I smiled. "She started reading Schnitzler and von Hofmannsthal."

When her pen had caught up with me, Martha looked up. "So it was as if Elena had just spoken her mind and that was it?"

"Yes. She seemed content. There's a certain . . . what shall I call it? . . . There's a certain searing glory to having taken a stand."

Martha nodded. "Did you see much of Elena between that time and when Elizabeth came back to New York?"

"Not as much as I would have liked. Miriam didn't have an easy pregnancy. She was never physically strong, and there were lots of problems." I remembered the queasiness, the sleepless nights, the poor appetite, the loss of energy, which she never fully regained, and which gave to the years that remained to her after Alexander's birth a kind of wistful insubstantiality, as if in giving birth she had used up the fire that had been her life.

"So you stayed around your own apartment a lot?" Martha asked.

"Yes," I said, "but Elena was consciously avoiding me, I think." Even as I said it, I could feel the strain of what now had to come. I had opened the gate, and I knew that Martha would not allow it to be closed again.

"Avoiding you? Why?"

"She was carrying a particular burden, and I suppose that since she knew I was having a little trouble with Miriam, she decided to keep it to herself, at least as long as she could."

Martha stared at me intently. "What burden?"

I hesitated, watching Martha's face. Such must have been the wanton stare of those who questioned Galileo. I glanced out the window.

"Please go on, William," Martha insisted.

I looked at her. "All right."

It had been in mid-December 1939. The Christmas season was everywhere, filled with those common yet relentlessly ironic scenes that only New York can provide — a drunken Santa Claus wobbling down the street, or one of the Wise Men, complete with purple robe and jeweled turban, wildly cursing a taxi driver. I had come to Brooklyn for an editorial session with one of the new authors Sam had assigned me, a slender young man who looked so much the sensitive, tubercular poet that I knew immediately he could be no such thing. We had finished early, and so, rather than return directly to Manhattan, I had decided to drop in on Elena.

I walked from Duffield Street to Columbia Heights, trudged up the three flights of stairs to Elena's apartment, and knocked at her door. I could hear her voice and also a deeper one. After a few seconds, the door opened and my father stepped out into the hallway, carefully closing the door behind him.

"What are you doing here?" I asked, astonished.

"I'm helping Elena over some trouble."

"What kind of trouble?"

"It's none of your business, Billy."

In one of those comic-opera turns which the mind can sometimes take, I remember thinking to myself that I had already written two books, one of them enthusiastically received, and that *I* would decide what was and was not my business.

"I think I'd like to see Elena," I said determinedly.

"You heard me, Billy," he said. "The fact is, she's already lost it, and I don't guess she wants a crowd of people around."

"Lost it? Lost what?"

My father's eyes widened. "You mean she didn't tell you?"

"Tell me what?"

"Elena's pregnant, Billy. At least she was. She miscarried."

I'm sure it took me awhile to grasp the news, and during those few seconds I must have appeared stupefied.

"It's that MacNeill guy," my father said. "He's the one who did it."

I was about to say something, although I have no idea what, when Elena opened the door. She looked drained of all color, pale and ghostly — a body left from a vampire feast. "Come in, William," she said softly.

With that, my father briskly stepped aside, following me into the apartment, where the three of us sat down in the living room.

Elena was dressed in a dark blue robe. Her hair looked matted and stringy; her eyes were glazed. More than anything, she seemed completely exhausted. She held a damp cloth in one hand and occasionally wiped her forehead with it.

"It started yesterday," she said.

"She called me this morning," my father said, "and I came right over." He hitched one of his thumbs beneath a suspender strap. "I was staying at the Edison," he added, as if I might want to verify it.

"I had already told him I was pregnant," Elena said.

I nodded. "And it's Jack MacNeill's?"

"Yes. He came over after the speech. He brought some roses."

My father sat back in his chair and folded his arms over his chest. "She don't want MacNeill to know, Billy."

"That's right," Elena said. "I didn't want anyone to know, at least until I knew what I was going to do."

"Did it ever cross your mind to marry Jack?" I asked.

Elena shook her head. "No."

"It was just a spur-of-the-moment thing," my father said casually. "You're a married man, Billy, you must know about that sort of thing."

I knew then why she had gone to my father in her trouble and had hidden it from me. The common ground that had always united them suddenly rose before me like the strip of an island as it first breaks out of the surrounding sea.

He understood the passionate quality of her impulsiveness, because it was exactly like his own. Elena's sudden decision to tour the country with Jack, to confront her critics, and then to take Jack to her once again was no different in its origins, or its irresistibility, than the impulse with which my father might pinch some shop girl on the road. She was like him; the same current flowed through her. And I was like my mother, cautious beyond imagining, a wire drawn tight.

I looked at Elena. "I didn't know you were still seeing Jack," I said lamely.

"I'm not," Elena said. "It was just that one night." She shrugged. "He came over after the speech, and that's when it happened. I thought I might keep the baby, but there's no need to think about that anymore now."

I was too numb to think about anything. "Well, don't you think you should see a doctor?" I asked.

"She saw one last night, Billy," my father said quickly. "Pal of mine, a guy I know from the Bronx. He came down here, and that was it."

"I see."

"We got everything under control, Billy," he added.

Elena smiled thinly. "Yes, we do," she said very softly, glancing toward the front window.

I stood up slowly. "Well, Elena, I don't suppose there's anything I can do for you."

"Been taken care of," my father said.

Elena looked up at me. "I do prefer that you keep this to yourself, William."

I nodded.

"Jack might feel . . . obligations."

"Perhaps he should."

"He should if I want him to," Elena said, "but I don't."

My father stood up and actually slapped me on the back. "Thanks for coming over, Billy," he said, as if he were ushering one of his better customers to the door.

I walked partway out of the room, then turned back to Elena.

"If you need anything, anything at all, I hope you'll let me know," I said.

She nodded. Then suddenly she stood up and rushed into my arms. I could not remember ever having been so powerfully embraced.

"I love you, Elena," I said softly.

After a moment she pushed herself slowly from my arms. My father stood behind her, as if ready to catch her should she stumble. She did appear to totter slightly as she stepped back, but regained her balance. She rubbed her eyes with her hands, then sank her hands into the pockets of her robe.

"Don't worry about me," she said. "The worst of it is over."

I touched her face. "Let me help you, if I can."

"If I need anything, I'll call," she said. Then she gently drew my hand from her face.

She never called me, at least about anything having to do with the miscarriage. I checked in on her several times during the next few days, and within a week Miriam and I had dinner with her. But the call for aid, pure and exact in its intent, never came. I suppose, as I told Martha that afternoon, that it was during the following weeks that Elena adopted that rigid sense of self-reliance which would finally sustain her through so much of what was to come.

"I am without spirit, soul, or any foreign anima," Dorothea Moore says in *Inwardness*. "I have only the bulk of a bulky thing, and pneuma is the hard bread I chew into a sodden mass, and God is the wine with which I wash it down." This is, of course, a terrible materialism, unacceptable to the faint of heart, but for Elena it was part of a larger contract she was in the process of making between her mind and reality, one which required her to cast off any but the hardest data and to shun even the most comforting of illusions. "The need to believe a thing," Dorothea continues, "is the least acceptable reason for believing it." These "things" constituted for Elena all manner of conjecture, faith, and an enormous assortment of ideas, which she dismissed with that word she often used in her later years, "etherealism."

Etherealism. The word caught Martha's interest immediately. "That's a judgment on ideas, isn't it?" she asked.

"I would say so, yes."

"But what about people? What you seem to be saying, William, is that Elena was getting rather hard in the way she thought about things, rather rigid."

"I would say her standards were getting higher."

"Was she getting more judgmental?"

"Yes. Why shouldn't she? Would you rather she had settled for Jack MacNeill?"

Martha smiled. "Why didn't she? He would have married her, wouldn't he?"

"Yes," I said. "But of course, Elena wouldn't marry him." I smiled. "Once, long after the miscarriage, the two of them were having an argument, and Elena told Jack that he had applied everything he had to politics but his mind."

"How did he react to that?"

"He let it pass," I told her. "Jack could never be intimidated by Elena. His own experience was too authentic, and he always considered Elena's too cerebral to be respected beyond all bounds."

Martha looked doubtful. "Then why did he make love to her that night after the speech? And why did she let him?"

"Because she wanted to," I said. "She said they both needed it, and that more than anything it was like a good cry."

Martha quickly jotted it down. Then she looked up at me. "Did she ever talk about that evening?"

"Yes," I said.

Elena had already gone to bed when he arrived, drenched by the predicted rain. She had not in the least expected him, as she told me later, and for a moment she had had the impulse to slam the door in his face like some dejected heroine in a movie melodrama. But she had caught herself in time and stepped back from the door to let him in. It was then she saw the roses, soaked and crumpled beneath his arm. "I never gave you flowers," he said as he handed them to her. "Too bourgeois." Then he told her that he had seen her at the meeting but had sneaked out of the room before it ended.

She left him in the living room, slumped in the chair by the window, as she made coffee in the kitchen. From there he related his trials in Spain. When she walked back into the living room, he told her what must have seemed to him at that moment the central secret of his life.

"I know that review must have hurt you a great deal, Elena," he said, "and I suppose that's exactly what I wanted it to do. You see, while I was in Spain, I couldn't think of anything but you. I felt like a dupe, you know? A sap. While Franco was taking Catalonia and the Loyalists were giving it to the *Deutschland*, I was completely preoccupied with a woman in New York."

Martha's pencil was flying across the page. I stopped to let her catch up. When she had, she looked up at me with a quizzical expression on her face. "Do you think — this may sound silly — but do you think that Jack hated Elena because he loved her?" she asked tentatively.

"Not exactly," I said. "But there is the line from Pope about one's becoming the thing one most abhors. Well, maybe when Jack found himself thinking about Elena when he should have been thinking about nothing but the Loyalist cause, maybe he resented that — resented the fact that he'd become something of a bourgeois romantic."

"Ah, yes," Martha said, as if a light had just gone on in her brain. "So Elena's speech must have really gotten to him, all that talk about nonmaterial needs."

I nodded. "It probably did," I said. "But you should be careful to remember that Jack MacNeill always believed in his own ideas.

He knew that he could be turned aside by a romantic notion, but only for a little while."

"So he didn't come back to Elena in order to apologize or anything like that?"

"Apologize for what?"

"For his review."

I shook my head. "He never believed *Calliope* was anything but a piece of obscure, breast-thumping nonsense, Martha, and he never took back one word of that review."

Martha nodded, wrote something down in her notebook, and looked back up at me. "So that review — it was not a subconscious effort to destroy Elena as a person?"

I shook my head. "No. It was an attack upon a book Jack felt to be utterly wrong-headed. He felt Elena had betrayed what he no doubt saw as her social duty. He felt that he had spent valuable time in Spain mooning over such a person."

"So he didn't spend his whole life loving Elena?" Martha asked.

"Absolutely not," I told her. "Jack was a very committed man, and when Elena took her interests away from matters of immediate political importance, Jack simply stepped aside." I glanced down at her notes. "Put down in your notebook that Jack MacNeill was as much his own man as Elena was her own woman and you'll be closer to the truth than you would be with any portrait of either one of them pining away for the other." I laughed. "Believe me, they didn't do that."

"Yes, all right," Martha said, accepting my judgment. "But did either one of them learn anything from this — what would you call it — this romance?"

"Elena learned something," I said. "She felt very stupid for getting pregnant, and I think because of that she began to think of her impulsiveness as something dangerous, something that could seriously mislead her."

"But how can you control your own impulsiveness?" Martha asked.

"By using your will," I told her. "And I think that for a while in Elena's life, she believed only in the will."

Even as I said this, however, it seemed to me that there was more to it than that, more to it than simply Elena's severe sense of self-reliance combined, as it was in her, with a deep distrust of her own impulsiveness. No doubt she felt very much alone after Jack left her, and no doubt that loneliness grew as she realized that she was carrying his child. But I also think that for a time she saw the baby as a way out of her dilemma, saw it as the one thing in life she might feel free to love with absolute heedlessness. In her short story "Work of Art," which was written only a week or so before her miscarriage, a connoisseur bestows just this kind of adoration upon an ancient urn because "it is complete in its beauty, flawless beyond particularities, so perfect that it seems unmade. Conceived without reservation, such a work can be loved the more for being mightier than our thought."

I will not say that when the baby died something in my sister died as well. But I do believe that with its loss Elena firmly turned away from those pursuits we term ordinary, and that she never sought them out again.

Thus when Elizabeth returned to New York, as I told Martha that afternoon, she found a friend less pliant than the one she left behind, less indulgent toward weaknesses she did not share, and thus less inclined to abide them patiently.

"Why did Elizabeth come back to the United States?" Martha asked. She was looking at me pointedly, as if there were some darker motivation than the most obvious. There wasn't, and I told her so.

"France fell," I said. "It's as simple as that." I shook my head. "I suppose it's hard now for anyone to imagine how dreadful the collapse of France seemed to us at the time." The very mention of it evoked once again the powerful dread that had seized us with the news. At the time, of course, the most grotesque German abominations had yet to be committed. Still, the fall of France cast a pall over our lives, heralding an unparalleled disaster. The shock was compounded by the images that swept over us, that appalling newsreel footage of Hitler standing on the esplanade of the Palais de Chaillot, leering toward the Left Bank at an Eiffel Tower which seemed, beneath his gaze, terribly naked and vulnerable. This vision of the unspeakable barbarian grinning maliciously within the heart of European culture offended even Harry, who in the beginning had espoused the standard defense of his class, that at least the Nazis had stopped the Communists in their tracks. For the rest of us, however, the invasion of France was merely the latest in a long series of German depredations, and I suppose that even Howard Carlton, standing utterly confused as German troops marched stiffly down the boulevard Saint-Germain, could feel the German noose tightening around him.

"And so they left Paris," I told Martha. "They packed their bags, took a train to Le Havre, and sailed back to New York."

"You met them at the dock?" Martha asked.

"No. They didn't tell us they were in the city right away. I suppose they were busy setting up their new apartment on Bank Street in the Village. Then one afternoon in mid-November Elena's phone rang and it was Elizabeth."

"Was Elena happy to hear from her?"

"Of course. We hadn't received a letter in quite some time. The Germans had entered Paris in June, and Elena hadn't heard a word from Elizabeth. It was a great relief to us all, but especially to Elena. You could hear it in her voice."

Martha looked up from her notebook. "Did she sense anything about Elizabeth?"

"I think she did," I said. "When I asked her how Elizabeth had sounded on the phone, she said that she had sounded just fine. But there was a tension in her voice, as if she were withholding judgment, or maybe just hoping for the best." I shook my head. "Of course, Elena was still rather out of sorts, herself. She had not been able to write anything but short stories since the miscarriage, and almost all of them had to do with some sense of loss or other. I suppose that those short stories are as spiritually autobiographical as anything she ever wrote, other than *New England Maid*. Not one of them is about a miscarriage, but that doesn't matter. The loss is everywhere."

"When did Elena actually see Elizabeth?" Martha asked.

"That same night," I told her.

It was already evening when Elena and I walked across the Village to the Bank Street address Elizabeth had given us. Alexander had been born only six months before, and I remember being preoccupied with various paternal concerns. Completely oblivious to how Elena might feel, I went on and on about my son, detailing his eating and sleeping habits. Still, she seemed to take a certain delight in my fatherhood, and I think that in the end she thought of Alexander as a good deal more than her nephew, particularly after Miriam died. But that evening, of course, it was Elizabeth who was most on her mind.

It was a four-story walkup, and I was winded by the time we reached Elizabeth's apartment on the top floor. Elena was visibly excited as she knocked on the door.

Howard opened it almost immediately. He was dressed in dark flannel pants, a white shirt, and a black suit vest. A cigarette dangled precariously from the corner of his mouth. He took it out by the tips of his fingers, a gesture that was as determinedly Continental as the thin mustache he had grown since we last saw him.

"Oh, it's Thursday," he said. "Elizabeth said you'd be coming on Thursday."

"Yes, it's Thursday, Howard," I told him.

He nodded slowly. He looked as remote as he ever had, his eyes full of the bafflement that pervaded his every mood, no matter how cheerful or downcast.

Elena peeped inside the door. "Is Elizabeth here?"

"Oh, yes, of course," Howard said as he stepped back into the tiny foyer. "Please, come in."

The apartment was small and somewhat cramped, filled with un-packed cartons and scores of canvases wrapped securely in brown paper and twine. There was a large sofa between the two front windows and a few small chairs scattered about. A lamp rested on the windowsill, the bulb beneath the shade shining into the room like a yellow eye.

"We've not really done much to settle in, yet," Howard explained. He glanced down the hallway to the left. "Elizabeth, come out. William and Elena are here."

I could see her coming toward us through the dark hallway. She was dressed in a gray artist's smock, and she looked generally disheveled and somewhat overweight. And yet her face was still quite lovely, though now it possessed only the kind of beauty that Swinburne gave to Faustine, the sort that in hell would be called human.

Elena rushed over to her and drew her into her arms.

"I was so worried about you, Elizabeth," she said. "We didn't know what had happened to you."

Elizabeth nodded. Her skin had a bluish pallor and her eyes were watery. At first I thought she might have had a bout of seasickness on the voyage over, but there was something almost broken in her manner, a distance and withdrawal. As Elena would later describe it to Jason, it was "the look of someone whose soul had drowned."

"I meant to call you before this," Elizabeth said weakly, "but I've been ill."

Elena gathered around her friend like a winter blanket and urged her gently toward the sofa, then eased her down onto it.

"It wasn't good over there, Elena," Elizabeth said. "It wasn't good at all."

"She means her painting," Howard said quickly. He pulled the cigarette from his mouth and crushed it into the glass ashtray in his other hand. "She had an exhibition, you know. At a little gallery in Montmartre." He looked at me. "It didn't go very well. It was really quite depressing for Elizabeth." He shrugged. "The reviews, you know. Very unfortunate."

Elena nestled in closely to Elizabeth and draped one of her arms lightly over her shoulder. "Don't worry about that sort of thing, Elizabeth." She offered a smile. "You're back in New York now. That's all that matters."

Elizabeth nodded tentatively, then stared down at her hands. They were trembling slightly.

"Actually, I'd like to see some of your work, Elizabeth," I said.

She looked up at me languidly, as if she were drugged. "See them? Why?"

"Because they're yours," I told her.

"Yes, good idea," Howard said. He walked over to a stack of paintings leaning against the far wall and began unwrapping them. Elizabeth looked on indifferently.

Howard quickly unveiled several canvases. Elena and I watched as he lifted one after another toward the light. Some were winter scenes. Some were of Paris street life. I recognized one as the gardens of Versailles. All the pictures appeared terribly gray and dreary, as if painted through filmy glass. The faces of the people suggested a kind of stricken panic, rather like those of Edvard Munch, their eyes crazed and sunken, their mouths open in gasps or screams or closed tight in mute horror. Had they been painted by anyone else, I would have dismissed them as too overtly advertising a fashionable despair — the grays too tedious, the black pure melodrama. But they were Elizabeth's, and because of that I marveled at their strangeness, as I'm sure Elena did. For after Howard had finished she turned to Elizabeth and asked her a series of routine questions about color and composition, avoiding the subject of her paintings' leaden mood.

Elizabeth answered quietly but with a shrug, as if her words were no more than table scraps thrown on some alley garbage heap.

"I'm not a painter," she said finally, dismissing any further discussion of her work, her voice rising once again with that older energy she had once possessed in Standhope. It was the last time either Elena or I would hear it.

"Actually," Elena said after a moment, "I was hoping to pry you away from Howard for a while so that just the two of us could spend some time together."

Elizabeth stared down at her hands again and said nothing.

"Not a bad idea, Elizabeth," Howard said. He turned to me. "We had a bright flat in Paris. Not far from the boulevard Raspail. Do you know it?"

I shook my head. "No. I've never been lucky enough to go to Paris."

Howard nodded, almost sadly, as if my misfortune were his own.

Elena continued to watch Elizabeth. "Why don't you come stay with me a few days," she asked urgently. "It would be wonderful to be alone together, just for a while."

Elizabeth looked up at Elena, her eyes listless, her head drifting to the left as if she could not hold it steady. "No. I wouldn't leave Howard alone."

Elena did not press the issue. She simply let it drop, one of those sins of omission which Dorothea Moore, in *Inwardness*, would later come so deeply to regret after her son's death: "Not long after Timon's death, I walked to the Louvre and sat and stared at the *Winged Victory* and thought how contradictory it was, this image of headless triumph, frozen in its broken arrogance, made accidentally great by its absurdity. And it seemed to me that what I had demanded of my son was not unlike this strange piece of sculpture, embodying both the idea and the reality, the dream of ascension and the earthly fall. Might my son have lived, had I brought him here, sat with him under my arm, inspected this shattered stone with him? I know now what I should have said: 'Timon, remain a man of earth, though your mother dreams you heavens.'"

They talked on for a time, Elena trying as much as possible to draw Elizabeth into a lighter mood. She even talked about *Calliope* a bit, describing the furor it had created in various circles. Elizabeth listened quietly but from a certain distance, as if she were listening to a radio report rather than to a friend she had not seen for years.

Elena continued on, however, as if she thought that the sustained sound of her voice might bring back the Elizabeth we both remembered. As she talked, her eyes turned down to Elizabeth's hands, to the trembling that occasionally seized them. And I suppose that it was then that Elena first understood that Elizabeth had sunk into the same disease as her father. There was no brown mug dangling from her hand, nor an assortment of empty bottles. But the physical evidence was in almost everything else about her — the stupor in her eyes, the slow measure of her voice, the swollen quality of her body, its alcoholic bloat.

Elena was still talking, stopping only to ask an occasional question of Elizabeth, when I walked into the kitchen, discreetly tugging Howard along with me. When we were out of earshot, I put the question to him directly.

"What's happened to Elizabeth?" I asked.

Howard's face was a blank page, utterly emotionless. "You might as well know," he said. "She's become something of a drunk."

"Yes, that's quite clear, Howard," I told him. "But why?"

Howard blinked slowly, then bit his lower lip. His voice was dry and flat. "She had this exhibition. She took it hard. They called her names. They said she had no talent."

I looked at him suspiciously. "That's not enough to change Elizabeth into what she is now, Howard."

He shrugged. "There were other things."

"Like what?"

Howard glanced about nervously, then slowly moved his eyes over to me. "I will stay with her, William," he said. "I will not desert her."

"That doesn't answer my question."

Howard drew in a deep breath and leaned against the small refrigerator that chugged ludicrously beside him. He had never looked more agitated.

"In Paris there was no place to get away from it. It was like New York, not Standhope. There was no way to get away from it."

"What are you talking about, Howard?" I asked.

He glanced away. "I took a lover."

It seemed so pedestrian a sin that I actually felt some relief.

Then Howard slowly turned toward me again. "This lover . . . It was a man."

It is difficult to imagine now how shocking such a declaration could seem in 1940. I was staggered by it.

"Elizabeth had to know, of course," Howard added, his finger nervously patting against the top of the refrigerator. "She had to know, you see. She'd already been drinking more than she should have, what with the reception of her work and all, and I guess, well, I guess it just tipped the balance."

I only nodded.

"But I won't leave her, William," he added quickly. "I won't do that." He took another deep breath, then let it out in a quick rush. "I suppose I've always known this . . . my . . . problem." He shook his head. "I don't understand it, William. I never have."

Every impulse in my heart urged me to gather Howard into my arms, but I could not do it. Instead, still aghast at what he had just told me, I abandoned him there in that little kitchen with the chugging refrigerator and strode back into the living room.

Elena glanced up at me as I came in. She forced a smile to her lips. "I've asked Elizabeth to do my portrait," she said.

"I don't do portraits," Elizabeth said, almost coldly.

Elena turned back to her. "What if I begged you," she said, using all her power to keep some lightness in her voice.

Elizabeth said nothing.

"I could come over some afternoon," Elena added quickly.

Howard drifted back into the room, his hands deep in the pockets of his trousers, his face filled with a longing to explain himself once and for all.

It was not an opportunity I felt inclined to give him. "We'd better go now, Elena," I said.

Elena slowly stood up. "All right," she said. Then she looked back at Elizabeth. "Promise me a portrait, Elizabeth."

Elizabeth nodded. "All right, I will," she said quietly.

Two weeks later Elena sat on a small stool as Elizabeth made one attempt after another to sketch her. Elena would later tell Miriam that that afternoon had been one of the saddest of her life. Elizabeth smoked so much that the cramped little studio seemed itself to smolder, and as Elizabeth dismissed one attempt after another a kind of desperation seized her. Her pencil strokes would become more and more violent, until finally she would rush to the bathroom and there, as Elena must have known, take a few quick gulps at the bottle she had hidden beneath the sink.

It was not until late afternoon that the portrait was finished, or at least declared so by Elizabeth, who, Elena said, appeared completely exhausted by the effort. "Her hands were trembling uncontrollably," Elena told me when she came by my apartment that same evening. "She slumped on the sofa and dropped her head into her hands.

Her face was covered with sweat, and she mopped it with her smock. Her hair was wet and matted. She just said, 'There, there, it's finished, take it' and went back to the bathroom again."

Then Elena showed the portrait to Miriam and me. I will never forget the shock of it or the awful emptiness in Elena's face when she displayed it. It was a portrait neither representative nor expressionist, only a hodgepodge of disconnected borrowings chaotically and randomly applied. But as a portrait of Elizabeth's terror, it was powerful enough. The background was a flat gray surface, with Elena's disembodied face floating in it like a ball on grimy water. Her eyebrows were done in bold black strokes and looked more than anything like the crows over van Gogh's field of corn. The eyes seemed lifted almost entirely from Munch's *Evening in Karl Johann Street,* while the surrounding face appeared as little more than strips of color ripped from those sides of beef which obsessed Soutine.

"She's at the very edge, William," Elena said. "What can we do?"

I found that I was as much at a loss as Howard had been two weeks before. "I don't know."

"I'm afraid for her, William," Elena said. "Very afraid."

But as the weeks passed and Elena made more and more attempts to break through to Elizabeth, that fear began to turn to anger. And as surely as Elizabeth had revealed her labyrinthine misery in her portrait of Elena, Elena came to portray her rage and indignation in the short stories she wrote during the long weeks before Elizabeth finally ended all speculation as to her redemption. They are singularly explosive tales of steadily accelerating disintegration and of the frustration of being caught in a situation that is not specific but cosmic and engulfing. In "The Lessons of the Road," a father becomes so indignant at his son's inability to master the rudiments of driving a car that he swerves it off the road, then collapses over the wheel in a fit of weeping while his son looks on, aghast. In "The Deadly Current," a lifeguard warns a young man of a lethal undertow and then finds that he cannot act to save him when the boy heedlessly moves into the deadly waters. And in Elena's most anthologized story, "Our Life Is Lived on Air," a good but deeply wounded doctor so relentlessly attempts to save a patient, and by that means, his honor, that the patient herself becomes exhausted by the treatment and finally dies from a weakness the doctor's tireless therapies have engendered.

By this time, of course, I had long ago told Elena what Howard had confessed to me in the kitchen that first day on Bank Street.

She had received the news somewhat less rigidly than I but with the same sense that it had probably had a devastating effect on Elizabeth. But for my sister, the real problem remained Elizabeth's recovery. She intended to make sure that Elizabeth survived. "No one should be destroyed by one relationship," she told me one evening as she sat in my apartment, Alexander cradled gently in her arms. "Not even one that ends so strangely." And I remember that she looked down at Alexander briefly, then slowly raised her eyes to me. She had a look of great willfulness in her face, as if nothing were beyond her power, as if Elizabeth could be brought back by Elena's effort alone. "I have to find the best way to help her," she said, "and I will."

There can be no doubt, of course, that Elena did try everything in her power to help Elizabeth. For months after Elizabeth's return from France, Elena made it her business to spend as much time as possible with her. Howard was becoming a less visible presence in the Bank Street apartment, and we later learned that he had already taken up with a composer who kept a kind of drug-crazed salon on Sullivan Street.

Thus Elena and Elizabeth had a great deal of time alone. They talked of many things, Elena later told me, but rarely about the most crucial thing: Elizabeth's increasing dependence upon the bottles of Scotch she hid in every conceivable nook and cranny of the apartment, and for which Howard continued to pay, telling Elena that no one should take from Elizabeth the only support she had.

But there can also be no doubt that at a certain point Elena determined to put into practice her sense of the necessity of personal will which had developed into a stringent element of her character. Like Dorothea Moore in *Inwardness*, she "shut out mercy as if it were a winter wind."

It was, in fact, the dead of winter, when she came to her decision. She was at my apartment, seated on the floor, bouncing Alexander playfully about, when suddenly she looked up at me with a thoughtful expression, as if she had been considering what she was about to say for a very long time.

"I think I've been blaming the wrong person for Elizabeth's troubles," she said. "Blaming Howard, when the real problem is Elizabeth."

"In what way?" I asked.

"Elizabeth has to get control of her life," Elena said firmly. "No one can do that for her. She has to do it herself."

"How?"

"Remember that day I brought you over to her house in Standhope? Remember how strong she was?"

"Yes, I remember."

"That's the real Elizabeth."

"I would like to think so."

"Believe me, it is. We need to remember what she had then, all that intelligence and will. That's what we have to appeal to in her."

"Instead of what?"

"Instead of letting her drift," Elena said. I could see her mind working. "And maybe with Howard gone, she's finally vulnerable. We can force the issue, tell her we've had enough."

"You have to be able to make something like that look absolutely real," I said.

"It will be real," Elena said. She stood up. "I'm going to do it now, tonight."

The night was rather dreary. A cold rain fell on us all the way over to Bank Street. Elena walked very briskly. "If this doesn't work, I don't know if there's any hope left for Elizabeth," she said.

"She definitely won't — as they say — take the cure?"

Elena shook her head. "No, I suggested that. Any sanitarium in the world. Elizabeth said no."

We reached Elizabeth's apartment a few minutes later. On the street outside, Elena paused, reconsidering her course of action.

"Elena," I said, "do you want to wait about this?"

She glanced up toward Elizabeth's apartment. "You haven't seen her in a while. She has deteriorated, William. I don't think we have much time."

"I don't know how things ever got this twisted, Elena," I said.

"I don't suppose anyone ever does," Elena said. Then she began walking up the stairs to the apartment, her pace much slower now than it had been on the street, as if with each step she expected to touch off a mine.

We could hear some rustling inside after we knocked at Elizabeth's door.

"She's hiding the bottles," Elena said wearily.

Then the door opened a crack, and Elizabeth's face was illuminated by a narrow band of light.

"Hi," she said weakly.

"William and I thought we'd come over and see how you were

doing," Elena said. There was no false cheerfulness in her voice. It was firm, even cold.

"Oh, okay," Elizabeth said. She stepped back and opened the door. "Come in."

The apartment was completely dark except for one lamp standing on a wobbly base by the window, its black cord dangling across the corner.

Elizabeth tried to smile. "Maybe you'd like something to eat?"

"No, thanks," Elena said.

Elizabeth nodded slowly. She was standing in the shadows, wearing that same gray painter's smock she'd had on the first day we had come here. She was nervously pinching at it, unable to move, waiting for direction.

"Well," she said finally, "why don't you sit down."

The apartment was bare except for two spindly wooden chairs which faced the sofa. There were ashtrays strewn everywhere — on the floor, the window ledge, the small table in front of the sofa. The entire place smelled like a cigarette which had been dipped in cheap whiskey.

Elizabeth glanced about the room. "They took the phone out," she said.

Elena and I sat down on the two chairs.

"William and I have come to talk to you very seriously, Elizabeth," she said.

Elizabeth looked up expectantly. "You know where Howard is?"

"No, we don't."

"He said he might come back."

Elena leaned forward, folding one of her hands in the fist of the other. "Elizabeth, you're in serious trouble. You need help."

Elizabeth nodded obliviously. "He was going to have the phone put back in."

"William and I have come to tell you that we will do everything we can to help you, but that you have to help us, too. You have to try to come out of this, Elizabeth."

"But, Howard . . ."

"Forget about Howard," Elena blurted out. "Forget about him." The anger in her voice was unmistakable, and even Elizabeth heard it.

"But he's . . . he's . . ."

"He's gone, Elizabeth," Elena said. "He's gone and he's not coming back."

It struck me, even then, that this was a lie, that Elena intended to isolate Elizabeth entirely, to convince her that she was utterly alone, and then hope that from that abyss she would return herself.

"Now listen, Elizabeth," Elena said. "We can move you someplace. Howard is not coming back. There's no need for you to stay here."

I sat watching Elena's plot unfold. She intended to make Elizabeth decide once and for all to do something on her own, to leave the apartment forever, and Howard and her bottles with it.

"William and I have a place for you," Elena said. "But we're not going to force you to go there. You can stay here by yourself if you want to."

Elizabeth turned toward the lamp, then raised her hand shakily to shield her eyes from its light.

"Howard is through with you, Elizabeth," Elena said brutally. "And I'll tell you this, if you don't come with William and me, we're through with you, too."

Elizabeth rubbed her eyes with her fists. "Maybe in the morning, when it's light. It's dark now, you know?"

"No, Elizabeth," Elena said, her voice as hard as steel on steel. "Now. Or never."

Tears began rolling down Elizabeth's cheeks. "It's too dark, Elena."

Elena's eyes grew strangely lifeless. "Now. Or I'm finished with you."

Elizabeth's head dropped forward and she wiped her eyes with the hem of the smock. She started to speak, but her voice trailed off in a low, repetitive whimper.

Elena stood up. "I've heard enough whining," she said. Then she turned those terribly remote eyes on me. "Haven't you, William?"

It was all acting of a desperate kind, and I could tell that she was having to use every ounce of strength within her to keep up this awful show. Still, even knowing that, her manner was shocking in its severity.

"Haven't you, William?" she repeated coldly, staring at me with a frightening sternness.

"Yes," I said weakly. I slowly got to my feet.

"Good-by, Elizabeth," Elena said. Then she turned and left the room. I followed behind like a stunned puppy, closing the door behind me. We walked down the stairs and out onto the street.

"That was quite a performance," I said.

Elena looked very shaken.

I draped my arm over her shoulder. "Maybe it'll work, Elena," I said. "Anyway, let's go back to my apartment. It's getting cold out here."

I gently began to urge her forward, when I heard a sound from above, a screech, as if a window had been thrown open overhead. Elena heard it, too, and we both turned back toward the apartment and looked up.

"Oh, God!" Elena cried.

Elizabeth was standing on the ledge above us, the wind billowing out her smock. She had stretched out her arms and was calling down to us. "All right," she screamed. "All right!" For an instant she seemed to hold herself firmly against the wall. Then she tumbled forward, her arms still outstretched, as though she had intended to take flight. She had turned over the lamp while crawling out the window and the cord had wrapped around her ankle. For the briefest moment it held her suspended from the window, and I saw Elena's hand fly up and hold in midair, her fingers stretched out toward Elizabeth as she dangled overhead. Then the cord released her and she fell.

We ran over to her, and Elena gathered her into her arms while I ran for help. She was still alive when the ambulance from St. Vincent's arrived a few minutes later. She was groaning softly, but she never spoke. Both Elena and I rode with her in the ambulance. Elena kneeled by the stretcher, clutching Elizabeth's head to her breast, her face so completely stricken that it seemed almost to lose its human quality, to take on an animal panic. Elizabeth continued to moan softly while the siren blared overhead. Then, only a block or so from St. Vincent's, the groaning stopped and she sank into a coma.

At the hospital she was wheeled quickly into the emergency operating room, while Elena and I continued to stand rigidly beside the ambulance. In the rain, I suppose, we looked like two rusty posts. After that, for what was probably several hours, we wandered about the hospital corridors or down the dark, wet streets of the surrounding neighborhood.

Toward dawn, Elizabeth was brought to a small, cramped room on the third floor. She was being monitored closely, a young doctor told us, and no one could be allowed to see her. Elena asked if she had regained consciousness, and the doctor shook his head in a desultory manner, as if such questions were no longer relevant. Two hours later, she died.

It was late in the afternoon when Martha asked me her question, but the morning storm had not abated. The wind still rocked the large windows, the clouds still hung heavily above.

Martha glanced up from her notebook. "Would you say, William, that Elena was tormented by Elizabeth's death, that she was tormented by guilt?"

"I would say that she was shaken by it," I told her. "I would say that she was profoundly saddened, of course. But tormented? I don't think so."

"Could you elaborate on that?" Martha asked immediately.

"Well, Elena felt that in forcing the issue with Elizabeth, she had made a mistake, had misjudged Elizabeth's weakness, and that this misjudgment had, in effect, caused Elizabeth's death."

"Isn't that guilt?" Martha asked.

"It might have been, if Elena had felt that she had done something wrong. But she didn't. She told me years later that she had done the best she could under the circumstances, that she had trusted her intelligence and that it had failed her. She had, she said, trusted her own perception of what Elizabeth could stand, and that she had misperceived to a tragic degree."

"It sounds either like guilt, William," Martha said, "or a neat way to sidestep it."

I smiled. "My sister felt betrayed, Martha, by her own intelligence."

Martha narrowed her eyes. "Wait a minute. Let me get this straight. You're telling me that Elena blamed her *mind* for what happened to Elizabeth?"

"Blamed herself for trusting it," I said.

"But that's like saying that her mind was separate from the rest of her," Martha protested.

"That tired old dualism, yes," I admitted. "But you have to understand that for Elena it was very important. It wasn't just a matter of looking for the mind's objectivity, it was a matter of looking into its capacity to form reliable moral judgments." I walked to the bookshelf across the room, took *Inwardness* down from it, and returned to my seat. "Listen to this, Martha," I said. I opened the book and read a passage from it: " 'I wanted my son to be brave and thought him cowardly, never recognizing that in standing up to me he was using all the courage he had. I wanted him to love the shape of things, but he admired their function, which was to him a shape of the most exquisite beauty. Give him possession of some ancient gold medallion and he would melt it down to make a spoon. He knew that what endures should equally sustain, that Mayan cups were loveliest when they brought water to a human mouth. Timon, your understanding was beautiful not because it was rare, but because it is silently affirmed by every human life.' "

I closed the book and looked up at Martha. "*Inwardness* is the story of a mother who relentlessly drives her son toward intellectual achievement, drives him so hard that, in a sense, she contributes to his death."

"Which is a little like saying that Dorothea Moore is Elena and that Timon is Elizabeth," Martha said authoritatively.

"It could be seen like that if the novel were nothing more than the action it presents," I told her. "But it is really about something else — about a woman's search for the intellectual foundations of moral certainty."

Martha nodded quickly, then wrote it down. When she had finished she looked up at me. "Go on, William."

"There's another line that's pretty important, I think," I said. " 'One must move inward by an outward thrust.' "

Martha looked puzzled.

"It took Elena a long time to realize what she had to do," I said, "that is, to realize that she had to separate herself from the rest of us for a while." I glanced up at the portrait of my sister Elizabeth had sketched. Elena had always insisted that it be hung conspicuously, usually in the front room of any place she lived.

Martha held her pencil bolt upright on her page. "You were saying that it took Elena a long time to realize that she had to separate from you, and others," she said. "Do you mean go to Europe?"

"Yes," I said. "It took her quite some time to make that decision." I regarded the portrait again, that vision of my sister as a mind adrift. "And I suppose, Martha, that it required another death."

* * *

He was found by the maid, lying face up on his bed, fully clothed, even down to his socks and shoes. There was a towel wrapped around his shoulder which was slightly stained with black. There was a bottle of dye on the bathroom sink. My father had just completed another of his deceptions, concealing his gray hair.

Since the owner of the hotel did not know that my father preferred his daughter to his son, he called me with the news, selecting the male named Franklin in my father's address book, rather than the female one. His voice was shaky.

"I'd like to speak with Mr. Billy Franklin," he said.

"I'm William Franklin."

"Are you related to Harry Franklin, the salesman?"

"I'm his son."

There was a pause, then he continued.

"Well, I've got some bad news, I'm afraid. Mr. Franklin died last night. Sorry. We found him this morning. He's at the hotel where he's been living for a few years. I guess you know that. So, you want to come down and get him, or what?"

He might have continued in this manner for some time had I not stopped him abruptly. "Call the nearest funeral director," I instructed him. "Tell them to come and get the body. I'll be by your hotel this afternoon to make the rest of the arrangements."

I decided to take the train over to Elena's apartment rather than telephone her with the news. When she opened the door she was dressed in blue slacks and a brown wool sweater with a thick broad collar. I had not seen her for two weeks, and she seemed to have made one of those little leaps in time, looking suddenly older than she had only days before. There were small creases at the sides of her eyes now, and her voice sounded just a half tone deeper.

"Just happened to be in the neighborhood, William?" she asked.

"Father died last night, Elena," I told her.

I expected her to collapse. I even began to stretch my arms toward her, as if anticipating her fall. There was no need.

She stepped back from the door. "The last few times I saw him, he mentioned that he was ill." She shook her head. "I guess I've been expecting this for a long time." She turned and walked into the living room. It was very disheveled, the chairs strewn with books and papers. The fronds of her hanging fern were dried to a rusty brown. The whole apartment looked like something out of Dickens, cluttered with eccentric mementos, my sister a scholarly Miss Havisham.

I plucked one of the leaves from the fern. It was so dry it practically turned to powder in my hand. I smiled lamely. "You have to water these things, Elena."

She had taken a seat in one of those beach chairs which Jack had given her long ago and which she had placed in the living room as if it were a chaise longue. She was pulling at her lower lip, her face calm and thoughtful.

I shrugged. "I can't pretend that he meant as much to me as he did to you."

Elena looked at me closely, as if studying my expression.

"You never cared for him at all, did you?" she asked.

"No."

"You begrudged him his life."

"I begrudged him his selfishness, Elena. Does that strike you as cruel?"

"It strikes me as banal."

I looked away. "I don't think there's any need to go into what I thought about our father."

Elena nodded. "All right, William," she said wearily. "What do you want to do?"

"Bury him, of course," I said dryly. "But where?"

"He wanted to be buried at the Mystic seaport, in Connecticut," Elena said.

"All right."

"Somewhere near Route One," she added.

I couldn't help it. I laughed out loud. "Are you serious?"

"That's what he told me," Elena said quietly. "He meant it seriously." She took a deep breath, then got to her feet. "Well, there's no need to wait around here discussing things. We have to go up to Mystic."

We borrowed a car from Joe Tully, one of those Chevy Blackout Coupés with a wooden bumper and no chrome at all. It was the late fall of 1942. We were at war, of course, and the signs of it were all about. Huge posters everywhere proclaimed the vigor of our patriotism. There were always knots of men hanging around the recruiting stations, and Fifth Avenue looked like an enormous hall of flags. Harry had already shipped out for the Pacific, and in the densely packed Selective Service station on lower Broadway it had been discovered that I had a precariously beating heart.

None of the trappings of such momentous times seemed very important the morning Elena and I left for Mystic, however. Miriam waved good-by from the stoop of our apartment, my ailing son perched on her hip. Then it was just Elena and me, heading out of the city and then up through Connecticut on that same road our father had driven so many times. It was a long drive, and for the most part a silent one. Elena sat quietly in the passenger seat, glancing at a hill or inlet from time to time.

We arrived late in the afternoon. The sun was already going down over the bay. It could hardly have been more beautiful: a swath of bright red, rising as if from the sea itself, spread out across the entire sky in seamlessly fading tones.

"Not a bad place to die, Elena," I said quietly as we began walking toward the hotel.

It was a small wooden structure with a porch that dropped to the right. It was painted light blue with a lavender trim, but despite the relatively gay colors, it looked worn and frazzled, much like the old people who sat listlessly in its tiny lobby. In such a weary galaxy my father must have been a blazing meteor. It became clear that he was beloved by the other residents as a lively, sporting figure, ribald as an old artillery officer, yet cultured, as one of them said, "like a retired actor, or something like that." He had told them whopping lies and they had adored him for it.

His body was still stretched out on the bed, but the owner, a small, bespeckled man whom the tenants called Mouse, had had the decency to cover it with a simple white sheet from which protruded at one end my father's neatly polished shoes and at the other his neatly polished hair.

I could hear Elena catch her breath when she saw him.

"I'll leave you two with him," Mouse said delicately as he shrank out the door.

"Well, there's the end of the tale," I said, glancing at my father wearily.

Elena looked at me coldly. "Why don't you try to respect him just a little, William."

I nodded. "Sorry."

She walked to the window and stared out at the port. A small sea breeze rustled her hair.

"Well, what do we do now?" I asked.

She did not turn around. "Go down and see if the owner has contacted a local funeral director."

"He has."

"Then why didn't they pick up the body?"

"He thought we might want them to wait. I think he's scared out of his mind that he's going to get sued for all this somehow. He's being very cautious."

Elena was still facing the water, half her body outlined by its dark blue background. "Have them come and pick him up, then," she said.

I walked downstairs and made the call. Within a few minutes they had come and bundled my father's body into a small station wagon which had been done over to resemble a hearse. As the car pulled away, I asked Mouse if there was a cemetery nearby from which the deceased could at least hear the traffic along Route 1. He looked at me as if I were an escapee from a madhouse. "There's one just up the road," he said, then retreated quickly into his quarters, no doubt carefully locking the door behind him.

Elena and I drove to it. It was a typical old New England cemetery, with a certain dignified modesty, the stones rather small and appropriately gray. From a distance, the cars along Route 1 could be heard as they swept north and south, headed for Boston or New York.

"It will do," Elena said. Then she walked slowly back to the car.

We made the arrangement the next morning, and on the following afternoon Elena and I buried our father after a quiet chapel ceremony which most of the people from his hotel attended. They sat soberly, staring at his coffin, and disappeared immediately after it was put into the ground.

For a time after they had left, Elena and I continued to linger by the grave. Elena leaned against a tree and stared gently at the freshly turned earth. I walked about at some distance, anxious to return to New York.

"Are you ready to leave now?" I asked finally.

Elena nodded but said nothing. Her grief was like black netting over her face. I could not share it. My father had always seemed to me a kind of clown, his life a parody of the person he should have been.

"You know, Elena," I said as we made our way back to the car, "he may have run up some debts around here. Perhaps we should check on that."

Elena continued to walk stiffly beside me. "He paid his bills, William."

"Outside the hotel, I mean. He could have stiffed the local grocer, something like that."

Suddenly Elena wheeled around and slapped my face with such extraordinary force that I stumbled backward.

"You have no right to talk about him like that!" she screamed.

I was thunderstruck. "For God's sake, Elena!"

She swung at me again. I dodged out of the way and stepped around her. "Stop it!"

"He didn't love you, William," she shouted. "So what? He didn't have to!" She lunged at me again, although with much less force than before, a kind of half swing, meant more to demonstrate her fury than to complete a blow.

"Now stop this!" I shouted. "For God's sake, what's the matter with you?"

She made a final swipe, her face red and her eyes filling with tears. I stepped forward and pulled her to me, holding her tightly while she sobbed.

"I'm sorry, Elena," I said softly. "Forgive me."

I felt her nod slowly against my shoulder.

Then I started crying, too, and the two of us slumped to the ground, gathered in each other's arms.

I don't know how long we stayed there. It might have been a half hour, it might have been much less. We finally struggled to our feet, however, and walked to the car, still clutching at each other as if afraid to let go.

Elena was very subdued on the drive home. She had been that way since Elizabeth's death. I suppose I hoped that her sudden outburst might have relieved her somewhat, washed away a portion of her accumulated grief, as if memory were a film of dust.

But such was not the case, and for the few years that remained until the end of the war, Elena held to her solemn mood. She visited Miriam and me often, of course, and she took great delight in watching Alexander develop from an infant into a child. But for all this, she remained steadfastly inward, wholly apart from the enthusiasms of the home front. She helped Joe Tully in his various antifascist activities and on two occasions spoke on the same platform with Jack MacNeill. Under Miriam's urging, she even wrote an anti-Nazi screenplay, but it was so talky and convoluted no producer would touch it.

In 1944, and after many false starts, Elena began another novel. Over dinner at my apartment, she stated her intention to write "something very quiet."

She worked steadily during the next year, and from time to time, while having a drink or taking a walk, she would detail certain aspects of what she called "the project." Bit by bit it emerged as a utopian novel of very curious intent. Rather than dealing with social and economic issues, Elena's novel would attempt to portray a world in which the mind had come to its perfection. Matters of material importance — the distribution of goods, for example, or questions having to do with the division of labor — would have no place in this work at all. Nor would there be any discussion of such ordinary concerns as family structure or sexual relations. "What I want to do," she told Miriam one afternoon as she sat across from her desk at Parnassus, "is describe a people who have, in fact, brought their minds to completion."

By February 1946 Elena had found a title, *The Inland Road*, but it was also clear that by that time she had found little else. In draft after draft, the book eluded her. Ideas came and went, and those which seemed firm at the point of inquiry dissolved under the flimsiest examination. Still, she kept at it, endlessly rethinking and rewriting until the book itself began to resemble, as she said in a 1975 interview, "a black funnel which simply whirled about in my head with no real substance whatsoever, just voices and shadows, nothing more." In the end she saved only a line or two from the entire manuscript, and these she typed out on a single piece of paper which she put in her desk and which remained there, in a plain Manila envelope, until the day she died.

I pulled that envelope out and brought it back to my chair while Martha looked at me warily, her face framed by the storm which continued to beat at the large window behind her.

"I think this may give you an insight or two, Martha," I told her.

"Into what?" Martha asked.

"Well, you're curious about Elena's leaving the country," I said. "I think, in part, this supplies an answer."

"But I already have an answer," Martha said. "You, yourself, have talked about all the sad things that happened to her from 1939 to 1946. I mean, Elizabeth's death primarily, but also your father's."

"But there's also this." I pulled the single sheet of paper from the envelope and read for the first time in almost forty years those two lines Elena had saved. They expressed, as clearly as she could state it, her final sense of what the people who lived along the inland road were like:

Close decorum they called love;
And learned judgment they called God.

I handed the paper to Martha, who read it slowly several times, then looked up at me.

"Well, I have to say, William," she said, "that I don't quite get the point."

"Elena left the United States in order to become like one of those people on the inland road," I said. "She left in order to become a person of learned judgment. She needed to get away in order to find that close decorum she required in her personal relations and which only distance could give her at that time."

Martha stared at me, positively stunned. A gust of wind hit the window to her left and she glanced toward it, held her gaze there for several seconds, then turned back to me. "Are you saying, William, that Elena didn't go to Paris because of all the tragedy that had occurred around her during the war?"

"Absolutely."

She looked at me doubtfully. "How do you know?"

"Because the look on her face the day she left for France was exactly the same look she would get each time she began a new short story or essay or novel."

Martha readied her pen on the page. "How did she look?"

"She looked like freedom, Martha," I said. "I can't be more specific than that. She just looked like freedom. Not excited or jubilant or full of mission. Not particularly solemn, and certainly not sad."

"Freedom," Martha muttered to herself as she wrote it down.

Elena left for Paris in the fall of 1947. I stood on the dock with Alexander crying in my arms and Miriam to my left and Sam to my right, looking vaguely disgruntled. "She'll become one of those goddamn Frenchified writers," he said gloomily, "just wait and see." He looked up at Elena, who was waving down at us from the passenger deck of the *De Grasse*. Four years later, when *Inwardness* arrived on his desk, he read it immediately and found his worst fears realized. "This goddamn thing's too cerebral," he said, thrusting the manuscript at me. "Too brainy. What's Elena doing over there, chitchatting with those Existentialist creeps at the Coupole?" He shook his head. "She's lost her edge, William. There's no bite in this book. Hell, it reads like one long pout." He never changed his mind about *Inwardness*, but he published it anyway and was amazed by its success.

But on the day she left, I would not have predicted that she would write anything in France.

"I hope Elena finds what she's looking for," I said as the ship drew away from us.

She landed at Le Havre, then practically followed the Seine to Paris, arriving there during the first week of November 1947. When Martha asked me whether or not Elena understood much about the political and social atmosphere of France at this time, I answered that I simply did not know. The political turmoil in Paris before the war had diminished during the long sleep of the German occupation. Then, with liberation, there had been a flurry of revenge against those who had collaborated with the Nazi regime. In her letters, Elena spoke with some familiarity of this recent history, commenting on the execution of Brassilach, which had occurred almost two years before, and then of the suicide of Brieu La Rochelle. She wrote of these people as if I should have known who they were, which, at the time, I did not, and her conversant knowledge of such events suggested that she had taken the time to learn about the France in which she now resided and that the moral questions involved in collaboration were of particular interest to her. In *Inwardness*, Dorothea Moore discusses the moral terror of occupied Paris more than once, and I think that the whole issue of principle versus expediency, which was so central to the literary collaboration of the Left Bank, preoccupied my sister and to some extent provided the atmosphere surrounding the more isolated question of Timon's death.

I did not see her for almost two years, although we wrote quite often, an exchange of varying quality. The letters seem to me now somewhat gossipy. Sam was having a torrid love affair during the first of those years, and more than a little space was dedicated to it. There was a bit of the travelogue, too, with Elena expounding on the various beauties of Paris. She visited Normandy and the Loire Valley, and there were chatty letters on these excursions. Once Elena saw Malraux at Deux Magots, and Sartre and Simone de Beauvoir seemed forever holed up in the basement bar of the Pont-Royal Hotel. Elena duly reported these auspicious sightings, but she never approached any of the literary lights of Paris, even though all her work had by then been translated into French and she had probably gained a small following of her own.

In the fall of 1949, I published *The Crossbow and the Lyre*, subtitled *The Romance of the Anglo-Saxon*. It was well received, attracting even sufficient notice to garner an invitation to a symposium on European literature which was to be held at the Sorbonne in Paris. I accepted, of course, and so in April 1950 I came to Europe for the first time and met my sister within the shadow of the Arc de Triomphe.

For some women, I suppose, the moment of supreme command comes while they are still in their teens, when their bodies shine with that incandescent beauty which only older eyes know to be almost instantly disappearing. For others, like Miriam, it comes when they are in their mid-twenties, when the last girlish effect flows imperceptibly into the flourish of completed womanhood. But for my sister, it came when she reached forty, and that glory, coming late, seemed all the more miraculous. She was dressed in a black skirt which fell almost to her ankles, and a white blouse, plain except for a ruffle of lace at the collar and the ends of the sleeves. A short black jacket with padded shoulders covered the blouse, and at her throat she wore a small cameo held by a black velvet band. She was carrying a burgundy handbag with a long strap. She smiled when she saw me, her eyes shining brightly under a pair of slender gold-rimmed glasses.

"Ah, William," she said softly as she pulled me into her arms.

For a moment we stood there, unable to separate, two strangely clinging figures holding to each other in the Tuileries Gardens, Elena's back to the Louvre, mine to the grandeur of the Place de la Concorde.

"I can't believe it's been three years," I said finally.

Elena pushed back a wayward strand of hair. "Too long," she said. Then she smiled and offered me her hand. "Come, let's stroll in the Tuileries."

"I like the glasses," I said as we began to walk together. "They make you look —"

"I know," Elena interrupted, "like a man. Distinguished."

I shook my head. "No, like a woman." I smiled. "Nobly planned, to warn, to comfort, and command."

"And that's from?"

"Wordsworth."

Elena squeezed my hand. "Would you like to see where I live?"

"If we can walk there," I said. "I want to see the city."

That afternoon she took me along one of the world's most scenic routes, and on those days now when I sit out on Elena's small porch and watch the sailboats glide along the bay and try to remember Elena at a moment of particular pleasure, I remember, along with others, that afternoon we strolled out of the Tuileries, down the quai du Louvre, and then along the Seine until we reached the great white façade of the Hôtel de Ville.

"I live in that direction," she said pointing to the right, toward an island in the middle of the river. "The spires you see just over the buildings, that's Notre-Dame."

We walked across the Pont d'Arcole and over to Notre-Dame, then into the garden behind it and across the small bridge to the Île Saint-Louis. Elena had an apartment on the quai d'Anjou.

"They say you live here," she told me, "if you can't decide between the Left Bank and the Right."

It was a small apartment, but adequate, with a tiny kitchenette and a separate narrow bedroom. It was stuffed with books, some of them in French, but most in English, most of them by Americans. Perhaps, even then, *Quality* was formulating itself in my sister's mind.

She had a small wooden desk where she kept her typewriter. From the window beside it, one could see the Seine flowing slowly by and beyond it the wall of graceful buildings that made up the Right Bank.

"It's very beautiful here," I said.

"Very different from New York."

"It's not as gray," I said casually. "It seems smaller. It doesn't have New York's . . . what would you call it? New York's monumentality."

Elena nodded.

"You don't feel as dwarfed," I added. "Paris doesn't look as if it's all about to fall on top of you, the way New York does."

Elena nodded again, rather listlessly, no more than polite under the barrage of my tourist's patter.

Finally I ran out of things to say. I could not hold back any longer. "Elena," I said, "when are you coming home?"

Elena removed her glasses and placed them on the desk beside the typewriter. "I don't know, William."

"You're not thinking of becoming a French national, are you?"

Elena shook her head. "No. One does not become French the way one becomes American. You can't just have some bureaucrat sign a paper, any more than you could become Jewish that way."

"So you will be coming back to the United States at some time?" I asked tentatively.

"I really don't know, William," Elena said. Then she stood up and went into the kitchen. She returned with a bottle of wine. "Shall we make a toast?"

"I don't mean to press you on this." I smiled. "It's just that we miss you, Elena. Especially me. I miss you."

"I feel the same way," Elena said. "But I still have some thinking to do." She uncorked the wine and poured each of us a glass. Then she lifted hers. "To a precious reunion," she said.

I touched my glass to hers. "Yes."

More than any place she had ever lived, Elena's Paris apartment seemed fully to represent her. The walls were bare except for a few paintings, which she probably had purchased from some sidewalk exhibition. A radio sat precariously on a small table in one corner, and near the fireplace was a large wing chair, clearly too large for taste but just right for comfort. A lamp stood beside it, the bulb shielded by a plain white shade. Beside the chair was a square wooden box filled almost to the top with manuscript pages.

I nodded toward it. "The new book?"

"Something I'm working on. A novel."

"Set in Paris?"

Elena shook her head. "Only partly." She took a sip from her glass, glanced out the window, her eyes following a barge as it made its way down the Seine, then turned back to me. "There's a darker side to nostalgia," she said. "Remembering the unrightable wrong."

I had no doubt that she was referring to Elizabeth. Her face was not drawn or strained; nor did she seem particularly distressed by this sudden allusion to the unfortunate circumstances that had finally culminated in Elizabeth's fall from the window.

"Do you think about her often?" I asked, almost casually.

Elena nodded. "I think about the situation, more than anything else. I don't just think about Elizabeth, and I certainly don't see that night over and over again in my mind. It's not like that." For a moment she searched for the words. "I think about the proper way something like this should be thought about. I'm curious about how the mind reacts to such circumstances. We tend to call such a response either guilt or indifference. But there's a great deal in between those two."

"Yes, I suppose so," I said. I took another sip from my glass, a gesture that seemed almost whimsical compared to the somberness that had overtaken my sister.

She looked at me seriously. "How about you, William? Do you think about Elizabeth very much?"

"Sometimes," I said. "I'm not overcome by it. I suppose I feel, well, just a kind of general sadness, perhaps a sense of waste."

Elena was watching me steadily. It was the sort of gaze that had always made me uncomfortable, as if my sister expected more than I could give and felt a kind of sober regret that I was both so limited, which was one thing, and so unconcerned by those limits, which was quite another. Elena did not expect you to answer her questions, as Jason wrote in his memoir, but she expected you to share them. When you did not, she could not wholly conceal her disappointment — the marathoner's regret for the short-distance runner.

I took another sip of wine, dodging behind my glass like a thief around a corner. "Well, so you're writing about Elizabeth, then?"

"Not exactly," Elena said. She seemed reluctant to go further. Finally she added, "But I think it has to do with Elizabeth, with certain questions her death brings to mind."

"Like what?"

Again Elena hesitated. She glanced once more toward the window, but this time her eyes did not linger there. "Do you believe in God, William?"

"No."

"When did you stop believing in Him?"

"I don't know." I shrugged. "Our household was not exactly what you would call religious."

"But the atmosphere in Standhope was somewhat religious. Everyone believed in God."

"I guess they did. What are you getting at?"

"Well, there must have been a moment when you suddenly said to yourself, as I did somewhere along the way, all right, there is no God."

"There probably was such a moment."

"Now, suppose something happened and you also came to say something else, if only inwardly, if only to yourself."

"Say what?"

"Say, all right, there is no meaning."

I shook my head. "You'd have to turn away from that sort of conclusion, Elena."

"Because you couldn't live with it?"

"Not happily."

"I'm not talking about living happily. I am talking about living at all."

"Are you asking me if I think there is any meaning in life, Elena?" I asked. Then I laughed. "That question is so grand that it is juvenile, the sort of thing one hears in freshman philosophy classes."

"Yes, that's true," Elena said. "But suppose you confronted a situation in which you had to be reborn morally, had to construct a moral world from the ground up. What would you rely upon to tell you what to do?"

"Experience. Learning. Who knows?"

Elena nodded. "All those things, of course," she said. "But how would they be put together? What would be emphasized? Which perceptions could be trusted as being objective? Where, in the end, does the mind meet the conscience?"

I wagged my finger at her. "You know, Sam warned me that the French air would get to you," I said, "that you'd end up in some cloudy philosophical mist and never write another word an American could understand."

The lightness of my remark seemed to pull Elena up short, almost as if she had taken it as a form of gentle scolding, the old professor warning his bright young undergraduate student away from mighty themes. She straightened herself slightly in her chair and crossed her legs.

"How is Sam, anyway?" she asked.

"He's so busy running the business of publishing that he hardly ever reads a book," I said. "Miriam's the senior editor now, and Sam even tacked a vice-presidency to her title."

Elena stared at me silently. Her eyes had a way of moving over you, as if molding your features as she looked at them, like a sculptor's fingers structuring the clay.

"Elena," I said, "I didn't mean to be dismissive about the things you were discussing."

"That's all right," Elena said. She smiled. "Where would you like to eat tonight?"

She never returned to the larger questions that were uppermost in her mind that afternoon and probably had been uppermost for quite some time. Instead we talked of Miriam and Alexander, Mary and Sam and Jack MacNeill. She even asked about Joe Tully. She did not mention her book again, and before we left for dinner that evening she gathered up the little box with its manuscript and tucked it into a drawer beneath her desk. I would hear no more of it until it arrived on Miriam's desk almost two years later.

We walked from Elena's apartment to the Left Bank, and in the Paris twilight, she pointed out the sights: the offices of Gallimard, her French publisher; the cafés Hemingway had made famous, the apartment of André Gide, Rodin's *Balzac*, standing in the open on a little island in the boulevard Raspail, as if it were of no more importance than a public fountain.

"I think I love Paris," I said.

Elena smiled. "Julien says that all men love Paris but the Scots."

I turned to her instantly. "Julien?"

"You will meet him," Elena said, and added nothing else.

She didn't have to, for in only a few minutes we were all sitting in the small restaurant Elena had selected near the Odéon. He was tall and rather somber, one of Elena's perennial older men, the only sort to whom, I think, she was ever really attracted after she had grown too old for Jack and for all his kind. He was wearing a plain dark suit to which he added absolutely nothing, not so much as a tip of handkerchief peeping from his pocket. He was almost entirely gray, but his face seemed somewhat younger, though plainly weathered, a bit by time, and as it turned out, a great deal by circumstance. To say the very least, he was charming, modest, soft spoken, his voice always whispery, as if insisting that no great importance should be attached to the things he said. He had a very slight French accent, but otherwise his English was impeccable. He even used the subjunctive correctly and was quite careful, even in conversation, that his infinitives not be split.

His full name was Julien Tavernier, and he had been a journalist before the war. After the Occupation, his newspaper had come under the editorial control of the Germans. Under such conditions, he had refused to continue in its employment. A rival at the paper had been discreetly informed on him, and he had been picked up by the police. Though not particularly political, he had been suspected of Communist sympathies, and during the first few days of his detention he had been tortured.

"It is an odd thing, torture," he said, rather matter-of-factly, later in the evening. "You're in a room, you see, and things are being done to you that are illegal. But since the mind is slow in understanding sudden changes in reality, you wait for some officer to enter the interrogation room. You know this will happen. You even know what this person will look like. He will be in uniform, with many medals. He will look about, scowling, and he will say; 'What is this? This is an outrage! This is not Turkey, gentlemen, this is France! Release this man at once.'" He smiled and took a draw on his cigarette. "And do you know, this does happen. This man of dreams comes into the room; he is in uniform with the medals. He does look about, and he is scowling, and he says, 'You are going too slowly. You must step up the procedure. We must have an answer from this pig by nightfall.'" He crushed his cigarette into the small glass ashtray on the table and laughed.

Still later he spoke of his first marriage, which had been a disaster. "My wife and I did not care for one another," he said, smiling delicately at Elena. "This made divorce thinkable. We did not have children, which made it relatively harmless. And we were not Catholics, which made it possible."

Through it all, Elena listened quietly, sometimes adding a comment of some sort, to which Julien usually gave immediate assent. Once she spoke at some length on the particular difficulties of expatriation, and Julien listened attentively, at times adding an opposing view, with the patience of the native before the alien's distress. "Your complaints are quite subtle, Elena," he said finally. "Usually Americans are most bitterly affronted by the harsh flavor of our cigarettes."

After dinner we found a sidewalk café and sat sipping drinks, while the traffic whirled down boulevard Montparnasse. Julien mentioned those more distant attractions which the fearful, nervous tourist might miss: Balzac's house in Passy, the tombs of the distinguished dead at Père Lachaise. "You should not spend all your time in the Louvre," he said. "It's a great palace, but a poor museum." He waved his hand. "And forget about Napoleon's tomb. All that dark marble. It is appropriate for an megalomaniac but most unsuitable for a man."

He shook his head. "Walk the streets. There, you will find Paris."

It was almost midnight before we left the café. I expected to take a taxi back to my hotel, but Julien put his hand on my shoulder as we walked down the boulevard and brought the three of us to a halt. He looked at Elena.

"Perhaps we should drive up to Montmartre," he said. "See the lights of Paris from the steps of Sacré-Coeur." He turned to me. "Would that please you, William?"

"Very much."

"Then it shall be done."

It took only a few minutes to traverse the city. I sat in the back seat of the car and listened as Julien and Elena pointed out various attractions. Then we made our ascent up the highest hill of Paris and parked under the dome of the basilica.

"You can see the entire city from here," Julien said as he got out of the car.

For a time the three of us stood staring down at the Paris lights. It was very quiet and it was very beautiful.

"I once thought of Paris as changeless, as immortal," Julien said softly, gazing out over the sea of rooftops. "And then the Germans came, and it was transformed into an evil city." He looked at Elena. "It cannot be reclaimed now. Not after the deportations. It has lost its virtue. Even the light is different. The silver's gone."

Then he turned quickly and walked back to the car. Elena and I remained on the steps of the cathedral.

"He is an interesting man, Elena," I said.

Elena glanced anxiously toward the car. "I'm afraid for him."

I took her arm. "Come, let's go back."

Julien smiled as we joined him. "Forgive my mood," he said. "I don't mean to be so dramatic." He shrugged. "It's just that coming over to the restaurant this evening I passed the Hôtel de Ville and all the flags were waving, the Tricolor, you know? It seemed so hollow. Everyone has forgotten what we did, we, the French, here and in Vichy. They have forgotten the collaboration, the roundups, the informants." He shook his head. "We are a forgetful people, we French, don't you think?"

"Like everyone else," I said. "The French are part of a forgetful species."

I glanced at Elena, then back at Julien. It could not have been more clear that they needed to be alone.

"I think I'll go back to my hotel now," I said. I faked a yawn. "I'm not used to these late Parisian nights."

My symposium had provided accommodations at the Grand Hotel. Julien and Elena let me off in front, and Julien got out and shook my hand, while Elena remained in the car. "Your dear sister has kept me from brooding too much," he said with a slight smile. "For this, I am grateful, you see?"

I nodded.

He placed his hand on my shoulder. "You Americans are better than I thought." He continued to watch me seriously, his hand gripping my shoulder more tightly. "You are in Paris only a few days. That is too bad. I must go to Stockholm tomorrow. But perhaps you shall return to France one day, and I shall see you then, yes?"

"I hope so, Julien."

He nodded. "Well, *bonsoir.*"

I never saw Julien again. A year later, Elena provided the details in a letter designed to convey the minimum of emotion:

I'm afraid this letter brings bad news. Julien died in his apartment a week ago. It appears to have been a suicide. The gas jets were opened. It was quick and painless, and I think it is very much what he wanted. He was so appalled by events surrounding the war that he found it difficult to separate himself from them. He entered what I would call a metaphysical loneliness. He called it "brooding" and liked to dismiss it as self-pity. But it was actually despair of the deepest sort, the kind in which there is no remedy by means of personal life. He lived in this dark cocoon. More and more in the past months, he could not get outside it. I tried to be of service. Possibly, I did not want to repeat any of the mistakes I made regarding Elizabeth. But I could not remake his country's past, which is, I think, what would have been required if he were to have been saved. I know your impulse will be to rush to Paris to comfort me. That is not necessary. Julien's death is very sad, but we had seen little of each other in the past few months. He had become increasingly remote, his isolation almost absolute. I can only think of his death as inevitable. I do not believe that death follows me wherever I go, or that everyone I touch turns suicidal. Such ideas are romantic and in the end suggest a grotesque sense of one's own power and importance. I am well, and working steadily.

In her biography, Martha reprinted this letter in its entirety. She saw it as emblematic of the icy state into which Elena had fallen since Elizabeth's death. As Jason once told me, this makes good reading but poor analysis, and I think that if Elena's letter can be said to suggest anything, it is the strength of character she had achieved at this point in her life. The letter reflects the meditative tone of a mind that had by then become infinitely enlarged by the act of meditation, a consciousness as repulsed by the melodrama of grief as it was, by nature, attracted to the sober contemplation of it. "When I think of Timon's grave," Dorothea Moore says in the final passages of *Inwardness*, "I do not think of its particularity. I do not think, There, below me, is my son, Timon, his features grotesquely altered by the opera of their decay. I allow no outward show to parody my inward grief, nor claim uniqueness for my loss, nor sound a trumpet to my guilt. Neither do I ask that all the world be reconvened into its primordial mass so that, beginning once again with the first light of that first explosive day, all that has come before could rearrange itself, twist and turn and wheel, and so at last, through lost millennia, deliver to my door this day a living son. Oh, Timon, I am sorry; but not alone for you."

My brief first visit to Paris ended only a week after I arrived. I saw Elena quite often during those few days, and on the last day of my visit we met at the rue Auguste Comte entrance to the Luxembourg Gardens, walked toward the palace through a profusion of mediocre statuary, and finally sat down at the edge of the Medici fountain. Elena appeared subdued. The unseasonable warmth that hung over Paris that first week in October had come to an abrupt end, and both of us could feel the first chill of winter as the wind swept through the trees.

"I should have brought a jacket," Elena said. She wrapped her arms around herself.

"Do you like the winters here?" I asked idly.

Elena nodded. "I'll miss you, William," she said. She reached over and took my hand.

I placed my other hand on top of hers and squeezed gently. "Come home."

Elena shook her head.

"You can bring Julien with you," I said.

"We're not thinking in those terms."

I did not press the issue, either about her returning to America or marrying Julien. She was forty. She would be childless in any event, and I suspected, beyond this, that she had also elected to live her life wholly free of those complex encumbrances which other people impose. At that time, I could not possibly have imagined the autumn loveliness that Jason Findley would bring into her life, changing it so radically, lending it that music which would finally rise from the pages of her last book.

I glanced about the gardens. Behind me, Delacroix's dastardly Polyphemus was about to crush Acis and Galatea, who hugged each other in pastoral calm, oblivious to the Cyclops's gaze.

"It's the only decent piece of sculpture in the whole garden," I said.

Elena did not seem in the least interested in my aesthetic judgment. She looked down at the water, then gently dipped her fingers into it.

"What are you thinking about, Elena?" I asked.

She looked up at me, hesitating a moment. "I'm thinking about what I've missed," she said.

"Missed?"

"Yes, missed," she said. "Family, children, that sort of thing." She smiled. "And I think it's probably worth it."

I took one of her hands and held it. "I hope so, Elena."

"My mind is alive, William," she said, her eyes shining with the joy of that good fortune, "and if I paid a price for that, I don't care."

In her face there was the oddest combination of newfound hope and past regret, loss and recovery, that I had ever seen. A fully developed consciousness is an awesome thing, and watching Elena at that moment in her life, one could almost feel the power of its tides.

THE QUALITY OF THOUGHT IN AMERICAN LETTERS

The usual revelers were on the pier the day Elena returned from France, vacationers and businessmen, along with a few reporters, the last surviving remnants of the ship news desk, who slouched about, chewing on cigarettes and looking bored yet dutiful.

Elena came briskly down the gangway of the *Flandre*, carrying only a single brown suitcase. She was wearing a black toque hat with a small feather at the side. She had come from a wintry France and looked rather like a bundle of moving woolens.

"There was a storm at sea," she said as she stepped up to me. "Everyone got sick." She put down her bag and drew me into her arms. "I'm so sorry about Miriam."

"She's gotten quite a bit worse since I wrote you," I told her.

She nodded, her face very grim. There was now a hint of silver in her hair, but surrounding the youth of her face it looked somehow impermanent, as if it had been spun there overnight and would be gone by evening.

"They're sure it's leukemia?" she asked.

"Yes, and a very rapid kind, evidently," I said. I bent down and grabbed her suitcase. "She'll be happy to see you, Elena."

Elena took my arm and we walked toward a row of taxis parked fifty feet away.

"Sorry about the storm," I said absently. "Would you like to go to my apartment first, freshen up?"

Elena shook her head. "No, I want to see Miriam, if you don't mind."

We were almost at the taxis when one of the reporters came charging up to us, firing questions as he trotted along.

"You're Elena Franklin, aren't you? Are you aware that Jack Mac-Neill is leaving the United States? Were you ever a member of the Communist party, Miss Franklin? Is it true that you wrote *Calliope* as an assignment from the Comintern?"

Elena looked at me aghast.

I stopped and turned to the reporter. He had a name tag on his coat. It said his name was Slattery.

"Mr. . . . . Slattery," I said, "my sister has returned to the United States because of an illness in the family. I would appreciate it if you would leave her alone."

Slattery grinned moronically. "Well, you know what they say, people's right to know, and all that."

Over his shoulder, I could see the other reporters laughing at him, at his youth and inexperience, that immaturity which they had long ago left behind but were still inclined to indulge. Elena, on the other hand, was not inclined to indulge it. She stepped forward and faced him.

"I had heard that Jack MacNeill was leaving the country," she said bluntly. "And if this is the way he has been treated, then I don't blame him in the least."

Slattery laughed. "Well, maybe he's got something to hide," he said. "Hell, maybe you do, too, Miss Franklin."

Elena looked at him as if he were a being from a more malicious world, one of those mischievous sprites who so bedeviled the Elizabethan mind. She had been away for so long that the terrible oppression of the early fifties had not in any real way touched her. It was now the spring of 1954, and the last wave of the decade's early madness was passing over us like a cloud going out to sea, retreating, but with a grumbling, quarrelsome thunder.

"Well, what do you say, Miss Franklin," Slattery asked in a mocking tone. "You work for the Comintern, or what?"

Elena did not answer. She turned quickly, walked a few paces to the taxi nearest us, and got in. I followed her immediately, of course, and within a few seconds we were riding across town toward Mount Sinai Hospital.

"You're lucky to have been in Europe for the past few years," I said.

"I read about it, of course," Elena said, "but it's different when you're suddenly attacked like that, accused of ridiculous things." She grimaced. "The Comintern. My God, how absurd."

I nodded. "Being accused is nothing. Joe Tully went to jail for eighteen months. You know what Sam did." I smiled. "Of course, Jack just told them to go to hell."

"And you?"

I shrugged. "Well, I was never political. I just had friends who were, and a sister."

"What about Miriam?"

"Oh, God, she was out in the thick of it again," I said wearily, remembering all the meetings and rallies and proclamations, that sense of heavy battle in which she had been engaged. "But not me." I shrugged. "Maybe Jack was right in what he said to me one night. He said that writing about dead poets makes you dead."

Elena glanced out the window at the line of storefronts and offices sweeping by. "I should have come home," she said quietly. There was more than a little self-accusation in her voice, more than a little moral doubt, the sort that remains like an ache in the mind. In Elena it surfaced oddly from time to time, in a line despairing of Mary Farrell's disengagement, for example, or still later, when she declared not long before she died that Jack MacNeill, for all his error and false hope, had won the championship of life.

Elena continued to stare out the car window a moment longer, then she turned back to me. "Tell me about Miriam," she said.

"Well, there's not much to add to what I've already written you," I said. "It's leukemia. They keep calling it 'cancer of the blood.' How terrible that sounds, like the blood stream is foul."

"What can be done?" Elena asked.

"Nothing at all, really," I admitted. "About six months ago she would get tired quickly. She didn't look healthy, but then Miriam always has a sort of pale look, despite her energy. That's what she lost first, the energy. Then other things began to happen. Loss of appetite, dizziness, that sort of thing." I glanced away from her, latching my eyes on the upper floors of Mount Sinai as they rose down the avenue. "It could have been a thousand little things, but it was leukemia." I looked at Elena. "She's sinking very fast now."

Even as I said this, I found something utterly unbelievable in it. That Miriam could go so quickly was inconceivable. I could not grasp that her enormous energy would desert her, that she would then be flesh alone, then void and without form entirely, as if uncreated.

"She's not in very much pain," I added. "They keep her sedated."

She was awake, however, when Elena and I came into her room a few minutes later. Her face was pale, waxy. When asleep, she looked like a carved white candle.

"Look who's come from Europe," I said as Elena stepped into the room behind me.

Miriam glanced up weakly and tried to smile. "Come to the death vigil?" she asked.

Elena said nothing. She walked over to the bed, bent forward, and gathered Miriam into her arms.

"I'm not taking it very well, Elena," Miriam whispered. "It's too slow, too slow. They should have put me in the oven, like the ones in Europe."

I turned away from her reflexively. "Oh, for God's sake, Miriam," I blurted.

Miriam kept her eyes on Elena. "William wants me to be strong," she said in a low, raspy voice. "But I've lost my strength, Elena, lost my spirit."

Elena took a white cloth from the stand beside the bed and gently wiped Miriam's forehead.

"Don't tell me that I'm going to be fine, Elena," Miriam said, almost bitterly. "Don't feed me that bullshit."

"I won't," Elena said firmly.

"William tried that for a while. So did these frigging doctors."

Elena continued to wipe her head but said nothing.

Miriam glanced about the room angrily. "Look at this goddamn place," she said vehemently. She glared at me. "I don't want to die here, goddammit!" she screamed.

"For God's sake, Miriam," I said again. I walked to the window and stared down at the roofs of the stubby surrounding buildings.

"Where do you want to go?" Elena asked quietly.

"Home," Miriam said. Then she closed her eyes and allowed her head to drop slowly onto Elena's shoulder. "Just let them give me something for the pain," she said almost in a whisper. "Just something for the frigging pain, then let me go home."

I turned back toward them. Elena had Miriam's head cradled in her arms. She was stroking her hair.

"Such a long way to come for a vigil," Miriam repeated. "One of those stupid Cunard liners with all the odd characters on it, right, Elena?"

Elena smiled slightly. "There were a few oddities."

Miriam nodded. "Rich old crones playing bridge, right?"

"Right."

"And in the lounge, some moron singing 'Besame Mucho' in a German accent."

"Exactly," Elena said. She drew her arms more tightly around Miriam's shoulders.

Miriam shook her head very slowly, already tiring, exhausted by her anger. "I scream at the nurses and at William and Alexander," she whispered, her eyes half closing. "I wanted to be strong, but I'm just a bitch, Elena, a frigging bitch." She began to cry gently. "No goddamn guts."

Elena wiped her face with the towel, then lay her carefully back down on the bed. Miriam's whisper was trailing off into silence as her eyes closed.

"She'll sleep for a while now," I said. "She always does."

Elena eased herself from the bed. "Is there some way we could get Miriam home?" she asked.

I shook my head. "No. It would be too hard on Alexander."

"Alexander is not the one who's dying," Elena said sternly.

I stepped to the door. "Come, let's talk about this somewhere else."

We walked down the hospital corridor to a small lounge. I bought us each a cup of coffee, and we sat down at a dreary metal table with a hard, formica top, the sort that makes the cold world of the hospital all the more cold.

"She's been this way for a while now," I said. "Very angry."

Elena stared down at her coffee.

"I've always loved her," I said. "I always will. But since she's gotten sick it's been hard to deal with her, hard even to like her."

Elena looked up slowly. "Perhaps they should have put her in an oven, then."

I was so shocked by Elena's remark that my mouth actually dropped open. I leaned toward her. "I know how I must look to you. Cold, indifferent, selfish. But the fact is, Miriam has been very difficult. Especially with Alexander. She's constantly after him. It's as if she thinks she has to lay down all the laws before she dies."

"What's wrong with that?"

"Well, it doesn't leave Alexander with very pleasant memories of his mother."

"Then Alexander is a shallow boy," Elena said, retreating not one inch. "What would he prefer, to have a mother who, with her dying breath, tells him a joke, or listens to his schoolroom gossip as if she gives a damn? Let him remember this: in the last days of his mother's life, she tried to teach him how to live."

I started to speak again but stopped, unable to explain myself, or Miriam, or, for that matter, anything at all.

"I don't mean to dismiss the problems you've had, William," Elena said.

"When someone like Miriam gets sick," I told her, "someone as strong as Miriam, you don't expect her to change so much, become so difficult."

"Miriam isn't just sick. She's dying."

"That doesn't change the way you feel."

Elena regarded me very seriously. "Miriam isn't dealing only with her own death, William, but with the death of her expectations. She didn't want just to live, she wanted to accomplish something. And now she sees herself dying. But she also sees the books she'll never write. She sees that sort of oblivion, too."

I pictured Miriam's unfinished manuscripts scattered about the tiny room she maintained as an office, all that work and ambition now come down to nothing.

"You have to make allowance for how much of a burden her hopes add to her dying, William," Elena said emphatically.

"All right, I can see what you mean, of course," I said. "But does that make any real difference in terms of bringing her home?"

"No," Elena said. "But still I think we might be able to manage it."

"She needs constant care," I said. "She's not even like our mother was. At least Mother was off in her own world. Miriam is very much aware of everything."

Elena said nothing.

"And I have a job, you know," I added. "I have to be at Parnassus all day."

"I will stay with Miriam during the day," Elena said.

"That could be a very difficult job."

"Maybe not so difficult," Elena replied. "I remember what it was like caring for Mother. It's not a bad experience to have again."

I glanced at my watch. "Let's go to the apartment while Miriam's resting. I'm sure Alexander's home from school by now. He'll be anxious to see you."

He was fourteen years old, a tall, graceful boy, with an elongated face and watery eyes, which gave him a look of perpetual longing and disappointment, though his manner suggested none of these.

"Aunt Elena," he said as he swept her into his arms. "It's good to have you back again."

He had prepared a light dinner for us, and as we sat together in the dining room he questioned Elena relentlessly about Paris, of which he had, of course, a romantically effusive view; about certain ideas in *New England Maid*, the only book of hers he had read, *Calliope* having been a bit too thick for his young mind, while *Inwardness* had had too little plot to keep his action-oriented reading needs alive; and finally about a host of less pointed topics.

They were still going at it when the phone rang an hour later, just as we were preparing to return to the hospital. It was Dr. Bergman. His voice was very calm as he brought the news to me. Miriam was dead.

I realized that the room was absolutely silent as I put down the phone. They were both staring at me, Elena and Alexander, their eyes recording the stricken expression on my face.

I nodded to them. "Yes," I said. "Just a few minutes ago. In her sleep."

I can remember only the most obvious details of the following two days. I remember Elena's taking long walks by the river with Alexander while I remained in the apartment, going through all the procedural matters that must be attended to on such occasions and which finally serve to delay by quite some time the full expression of one's grief.

She was buried in Hoboken, New Jersey, in a public cemetery there which she had seen only once, years before, but which had appealed to her far more than the packed burial grounds of New York. The service was brief, as she had requested. She had only a brother left, her parents having died some years before. She always referred to him rather dismissively as "the engineer," but he was quite intelligent, though somewhat lusterless. At Miriam's grave site, he told a few quiet stories about their childhood together, then disappeared into the surrounding circle of her friends. Elena also said a few words, as did Sam Waterman. But quite privately Miriam had asked her favorite author, the one with whom she had most enjoyed working, to deliver what amounted to a eulogy. This was Jason Findley, a displaced Southerner, in whom Miriam, perhaps, saw a kindred spirit, another exile from a distant world. Each was imbedded in a cultural inheritance that seemed very remote indeed from that of modern America. Where Jason looked back to the imagined beauties of what he jokingly referred to as a "jonquiled and be-juleped South," Miriam, ever the idealistic communitarian, dreamed of the idyllic peace that must have flourished in the valleys of Judea.

Jason was the last to speak. He wore an elegant black suit, cut perfectly to his tall, slender figure, and stood beside Miriam's grave with his hands folded primly in front of him. His voice was soft but sure, and when he spoke he seemed to look everyone around him directly in the eye.

"Miriam was a very strong woman, as I'm sure all of you know," he said, "and so I won't tell you how gentle she was. Miriam wasn't gentle. She was hard as nails. She worked at everything obsessively, like Saint Thérèse on her *Histoire d'une âme*. She was a kind of Jewish Jesuit when it came to commitment." He smiled. "I won't tell you she was tolerant, either. She was intolerant, especially of laziness, shoddiness, ineptitude. She didn't have the kind of moral waffling that poses as understanding and so forgives everything. She would say of an evil thing, 'This thing is evil.' "

He glanced around at all of us, the look on his face somber but somehow uplifting, as if he felt good about the world because he felt good about Miriam.

"This woman had opinions, and she wouldn't shut her mouth. She thought religion was a carnival oddity and most of what the world talked about, sheer nonsense. She was very political, but even in this she had a literary bent. One evening when I was at her apartment along with her husband, William, something was said about that occasion some years before when one of Franco's brigands had given a speech with the great Spanish philosopher Miguel de Unamuno sitting mutely right behind him. It seemed that this commander had had an eye patch and had lost one arm, and I remember that Miriam noted just how physically he represented, as she put it that night, 'all that is blind and crippled in the fascist heart.' "

I remembered that evening very well as he spoke of it, and for the first time since her death, I felt my loss completely.

"That's the sort of thing Miriam would say," Jason continued, "the sort of thing she would feel."

He stepped aside with solemn deliberateness, as if this gesture of taking one long step away from Miriam was his way of saying, finally now, good-by.

Within a few minutes it was over, and we all straggled down the hill to our cars. Mary walked beside me, with her four-year-old daughter, Martha, in tow. Elena walked with Jack MacNeill, her hand tucked beneath his elbow. Sam and Jason strolled along together, talking quietly. Besides these, there were a few others, mostly a smattering of Miriam's authors, all of them fittingly subdued in the presence of what they must have thought of as the powerful publisher, Sam Waterman, the radical novelist, Jack MacNeill, and the legendary expatriate, Elena Franklin. One of them later wrote a poem about the funeral, a very bad one, as it turned out, but published anyway. It was entitled "Luminaries in their Mourning," and it stretched its feeble ironies to the bone. Still, I saved it through the years, then finally added it to that huge collection of Miriam's unpublished manuscripts, an award, perhaps, for all the sleeplessness and anxiety and hard labor that had gone into creating them.

After the funeral, we "luminaries" returned to my apartment. It felt terribly empty without Miriam pacing through it, whispering bits of dialogue to herself. And yet, her death had also liberated the space within the rooms, opened it up to an uncomplicated light, as if her long dying were no more than clutter, an episode of disarray in the long *pax et ordo* of my life.

For a time we all sat around the dining room table, drinking coffee and talking quietly, as people do on such occasions, as if we do not wish the dead to know that we have gone on living.

Jack sat to my right. His hair was now completely white and very beautiful, the crowning touch to a handsomeness that had graced him all his life. Jason sat next to him, and directly across from Elena. From time to time he would glance at her.

Only Sam was unbuttoned. He played on the living room floor with Martha Farrell, grinning delightedly as he rolled her right and left across the carpet or slapped gently at her hands in a game of pitty-pat. It was a relief for Mary, who'd been at her wit's end with Martha all day. She was clearly tired of motherhood by then and looked dry as a pretzel; but her tongue was as sharp as ever.

"I'll sell you that kid for a good price, Sam," she called to him from the dining room.

Sam shook his head. "I got plenty of time to make one of my own, dearie."

Mary turned to Elena. "How about you? I'm talking a bargain here."

Elena smiled faintly but said nothing. She appeared a somewhat more reserved person than she had been in Paris, one who increasingly kept her counsel — something I have no doubt that Jason saw that afternoon, and instantly admired.

Still, he always directed his attention to someone else, Mary or Jack or me, while guiding them away from Elena in a movement which was, I think, essentially a feint.

"When are you leaving for Europe, Jack?" he asked.

"Two weeks," Jack said. "I have a little place in Wales. A cottage by a lake. Perfect for thinking and writing. A friend owns it."

Jason nodded. "Sounds very good indeed."

Jack shrugged. "Well, what do I have to hang around here for? The reactionaries are in the saddle."

"Wait them out," Mary said. "What the hell, this'll blow over in a few months. We're in the tail end of it."

"I'm not so sure," Jack said.

"Christ, Jack," Mary said, "they'll make a hero out of you before long. That's the way things are, fickle." She turned to Elena. "How about you? You going back to France?"

"I'm not sure," Elena said.

Jack smiled at her. "Well, you could always live with me in my little cottage in Wales. We could walk by the lake. Even resume old passions, perhaps."

Elena shook her head. "Too rainy."

Jack nodded quickly, then turned away.

"She's a European now," Mary said. "One of those literary ladies."

Jason leaned toward her slightly, and for the first time that afternoon addressed her directly. "Are you tired of Europe?" he asked.

"Yes," Elena said.

He smiled softly. "Curious how modern man has forgotten that in ancient times exile was considered the most severe of punishments."

Mary laughed. "Well, that was before they started serving meals in the air."

Jason laughed at that, but only politely. He kept his eyes on my sister. "So you are going to stay in New York?"

"For a while, I think," Elena said.

Jason sat back in his seat. "Good," he said. He stood up slowly. "Well, I'd better be going now." He shook hands with each of us, last of all with Elena. Then he left.

For a time the rest of us continued our conversation, though we were all so busy shuffling around Miriam's death that talk became a kind of dodge.

Finally a certain weariness overtook us all, and we trooped down to Sam's car. He drove Mary and Martha to the airport, leaving Jack and Elena and me standing on the sidewalk, waving at them. Mary hoisted her daughter up to the back window, grabbed her wrist and waved it for the little girl. Martha grinned and pushed her nose up against the glass, making a pug-nosed face as the car pulled away.

"Well, I'd better be going, too," Jack said to Elena.

"It was good seeing you, Jack," Elena said.

Jack took her hand. "You know, you could come and stay with me in Wales sometime," he said. "No one would think the worse of it." He looked at me. "Right, William?"

"Not in the least."

Elena gently pulled her hand from his grasp. "I'd better stay here for a while."

"Are you sure?" Jack said with a slight smile. "Think how we could liven up poor Wales."

Elena shook her head. "I'm sure."

"All right," Jack said, "I won't press you. But I hope you'll come and see me off. I'm leaving on the twentieth."

Elena smiled. "You didn't want me to see you off when you left for Spain," she reminded him.

"I've changed," Jack said. There was still a kind of yearning for her in his eyes, the sort that seems not so much a matter of passion as of stubborn pursuit. There was no doubt that he still loved my sister, though not with an unbearable need. Instead, I think, she continued to possess the powerful allure of something we have lost. "Anyway," he said, "I'm off to Wales on the twentieth."

"I hope you like it there," Elena said softly.

"I suppose I will," Jack said. "I would very much like it if you would come and see me off."

"All right," Elena said, "I will."

I went with her the day she did. At the pier Elena gave Jack a single long-stem rose, which he flung back at the reporters hounding him as he went up the gangway. "Here," he said, "America needs all the beauty it can bear." The remark made minor literary history. When I read it now in yet another chronicle of the period, I no longer see Jack as the singularly resilient person he was but just as a figure made famous by a single dramatic moment in his life, reduced to cliché by a gesture he thought far less significant than even the least significant of his works. "I have become a single line," he told Elena not long before he died.

After the ship pulled away, Elena and I took a train uptown, got off at Columbus Circle, then walked for a while in Central Park. We sat down at a bench near the Sheep's Meadow, perhaps on the very bench we had taken so many years ago when I told her that she need not be ashamed of a single line in *New England Maid*.

"Have you decided when you'll be going back?" I asked.

"No."

Elena looked at me. "Americans want so much to be good, William," she said. "Have you ever noticed that?"

"It's part of their naiveté," I said.

"It's not naiveté, William, it's desire."

Whether this interpretation was true or not, she never abandoned it. It surfaced once again in the opening chapter of *The Quality of Thought in American Letters*. For there she chose John Woolman, that gentle Quaker parson of endless moral striving, as the figure with whom to begin her exploration: "All his life, Woolman acted against the currents of his age, defending those without defenders, asking questions that prudence would have silenced, making of our mortal clay at least a dream of paradise. He extolled the subtler acquisitions of the soul over the grosser ones of the hand. He turned resolutely away from the imperial politics of Winthrop and the closed theology of Edwards, fighting their fires of conquest and judgment with the cool water he presumed to flow from a righteous stream. In doing so, he came to voice, in the early morning of our history, those questions of justice and equality which Jefferson would later raise so powerfully, and in the raising, as Frost wrote, set our minds ablaze for a thousand years."

D o you think that when Elena came back to the United States in 1954, she intended to stay here?" Martha asked.

"Yes, I do," I told her. "But I'm not sure she had *Quality* in mind at that time. She certainly didn't mention it."

She leaned back in her chair. It was one of our last interviews. Elena had been gone now for almost a year. Her small flower garden looked lonely and untended under the spring sun. From where I sat in the back yard, I could see Elena's day lilies tossing in the breeze that swept in off the bay. She had insisted on planting them, even though Jason had dismissed them as "cotillion flowers." Elena always got her way with Jason. "She was the volcano," he wrote in his memoir, "and I was falling ash."

Martha touched the tip of her pencil to the note pad in her lap. She would come here for a final interview only six months later, looking very proud of herself, convinced that her biography of my sister was a true literary triumph, a book almost as great as its subject. On her last visit she said it needed only "a few loose ends tied up, you know, scholarship-wise."

"How would you describe Elena's mood as she began *Quality?*" she asked. She slowly tapped her pencil against her ear and waited for my answer. She had developed several such donnish mannerisms since beginning her research. I half expected her to bring a goose quill and inkwell to our final rendezvous.

"I would say that Elena was full of energy," I told her. And I suppose it could be said that it was the energy of *Quality* that I found most striking when I read the manuscript for the first time. I remember looking up from the pages from time to time just to take a breather from the relentlessness of its prose, at once so alive with raging admiration and yet so expressive of bottomless disappointment, simultaneously floral and coolly analytic, centerless, yet deeply centered within the shifting lights and mingled textures of my sister's mind.

"Yes, I would say that she was very full of energy," I repeated as Martha looked up from her pad.

"When did you first realize that Elena had embarked upon a new book?" Martha asked.

"In the spring of 1956."

We were sitting with Sam in Washington Square Park. Perhaps she had already been thinking about the book for some time by then. There were, after all, those stacks of books in her Paris apartment, almost all of them American, and looking rather like expatriates themselves as they rested beneath her window. Elena herself did not seem to know when the idea struck her. "Somewhere along the way," she said in the 1980 interview, "I recognized that taken as a whole America's tendency to encourage endless striving constituted a form of moral intelligence which was genuinely great, both in its drift, to use a phrase from Walter Lippmann, and in its mastery, and that American failure contained within it an element of poignancy which flowed more than anything else from the predicament of an early dream."

Thus on that spring day in 1956, my sister had perhaps no more than the vaguest notion of the sort of book toward which her mind was tending, and to which she subtly introduced Sam and me as we rested in the park that afternoon.

It had been over a year and a half since Miriam's death, and a great deal had transpired. Sam had finally ended his long bachelorhood by marrying the young woman with whom he had been tempestuously involved for six or seven years. She had all too promptly borne him a daughter, Christina. Elena had taken an apartment in Brooklyn Heights and had published several essays and short stories but had begun no larger work. Alexander and I had learned to adjust to Miriam's absence and, despite the tremors of his adolescence, maintained a respectful congeniality toward one another. I had left Parnassus and was teaching at Columbia.

And so the year following Miriam's death had been a rather peaceful one for our circle of friends. The heavy sediment of middle age was drifting down upon us. We would all continue now along a graceful road, so I supposed, each of us mindful of our own good fortune as we drifted into a gentle elderliness, the sort, as Horace says, "not unbefriended by the lyre."

Sam and I had walked quite a way down Fifth Avenue to meet Elena that morning. It was a Sunday, and the avenue was almost deserted. Sam placed Christina on his shoulders and bounced her playfully.

"I suppose Elena's going to stay in New York for good now," he said. He took a handkerchief from his jacket pocket and swabbed his head, which was almost completely bald now.

"I think so," I told him.

Sam nodded. "Good. *Inwardness* was a mordant French concoction, the type they love over there — sour in a sweet kind of way."

I had no idea of what he was talking about. But long ago he had predicted what *Inwardness* would be, and he did not intend to alter his opinion of the book merely because he had been wrong. The book would alter. It would be what he had said it would be. That was that.

"Have you seen her new place?" I asked him.

He shook his head. "Too busy. Kids are a lot of work, William, even when you have a nanny."

We passed under the Washington Square arch a few minutes later and took a bench alongside one of the walkways. Through the drooping limbs of the oaks, elms, and yellow locusts, we could see Garibaldi standing proudly to the east, not in the least unnerved by the drab façade of NYU.

Sam put Christina down on a plot of grass and watched as she tumbled about. Street musicians were playing here and there, but it was an amateur juggler who caught her eye, mainly by continually dropping his pins.

"The Village has changed, William," Sam said as he leaned back into the bench.

"Everything does," I said.

"It was something back when they were publishing *The Quill*," he added. "And nobody ever thought of moving to Connecticut." He pulled down his tie and flung one arm casually over the back of the bench. "Now it's rock and roll, and gangs roaming around like tribes of savages." He shook his head. "Maybe it *is* time to leave New York."

I smiled knowingly. "Are you leaving, Sam?"

"Not for good," Sam said. "But I've bought a little place up on Cape Cod."

I laughed. "That's even farther away than Connecticut."

Sam shrugged. "What the hell." He stared out across the park. "I guess I'm satisfied." He glanced down at Christina and grinned. "I made a pretty one, didn't I?"

"Yes, you did."

He looked at me thoughtfully. "When you have children, you realize what a wilderness it all is, William, what a wilderness they must go through."

"We got through it," I said. "So will they."

"I suppose so," Sam said. He reached down to stroke Christina's hair, then straightened himself up again. "There's Elena," he said.

She was walking toward us, weighted down with a large shopping bag. She lowered it heavily to the ground when she reached us.

"I made a stop at the library," she said breathlessly as she sat down. "Sorry if I'm late."

"Howells, Twain, Van Wyck Brooks," I said as I fumbled through her bag. I picked up another volume and held its spine up to get a better light. "*The Damnation of Theron Ware.*" I dropped the book back into the bag and picked through the rest. Some were famous titles, others less well known, and still others obscure, at least to me.

"Are you reading for anything in particular?" Sam asked Elena.

"Just reading," she said.

Sam was already smelling a purpose in her labor. "For no reason at all? No ulterior motive?"

"Not one I fully understand."

Sam watched her suspiciously. "Not a foray into nonfiction, I hope."

"Possibly," Elena said.

Sam shook his head. "You're a novelist, Elena. Why do other things?"

Elena said nothing.

Sam cleared his throat, a gesture of paternal disapproval he often used with writers. He had once expressed so much inarticulate disapproval at something Jason Findley was telling him that Jason had actually risen, walked to the pharmacy down the street from Parnassus, and returned with a throat spray.

"Well, as your publisher, Elena," Sam said, "I think I have some right to be given an idea of what you're up to."

"A book on American writing," Elena said.

Sam shook his head. "That's been done about a thousand times," he said, as if such information would be news to my sister. "Ever heard of Vernon Parrington, Moses Tyler?"

Elena smiled. "Is there something you're trying to tell me, Sam?"

"Just that those guys can't write novels" Sam said, "but you can. Why mess with this other stuff? It'll just confuse you."

"I don't think so," Elena said.

Sam doubted it. "Well, why will your work be any different from the others?"

Elena did not skip a beat in her reply. "Because it will be mine."

Sam nodded wearily, snatched Christina up, and began bouncing her on his knee. There was really nothing more to say to Elena on the subject, and so rather than continue in a direction that could only end in dispute, he quickly opted to engage his daughter, who was, at least at that point in her life, the sort of female he could handle.

While Sam played with Christina, Elena and I chatted casually. I mentioned a teaching offer I'd received from a Midwestern university. "I thought about taking it," I told her, "but I decided against it."

Elena smiled. "You're the complete New Yorker now," she said. "You couldn't live anywhere else." Years later, when she visited me for the first time in my new apartment in Cambridge, she brought a huge poster showing the Empire State Building at night. "So you don't forget your roots," she said as she taped it to the wall.

After a time, Christina became cranky, and Sam fled across the park in search of a taxi.

"He's quite the incompetent father," I said, watching him. "Panics at the slightest thing."

Elena nodded. "Well, he's used to having a lot of help. I'm not sure he could get along without it anymore."

I laughed. "He wanted a kid, now he's got one," I said. "Why he wanted one, I'll never know."

Elena looked at me as if she found my remark quite unusual. "He was lonely, William."

I shook my head. "You learn many things when you have children,

Elena, and one of them is that they are no solution to the problem of loneliness."

"So when Alexander grows up and leaves, that won't bother you?" she asked.

"I'll miss him," I said, "but I won't be lonely without him, because I won't be any more or less alone." I stood up and stretched my arms out. "Let's take a walk."

Elena grabbed her bag of books. "Where to?"

"Oh, just around," I said, taking the bag from her as I started off toward the opposite side of the park. "How about you? Do you need a companion? Husband? Lover?"

"Something of that sort," Elena said. She smiled. "Does that seem so shocking?"

I shook my head. "Of course not."

We reached the southern edge of the park, and up ahead I could see a long line of paintings displayed on a wrought iron fence, the sort of art the universal tourist buys, whether munching a hot dog on MacDougal Street or a croissant in Montmartre.

"My God, Sam's right," I said. "The Village has changed." I took Elena by the arm and steered her eastward toward Fourth Avenue. "Perhaps you have, too, Elena. I remember sitting with you in the Luxembourg Gardens only a few years ago and you said that you'd missed a few things in life, but that you could get along without them."

"I have, and I can," Elena said. "But I don't want to." She stopped suddenly and there was an unexpected fierceness in her face. "I'm forty-four years old, William. I'm not ready for my dotage." She glared at me. "I intend to enjoy what I can. Why should my work defeat everything?"

It was only three months after our walk in the Village that Elena met Jason Findley again. In the meantime, she had been actively pursuing those invitations and gatherings which would most likely have put her in touch with interesting men, "the intellectual equivalent of occupying bar stools," as Mary so bluntly put it in a letter to her at that time.

Still, for all this effort, she had had little success, and by the fall some of her energy had clearly dissipated. The need remained, however, and because of that, she showed up at a party at Sam's penthouse apartment in the fall of 1956.

It appeared that everyone else on earth had shown up at Sam's party as well. There were crowds around the buffet tables and the makeshift bars, crowds roaming through the tiny art gallery and somewhat larger library, crowds milling about in the foyer, and probably in the laundry room as well. Somewhere in all that teeming mass was Jason Findley, and by some act of either accident or design he spotted Elena and immediately approached her.

I was seated with her on a sofa in one of the more remote corners of Sam's cavernous apartment. It was as far away as we could get from both the string quartet and the smell of hot hors d'oeuvres. Elena was already getting fidgety, but she seemed to calm down as Jason came up to her.

"Good evening, William," he said, bowing slightly. "And to you, Miss Franklin." He smiled. "May I call you Elena?"

"Of course," Elena said. "Would you like to join us?"

"I would, yes," Jason said. He took a chair from a few feet away and brought it over to us, sitting opposite the sofa, his legs crossed and pulled under the chair to keep them from looking, as he said, like a raised drawbridge.

"Rather crowded, isn't it?" he said. He was fifty-seven but always appeared somewhat older, or perhaps simply more experienced. It was as if by writing his history books he had lived more lives and now looked back at you not through his own life alone but through vast distances in time.

"I feel as though I know you, Elena," he said. "I've read all your books and learned quite a lot from them. I remember the whole episode with *Calliope*. They bounced you around a bit on that one, didn't they?"

"Yes," Elena said.

"You had one thing on your side, however," Jason added. "Your detractors were fools."

"Not all of them," Elena said.

"No, not all," Jason admitted. "Of course, one's enemies never are entirely foolish." He smiled. "That's one of the more disturbing elements of life." He took a sip from the glass of wine he had brought with him. "Are you working on anything now?" he asked her.

"Nothing in particular," Elena said. "Just some research. And you?"

"Just finished a book on John Randolph. Parnassus has it now. I suppose it's in good hands."

"Yes, I'm sure it is," Elena said.

"You were just back from France when I saw you last," Jason said. "I'm happy to see you've decided to stay with us. As I said to you before, I believe, exile's not all it's cracked up to be."

"No, it isn't," Elena said.

"Of course, I'm a bit of one myself. Southerner, you know."

Elena nodded. "How did you happen to come north?"

Jason laughed. "Well, I was born in the Mississippi Delta, like Basil Ransom in *The Bostonians* — both of us beached and forlorn in the North."

"Do you feel that way?" Elena asked immediately. "Beached and forlorn?"

"Well, maybe that's a bit too strong," Jason said. "The fact of the matter is, no one made me come up here, it was all my doing. I fled the South like it was a house on fire."

"Rather like you did Standhope," I said to Elena.

Jason nodded. "Yes, like that. I hated it down there. All I thought about was escaping." He cleared his throat softly, then went on. "I was the only son in an old family that had gone entirely to seed. We lived in a crumbling mansion. A family of sparrows was nesting in a hole in my bedroom wall." He laughed. "You wouldn't have seen that at Tara. Anyway, we'd lost everything in the war. The Civil War, I mean. We'd deserved to lose it, but we'd never have admitted that."

"Why not?" Elena asked.

"Pride," Jason said. "Pride's a big thing, especially down there." He shifted in his chair to release the tension in his legs. "You know, in the Salem witch trials there was a man named Barrows who'd falsely accused his wife. Well, as it turns out, he was convicted of witchcraft not long after his wife was executed for it, largely, I might add, on his own testimony. Anyway, he was sentenced to being pressed to death, and when it was almost over somebody came over to him and said, 'Well, George, is there anything you want?' And Barrows said, taking all his guilt, you know, admitting it, he said, 'More weight.'" Jason leaned back in his seat. "Now that's the way my family should have acted. They should have said that they deserved their destruction. Instead, they just became bitter about it."

"And that's why you left?" Elena asked.

"Well, that was certainly part of it," Jason said. "Of course, I was only fifteen at the time, so I had the general adolescent heat that most boys do." He smiled. "I was certainly touched by that current, you may be sure." He looked at Elena almost impishly. "But only at the fuse, if you know what I mean."

Elena laughed, and so did I.

"I don't suppose that was part of the reason you left Standhope, Elena," Jason said.

"You might be surprised," Elena said.

"You know, when I was growing up, young men never suspected that young women might feel as . . . shall we say, turbulent as they."

"They did in medieval times," Elena said. "There was a word for it. *Furor uterinus,* fire in the womb."

Jason looked at her intently. "And was that considered a pathology?"

"Not exactly," Elena told him, "only an appetite, but singularly difficult to control."

Jason nodded. "Well, that it certainly was with me. I was in a terrible rage, or frustration — whatever. I'm sure that that was part of my need to leave the South. I felt completely smothered, physically smothered, like when I was a boy I used to go out to the corn crib and jump in, sinking all the way down in the shucks and husks, so far down it felt like drowning."

"Yes, that was like Standhope," Elena said.

"At the time, of course, I never would have guessed that New England had such prisons, too."

Elena looked at him in disbelief. "Really?"

"We all think that ours is the only cell," Jason said. "Or at least, I did. My God, I felt that any place on earth would be freer than the South. But, to my adolescent mind, New England seemed the best place on earth to run to. When I decided to get the hell out of the South, all I could think of was the North. Never the West or the Midwest; always the North. I yearned for snow and ice and bitter winds — anything but that sweltering basin I'd lived in all my life." He shrugged. "So one night I just up and did it. I walked out and looked up at the stars to see where the North was, exactly, then jumped on the first train that came by going in that direction.

It took me all the way to Washington, D.C., without a stop." He placed his glass down on the table beside his chair, took out his pipe, and began filling it, watching Elena as he did so. "Do you and William still have family in Standhope?"

Elena shook her head. "No. Except for William's son, we're the last of the Franklins."

I looked at her and smiled. "Well, there may be one or two left somewhere in Rhode Island."

"Not in touch with them at all?" Jason asked.

"Never," I said.

"Are you in touch with your family?" Elena asked Jason.

"I do keep in contact with some of them," Jason said. He tamped the tobacco down tightly into the bowl of his pipe. "Cousins here and there, scattered over Dixie." He smiled. "They're all probably pretty busy these days keeping the Negroes down." He lit the pipe, took a few short puffs, then lowered it from his mouth. "I got the impression from *New England Maid* that your home life was rather unusual, Elena."

"It was," Elena said.

"Mine too," Jason said. "They had suffered a malaise for what seemed like generations." He then described the nature of it in a somewhat comical fashion. But despite the joking manner in which Jason portrayed the deep sleep of his progenitors, something of the sorrow of their plight rose from it and moved deeply into Elena's mind, to emerge finally once again in a passage on William Faulkner in *Quality:* "One detects in so many of these strangely moving tales, as well as in the general sensibility of Quentin Compson, a tidal dissipation, an atrophy of will welded to a galvanizing passion, a heart at once broken and rebellious. The voice is unique in American letters, full of the rage of its retreat. It is the whimper, one might say, of a volcano."

"So they just mostly sat out life," Jason concluded with a quiet chuckle. "You know, listlessly, like it was one long advertisement for something they couldn't afford."

Elena was watching him very closely, taking in the entire man, everything from the look of his body, so very erect in his chair, to the sound of his voice, soft and unassuming, to the gentle humor of his mind, its kindly self-deprecation combined with an absolute authority.

He shrugged. "You'd have thought nothing could rouse them, my family. But when I left home, being the only son, you know, this desertion hit my family like chain lightning. My father simply would not stand for it. He came raging North like some crazed Paul Bunyan, striding across the hills, knocking over buildings, scattering the terrorized populations of countless Northern towns." He laughed. "He wanted his son back, you see. I was the only thing on earth for which he could generate any passion whatsoever." He took a puff from the pipe. "Hell, he even hired a bunch of gumshoes to find me. They tracked me like a pack of Shawnee scouts. Why, sometimes they'd show up at some flophouse I was staying in and give everybody the third degree, rough up the bums and derelicts, you know. Nobody to stop them."

A waiter passed and Jason took a glass of wine from the tray and took a sip. "Good stuff. Sam spares no expense. You have to hand it to him. I guess we're all lucky to be at Parnassus. That the way you feel, Elena?"

"Did he find you?" Elena asked. "Your father?"

Jason nodded. "Yes, he did. Can you believe it? He found me in a little hotel in the Village. I'd been living there for a month, working as a sweeper in a bathhouse. I didn't care. Just to be in the Village was all that mattered." He smiled, remembering it. "I saw Floyd Dell one time, and a portly fellow who looked a whole lot like Henry James." He grinned boyishly. "Friend of mine punched me one day and said, 'Look there, it's Isadora Duncan,' but it was just some stripper he knew from a burlesque show."

"You said your father found you," Elena said, coaxing him back to his narrative.

"Yes, and we had a talk in my room," Jason said. "We made an agreement. Sort of a strange one, but it worked for us. He agreed to live without me, if I'd agree to come back before he died." He looked down at his hands, his mind now captured by that distant moment in his life. He was silent for several seconds, then he glanced back up at Elena. "Well, I did go back. About two months before I left for the war."

He stopped then and stared into his glass.

Elena smiled. "I'd like to have the whole life in one telling, if you don't mind," she said.

Jason smiled back at her. "Well, I had the usual experiences in the war. Took a bullet in the thigh, but I was never gassed. I got back to New York in 1919." He chuckled. "Fancied myself an actor. I married a young actress named Jill Thornton, who had a stage name that was truly ridiculous: Eureka Patterson. Can you imagine the credits? 'And Eureka Patterson as Ophelia.'" He laughed and shook his head. "But, my God, I loved that girl. She decided to go to Hollywood. She was tired of bumming around Broadway. We got divorced over that. I didn't want to go to California." He mused a minute, and then his eyes brightened. "And you know, once in a while I'd see her in a movie — just an extra — I'd see that face staring back at me from a crowd in a Roman coliseum or the streets of some dusty cowboy town . . . poor Jill, in a toga or with a bonnet strapped to her head." He shrugged. "I have no idea what happened to her." He stopped again and looked at Elena. "Do you really want the whole life?"

"Certainly," Elena said lightly. "It's interesting."

"If I give you mine this evening," Jason said, "will you promise to give me yours over dinner next Saturday night?"

Elena did not pause a moment in her reply. "Yes."

"Good, then it's a deal," Jason said. "Now, where was I in the great epic that is my story? Ah, yes, divorced. I still thought I wanted to be an actor, but it was a crazy idea. I didn't like the rehearsals, or learning the lines, or the tension of opening night, or the party after it. I didn't like the people who liked these things. So in the end truth dawned and I left the stage. I was never much more than a spear carrier anyway."

"So what the stage lost, the historians gained," I said.

"Well, not straight away," Jason told me. He turned back to Elena. "The divorce hit me very hard. I was raised a strict Southern Protestant, which is a whole lot, believe me — like being raised a Catholic. You have God's eye watching you every minute, and sin is like polluted blood running through your veins, and in everything you do, everything you are, there is not so much God's love as his disappointment." He shrugged. "It becomes your disappointment, too, and I took my divorce very hard because of that, a real spiritual failure." His eyes narrowed, as if he were trying to peer directly into my sister's mind. "Fact is, I had a couple of fantasies. Not the usual kind, though, nothing to do with beautiful women, or spike-heeled shoes, or anything like that." He smiled. "I had a fantasy, you see, that I would live my whole life with the woman I loved, that I would have children, and that they would be able to say of me that I was the one who never left them.

"Of course, that didn't pan out. So if you want to know the truth about it, well, I sort of hit bottom after that. I took a little room off Sullivan Street and started drinking. It really wasn't even a room; it was a dank, stinking cellar I paid maybe ten cents a month for. There was a boiler in it and a single lamp, but the plug for the lamp was a long way from the boiler, so in the winter I had to choose between keeping warm and using the light to read by." He laughed to himself. "I chose heat every time, Elena, every time. And I think that proved that nature opts for a thick coat of fur rather than intelligence, for comfort rather than knowledge . . . and so, if you follow me, the origin of illusion is in our very genes and chromosomes."

He waited a moment for Elena to respond to this, but when she didn't he went on. "Of course, the library had light and heat. I began to read. It became a real passion for me. I found that I preferred history books to everything else, so I read a great many of them. And you know what they say: He who greatly reads will one day wish to write. Well, that's what happened to me. I decided to write my own history of the United States. I worked very hard, and seven years later I finished *The American Experience.*"

"Which, as they say in publishing," I added, "became an instant classic."

Jason nodded. "In a way, yes." He smiled. "And I started publishing fairly regularly after that. Then I got a job teaching at Columbia."

"Do you like it up there?" Elena asked. "William does."

"It'll do," Jason said. "They don't work me too hard, and I'm becoming the mossback of the department." He regarded Elena almost sadly. "To the new historians, I'm old hat, a Whig, a poor cousin of Macaulay. My concerns — with death and time and tragedy — are ones my colleagues don't consider very great, or even very relevant. They say — and they mean this in a derogatory way — that they are only, you know, poetic."

Elena was looking at him very intently when he finished. "If you are very lucky in your life," she would later write, in the words of Manfred Owen speaking to his daughter, "then from time to time all that you have learned will become a kind of love, as if in grand rebellion against your cynicism, and you will realize with infinite surprise the boundless depths of your sympathy. You will sense that compassion toward which all our faith and hope are tending, and you will understand that it was all worthwhile." That happened to me only once, shortly after I realized that Elena was dying. I don't know how often it happened to my sister, but as she watched Jason, I think that she at least suspected that in him she had found a man who had felt it too.

For the next few months, Elena and Jason met frequently for dinner or the theater, usually capping the evening with a late-night drink in Brooklyn Heights, then a stroll along the promenade — so beautiful at night, the black plain of the East River set against the glittering cliffs of Manhattan. Finding a more romantic locale would have taxed the best minds in Hollywood.

These must have been very peaceful walks, and I think something of their calm as well as what must have been their edgy expectation made it into the opening passage of *Quality:*

> They came as the inheritors of two forms of knowledge. The one had been gained by the history of bitter seamanship, a knowledge of winds, currents, and deadly shoals, of discerning one's place on earth from the stars, a knowledge steadily increased from the time the Carthaginians set sail from northern Africa. And to the limits of their materialism, they joined another form of understanding, sprung from the soil of a Roman Palestine. They answered the call of a prophet dead almost two thousand years yet alive in a promise that beyond the world of the flesh there was a world of the spirit, one assailed by the depredations of Bishop Laud, from whom they had fled across the Atlantic to confront a forest standing frozen in the November chill. Unlike their predecessors hacking out a village in the swamplands of Virginia, they had been driven to this bleak coast, divested of everything but two sustaining notions: that the body should survive as long as possible and that the soul should never die. One-third of them were truly Pilgrims, while the rest were scraped up from the detritus of England, victims of royal folly, tangled economies, cruel imprisonment. All together, they

must have been a dreamy lot, though with separate dreams, some casting their eyes toward heaven and some toward their neighbor's purse. Here the American mind began, stripped bare by confiscations of both property and heart, ignited not by a unified vision but by a multiplicity of need.

In the spring of 1957, when Elena and Jason were beginning to spend time together, there was a steady sense that they had found each other in the eleventh hour of their lives and that they should take great care not to injure a relationship that both of them expected to be, for better or worse, their last. Because of this, in those first few months, they approached each other gingerly. Jason rather carefully avoided a too ardent inquiry into my sister's expatriation or her affiliation with the Left of the thirties, of both of which, I am sure, he disapproved. For her part, Elena carefully avoided any criticism of those ideas of Jason's which, even then, she thought of as romantic: his preoccupation with military exploit, though he was himself a pacifist; the sudden bursts of Southern chauvinism which rose in him when someone dared slight the South, though he railed against its backwardness continually. These were the contradictions most central to his character, against which his mind battled constantly but with little success, and for which Elena had the deepest sympathy as long as the lines were clearly drawn. In Jason, as it turned out, they were not.

As much as a year after their first meeting, Elena and Jason still remained decidedly cautious with one another. Jason had read the first few chapters of Elena's first attempt at *Quality* by then, had praised it, of course, but no doubt more moderately that Elena would have liked.

We were together at Sam's house on Cape Cod when this icy restraint between them broke for the first time. Sam had bought the house some time before but had used it very little. Instead he had made it available to a chosen few of his authors, Elena and Jason being foremost in that company.

It was in September when we drove up to the Cape in Jason's car. Alexander was quite the independent young man by then, and I suppose a weekend alone in the city, with his watchful father on Cape Cod, almost three hundred miles away, must have seemed like the answer to his late-adolescent prayers.

In any event, Jason, Elena, and I had the run of the house for that first week in September. We could stroll the beach, walk the flats when the tide was out, or simply lounge on the lawn, taking in the sun. The relief it afforded us from the claustrophobic atmosphere of the city was exhilarating. I think that even Elena was surprised by how much she enjoyed the lovely spaciousness of Cape Cod, that unlimited openness which pervades it, as if it were the borderland, as she once said, between the merging infinities of the sky and the sea.

In the morning Elena would work on *Quality*, either typing out her notes or rereading those parts of her manuscript which she thought unfinished. Jason was at work on a critical analysis of Alfred Mahan's *Influence of Sea Power upon History*, while I continued my investigation of the poet George Crabbe.

But by afternoon all of us were intent upon putting these labors aside, and so we would stretch out on the lawn, sipping wine or lemonade, and talk about whatever came to mind.

Jason always took the hammock on these occasions, swaying casually back and forth with one hand behind his head. He looked, Elena said, like an old campaigner, full of the fire and smoke of long-forgotten wars. He talked of Austerlitz and Trafalgar, Gettysburg and Cold Harbor, as if he had himself engaged the enemy on these historic sites. The horror of battle, and its exhilarations, lent an agonizing glory to his tales, and more than anything else about these afternoons I remember the somber allegiance Jason forever bestowed upon the weary, ghostly legions who had marched into the Crater or out of Stalingrad.

"And I wonder, Elena," he said cautiously one afternoon after we had all been on the Cape together for over a week, "I wonder if your work on Stephen Crane in the new book, if it can be complete without some knowledge of the actual writings on combat experience."

Elena was sitting in a lawn chair, her back to the bay. There was a magazine in her lap, and its pages fluttered sporadically in the breeze from off the water.

"You don't consider the works of Stephen Crane 'actual writing,' Jason?"

"I mean nonliterary, of course," Jason said. He looked at me. "Blunden's *Undertones of War*, for example." He turned back to Elena. "Blunden actually experienced the war he wrote about. But Crane? He was too young to have fought in the Civil War."

"Well, my book is about American literature, Jason," Elena said casually. She glanced back down at the magazine in her lap. "It's not about the American military experience."

Jason laughed lightly. "Well, I don't just mean military experience either," he said. "I mean all those other kinds of writing that go into the making of a national intellect."

Elena looked up again. "Like what?"

"Well, the work of Parkman and Prescott in history, for example, and Helper and Fitzhugh on the antebellum South, and not just Sarah Jewett or Emily Dickinson, but maybe the letters of Abigail Adams, too."

"I see," Elena said. "But I am writing on American literature, Jason."

"Which has to include other things, Elena," Jason said emphatically. "You can't just deal with, say, Jonathan Edwards as if he represents Puritan literature. There are the diaries of Michael Wigglesworth and Samuel Sewell. They were Puritans, too."

Elena closed the magazine. "Jason, a long time ago Jack MacNeill tried to tell me the book I should write."

"I'm not telling you what to write at all," Jason said, "just that even a work on literature is incomplete if it avoids other kinds of writing. It doesn't have to concentrate on them, of course, just take them into account."

Elena glanced over to me. "Do you agree?"

"It depends on what you intend," I said. "A very substantial book can be written on literature alone."

"But not a great one," Jason said. "There are great works of literature, but no great ones about it. Do you know why?"

Elena smiled indulgently. "Please tell us, Jason."

"Because they are, by their very nature, derivative works, you see? They are one step removed from the real source of greatness."

Elena looked at him doubtfully. "Which is?"

Jason smiled, almost playfully. "Well, you're a novelist, Elena, you must surely know the answer to that."

"I'd like to hear it from you."

"Well, I'd say it's a freely roaming intelligence," Jason said, "one that can make its own parameters as it goes along, which can move in sudden, odd directions, take on a sweeping scope, rather than one that is already determined by a too tightly defined subject matter."

"And what about your books?" I asked. "Are they too tightly defined."

"I suppose they are," Jason said, "— except *The American Experience*, which had the advantage of having been written when I was young." He smiled. "There's a little sweep in that one, a little boldness that age and caution have drained away."

Elena stood up. "Who's for a stroll to the jetty?"

It was almost an hour before we got back to the house. Then we had dinner, and after that Elena retired to her room while Jason and I continued sipping brandy in the living room. Jason and Elena always retained separate rooms, at least when I was with them, and that night I could hear Elena padding about behind her closed door, then typing for a few minutes, then shuffling papers, then pacing the room again.

She did not come out again until almost midnight. Jason and I were by then deeply in our cups.

"I just wanted to tell you, Jason," she said, "that I've been thinking about what you said this afternoon, and that I think you're right."

"Good, good," Jason said casually. His head lolled to the right. "Nothing to get all spinned around about, in any event."

"Anyway, thank you," Elena said. Then she turned and walked back into her room.

The next morning, after we'd all had breakfast, I happened to glance into Elena's room as I passed it on the way to mine. She had scattered the pages of her manuscript all about, and I could see all those heartbreaking black X's she had cut across page after rejected page. From the look of it, nothing whatsoever had survived the deep surgery of her mind.

Martha drew the book from its place on my shelf, returned to her seat, and opened it. "So this is it."

Resting on Martha's lap, it did not seem so large. On the front there was a rather blurry representation of the American flag, further concealed under the massive lettering of the title. Sam had insisted upon this dramatic rendering and Elena had gone along reluctantly, commenting that the cover of *Quality* looked like the front page of a tabloid.

"I can't imagine beginning such an enormous project," Martha said. "I can't imagine coming up with the design."

"I don't think Elena did that."

Martha looked up. "She didn't have an outline for *Quality?*"

"Not a specific one, no. I think she allowed the book to surprise her."

Martha looked as if she doubted me. "But nowadays, you have to have a very clear idea of what a book will be before you begin it."

"Which may be why so few people will read it when it's finished."

Martha scowled. "I've never met anyone so down on modern scholarship, William."

I smiled. "Well, chalk it up to the grouchiness of an old man."

It was obvious that she intended to do no such thing. She regarded me warily. "You know, I have a suspicion that when my biography of Elena is finished, well, that you may not like it."

"I wouldn't let that worry you, Martha."

She shifted uneasily in her chair. "Yes, but, that would be a blow, wouldn't it, I mean for you to —"

I raised my hand to stop her.

Martha smiled. "Yes, you're right." She opened *Quality* to the first page, looked at me knowingly, then read the first line: "From ten miles out to sea, the land that greeted them could have looked more forbidding only had it been aflame." She lifted her eyes toward me. "Who does that sound like to you?"

"Jason Findley," I said. "Elena never denied his influence, especially over the first third of the book."

"Would you say the first third was a collaboration?"

"No. The ideas were Elena's. But Jason guided her research initially, particularly into areas beyond literature. I think he even perceived that as his major function."

"Would there have been a book without him?" Martha asked bluntly.

"Yes," I told her, "but it might not have included such things as the story of Mary Rowlandson's captivity or Thomas Morton's Maypole. Jason knew thousands of such minor historical episodes, and he showered her with them."

"What is Elena's?" Martha asked.

"Everything else," I said. "But particularly the ideas." I leaned over and took the book from Martha's lap, then flipped through it. "Take Dreiser, for example," I said. "Listen to what she writes about him." I read aloud: " 'The primary difficulty in Dreiser's vision is that his sense of fatality lacks the complexity of a profound intelligence. At times, and particularly in *Sister Carrie*, it seems little more than an overly elaborate defense of the simple-minded view of that judge in Butler's *Erewhon*, for whom luck is the only human quality worthy of veneration.' " I closed the book and looked at Martha. "Elena goes on from this to write an entire essay on the nature of fortuity in American letters." I shook my head. "Under no circumstances could Jason Findley have done that." I stopped for a moment, suddenly seized by a memory of Elena near the end of her long labor on *Quality*, sitting at her desk, her glasses resting on her lap as she leaned back to rub her eyes.

Martha seemed alarmed by the sudden pause in my speech, suspecting, as she must have, that it was perhaps a subtle prelude to a stoppage of the heart. "William?"

I closed my eyes slowly and rubbed them, just as I imagined Elena doing. When I opened them, Martha was halfway out of her seat, one hand extended toward me.

I smiled. "I'm fine," I said. "I was just remembering how weary Elena sometimes looked while she was writing *Quality*, especially toward the end. And I was also thinking how very lovely that weariness was. Do you know what she said about Melville? It could be said about her, too, you know."

"What do you mean, William?"

"She said that he had the beauty of a grave resolve. So did my sister, I think."

Martha eased herself back into her chair. She looked rather addled, no doubt grasping the alarming fact that were I to die, a very important primary source would be snatched from her.

"Relax, Martha," I said, adding a little wink. "I'm eighty, but I'm not going yet."

Martha nodded quickly, unamused, then glanced out toward the small, weedy garden that rested between the house and the beach.

"When I interviewed Jason a few months ago," she said, "he told me that he thought of Elena almost all the time."

"That was gallant of him."

"Do you think he was telling me the truth?"

"I have no doubt of it at all," I said. "He loved my sister." I lifted my hand and swept it out slightly. "This is where they had their best years, those summers in this house." I laughed. "I remember the second one we spent here better than the rest. It was the summer of 1959. Elena was at work researching her far more expanded version of *Quality*. Jason was putting the finishing touches on his latest effort. They were very happy together that summer."

I could remember it very well. It was the summer they planted the flower garden. We had come up toward the end of May. Alexander had come along, too. He had finished his freshman year at New York University, and he'd brought Saundra, the young woman he would soon marry, and also a young man named Roger Whitman, a fellow student at NYU. Saundra was very personable and accomplished, a music major who dreamed of becoming a concert pianist. Roger, however, dreamed of nothing whatsoever, and we were all amused by his immense indolence. It so happened that Elena was researching the twenties at that time, and I have always believed that Roger's languid manner must have fit right in with the era she was studying. Even now I think of him when, from time to time, I take down *Quality* and read a passage or two from her section on the twenties:

> It was an age that encouraged the adoration of a certain kind of writer, who laughed at work and slow increase while swigging gin in dark speakeasies where papier-mâché grapevines framed wall-sized pictures of the Bay of Naples. Even a frivolous time must have its hero, and for the twenties it was the sort of character who looks for an inheritance as his salvation as surely as others look for work, who exalts money and even grovels for it, as Amory Blaine does in *This Side of Paradise*, but who sneers at the labor that earned it.
>
> Beside this listless, supercilious creature, the characters of Sinclair Lewis burn with an almost holy flame. One finally comes to respect the plodding Dodsworth, the grasping Babbitt, and even the naive Carol Kennicott, whose sleepless reformism is as noble as it is ridiculous. At least these people acknowledge, however unintentionally, the truth that effort is a moral and a biological imperative, that growth comes only through extension, and that if this were not so, then life would not have evolved beyond the humblest glob of undirected protoplasm.

Roger Whitman was probably as close as any human could have ever been to a glob of undirected protoplasm, but even he could not spoil that summer. For a while he and Alexander lazed on the beach below the house, Alexander attempting to rouse him to the effort his sophomore year would require. Elena and Jason and I smiled to ourselves at both Roger's effete malaise and my son's evangelical relentlessness in trying to dispel it.

"I must say that I'm proud of Alexander," Elena said on one occasion. We were busily breaking ground, readying the garden for the first planting. Elena was dressed in a cotton blouse and flannel pants rolled at the cuff. She looked, Jason said that day, like a Norman farm woman, thinner, perhaps, but with that same outdoor bloom of health.

"Proud of him?" I asked. "For what?"

"The way he's determined to turn his friend around," Elena said. "It's admirable."

"I can't imagine why he's taken up with that boy," I said, shaking my head. "I think he should expend his reformist efforts on less intractable subjects, like war and poverty."

"Speaking of war," Jason said, without looking up from the plot of ground he was hoeing, "I brought you a copy of von Steuben's *Regulations for the Order and Discipline of the Troops in the United States.*"

I looked up. "Me?"

"No, Elena," Jason said. He laughed. "I can't imagine you reading von Steuben, William." He turned back to Elena. "Also various works by Jonathan Dickinson, Freneau, and Odell. They should help you figure out the Revolutionary period."

"Yes, good," Elena said. She continued raking her square of ground. "It should also be a nice contrast to my notes on the twenties." She looked up and smiled. "And then, of course, I've got to deal with *The American Experience* by Jason Findley."

Jason covered one of his bulbs and patted the ground softly. "I prefer perennials."

"Less work involved," Elena said. "Don't have to replant every year."

"Yes, but in the idea, too," Jason said as he got to his feet. "You know, the business of something continuing to provide beauty year after year. I like the way they stand, symbolically I mean, for perseverance."

Elena laughed. "Of course, you wouldn't want to pursue that too far, would you? Imagine the perseverance, for example, of crab grass or dandelions." She shook her head. "That's the problem with romantic symbolism. It's not pared down, not precise." She scowled. "It's all moonlight and magnolias."

"Don't be so harsh, Elena," Jason said. He slapped some of the dust from his pants. "People shouldn't expect information from a poet."

Elena looked at him quizzically. "What, then, should they expect?"

"Sentiment," Jason said. "It doesn't matter what the truth is. It only matters that the feeling is genuine."

Elena frowned. "I don't believe that," she said. "If that's true, then what's the point of thinking?"

Jason smiled. "Well, what is thinking, anyway? It's only the arrangement of sentiment, nothing more."

Elena started to speak, but Jason lifted his hand. "There's no such thing as thought, Elena, there is only intelligent feeling."

Elena looked at Jason as if she had just discovered an alien presence in his soul.

"I don't believe that," she said.

Jason shrugged, picked a bulb from the seed pouch which hung from his neck, then bent down and began digging a shallow hole.

Elena continued to stand above him, looking down.

"Did you have the same attitude toward thinking when you wrote *The American Experience?*" she asked after a moment.

Jason did not look up from his planting. "Of course," he said. "I've always had that attitude."

Elena watched Jason as he casually went about his gardening that afternoon, walking in a squat as he planted one bulb after another up the long row we had already cleared. "Much in him remained but weakly formed," she would later write of the poet Joseph Rodman Drake, "as if at the moment of creation, nature had withdrawn something, stubbornly withheld that which might have brought him to completion.

I have always believed that Elena wrote this passage, about a man of sadly scattered gifts, with Jason in mind, and that the process which ended in her writing it began that afternoon in the flower garden by the bay.

Perhaps they should have had their battle that very night, sent plates and coffee cups crashing. Perhaps if Elena's "close decorum" and Jason's determined civility could have been laid aside for one instant of combat, then much of their later pain might have been averted.

I don't know what my sister might have surrendered to Jason in such a battle, or to what difficult lengths she might have gone to indulge him. But to suggest, as Martha does in her biography, that Elena would never have tempered her opinion as to the intellectual paucity of *The American Experience* is to render my sister so one-dimensional in her intellectual integrity as to strip her of her human needs. Elena loved Jason Findley more than she ever loved another man. She would not willingly have allowed a simple difference in ideas to have destroyed their relationship. Martha may portray my sister in heroic isolation, but in reality Elena did not want to end her days alone on Cape Cod, and certainly she would have preferred to spend them with Jason rather than with me.

And so Elena moved very cautiously indeed for the next year. She had read *The American Experience* years before and delayed rereading it as long as possible. Perhaps even on that day, as we were planting the garden, she already suspected that "romantic wooliness" which dominated Jason's thought, and in turn, his work. But if that were so, she kept it honorably to herself, as Manfred Owen does, "not as one who avoids an unpleasant truth, but as one who understands that the precious things of life form a tapestry rather than a hierarchy, and that of all the things we deem worthwhile, the values that contra-dict our love remain the most difficult to enforce."

Still, no matter how difficult, the judgment had to be made, and by the time Elena turned fifty she had begun the long process of making it. It was still an entirely inward affair, of course. My sister made sure no hint of it emerged. As a result, when Sam threw a party for her on her fiftieth birthday, she appeared content with the life she had made for herself. But it was all a show, as she would later admit, all a pointless show.

The party was held in the afternoon. It was winter, and snow blanketed the ledges outside the arched windows of the Parnassus Press executive meeting room. Sam had asked Elena and Jason and me to come in a bit before the party started. He took us to a small room and unveiled the portrait of himself he had commissioned. It still looks down on that long oak table where Christina now presides, but it will always seem to me, in its hopeless exaggeration, uniquely Sam's.

"Well," he said, "what do you think?"

Elena took her glasses from her purse and put them on. Then she carefully surveyed the portrait. "You look . . . how shall I put it . . . you look *in charge*, Sam."

A huge smile swept over Sam's face. "That's exactly right, Elena, exactly right."

Jason nodded and puffed his pipe. "Saladin himself could not have looked more regal."

Sam's glance slid over to me. "How about you, William?"

I put my arm over his shoulder. "It bears a resemblance to its subject," I said, patting his ample belly, "but I think the artist was more successful in taking off a few pounds than you have ever been."

Sam nodded gravely. "I told him to do that, shave off a few pounds. In a thousand years, who'll know the difference?"

"Absolutely," Jason said. "Washington had the artist remove his facial scars, and no one ever accused him of being a liar."

Sam punched me lightly on the arm. "There, you see?"

And with that Sam ordered the portrait transferred to the meeting room and hung. When the task had been completed, he slapped his hands together and stepped back to admire it. For a moment he seemed almost mesmerized, his eyes locked on that other set of eyes that stared back at him. Then he wrapped his arm around Elena's waist and drew her to him. "Well, Elena, the grapes have ripened nicely on the vine, aye?" He gave her an affectionate little hug. "Come, let's join the party."

Elena and Sam moved down the hallway, and Jason and I strolled along behind them. The walls of the corridor were decked out with photographs of the prominent authors Parnassus had either nurtured from their beginnings or lured away from other houses by treating them with more respect and even, at times, more money. It was an impressive array, for much that was worthwhile in American letters since 1934 had been published by Parnassus, and as Sam strode down the hall with Elena in tow he looked very much like one of those captains of culture he could now claim with some justice to be.

He stopped at the large double doors of the reception room and turned to Elena.

"Happy birthday, my dear," he said.

Elena smiled. "Thank you."

Sam kissed her. "We've worked well together, don't you think?"

"Yes."

"Take this little party as a token of my esteem," Sam said. Then he swung open the doors.

There must have been two hundred people milling about, and for the next hour or so Elena strolled among them with Jason at her side, not at all discontent in that role.

"She looks very happy these days," Alexander said as he walked up to me. Saundra was with him, looking a bit intimidated by the scale of the occasion. She was still a shy young woman, and she appeared almost to tremble in Elena's presence.

"I think she is happy," I told him.

Alexander took a sip of wine. "Do you think that'll harm her work?"

"I don't think happiness ever harmed anything, Alexander," I said. I looked at Saundra. "Do you?"

Saundra shook her head. She had one of those highly animated faces, the sort in which every emotional nuance displays itself, no matter how simple or complex.

"They look very beautiful together," she said as she glanced at Elena and Jason. She tucked her arm playfully in Alexander's and smiled at me. "Do you suppose Alexander and I will ever look like that?"

"If you're very lucky," I said. Then I edged away, leaving them their illusions.

Mary Farrell came plowing through the great doors only a few minutes later, wrapped in vast loops of brown fur.

"My God, William," she said as she rushed up to me, "Elena is fifty and I am fifty-five, and look at this, will you." She drew a photograph from her handbag. It showed her daughter, Martha, standing in robe and mortarboard, a proud graduate of Hollywood High. "I have a daughter who is practically a woman." Her hair was streaked with more than a little gray now, but otherwise she looked somewhat less parched than before and her mood seemed less acrid, as if her body and her mind had finally come to some agreement as to their future course.

"Is your husband with you?" I asked.

Mary smiled. "Why no, William. Should we have an affair?"

I laughed, but a bit self-consciously, unsure of whether or not she meant it, and certain only that I would have gone with her in an instant if she had.

"Speaking of affairs," Mary said, "this thing with Jason has been going on for a while."

"Yes, it has."

"All smooth to the naked eye?"

"I think so."

"He's not blinded by her light?"

"He has one of his own."

"Not pulling a MacNeill and trying to get her to do things he can't do?"

"No."

Mary looked suspicious. "Sounds a bit idyllic for my taste."

"Well, you always did like tragic endings, Mary," I told her.

She glanced across the room. Elena had seen her and was coming quickly toward her, with Jason at her arm.

"Do you like him?" Mary asked me quickly in a whisper.

"Very much."

"I had no idea you were coming, Mary," Elena said delightedly as she drew Mary into her arms.

"All the way from California," Mary said. "Just me and my minks." She stepped out of Elena's embrace and looked at Jason.

"Hello," Jason said, somewhat shyly.

Mary looked him up and down. Then she looked at Elena. "Looks stable enough, Elena," she said. "Does he have good teeth?"

"Reasonably good," Elena said.

Mary was about to reply, when suddenly the lights went out. Then the doors opened and a huge cake was wheeled in, glowing brilliantly with fifty candles. At a signal from Sam, the crowd began singing "Happy Birthday," and Jason bent forward and kissed her.

"I think a short speech is in order," Sam said once the singing had stopped and the lights had come back on. "What about it, Elena?"

Elena walked to the front of the room, briefly surveyed the large crowd that had gathered to honor her, and for one of the few times in her life spoke extemporaneously.

"Long ago, when I was a little girl," she began, "I wrote a poem, which one of my teachers didn't like. Her name was Mrs. Nichols, and a few years after we had our little conflict, she left Standhope. It was evidently quite a show at the railway station that day. Mrs.

Nichols was screaming at her husband, causing quite a commotion. Then the train pulled up and she disappeared into it and was never seen again." She smiled quietly. "From time to time when I leaf through my yearbook, I always pause at the picture of Mrs. Nichols. It's one of those pictures you can't forget, one that, as you look at it, you want to come to life. You want those gray features to take on human colors, you want to hear her speak: 'Remember me. I am Mrs. Nichols, who left in such a huff one day and was never seen again. Listen now, this is what I did. This is what happened to me.'

"In the end, I think, every life is like that, a story. Some are more interesting than others, but all of them can be regarded as tales of some kind. When we do that, see our lives as if they were the creations of someone else, as if we were figures in a novel, then I think we can get some perspective on ourselves. Am I really a hero or a villain, a wise man or a fool?" She laughed softly. "At fifty I can look back on my own life in that way, as a story which began in 1910 and which has lasted until now." She lifted her gaze toward the rear of the room where her oldest friends had arrayed themselves. "I can't come to any judgment about it, however, except to say that, from this place, from this moment, it seems to have been enough. And I could say this, that it has been enough, even if it ended before dawn, even if there were nothing more."

She stepped into the crowd and began making her way slowly toward the rest of us, shaking hands as she edged her way through. She seemed quite content, and from the perspective of that moment — and even as I now remember it — it would have been impossible to imagine that only a few years later Manfred Owen would declare in a voice that was clearly Elena's that of all human states, serenity is the least admirable, and that at fifty he had looked back upon his life and seen only charred or burning fields.

But the fields were burning, as I told Martha that same afternoon, even if only in my sister's mind.

Martha cleared her throat pointedly. "But wouldn't you say that Jason and Elena were still happy together the day of the party?" she asked.

"Relatively, yes," I said.

"Why only relatively?"

"Because despite what Elena said that day," I told her, "despite the fact that she no doubt believed it herself when she said it — despite all that, Martha, it was not enough."

"You mean Jason was not enough?"

"I mean that whatever it was she had in her life, whatever Jason was to her, it wasn't enough."

"Was that obvious at the party?"

"No."

"When did it become obvious?"

"There were little signs."

"Like what?"

"Well, once when we were at dinner," I told her, "Jason began a long story about the last hours of John C. Calhoun. It seems that Calhoun was completely lucid until the exact second of his death. The doctor, Jason said, even told Calhoun when his pulse had stopped, and Calhoun had simply nodded and waited for his life to end, quite calmly waited." I could see Elena's face before me, staring oddly at Jason as he wound his story to an end. "Anyway," I said, "Jason told this anecdote in his usual style, very full of drama. He was relishing the tale himself, completely captivated by it. But when he finished, there was a short silence, and then Elena said crisply, 'What's the point, Jason?' "

Martha nodded. "I see."

"Do you?"

"She meant that he was too verbose, too florid in his style," Martha said confidently. "That he was always losing his place, getting all tied up in his language."

I shook my head. "No. She meant that his stories had no point, that they related to nothing, that they were only connected to his own sense of the dramatic, and that beyond this very subjective sort of appreciation, there was nothing."

"Well, what did Jason say?" Martha asked.

"Nothing much. He just shrugged it off. He laughed and said that he wasn't sure there was a point at all. He didn't seem bothered by it."

Martha jotted something in her notebook, then looked back up at me. "That's it? The only sign of what was happening, just that question, 'What's the point?' "

"No, there were others," I said. "For example, Alexander and Saundra were married not long after Elena's party, and within a year my grandson, David, was born. Elena began to spend a great deal of time with the three of them and a great deal less time with Jason."

"Did he resent that?"

"I don't think so. He had his own work. Whatever else may be said about Jason, he didn't need Elena to complete himself. He had his life, his work. He never gave them up to my sister."

"I see," Martha said.

"Of course, at that time, the worst hadn't happened," I added quickly. "But later Elena began to work on that section of *Quality* which dealt with America's vision of itself. And that brought her, at last, to *The American Experience*."

Martha nodded. "Ah, so that's where the conflict really began, over *The American Experience*. That's when she found it necessary to desert him."

"Well, perhaps," I said dully.

Martha looked at me very pointedly. "I know you disagree with my approach, William," she said, "this theme of mine, about desertion. I know you disagree with that."

"Yes, I do."

"Why?"

"It's too convenient, I think. But more than that, I think it may be basically false."

"But people deserted Elena, didn't they?"

"Yes."

"Doesn't that matter?"

"It matters, perhaps, but it did not make her an artist."

"Then when she deserted Jason, that was not a kind of subconscious revenge?" Martha asked.

I shook my head. "I don't think so."

"Then why did she leave him?"

"Because she came to see him more clearly. Is that wrong?"

"What did she see?"

"The clouds within his mind."

Martha quickly scribbled the phrase in her notebook. "And that caused her a great deal of trouble, that insight?"

"Yes, it did."

"And for Jason?"

"Oh, yes," I said immediately. "Very much for Jason."

I could recall the first time his distress became apparent. The three of us, Elena, Jason, and I, had planned to have dinner together at a restaurant in the Village. I had arrived around seven and was seated in the lounge with my wine, nibbling at a bowl of peanuts, when I saw Jason come in. It was autumn, and I remember that a very hard rain had been falling all day. Jason was drenched. He shook his umbrella vigorously, then hung his sodden overcoat on a rack by the door.

I waved to him and he came trudging heavily toward me, as if slogging through a field of mud.

"You look as though you could use one of these, old boy," I said, lifting my brandy. I was in a very cheerful mood. I had spent the entire day with my grandson and the afterglow was still upon me.

"Yes, I think so," Jason said wearily. He slumped down in the chair across from mine and shifted about in it, trying to find a comfortable position. There was a creakiness in him that I had not noticed before. He looked rather like an old house, chipped and peeling. One could almost see the places where the wind came through.

"Elena's not coming," he said. "She called me this afternoon to let me know." He glanced about irritably. "She's gotten caught up in some research and doesn't want to leave it."

I smiled. "Ah, so that's it. The Great Book. She's getting to be something of a caricature of the obsessed scholar, isn't she?"

"Yes, she is," Jason said crisply. "I've gotten used to it over the past few years, of course, but it gets worse and worse." He glanced quickly about the bar. His edginess was unusual. It was as if a little animal were clawing at the basic calm of his temperament.

"You seem a bit distracted, Jason," I said.

He turned toward me. "You've never written on anything American, have you?" he asked.

"No. It's strictly English literature for me, except for an occasional review."

"Has Elena ever commented on your work?"

"From time to time," I said. "Sometimes favorable, sometimes unfavorable."

"How many books have you written?"

"Five."

Jason nodded. "You're like me, sort of a plodder. You're not like Elena."

"I have never been like Elena."

"She doesn't work like a scholar at all, William. She works like a revolutionary, with fanatical purpose. If she built bridges, there'd be no river on earth without one."

I remember thinking at that moment that he looked curiously emaciated. Even his language sounded pared down.

I leaned across the table toward him. "What's the matter, Jason?"

"Your sister is obsessed."

"You should be able to understand that."

"It's not just the incessant work, William," Jason said, "it's the way she goes at it. In the beginning, she would ask me something, and I'd give her an answer. She knew I was very learned in the field. She took the answer. Now my opinions seem to mean very little to her."

I forced myself to smile. "Well, Jason, you know your Plato: opinion is, after all, the lowest form of knowledge."

Jason's face darkened. "There is such a thing as informed judgment, isn't there?"

"Of course."

"And shouldn't it be trusted?"

"Well, that depends."

Jason looked at me irritably. "On what, may I ask?"

"On just how learned it actually is."

Jason's eyes narrowed. "Well, what about my judgment? Does that mean anything?"

"Of course it does."

He seemed on the verge of explosion, an attitude alarmingly out of character.

"Look, Jason," I said, "I've been through this sort of thing with Elena before. There's a rising passion as the work progresses, then it crests and everything goes back to normal."

Jason looked utterly unconvinced. "And what is normal? Is respect normal?"

"For Elena? Yes."

"Perhaps for you, William," he said with sudden, deep bitterness.

"Are you saying that Elena has lost respect for you, Jason?" I asked.

He actually laughed. "My God, how stupid I can be." He was about to add something else when the barmaid stepped up. Jason ordered a Scotch. Then he turned back to me.

"You know, William, a man can go through his entire life thinking that he is one sort of person, and then discover that he is quite another." He shook his head. "That's me, you know. I've done that."

"In what way?"

He shrugged. "Well, I've always been a rather vain man, I suppose. But I've always thought that this part of me was offset by a certain generosity, a certain kindliness."

"Isn't it?"

He shook his head again, and his eyes closed slowly. "No, I don't think so."

The barmaid brought the Scotch and Jason drank it down quickly.

"I've become a victim of my own charm, William," he said. "I've used it like a pose. I've filed down my rough edges with it, filed them down so well that they've almost disappeared."

"I don't follow."

He smiled. "I'm not surprised. I'm talking to myself, you see. It's an interior monologue." He motioned for the barmaid and ordered another Scotch. "Do you know what Goethe's last words were, William?"

"Yes," I said. "It's a well-known anecdote. 'Mehr Licht,' more light."

"Have you brought more light into the world, William?"

The question was so grand that only a modest reply was possible. "Perhaps a little," I said.

"And your work," Jason said. "Does it ever look like a sham, a deception?"

"No."

"Good for you," Jason said. He smiled quietly as the barmaid brought his second drink. He lifted the glass. "To the truth of the work, then," he said, and tossed off his Scotch.

"Perhaps we should order dinner," I suggested.

Jason laughed. "You don't have to worry about my getting drunk in a public place and making a fool of myself, William. I haven't done that since I was a very young man with a wife in Hollywood."

I continued to watch him closely but said nothing.

"You don't believe me, do you?" Jason asked.

"Of course I do."

Jason looked at me very gravely. "I never willingly lied, William," he said, almost pleadingly. "I never willingly distorted."

I leaned toward him. "What is this all about?"

Jason shook his head. "It's just too embarrassing," he said with a mocking smile. "Just too embarrassing."

"What?"

For a moment he seemed determined to tell me. I could see the resolve clearly in his face, and an instant later I saw it just as clearly disappear.

"It's not your problem," he said as he slowly got to his feet. "It's not even Elena's problem. It's mine."

I stood up, too. "I'm totally at sea in all this, Jason," I told him.

Jason nodded quickly as he laid a ten-dollar bill on the table. "I'm not surprised," he said dryly. "Sorry I can't stay for dinner."

I took hold of his arm. "I'm your friend, Jason."

"Yes, of course," Jason said, almost sharply, as if such indulgence offended him. He hesitated, and then regarded me intently. "You wouldn't think of me as a violent man, would you, William?"

"No."

Jason looked at me as if I were the shallowest person on earth. Then he turned and walked away.

I suppose that had Jason been a less understated man I would have let the matter drop, simply gone home and slept off my concern. But his agitation was so contradictory to his usual calm that my alarm increased after he had left the restaurant. I sat nursing a second brandy and replaying our conversation. The mystery only deepened, however, and before long I had to find the answer.

I went first to Jason's apartment, but he was not in. So I went to Elena's in Brooklyn Heights.

She opened the door immediately. She was dressed in a long skirt and bulky sweater. She tugged her glasses from around her ears and look at me quizzically.

"Didn't Jason tell you that I couldn't make it to dinner?" she asked.

"Yes, he did," I told her. "He seemed out of sorts."

Elena nodded. "He probably was." She opened the door and stepped back to let me in.

I walked through the short hallway and into Elena's combination living room and office. Her desk was at the side of the room, near the window. It was covered with papers, and her old typewriter, the one my father had given her so long ago, sat open on it. The manuscript of *Quality* was sitting on the wide windowsill beside the desk. It was perhaps six inches thick.

Elena was entirely calm, quite different in her mood from Jason. "This afternoon Jason and I fought like a couple of teenagers," she said, shaking her head. "It was ridiculous, really. I think we're both ashamed of ourselves. Sit down, William."

I remained standing.

Elena walked to the fireplace and leaned against the mantel. "I'm too old for this sort of thing, and I won't put up with it."

"I don't mean to pry," I began, "but could you —"

"Of course you mean to pry, William," Elena said firmly. "Every life is a soap opera but our own." There was a harshness in her voice that I had never heard before.

"I could leave now, if that's what you want," I said.

Elena waved her arm dismissively. "Oh, for God's sake, sit down, William. I don't need another display of wounded pride today."

I sat down on the sofa.

"We had a fight," Elena said. "It's just that simple. I happened to mention some doubts I had about some of the things he'd written in *The American Experience*." She glanced angrily toward the window. "His response was hysterical."

"That doesn't sound like Jason," I said.

Elena remained on her feet. She glared down at me. "I don't care how it sounds, that's what happened."

"Well, what exactly did you say?" I asked cautiously.

She was about to answer when there was a knock at the door.

"That's probably Jason," Elena said. "He called a few minutes ago." She did not move.

"Should I leave?" I asked.

"No," she said. She walked slowly to the door and opened it. From the living room I could see Jason standing in the doorway.

"William's here," Elena told him. "Do you still want to come in?"

"Yes, I do," Jason said. His voice was very soft. She stepped out of the doorway and allowed him to pass in front of her.

Jason nodded to me as he walked into the living room, then he turned to Elena.

"I've come to apologize," he said.

"I accept," Elena said coolly. "Now you can go, if you like."

"No, Elena, I can't," Jason said. "Now I have apologized to you, and I think we both know that I am not the only villain of the piece."

Elena walked across the room and took up her position by the fireplace again.

"You expect an apology from me?" she asked.

"Yes."

"For what?"

"For hasty judgments, Elena."

"About what?"

Jason shook his head despairingly. "You know exactly what I'm talking about." He looked at me. "She believes that *The American Experience* is — how did she put it? A work of rhetoric, not of history." He looked at Elena. "Isn't that about right?"

"Yes," Elena said firmly.

Jason glanced at me helplessly, then he turned back to my sister.

"You've learned a great deal since you started your book, Elena," he said, "but you shouldn't believe that you've learned everything."

"I don't."

"Not about American intellectual history," Jason added, "and not about me." He turned to me. "She thinks I glorify war and violence in my books."

"Wittingly or unwittingly," Elena added.

"She says this about a pacifist," Jason said, still looking at me.

Elena rolled her eyes toward the ceiling. "Jason, there's no need to go over this again."

Jason continued to stare into my eyes. "How can she believe such a thing?"

I looked into Jason's face, and I realized that what my sister had discovered was the truth. There was a violence in his soul which he had spent a long, heroic life suppressing. It had been born, no doubt, in the rage he had known in his youth, the rage to escape from the heavy wool of family and regional loyalty, which only the force of a violent temperament could have overthrown. But the violence had remained, in the long passages of cathartic battle and massive destruction that flared up in his work — the almost loving portrait, for example, of the burning of Atlanta. Elena had seen this, had seen how his early hatred and the need to control it had "continually shifted his work," as she wrote in *Quality*, "between roseate romanticism and a terrible swift sword."

When I made no response at all to Jason's question, he turned back to Elena.

"Do you think my whole life is a charade?" he asked. "Just one long hypocrisy?"

"No, Jason," Elena said. She glanced toward the window. "Perhaps you'd better go."

"No!" Jason said. He walked over to the window and picked up the manuscript of *Quality*. "Do you think there are no errors in this goddamn thing?"

Elena turned toward him. "Put it down, Jason."

Jason waved the pages in the air. A few slipped from the stack and scattered across the floor in front of him. "Your mind is a knife, Elena," he shouted. "Just a knife to slash things with!"

"Put that down," Elena said firmly. She took a step toward him.

Jason continued to wave the manuscript. "What if I were to throw it in the goddamn fire," he threatened.

I stood up. "For God's sake, this is not a scene from Ibsen," I told him. "Put it down."

Jason glared lethally at Elena. Then, in what must have been for him a gesture as uncontrollable as the movement of a planet, he hurled the manuscript at my sister. The pages flew into the air all around us, then fell to the floor.

Elena did not move. Nor did I. We simply stood silently and watched as Jason walked slowly to the door. When he reached it, he turned around.

"Elena," he said softly.

She walked over to him and opened the door.

"Good night, Jason," she said.

Jason stepped into the hallway. "I'm sorry," he said.

"So am I," Elena said. Then she closed the door.

She walked back into the living room and without a word began gathering up the pages of her book. She was trying very hard not to cry.

"Maybe this can all be forgotten," I said lamely.

Elena did not look up from the floor.

"Maybe you could indulge him a little," I suggested.

"No," Elena said sternly.

"Just a little," I said. "Why not?"

"Because that is not my function in life, William," Elena said. She picked up the last pages, took the ones I had gathered up from me, and laid them all in a stack on the mantel. Standing there in her long black skirt, the marble mantelpiece behind her, a fire at her feet, she looked very much, as she had once jokingly described herself, "like an English murderess."

"Would you like a drink, William?" she asked.

"If you're having one."

She walked into the adjoining kitchen, and from my seat in the living room I could hear her drawing the glasses down from their shelf. Years later, she would tell me that those few moments alone in the kitchen had been among the most terrible of her life, that she had thought of nothing but Jason, and that she had had to fight every impulse within her not to rush down the stairs and bring him back.

"Brandy for you, of course," she said as she walked back into the living room and handed me my glass.

"Yes, thank you," I said.

"You know, Miriam and I used to have some pretty bad rows," I said, almost lightly, "and we always got over them."

Elena sipped her wine slowly, watching the fire.

"We just simmered down after a while," I continued. "By the end of the day, we always loved each other again."

Elena nodded in that desultory fashion of hers, an indication of neither argument nor agreement but only that her ear had received my voice.

"And of course, after a particularly bad squabble —"

Elena lifted her hand. "Enough, William."

"Sorry," I said quickly.

She took another sip of wine. "I wish I could just forget about it," she said after a moment. "Forget about his books, his contradictions." She looked at me. "But I can't."

I leaned toward her. "Why not, Elena?"

She smiled, but very sadly. "Because I know them too well," she said. As she sipped her wine and watched the fire, she seemed to possess rather painfully that form of surgical understanding which in *Quality* she ascribed to Henry James, "the peculiar human cost of a great intelligence."

For the next three years, Elena worked more or less continually on *The Quality of Thought in American Letters*. She and Jason resumed contact, walking cautiously together along what Jason romantically called "a delta made of old erosions." They would sometimes have dinner together, usually in Brooklyn Heights so that Elena could return to her work immediately after. Occasionally he would lure her out of the city — a day at the Danbury Fair, for example, or a trip to the Hamptons — but they never shared the house on Cape Cod again. Elena would sometimes go alone, sometimes with me, sometimes with Alexander and his family. In Martha's biography, my son is quoted as saying that even on the Cape Elena seemed preoccupied with *Quality*, and this is quite correct.

Still, she maintained a determinedly routine existence, working her usual full day and having dinner in at night. There was a reclusive aspect to her personality during this time, an obsession with her research that lent at least an inner passion to her life. "There is a power in his dislocation," Manfred Owen says of the painter, Kramer, in Elena's last book. "His brush strokes are raised veins."

There was a power in my sister's dislocation, too, but it exacted a price. I remember that on the day Jack MacNeill returned to New York, he and I arranged to meet Elena in Bryant Park. It was a beautiful spring day in 1965, and even the derelicts who drifted along the shaded walkways appeared to enjoy the warmth and greenery. Jack looked quite refreshed after his long exile, and he was talking in a very animated way about the Welsh coal miners, when he looked up and saw my sister moving in our direction, in that erect posture of hers. We both stood up at her approach. As she came nearer, she held back for just an instant, then rushed into Jack's arms and burst into tears. At first I thought this no more than a tearfully joyous reunion. But Jack knew otherwise. He caressed the back of her head with his hand and pressed his mouth to her ear. "All that thought and concentration, Elena," he whispered. "It will kill you in the end."

For the most part, however, she had held up under the stress, and at every stage of the work she kept herself in check by a few simple rules. "My one guiding notion," she said in the 1980 interview, "was that I would refuse to create a situation in which thought could not triumph over information. If I had one general rule of a technical nature, that was it. As for aesthetic principles, I was guided by my belief that in the perception of things human there is an inescapable sympathy, which the French call *pitié* and the Jews call *rakhmones*, whose absence will weaken even works of the highest technical craft, and whose presence will ennoble the humblest platitude."

For Elena, I think, the writing of *Quality* became that legendary city of sanctuary which is everywhere a part of our ancient lore. She went to her labors for the safe harbor they provided, and even the most tiresome and painstaking of her researches — the long slog through the historian John Fiske, for example — were in fact less arduous because of that. Thus, year after year, she moved into what she later called in *Quality* that "*disciplina arcani* through which all serious thought must pass as it moves between the shifting fluctuations of the temperament and the grave and stable greatness of the mind." Great scholarship was what she wanted, but with a human face.

Her own face changed markedly during this period, though it retained its singular grace. Her eyes lost some of their earlier glow, deepening into an opalescent blue, but the creases about them merely gave her a more forceful aspect. She kept her hair in a bun, and it turned increasingly gray, first along the sides of her head, then everywhere. She wore her glasses more often — the sort called "granny glasses" by young people at that time — and kept two identical pairs with her at all times. She began to favor calf-length dresses almost exclusively, and always dark, one might almost say matronly, colors.

She was dressed in just this way on the day Jack MacNeill returned to Wales, in the autumn of 1967. He had been able, as he said, to endure America for only two years. Elena thought differently, however. It was not America that drove him away, she said, it was just Jack's need to go somewhere again, anywhere, even back to Wales, which, as it turned out, he only used as a sort of home base for excursions to the Continent.

As he stood on the curb outside Elena's apartment, a single suitcase in his hand, the door of the cab already flung open, he looked very much the Jack of old, talking energetically about the explosive situation in France at one moment, his unabashed need to see Paris again at the next. As he shifted about arbitrarily from politics to wanderlust, he reminded me of the twin hills of Mount Parnassus, the one devoted to heedlessness, and the other to solemnity.

"Too bad you can't come along, Elena," he said with a boyish wink. "But of course, we've played this scene before."

Elena nodded silently. Her hands were folded in front of her, and a long shawl hung from her shoulders. In such a pose, and with her face so somber, she looked as Jason once described her, "like one who might at any moment turn into allegory."

"Don't guess you'll change your mind?" Jack asked.

Elena shook her head. "No."

Jack shrugged. "Well, I may come back soon. A little college in Connecticut wants me." He laughed. "I've become something of a historical figure, you know. They revere me now for the things they hated me for ten years ago." He reached over and took my hand. "So long, Bill."

"Take care of yourself, Jack," I told him.

He drew Elena into his arms and kissed her.

"Good luck with the book," he said.

Elena smiled. "Enjoy the barricades, Jack."

Jack laughed, then disappeared into the cab. Just for old times' sake, he threw his hat out the window and into the air as the car pulled away.

I picked it up, and Elena and I walked back into her apartment. Stacks of her manuscripts were scattered about, and for some reason they reminded me of the way Miriam's office had often looked, disheveled to her eye, no doubt, but ordered to her mind.

I casually picked up a few pages from one of the stacks. "Funny how this makes me think of Miriam," I said. Elena was busily packing one of her suitcases for the drive we were about to make to Cape Cod. "Miriam comes to mind quite a bit now. She disappeared entirely for a few years, but she comes back to me quite often." I smiled. "As if resurrected, somehow, or maybe now that I'm getting old I can just feel her waiting in the wings."

Elena said nothing. She continued her packing.

I walked over to her suitcase and dropped my camera into it. I had just taken a photograph of Elena and Jack as they stood beside the cab.

"I think that'll be a good picture, Elena," I said casually, "the one I just took of you and Jack."

"Good," Elena said indifferently.

I looked at her closely. "Anything wrong?"

She dropped a folded sweater into the suitcase, then closed it. "The book is finished, William," she said. "I'd like you to take it up to the Cape this week and read it."

"All right."

Elena snapped the latches shut. Then she straightened herself and looked at me. "No holds barred in your criticism," she said.

"As always, Elena," I told her.

It took me the next three days to read it. Elena was walking on the beach below the house when I finished. I glanced up from the last page and saw her there, wrapped in a sweater, her skirt falling almost to the sand. She was facing the bay, and the water was flat and gray before her. It struck me then that she was rather like her latest book, a creature of disparate cords which had been wound into a sturdy cloth, and that she would remain so always, regardless of all that would swirl around her, like a stone held firm, rather than dislodged, by the tumult of the stream.

As Martha scribbled something in her notebook, I glanced up at the bay. A single sailboat could be seen between the beach and the distant shores of Provincetown. The wind was buffeting it badly.

"It must be cold out there," I said quietly.

Martha looked up. She had not heard me. It was late in the afternoon and she had arranged to take a plane back to New York that evening. Because of that, she was eager to get as far as she could during the last few hours of our next-to-last interview.

"How would you describe Elena's mood after finishing *Quality?*" she asked.

"She was tired, of course," I told her, "but she was not in any sense depressed."

"Was she apprehensive?"

"Of course. What writer isn't?"

"About the book's reception?"

"Yes," I said. "She knew that there were things in it that could, and probably would, draw a great deal of fire."

"Like what?" Martha asked, as if she thought *Quality* a perfect book, beyond all criticism, which, of course, it wasn't.

"Well, her inability to resist a quip from time to time, for one thing," I smiled. "Of course, your mother would have understood it." I stood up and took a copy of *Quality* from the bookshelf, then sat back down and began to flip through it. "Here's something, for example."

Martha brought her pencil to the ready.

"There's a section on Hemingway," I said, "and in it Elena says this." I began to read: " 'In certain works, Hemingway's power to convey the grit of experience becomes his weakness. He offers minute detail at the expense of a broader generality, so that one comes to suspect an eye that sees everything but a mind that senses nothing.' " I closed the book. "She came to think of lines like that as petty and probably wrong-headed."

"I see," Martha said.

"And then there were others that erred in another direction, like when she wrote that Edgar Lee Masters 'sensed the waste within the plenitude.' " I shrugged. "Maybe he did, but Elena later thought such phrases stupid."

Martha looked shocked. "Stupid?"

"Yes, stupid," I repeated.

Martha stared at me, aghast. "It's difficult to think of that word in connection with Elena."

I laughed. "You can think of that word in connection with anyone, Martha."

She nodded quickly, then glanced down at her notes. "So how would you describe her mood generally then?" she asked. "I mean, after she finished *Quality?*"

"Well, she seemed pleased that I had liked the book," I told her, "and she was pleased that Sam had liked it, too. Of course, *Quality* was way over his head, but Sam had a canny editorial sense. He didn't have to understand a book, and he certainly didn't have to like it, to sense when he had an extraordinary work before him."

"How strange," Martha said.

"Yes. Of course, he wasn't always right — just often enough, as Elena once said, to make it eerie."

Martha quickly wrote down Elena's remark. Then she looked up at me again, hungry for the salient fact. "So, in general, you'd say that Elena was happy with what she had accomplished in *Quality?*"

"Yes, I think she was."

"Quite content with herself?"

I started to nod reflexively, but something held me back, and I instantly remembered something Manfred Owen tells his daughter: "There is a form of serenity," he says, "that is nothing more than the highest level of despair."

I looked at Martha quizzically. "Content with herself, did you say?"

"Yes."

I shook my head. "I don't think I could go that far."

"Why not?" Martha asked. "She'd just completed a great book. You had liked it, and so had Sam Waterman. It was due to be published the next year. Why would she not be content?"

"You know, Martha, that is a very good question," I said. And I meant it.

Martha looked pleased. "Well, do you have an answer?"

"I'm not sure," I told her. "But I just can't say to you that Elena was, as you put it, content with herself."

Martha tried to offer me a way out. "Well, you've already said that she had qualms about some of the things she'd written in *Quality*."

"Yes, but it was more than that," I said. "Every writer realizes how much he would change a book the day after it's published."

"So her — what would you call it? — her discontent was not about *Quality*?"

"No, I don't think it was," I said. I glanced down at the copy of *Quality* in my lap and saw the Parnassus logo staring up at me: a mountain shrouded in clouds, a single bolt of lightning striking down toward a plain. I shook my head. "No, it wasn't the book." I stood up, walked to the bookshelf, and replaced it there. Then I returned to my seat, still preoccupied with Martha's question. It was only then that a particular incident occurred to me. It had never seemed inordinately telling before, and so I had more or less forgotten it. But now, with Martha staring at me as if I were slightly cracked, it drifted back, in that whispering voice the mind uses from time to time when it is helping you along, and the minute I heard it, I could sense an enormous shifting in my perception of my sister.

I glanced toward the bay, then quickly back to Martha. Her face was very serious, and I suppose she could tell that a great deal was going on in my mind.

"Yes, William?" she said.

I shrugged. "It was just a remark Elena made not long before *Quality* was published," I said. "Just a remark made at dinner, which got buried under all the activity that followed the publication of the book, all that incredible hoopla which Sam did everything he could to create."

"And what remark was that?" Martha asked quickly.

"Well, I was having dinner with Elena and my son," I began. "He'd just passed the New York bar and was working on Wall Street, something which both Elena and I thought rather disreputable but had the good sense to keep our mouths shut about."

Martha nodded quickly. She did not care for introductory remarks. She wanted the heart of the matter, and it was obvious from the tension in her face that she wanted it without delay.

"Anyway, he was very full of himself," I continued, "and he'd just read *Quality* and was going on about it, praise on praise." I could see the entire scene clearly in my mind, the three of us seated around a table in a restaurant, waiting for Saundra to arrive, and Alexander relentlessly showering my sister with praise that was unnecessarily effusive but certainly sincere. "For her part," I said, "Elena sat casually in her seat, one arm slung over the back of her chair, listening politely but with a certain aloofness."

"Aloofness?" Martha asked.

"Yes," I said. "You know, the sort of dignified silence that is the only permissible response to an exaggerated compliment."

Martha nodded. "Go on."

"Well, Alexander then singled out the particular aspect of *Quality* he most admired," I told her. "It was what he called the analytic quality of the book, its sharp precision."

"Well, it certainly has that," Martha said.

"Yes, it does. But I could see that Alexander's comment bothered Elena. As he went on, she became noticeably agitated, and just before Saundra came into the restaurant, she held up her hand to shut Alexander up and she said, "Remember, Alexander, one does not find the truth simply by splitting veils.""

Martha regarded me expectantly for a moment, waiting for me to continue.

"That's it?" she asked when I added nothing else. "That's the whole anecdote?"

"I'm afraid so."

"Well, what does it mean?"

"I'm not sure, Martha, but I believe that it fits into her life somewhere."

"Can you be more specific?"

I shook my head. "I wish I could, but everything seems to be floating right now."

It was still floating when I drove Martha into Hyannis sometime later. I felt very tired by the time I got back to the house. It was not a specific weariness, just a general sense of being adrift in insubstantial atmospheres. To escape the discomfort of that feeling, I went to bed early, found that I could not sleep, and rose again. I sat for a long time in the back room, with nothing but the blackness of the nocturnal sea before me, that utter blackness which is like no other.

After a time I took down Elena's copy of *Quality* once again, reading at random but searching for a clue, as some deranged Christian mystic might roam through the Bible, turning over verses, looking for the guidepost from the hand of God. Only one passage struck me, the final one of the book:

> When one searches through the letters of our nation, its thought as written, spoken, or in law decreed, one finds no single strand of steady and precise reflection. Rather, the mind that presents itself to our concentration is one of shifts and undulations, full of praise and squabbling, duty and resistance, a consciousness vaguely groping for half-imagined answers to the questions of freedom, fulfillment, and existence. To these timeless questions, our men of thought have attached issues of justice and retribution, privilege and equality, labor and creation, community and individuality — these and scores of others, which are little different from the common thought of man. The study of our letters, therefore, suggests the weaknesses of our probing, both singly and as a people. For on this abundant continent, all things have been emboldened except the mind, and thus we have remained no more intellectually enriched than the far less privileged body of mankind. We have learned how to possess, but not how to nurture; how to acquire, but not how to cast aside; how to calculate, but not how to think.

I closed the book, alarmed by how stern that passage was, how severe and unforgiving. I opened the book again a few moments later and reread the paragraph. I looked carefully at each phrase, foolishly convinced that somewhere in the words was the key to her life. Here was the Rosetta stone lying open in my lap. I read it again and again, each time more slowly, pausing after each sentence as if waiting for an echo.

Suddenly, I saw Elena as she appeared on the cold, blustery day we buried Mary Farrell. The service was held in a chapel near the coast of Maine. I had an image of Elena rising and walking to the altar. I could feel the hush of the crowd as she moved forward. At the altar, she set her eyes firmly on the people who waited before her, her hands plunged deeply into the pockets of her black wool coat. And even as I sat in the back room of her house on the Cape, I could feel myself leaning forward to hear her, just as I had done that day in the freezing chapel. I knew that I was approaching what she must have meant, first in *Quality,* when she wrote of a material abundance which had done nothing to enrich the mind, and then, later, with Alexander, when she had alluded to the limits she had discovered in her own scholarship. It was clear that she was after larger game now. But I could not exactly name it. In my mind I saw her once again as she stood behind the altar. She took a deep breath before beginning. Then she spoke, and I knew it, the secret of my sister's mind.

The *Quality of Thought in American Letters* was published by Parnassus Press in the fall of 1968. It could hardly have been issued at a better time. The nation was reveling in an orgy of self-immolation over poverty and racism and the war in Vietnam. Elena's book could only be seen as another log on that fire. It was snapped up by student and teacher alike, quoted continually by the new wave of young historians, sociologists, and literary critics, hailed as a monumental attack upon the very foundations of American intellectual achievement, and generally regarded as a sweeping work of literary, historical, and intellectual criticism, a work of enormous insight and deep disaffection.

It would be disingenuous to suggest that Elena found any of this a surprise. Certainly she knew what was in her book, and certainly she had by then had enough experience as a writer to know, as she said in the 1980 interview, that "that which is written is not necessarily that which is read." But I believe the extent of the notoriety the book achieved did genuinely astonish her. She was deluged with requests for her attendance at various rallies, forums, symposia, and conferences. She received teaching offers from fourteen universities, was written about in the popular press (*Time* called her "the femme fatale of American letters" but at least buried the story in the back of the magazine; *Newsweek,* on the other hand, put her face on its cover), she even appeared on television one Sunday afternoon, looking very pale and edgy under the white lights.

For a time the enormity of all this seemed to distract her. She took a certain delight in the book's success. She began work on a two-volume edition of her essays and short stories, a project Sam rushed into print, hoping to capitalize on *Quality's* extraordinary success. She spoke to most of the groups that asked her, at least attempted to reply to her steadily increasing mail, and in general worked feverishly to measure up to what seemed expected of her.

Inevitably, however, the wave subsided, and as it did those concerns which had risen in the last passage of *Quality,* but which had been buried under the flurry of public acclaim that followed its publication, began to emerge again in Elena. She talked insistently about methods of literary and historical analysis. Epistemology became a passionate interest. She discussed the classics of moral philosophy as if she had only recently discovered them. As a mind, she was very much alive.

But she also grew more aloof. The early energy she had poured into the essay and short story collections quickly dissipated, and Barney Nesbitt, her latest editor, began to complain that Elena was intentionally avoiding him. Once, during a luncheon, he suggested that she might have caught what he called the "star syndrome."

"Maybe she thinks she's too big for Parnassus now, William," Barney said.

I shook my head. "I don't think so."

"Really? Well, she doesn't return my calls," Barney said. "I'm her editor, William, not some starry-eyed groupie, you know what I mean?"

"Of course."

He smiled, leaned across the table, and patted me on the shoulder. "Do what you can with her, will you, old boy? She shouldn't let fame go to her head. Like the Romans say, it's fleeting."

I nodded. "I'll talk to her."

But when I next saw my sister, I found that it was almost impossible to talk to her about anything even remotely touching on her career. Instead, over an extended dinner, she talked about Elizabeth and Julien Tavernier, about fatality and moral choice. She mentioned that she had written Jack MacNeill and was planning to visit him in Wales and that Mary had written her. But they seemed no more than distant references to her now.

Finally, I had had enough. I interrupted her in mid-sentence, actually grabbing her hand as I did so. "What are you looking for, Elena?" I asked.

To her credit, she did not pretend that the question surprised her; she simply answered it. "I don't know," she said.

"You must have some idea."

She thought about it for a moment but came to no conclusion. "Maybe you just go through times when what's killing you, William —" She stopped, as if she had grasped it. "When what's killing you is your life."

She flew to Wales a few weeks later and spent almost two weeks with Jack MacNeill. But when she came back to New York, she looked anything but refreshed. As it turned out, Jack had had a slight stroke only a month or so before her arrival. It had not permanently damaged him, but Elena could see other distressing effects — a certain weariness and dread, as she described it, a premonition of the end.

"He looked a great deal older," Elena told me on the evening she returned. She looked at me as if hoping I might have some answer for all our inevitable decay. "He got very maudlin one evening," she went on. "He said he was just a flicker now, not a flame, just part of the effluvia left in the wake of a revolution that never happened." She shook her head. "It should not end this way."

Elena remained in this somber mood for almost two years. There were no fits of uncontrollable depression, no excessive reclusiveness, and certainly no sudden explosions of rage or resentment, but her work grew darker, and the stories she wrote during this period are filled with a straining after an impossible exactitude. In "The Treatise," an old professor spends his last days perfecting an essay begun in his youth; it remains unfinished when he dies. In "Attorney's Fees," a brilliant lawyer searches for that one precedent which on its own will win his case, rejecting all others because, as he says, "I am sick to death of standing on the trap door of ambiguity." And in "Just a Line or Two," a college student attempts to explain his decision to leave school to his father with such complete precision that it cannot possibly be misunderstood, but finds after reading the final draft of his letter that "there was nothing in it at all, except maybe a dreadful opacity resulting from my yearning to be clear."

Elena was probably at work on the final version of "Just a Line or Two," in March of 1971, when Mary Farrell died in San Francisco.

It was Martha who telephoned to let me know. I was sitting in my apartment, chuckling over the schoolboy gossip in a letter from David, when the phone rang. I suppose there was still an edge of amusement in my voice when I answered it.

"Mr. Franklin, this is Martha Farrell, Mary's daughter," Martha said. It was typical of Martha to introduce herself this way. I had met her many times, of course, but until she got her doctorate, she always addressed me with much formality.

"Well of course, Martha," I said cheerfully. "How are you?"

"I wanted to let you know that mother died yesterday," Martha said calmly.

All the world seemed to grow silent for the second or two I stood with the phone pressed to my ear.

"I was at Berkeley when it happened," Martha added matter-of-factly.

I finally found my voice. "I can't tell you how sorry I am, Martha."

"You know, she had this small farm in Maine," Martha said. "It was my father's old place, or his father's, or something like that. It goes back for generations. Anyway, there's a little chapel on it, evidently. Unless somebody's torn it down or something. Well, my mother visited it once. I guess she fell in love with the place. She's put it in her will that she wanted to be buried there."

"I see."

"It's not far from Portland."

"So, you're going to bring the body back East?"

"Yes," Martha said crisply. "I think we can have the funeral a week from today. I suppose some of you would like to come."

"Of course."

"Well, just let everybody know about my mother," Martha said. "I'll send you all the details about the place in Maine. And I guess I'll see you in a week."

"Yes, you will," I told her.

"And by the way," Martha added quickly, "I think that my mother would have liked your sister to speak at the ceremony. There's no minister, or anything like that. You know how Mother felt about religious things. But I do believe that she'd have liked for Elena to say something."

"I'll tell her."

"Good," Martha said. Then she hung up.

I called Elena right away. She received the news of Mary's death quite calmly. Her voice remained cool, measured, betraying nothing excessive in her grief. "Is she going to be buried in California?"

"No. A little chapel not far from Portland, Maine."

"Oh yes, she once told me about that place," Elena said.

"We'll fly up. Sam will probably want to go with us."

"Yes, of course," Elena said. In my mind I could see her standing by the window, the phone trembling slightly in her hand, using all her strength to steady her voice.

"Martha would like for you to speak, deliver the eulogy," I told her.

"All right," Elena said.

I started to tell her more, explain that Mary had simply died in the park while staring out toward the bay, but I heard the receiver click down on the other side. Clearly Elena had already heard enough.

We all flew up to Maine the next week, Sam and Elena and me. Elena sat silently beside me on the plane. Several times she drew a few pages of lined paper from her purse and read them over to herself, making small changes with her pen. It was clear that she had given these remarks a good deal of thought.

Martha met us at the airport. She seemed pleased to see us, particularly Elena. I suppose that by then she thought herself rather a fan of my sister. She had read all her books and could discuss them with considerable knowledge. But she was not fawning in the least. Martha was far too much like her mother ever to play the sycophant. "Everything's arranged," she said, "and I hope it all goes off with a minimum of confusion." I almost smiled at the directness of her manner. Mary would have understood it, perhaps even admired it, in anyone but her daughter.

Elena suddenly moved forward and drew Martha into her arms. "I loved your mother very much," she said.

Martha smiled sadly. "Yes, I know." She drew back, then took both Elena's hands in hers. "You know, Mother and I weren't that close, in some ways," she said. "I always thought she could have been so much more."

Elena drew her hands slowly from Martha's grasp and sank them into the pockets of her coat. "We can never know what is possible for someone else, Martha."

Martha's face tightened. She understood that she had been gently scolded. "Well, I suppose we should go to the chapel now," she said, avoiding any further discussion of her mother.

It was a small stone church. Mary's coffin had been placed at the front, below the raised pulpit. It was covered with roses. There were no other flowers. Long before, Mary had decreed that her coffin be closed, since even in death she did not want her wrinkles to show.

The chapel was almost completely full. Even so, it was a small assembly. A few people had flown in from California. They were quiet and well-dressed, and in their manner appeared more to have been the friends of Mary's husband than herself.

The ceremony began with a song played on a beat-up piano by an old woman Martha had hired for the occasion. Mary herself had selected the song, however. It was "Hail to the Chief," and when it began, a round of quiet, nervous laughter swept the crowd.

Martha was smiling as she stepped up behind the lectern when the music stopped. "My mother was not high on ceremony," she said. "She planned this funeral to be a simple affair. She only wanted one person to speak, Elena Franklin." She glanced back at us.

The crowd shifted uneasily as Elena rose and walked to the front of the chapel. When she reached the altar, she turned slowly and lowered her hands into the pockets of her coat.

"I suppose that if I asked any one of you to describe Mary Farrell," she began, "at least part of that description would include her wit. She made it that part of her we remember most. Yet I think she knew how cynical and blind wit can be if it is not joined to other virtues."

She stopped and glanced quickly at Martha, who sat in the first row, then back up at the rest of us. "Thought is the greatest achievement of the mind, hope the greatest achievement of the heart, and goodness the greatest achievement of the will. When wit diminishes any of these, it reduces our humanity. This was sometimes the case with our friend, as it is the case, to more or less degree, with all of us. The point, however, is that Mary used her wit to reveal herself, not to conceal. She had the peace that comes from being exactly what she seemed. She accepted her limits and ignored her possibilities. Her knowledge of herself was very deep, and she possessed what Emily Dickinson called 'apocalyptic wisdom,' the sort that will not be diverted from the terrifying implications of its understanding. She had stared down into that abyss from which so many turn their eyes, and in the face of that knowledge, her wit became her means of survival. It did not relieve her of her pain, but it kept her from imposing it on us.

"It has been said that a book can never be both great and angry, and the same can be said of a life. Anyone who knew Mary knew there was anger in her. Part of it flowed from the simple fact that she was a woman who understood the peculiar contradictions of that estate. She knew that the man's world in which her life was imbedded would praise her dutifulness, then allow her only trifling duties; extol her intuitiveness, then bar her from the harder world of fact by sneering at her illogic; exalt her sense of service, then feed upon it. Particularly in her youth, Mary felt the constriction of her womanhood. But she also felt the larger human failure from which it came: the casual abandonment of that principle of moral thought which requires consistency between the admiration of a virtue and the treatment of it. And I think that she saw this as part of a larger debility: an indifference to suffering that is not your own. 'Every man is an island,' Mary used to say, laughing as she did so, 'so make sure you check for whom the bell tolls, because if you're lucky, it may not be for you.' "

There was a smattering of subdued laughter, and Elena waited for it to subside. Then she continued.

"This distrust of human nature was as deep as Mary's cynicism ever went, but it was deep enough to hold her in its grasp. It drove her into a life that could only look apathetic to those who viewed it from a distance. She married, as she always said, 'quite often and quite well'; and to her oldest friends, this seemed emblematic of a larger self-indulgence. But there must be a place in the world for the unbeliever who cannot hide his unbelief or act against it, for the one who loves nature but cannot be a pantheist, who dreams of human community but cannot be a Communist, stands in awe of creation, but cannot leap from bafflement to God. Mary was one of these, and she paid the price of all those like her. She never knew the glory of fighting for a great idea, nor the pain of abandoning it. Such is the penalty of disengagement, and none greater should be asked of anyone."

Elena glanced about the chapel, then drew her hands from the pockets of her coat and grasped the sides of the lectern. "The essential quality of goodness," she said, leaning forward, "is its sense of preservation. Because of that, it must have already seemed an ancient value to the first human being who consciously possessed it. It seems to me that we must judge a life not by what it spent but by what it saved. This is no easy task. It is our duty to know as much as we can of what the mind and heart can teach us. To accomplish this, of course, we have only those powers of thought and feeling which have been given us imperfectly and which remain, as Mary surely knew, at once both crippled and supreme. I will leave the question of the goodness of Mary's life to you, and I think that you could not more honor her — and certainly not more please her — than by attempting quite seriously to answer it."

She nodded slightly to the crowd as she stepped down. Then she returned to her seat and sat silently beside me while the final stages of the funeral were concluded. And I suppose I should have known then what I only learned years later, as I sat in the darkness with *Quality* on my lap and the memory of Elena's remarks at Mary's funeral in my mind. I should have known that for all her outward calm as she sat beside me, her features almost melding with the frozen beauty of the New England countryside that surrounded her, I should have known that her mind was on the road again, that it had turned onto another path, one which had led her to the most difficult of our questions, the one least accessible to our methods of approach: How can our knowledge make us good? In its own way, this was the only question my sister had ever asked, and now she was asking it again, not by going forward, but by returning, first, as a human being, to the rudiments of life, and then, as a writer, to the simplest of all tasks.

TO DEFINE
A WORD

I did not see Elena for almost a month after Mary's funeral. Nor did I call her or make any attempt whatsoever to contact her. If I had learned anything at all about my sister, it was that she sometimes needed to be alone. All my life, it seemed to me, I had offered unnecessary aid. There would be no more of it.

Still, I remained keenly interested in her next step. I knew there would be one, but I had no idea what it might be.

Then one afternoon when I met Sam for a drink after my classes at Columbia, a little light broke on the matter.

"By the way, William," Sam said, "I got a call from Elena yesterday."

"Really?"

"Have you talked to her since we got back from Maine?"

"No."

Sam looked at me suspiciously. "You two didn't have some kind of argument, did you?"

I laughed. "Not at our age, Sam. What did she want?"

"She was asking about that house of mine on the Cape," Sam said. "She said she might want to buy it." He took a sip from his drink. "Sort of surprised me, since she hasn't been up there all that much since she broke off with Jason."

"Do you want to sell it?"

"I told her I'd just let her have it for the summer, if that's what she wanted, a brief vacation out of the city."

"And what did she say?"

"She said no, that she wanted something, you know, permanent."

"You mean, leave New York?" I asked. I shook my head. "She'd never do that."

Sam smiled that old sly smile of his. "Why not, William, you are."

"What are you talking about?"

"That Harvard offer. You'll take it."

"How'd you know about that?"

"I have my sources," Sam said. He gave me a cunning wink. "You'll take it, William. I know you will. Because you can't turn it down. Not Harvard. Teaching there will finally legitimate your career, all your work."

I waved my hand dismissively. "Ridiculous."

Sam watched me knowingly. "You're still basically a little boy from Connecticut with a traveling salesman for a father and no prospects of your own," he said. In the twilight years you need a little affirmation. Harvard will give you that. It's bullshit, but it's gold plated."

"Maybe it's not that at all, Sam," I said, weakly defending myself. "Maybe I just need a change."

Sam took another sip from his drink. "I need a change myself," he said. "I'm seventy-two, William, but I can still get it up."

"Congratulations."

"I still have some life, but I'm tired of Parnassus. I'm going to turn it over to Christina." He scratched his chin. "I'm going to grow a beard, a big white one, just like Santa Claus, and then I'm going to give some things away. Like that little house of mine on Cape Cod."

"She would never take it," I told him.

"Not free, she wouldn't," Sam said. "But — how shall I put it — she'll get a bargain, you know?"

I nodded.

"You know why I'm doing this?" Sam asked. "Because you're going to Cambridge, and I will not have Elena living alone."

"Maybe that's what she wants."

"It's just a two-hour drive from Boston to Cape Cod," Sam said. "I'm sure you'll make it often, am I right?"

I smiled. "I'll try."

He slapped the table with his great open hand. "Good."

"It's funny, Sam," I told him, "I never figured you for early retirement, and certainly not for divestiture."

"I'm going to Israel," Sam said. "I'm going to plant a tree and give away some money and live on a kibbutz and tend the children while their parents farm."

"You're *not* serious," I blurted. "For God's sake, you're a native New Yorker. What the hell are you going to do in a desert village?"

"They ship in movies," Sam said.

"Do they ship in nightclubs?"

Sam leaned toward me. "You've always thought me a vulgarian, William. And you're probably right, at least in some ways. But there's another side to every coin. I'm going to Israel — that's a fact. And you're going to Cambridge and Elena is going to Cape Cod."

He left for Israel three months later. A huge party was thrown for him at Parnassus, during which he formally turned over control of the house to his daughter.

"I think Christina may not put up with some of the old guard," I said to Elena as we stood together in the crowd.

Elena looked up at me. "I will miss Sam." She smiled slightly. "And I will miss you, William."

I had already accepted the post at Harvard and taken a small apartment on the Charles. Sam had been right about me, but he had been wrong about Elena. She had decided not to move to Cape Cod.

"Well," I said, "I have another full week before I move. We should paint the town."

Elena surprised me by liking the idea of a farewell celebration. "It could just be the remnants, William, just you and me and Sam," she said.

A week later we all met outside Parnassus. Sam was dressed to kill in a black tuxedo. I wore my standard dark gray suit, and Elena wore a long dark dress and black cape. She spun around for us, there on the street, the hem of her cape lifting to the air.

We began with dinner at Le Pavillon, an extravagance I had not expected, even from Sam. Then there was a round of dancing at the Waldorf, and I remember that Elena seemed almost girlish, the way she dipped and whirled in Sam's arms. We ended the evening with drinks in the Palm Court at the Plaza, while the pianist played the full list of songs that Sam had previously selected. By midnight we were exhausted as we struggled down an all-but-deserted Fifth Avenue. Sam had loosened his necktie, and its separate strands blew gently in the chill night breeze. Elena had slung her cape over her shoulder and was holding it with the peg of a single finger.

"What I can't get over," Sam said, stopping to gaze down the wide, empty boulevard, "is how quiet New York can get on a night like this." He looked at Elena. "It's the world's largest ghost town."

"You'll miss it," Elena said.

Sam smiled and draped one enormous arm over her shoulder. "Barney said something a little disturbing to me, Elena."

"What was that?"

"He said you weren't working on anything."

Elena smiled. "Well, that's Christina's worry now."

"I'm not talking about making more money off you, my dear," Sam said, "I've made enough." He looked at her very intently. "I'm talking about your health, Elena, your mental health."

Elena's face suddenly darkened. "Let's not spoil the night, Sam."

"I leave tomorrow," Sam said. "Do you think I should leave without saying a few important words to a friend?"

"I'm fine," Elena assured him. She looked at me, as if for aid.

I stepped forward. "Come on, Sam, let's not get maudlin."

Sam's eyes widened. "Maudlin? I'm talking about Elena's life." He squeezed her shoulder. "You don't travel in a very big circle, Elena. Who do you have in the world? Just me and William. Now I'm going to Israel and William's off to Cambridge. Where does that leave you?"

"Please, Sam, I'd really like for you to stop now," Elena said firmly.

Sam straightened himself, then pulled an envelope from his coat pocket. "This is a contract, all made out," he said. He handed it to Elena. "It just needs your signature."

Elena glanced at the envelope but said nothing.

"It gives you that house of mine on Cape Cod," Sam said, "the one you asked me about. It gives you that, Elena, in exchange for the right to publish your next book. Any book. I don't care what."

Elena smiled softly. "There may not be a next book, Sam."

Sam shrugged. "Well, I may be dead, shot by some goddamn terrorist, by the time you find that out."

Elena shook her head and held out the envelope. "No thanks."

Sam did not take the envelope from her hand. "There is a custom among the Jews, Elena, called the Year of Jubilee. During that time, all debts are forgiven." He placed his hand softly on the side of my sister's face. "I owe you a great deal. You helped to make Parnassus." He smiled. "But you also owe me, because Parnassus helped to make you." He nodded toward the envelope which Elena continued to hold out toward him. "You sign that contract, and we'll call it even." He drew Elena into his arms. His eyes were glistening. "Tonight is our Year of Jubilee, Elena," he said. "I want to leave with all my debts paid."

Sam Waterman was dead by the time *To Define a Word* was published, but in at least one passage within that book, he lives. "Perhaps I could have had a perfect friend," Manfred Owen says of the painter Kramer, "someone the crooked had by force or guile made straight, someone made good by unquestioned zealotries — a voice lost in anthems, a hand lost in salutes; but I had this floating You, Kramer, a beam more strong because composed of scattered light."

Elena signed the contract then and there, with a pen I handed to her. She used Sam's back for a table, and she kissed him when she was through.

We took him to the airport a week later. He was in a jovial mood. He talked about how he was looking forward to the life he imagined lay ahead. He seemed oblivious to what it implied — the boredom and routine, the heat and dust, the petty squabbling of the kibbutz council — everything so trivial, it would seem, compared to the enterprises in which he had been so long engaged. I laughed and quoted Byron as the plane taxied away: "Fools are my theme, let satire be my song."

Elena turned toward me. "You *have* grown cynical, William."

"Mark my words, Elena, Sam will be back in New York within a year."

She nodded. "Maybe."

"Where else can he get really first-rate Châteaubriand?"

Elena laughed and took my arm. "When are you leaving for Cambridge?"

"First of the month," I said. "Care to come along?"

"No."

"May I leave you with a little advice then?" I asked, keeping the lightness in my voice.

"Please do."

"Find something to work on. Start a new book, a new short story. Start a new essay. Start something, anything."

She looked at me and smiled. "Is speed everything, William?"

"Elena, at our age, to hesitate is to die."

She shook her head. "I'm not sure that's true. At our age, or any other."

"You haven't written a word that I know of since you finished *Quality*," I said.

"No, I haven't."

"May I ask, as a brother, why that is?"

"Because I haven't found anything I particularly want to write."

"Are you looking?"

"Yes, I am," Elena said. "But not quickly. Not anymore." It was clear that she did not intend now or ever again to be rushed ahead. Not by me; not by anyone. Later, she would make this explicit in chosing a line from Chaucer as the epigraph for *To Define a Word*: "He hasteth well that wisely can abide."

It was in the dead of winter when Martha came to Cape Cod for her last interview with me. I picked her up at the airport in Hyannis, then drove her back to Elena's house in Brewster, the house I owned now, since she had left it to me.

Martha was bundled up in a host of coats and scarves and sweaters. She had flown in from California, and the East Coast seemed all the colder to her. "How do you stand this weather?" she asked as soon as I came through the doors of the terminal. She was bobbing on her feet and slapping at her shoulders with her gloved hands. "The cold and the isolation," she went on. "Did Elena really want this?"

I nodded. "In her last years, I think she did."

Martha quickly grabbed her two bags. "Well, let's go."

There was a thick fog that day, gray and persistent, the sort that, after a time, makes you feel that the earth you stand on has somehow been torn out of the planet and that you are now suspended eternally in a ball of clouds.

Martha peered out the window as we drove slowly down Route 6A. "I've run into a blind spot," she said.

"What kind?"

"Eight years in Elena's life. The time between when you left for Cambridge and she spent her first winter up here."

"Yes," I said, "I know what you mean."

Martha turned toward me. "She didn't decide to live on the Cape year round until she . . . she . . . how should I put it?"

"Until she began to die."

Martha nodded delicately. "That winter she spent here — that would have been the winter of 1975 — that's when she began *To Define a Word*, right?"

"Yes, I think so."

"Well, I've found out a lot about that time," Martha said, "but the eight years immediately before it, they elude me, William." She looked worried. "I really hope you can help me. After all, we're approaching the finish line now, aren't we?"

It did not seem the most felicitous of terms, finish line, but I suppose it had to do. "If you're looking for tragedy in the end, Martha," I said, "disillusionment and hopelessness and all that sort of thing, then I'm afraid you've studied the wrong life."

Martha shook her head. "I'm not looking for anything except the truth."

We rode on silently for quite some time. In my mind I could see Elena standing on the curb outside my apartment on the day I left for Cambridge. It was in the fall, and she was wearing one of those heavy sweaters she always preferred, the ones with the deep pockets and thick collars. This particular one was buttonless, with a belt tied at the waist, and I remember that it seemed better suited to a younger woman than my sister. Her hair was almost completely white by then, though her skin remained very soft and smooth. She always looked very much as David once described her, like a young actress trying for the part of an older woman.

I glanced over at Martha. "Those years you're talking about," I said, "I think Elena wanted them entirely to herself."

Martha instantly snatched a pen and notebook from her coat pocket. "Go on."

I shrugged. "Go on to what?"

"With your story."

I tightened my grip on the wheel, steadying the car as we headed into a pocket of denser fog. "I'm not sure I have a story."

"Well, you said that Elena wanted those years," Martha said, coaxing me on. "What did she want them for?"

I could feel my mind pushing backward again. Elena was there on the curb, wrapped in her enormous sweater. David was bustling about the car, strapping boxes to the top. Elena smiled and said that we looked like a couple of refugees, and then David stepped over to me, put his arm around my shoulder, and said to Elena, "You'll miss this scholarly old buzzard, won't you?" And I remember that Elena's eyes moved slowly toward me, her face very calm and thoughtful as it silently answered my grandson's question: no.

I relaxed my grip on the wheel as we came out of the fog. "I think she wanted to be entirely alone," I said. "She wanted to think, Martha, just to think deeply and for a long, long time."

Martha wrote it down. "But that was sort of a pattern with her, wasn't it?"

I shook my head. "Not really," I said.

Martha looked surprised by my answer. "But what about all those other times, her reclusiveness when she was writing *New England Maid*, and then later, the year or two just before she finished up *Quality?*"

"I suppose that can look like a pattern," I admitted, "but this time it was different, I think, because Elena wasn't working on anything, on any book, I mean." Again I could see her standing near the car as we pulled away. She raised her hand slowly and waved. A swirl of leaves rushed toward her, blown by a sudden gust of wind. She stared intently down at them and did not look up again before we had turned the corner and she was no longer in view. "She was not working on a book," I said to Martha, very certain now that I was right. "She was working on her mind."

And that is what she did for the next eight years: she thought about how to think. She continued to live in Brooklyn Heights, in her small, well-furnished apartment on Columbia Heights. Jason sometimes visited her there, but aside from him very few people saw her. Barney Nesbitt complained, grew disgruntled, accused Elena of wasting away. He wrote me letter after letter warning me that she was going crazy all alone. But I had by then learned not to be alarmed by such things. His portrait of her walking in solitary preoccupation on the Promenade, with all of lower Manhattan staring gloomily down at her from across the river, did not disturb me at all. She had what she needed, she had herself.

Which is precisely what I told Martha as we pulled up in front of Elena's house.

Martha smiled, a bit indulgently. "That's just a little glib, don't you think, William?"

I put the car in gear and turned toward her. "Does it matter that it's true?"

Martha looked skeptical. "Surely you're not saying that it was only very late in life that Elena learned to like herself."

"Of course not. I think my sister was one of those very fortunate people who like themselves from the beginning and never stop liking themselves."

Martha drew the collar of her coat more tightly over her throat. "Can we go in the house now? It's really dreary out here."

I built a fire in the front room, and Martha and I sat down together. There was a small table between our two chairs, and I had placed a bottle of brandy on it. I poured a snifter for each of us.

"Take this, Martha," I said. "This is the sort of drink that warms the blood and mellows the spirit."

Martha smiled, took the glass from my hand, and downed it in one gulp. "Yes, very good."

"I didn't realize you were such a longshoreman when it came to booze," I told her.

"A woman has to learn to drink, William," Martha said. "It pulls men up short, makes them realize you're not to be screwed around with."

"I see."

Martha nodded firmly. "Once you realize that people think in symbols, you have to get your symbols straight, and make sure everyone else does, too."

I smiled. "I never doubted that you were a formidable person, Martha."

Martha poured herself another brandy. "Good." She took a small sip and laughed. "You didn't think I was going to down it like the first one, did you?"

"I'm only an observer here," I said.

Martha laughed lightly. "I'll miss you, William. I'll miss these interviews." She put down her glass. "This is the last one, I'm afraid."

"Really?"

She nodded mournfully. "I've spent the advance, or most of it. I simply can't afford another plane fare back to the East Coast."

"I'm sorry to hear it."

"Well, it has to be. We'll correspond, of course. I still have many questions. But for now, it's those mysterious eight years."

"Which are not very mysterious," I said. "They're really not. Sorry."

Martha shifted uneasily in her chair. "I'm not altogether convinced of that, William." She glanced down at her notes. "After you left New York for Cambridge, when was the next time you saw her?"

"Perhaps a month later," I told her. "She came to my apartment. She brought a poster of the Empire State Building and taped it to the wall."

"How did she look?"

"She looked quite well," I said.

"Not distressed in any way?"

"Why should she have been distressed?"

"Well, for one thing, she was suffering from a pretty severe case of writer's block, wasn't she?"

"Not that I know of."

Martha's eyes widened. "William, Elena hadn't written a word since *Quality*. What would you call that, if not writer's block?"

I leaned forward, jostling the table a bit as I did so. "Martha, my sister was not interested in writing anything."

"How do you know that?"

"By her manner," I said. It was a vague answer, of course, yet, her manner was the only thing I had to go on.

Martha blinked rapidly. "Manner? You mean her behavior?"

"I mean the sort of grace she had at that time in her life," I said. "All that frenetic need to be engaged in something had simply disappeared." I smiled. "It struck people as very odd, no doubt. Jason thought Elena suicidal."

"And you didn't find that alarming?"

"No. I knew it wasn't true," I said. "And so did good old Jack MacNeill." I remembered the telegram he had sent to me shortly after Elena had visited him in Wales: "Know how you must feel re Elena STOP. Keep in mind STOP. In order to open again a flower must sometimes close STOP." I stood up, walked to Elena's old desk, and took the telegram out of the top drawer. "Here, look at this," I said as I handed it to Martha.

Martha read it, then looked up and smiled. "Well, the image is hackneyed," she said, "but the sentiment is lovely."

I nodded and drew the telegram from her hand. "True, too."

"All right, then," Martha said, "what were those years all about, William?"

"I told you. They were about the mind," I said flatly. "My sister's mind — not a small or simple thing, as you already know."

"So she was thinking? Just thinking?"

I smiled. "Well, as Sam used to say, that ain't chopped liver."

Martha laughed. "No, I guess not." She reached for the brandy and poured herself another drink. "Do you mind?"

"Of course not."

She took a sip from the glass, then placed it back on the table and took up her pencil. "Now, what were you saying about chopped liver?" she asked with a grin. "I mean about Elena's mind. She was working to expand it?"

I shook my head. "To reorient it."

"Seek its limits?"

"No, Martha," I said, shaking my head again. "One thing is certain about Elena. She had her politics, her much-talked-about feminism, and a host of other ideas. But more than anything else, my sister believed in a considered life."

Martha raced to get it down. Then she looked up at me. "Well, that's not a new idea, is it?"

"Not at all. But it is a very powerful one when, more than any other single notion, it informs a life."

Martha smiled rather sweetly and took another sip from her glass. "This goes down very smoothly."

"Yes, it realizes its function that way."

"How Aristotelian, William."

I looked at her closely. "How will you realize yours, Martha?"

Martha lowered the glass. "What?"

"That's the question *To Define a Word* asks more often than any other," I said. "How may I be a human being?"

"Well, by just living, right?"

I shook my head. "No, by thinking about life."

Martha was going to reply, but I turned away and looked out toward the road that passed in front of the house. The fog was lifting now, and I could see the gray shingles of the cottage across the street, dark and wet, even through the haze. I remembered that one morning, early on, when Elena was still able to get around, we drove to the Brewster Ladies' Library, where she had been asked to deliver a brief address. It was foggy, and very chill and damp. Elena watched out the window as we drove along.

I turned back toward Martha. "Do you remember that essay Elena wrote about Sam Waterman when he died, the one about the bitterness of old age?"

Martha nodded. "Yes, I do."

"Elena never felt that, the bitterness," I said. "And the reason is that she had taken those seven years to decide her course." And at the end of that time, she had given away almost her entire library, quite a few of her records, and even that violin she plucked at sometimes but never really learned to play. "You know what Manfred Owen says to his daughter in *To Define a Word*," I asked Martha. "'You have lived your life like a pinball, knocking left and right, banging into walls, ringing pointless bells.' Remember that?"

"Yes."

"We all do that, to some extent," I said. "Elena believed that she had lived that way for quite some time. She intended to stop."

Martha smiled cunningly. "So she chose at last."

"Chose what?"

"Between passion and control, she chose control."

I poured Martha another drink. "Why does that sound so terrible, when you say it?"

"But that's what she chose, isn't it?"

I handed Martha her glass and poured one for myself. "Not long before Elena died," I said, "I walked into the back room, the one you and I have sat in so often, the one that looks out on the water. She was lying down on a small bed I had moved in there. Her breathing was becoming difficult. I wanted to lighten things up a bit, so I slapped my hands together and said — in a mocking voice, you understand — I said, 'So, Elena, what have you learned from life, aye?' And I remember that she turned to me slowly, her face very serious indeed, and she said, 'I have learned how difficult it is to live an intelligent life.'"

Martha lowered her glass. "So that's what she came here to discover? How does one live an intelligent life? That's the question she answers in *To Define a Word?*"

"No, that's one of the question she asks," I said. "Look at it this way, Martha. *New England Maid* was a reaction to her youth. *Calliope* was a way of dealing with human catastrophe and its moral implications. *Inwardness* examined what moral responsibility is. *Quality* was about the actual, reducible intelligence of our literature. And then, after all that, *To Define a Word* asks about the nature of a moral life." I took a sip of brandy while Martha pondered my assertion. "If you are looking for a pattern in Elena," I added after a moment, "look for the pattern in her mind."

Martha winced. "Going after my desertion theme again, right, William?"

I let that pass and pressed on toward my point. "Don't you see, Martha?" I asked. "She demanded two things of herself, and of everyone else for that matter: knowledge and goodness."

"Did she think that there was a contradiction between the two?" Martha asked.

"She knew that they were not the same," I said.

"So this passion and control duality, which Jack talked about, that was nothing?"

"It may have been true in terms of certain elements of my sister's personality," I said, "but it had little to do with her mind."

Martha raised a finger in protest. "Yes, but William —"

"I know what you're going to say, Martha," I interrupted, "and I can only tell you what I believe to be true of Elena: that the story of her life is the story of her work, and that the story of her work is the story of her mind." I smiled. "Can you follow that?"

Martha grinned impishly and actually winked. The brandy was clearly getting to her. "Only with difficulty, old fellow, only with difficulty," she said.

I poured myself another drink. "Look Martha . . ." I began, then stopped. How could I explain to Martha something I only dimly perceived myself.

"Yes, William, go on," Martha said, lifting her glass slightly as she eased herself backward in her seat.

I shook my head. "I can't." Suddenly I saw Elena looking back at me from the jetty again, wrapped in a huge scarf, her white hair in a bun behind her head, quoting Jason with a small, sad smile: " 'Death completes no circle save the most banal.' "

"William," Martha said, "you were saying."

I shook my head. "No, nothing."

"But it was quite interesting and I'd like to get it down."

And Elena had eased herself down from the rocks, offering me her hand. It had seemed very cold when I took it.

"This duality," Martha sputtered, "this business of — what would you call it — the mind and the heart."

I could not stop my head from shaking as I continued to answer Martha. "No, nothing. Nothing at all. No. No." My voice was like a bell tolling in the background, and I saw Elena at that moment when I lifted her from the jetty and put her down again on the sand. She had taken her hand from mine and lifted it toward me and touched my face. "Ah William, my noble knight."

"No, nothing, Martha, nothing," I said, very quickly. And then suddenly I began to cry.

Martha shot forward and took me into her arms. "Oh, William, I'm sorry," she said, hugging me gently, playing kind Cordelia to my wailing Lear. "I didn't mean to press you. I'm sorry. I won't ever do that again."

For the next two days, we tiptoed around each other, Martha asking only the most trivial questions, carefully keeping the floodgates tightly closed.

She left on Monday, insisting on a cab. She hugged me tightly before she left and waved from the window, a huge smile pasted to her worried face. She looked back as the cab pulled away. Her face was gray behind the glass, but I could see the kindness in her eyes. I could also see myself in her mind, an old man smitten with God knows what depths of belated passion and remorse, living now in a lonely house, waiting only to die as Thomas de Quincey had, whispering desperately into the night, "Sister, sister, sister," his last words.

I suppose it was Sam Waterman's death that finally determined Elena to take up residence on Cape Cod. It was something he had always wanted her to do, and so she did it for him. But what began as a gesture of remembrance and respect ended in a deep commitment to the little house Sam gave her, and to the particular loveliness of Cape Cod in winter, bleak as Hardy's Egdon Heath, and as beautiful.

Only three months after leaving the United States, Sam began to get edgy. He fired off letters to his spies at Parnassus, and, like good lieutenants, they told him what he both wished and dreaded to hear: that Christina was recklessly dismantling the empire he had so laboriously created, that she was arrogant, headstrong, and domineering (as if their former master had not been), that she was idiosyncratic in her editorial choices, that she was lavishly supportive of minor talents and niggling in her treatment of established ones (never mind that Sam had resplendently supported a talentless poet because he had a blind daughter, but at the same time refused to consider the work of a Pulitzer Prize winning novelist because he dressed "like a deranged gigolo"), and finally that she was promoting personal causes, particularly feminism, at the expense of sane business practice (it need hardly be added that Sam had consistently committed the same offense during the thirty years he controlled Parnassus, moving from the socialism of his youth to the vitamin fads of his old age).

Thus, while Sam considered his own faults as mere extravagances of nature, these same failings in his daughter were seen as unspeakable perversities. The letters began, and once begun, never stopped. It is a dreadful correspondence, the anger of the one continually feeding the anger of the other. As in all such cases, the lawyers were ultimately brought in to cool boiling tempers, but succeeded only in turning up the heat. Finally, Sam launched his ill-fated lawsuit, floundered as it floundered, and grew exhausted with a battle he could not give up.

He died in the spring of 1975, a bunch of legal papers crushed in his hand. He had gone for a walk on one of the dusty roads that surrounded his kibbutz. A routine army patrol found him, loaded his body into their jeep, and drove him back to their encampment. A young UPI reporter there took one look at the craggy face and knew he had a story on his hands. Only a few hours later those people to whom it mattered knew that Sam Waterman was dead.

He was, of course, brought back to New York. There was a large public ceremony, then a much smaller one at Parnassus — small at least by Sam's standards, perhaps five hundred people. Some of the greatest names in literature were there, bumping into each other at the enormous buffet Sam had insisted on in his will.

Most of them even had the decency to show up at the cemetery sometime later. When I arrived, Christina shoved me toward a group of men who stood just beyond the grave site. "You'll be part of the minyan," she said authoritatively. I shook my head. "Christina, I'm not Jewish." Christina smiled. "That's okay, William," she said. "We fudge a little on this issue, especially when it's an old friend."

So I stood on that warm summer day with my hands folded in front of me, and listened to the ancient rhythms of the Kaddish, and said good-by to my old friend. Elena watched me from across the way, with Jason standing to her right and Jack to her left — a romantic circumstance about which Martha made far too much in her biography, but which had a certain poignancy even so.

After the funeral, Jack and Elena and I went out to dinner. Jason had work to do, he said, but no one really believed that, especially Elena. He was still, even after all this, edgy around her. He was writing the part of his memoirs in which she played a prominent part, and I suppose he found it painful to be near her.

So it was just the three of us. We went to a small restaurant on the Upper West Side. The neighborhood was growing chic by then, filling up with cheese stores and boutiques, a kind of half-baked boulevard Saint-Germain, as Jack called it.

When we had ordered dinner, Jack chuckled softly. His hand trembled at his mouth, the aftermath of a second stroke. "Sam was the most restless guy I ever knew," he said. "Did he rest even in Israel?"

"I doubt it," I said. "Rest would have killed him."

"Rest did kill him," Elena said.

Jack regarded her quietly. "Well, you'd better be careful then, Elena, because I hear you've been resting a lot." He smiled. "Have you retired from life?"

"No."

"Well, look at me. I was out there in that godforsaken little hole in Wales," Jack said, "— you know it, Elena, you came there —

and while I was there, I got in five newspapers and seventeen periodicals a week. Did you know that?"

Elena glanced down and unnecessarily smoothed her napkin. "No, I didn't, Jack."

Jack turned to me. "That's — let me see — that's twenty-two different publications a week. I was not retired from life." He looked at Elena. "You understand my point?"

Elena smiled affectionately. "Better than you know."

"The fact is," Jack went on, "the world still has to be saved. You know why we fought so hard in the thirties? You know why we wanted to save the world then?"

Neither of us answered him.

"Because we knew that if we didn't," Jack said vehemently, "we'd have to grow old in this one." He rocked back in his seat, squinting at me fiercely. Then he laughed and turned to Elena. "There's no fury like an old fury, right, Elena?"

"No, there isn't, Jack," she said gently. "None at all."

He leaned forward and kissed her. "I'm back in the USA for good, now. Hell, I'm going to kick some more ass before I die." He wrapped his arm around Elena and squeezed her. "Would you like to join me, my dear?"

I think she surprised him with her answer. "No," she said, quite firmly.

Jack smiled and gently drew away. "Well, I've grown more tolerant with time," he said to her. "You have to find your own way." He looked over at me. "I don't know where our life comes from, but it has to *go* somewhere, doesn't it?"

I nodded. "Of course."

He turned back to Elena. "Quick answer from Cold Bill. He makes it sound like such a simple truth."

But of course it wasn't simple at all, as any freshman philosophy student would have known. And I remember thinking as I watched Elena and Jack through the rest of the evening that there was something in their lives that transcended mine, that they looked down on me from a higher shelf. To Jack I would always be Cold Bill, someone who, for all his accomplishment, remained a man of missing parts. And for Elena I would forever be cast in the role of sidekick brother, an intimate in certain parts of her life and an alien to others. I had grown old among these unhappy truths, grown so accustomed to their ache that they ached no more, and I was at last at home with my enfeeblements, warmed by their long companionship, as one might grow kindly toward his limp, or listen with affection to the murmur in his heart.

It was still fairly early when we finished dinner, but Jack was already tired. "The sap is drying up, William," he said to me as I held his coat for him at the door. Then he turned to Elena. "It's good there's a few people left who remember when it wasn't."

Traffic on the street was at a monstrous roar, and Jack's rather shaky voice could hardly be heard above it. He tried to shout, but the effort exhausted him and he finally shrugged helplessly, and walked to the curb to flag a taxi.

In a moment he was gone. Elena and I stood together on the sidewalk.

"Are you going back to Cambridge tonight?" she asked.

"Yes."

"Well, you may be seeing more of me in the future."

"Really? Why?"

"I've decided to take that house of Sam's on the Cape," Elena said. "Not for good, of course, only for the winters."

I could not have been more pleased. "Well, we'll be neighbors of a sort then, won't we?"

"I suppose so," Elena said. She glanced away from me. "I only made this decision just now. I'm not used to it yet. And of course, this should not be thought of as retirement."

"The last eight years have been your retirement," I said.

She shook her head. "You're wrong, they haven't been."

"What was it then, a search? How romantic."

Elena laughed. "A search? How banal. No, just a reorientation."

"Not of your personality, I hope."

"No, of my consciousness."

I smiled. "That sounds a little grand."

"Well, I can't help that. It's all we have, William, our consciousness. We should keep it tuned, don't you think?"

"And now you think something's clicked and you're ready for winter on the Cape?" I said brightly.

"Yes."

"When do you intend to move?"

"Perhaps within a month," Elena said. "I have some things to settle."

"Well, call me when you're ready," I told her. "I'll come down and drive you up there. I always welcome an opportunity to come back to New York for a day or so, and the drive up to the Cape should be pleasant, considering the company."

Elena smiled. "That would be nice, William, the two of us driving up together."

She called during the first week of September, and over Labor Day weekend I drove down to New York, checked in with Barney Nesbitt, who was editing my new book, a collection of essays on the English Romantics, and then drove Elena up to the Cape. It was a brilliant fall, almost as radiant as that other one, long ago, when we had stood in the Standhope railway station, waiting for a New York train.

Elena turned from the window and smiled when I reminded her of that. "My God," she said, "how could anyone have ever been that young?" She glanced toward the rear seat. There were only two suitcases there, along with her typewriter and those two reams of plain white bond upon which during the next year she would write the first draft of *To Define a Word*. "Traveling light again, I suppose," she said.

"Well, you've not accumulated much, Elena," I told her, "just a noble reputation."

"That sounds rather final," Elena said.

"It's too late to blow it now, my dear."

"I could write a foolish book."

"You'd be forgiven for it," I said. "People would scratch their heads and ask what happened, but in the end they'd let it pass."

"Chalk it up to my senility."

"Or to the weepy sentimentality that comes with old age," I said. "That's what I'm most in danger of, I can tell you." I shook my head. "Barney said that my essay on Byron was breathless as a schoolgirl."

Elena did not seem worried. "Barney is witty but he's shallow, William."

In this mood, Elena seemed extraordinarily alive. She talked on about Barney Nesbitt for a while, speculating on the differences between learning and wisdom. She talked about David, about how she hoped that he would remain in New York, perhaps go to Columbia. After that, she simply wandered through any topic that struck her as worthwhile.

We arrived at the house late in the afternoon. I had made an early morning appointment with a student for the next day and so had to return to Cambridge. Still, I wanted to see Elena safely installed. I helped her with the two bags and the typewriter, then joined her for a quick cup of coffee.

"I could linger a bit longer if you like," I offered.

Elena shook her head vigorously. "No need at all, William," she said. "This place is like a second home to me. I'm perfectly fine."

"I wouldn't mind staying, just to make sure everything's in working order," I said.

"No, that's all right," Elena said. "You go ahead back to Cambridge now."

It was evident that she was anxious for me to leave. She wanted to enjoy the solitude the house offered her, that "awayness" which Manfred Owen requires in *To Define a Word*.

I left just as the sun was beginning to set. Elena stood on her porch and waved to me as I got into the car. Once behind the wheel I leaned to the side, expecting to see her still there, her hand in the air, with the sky like a golden bowl behind her. But she was gone.

Elena was already at work on *To Define a Word* when I saw her again. About a month after moving in, she called to invite me out for the weekend. I drove down from Cambridge on a Saturday morning, and as I walked up to her door, I heard the sound of her typewriter clattering away from within. It was a heartening sound. The recognition that she was at work again lifted my spirits, and I remember bouncing jauntily up the flight of wooden stairs that led to her house.

She opened the door almost immediately. She was wearing a long robe, and the light flooding in from the windows behind made her look as if part of her already belonged to another world.

"I heard your typewriter as I pulled up," I told her.

She smiled. "Well, you can notify our mutual acquaintances in New York. I'm sure they'll be relieved."

She stepped back and allowed me to enter. She had bought a few paintings from local artists, replacing some of the more dubious ones Sam had purchased years before. But otherwise, very little had changed.

She led me into the back room. "I use this for my office."

She had moved in a small desk from one of the bedrooms. Her typewriter rested upon it, and beside the typewriter, a manuscript perhaps an inch thick.

"The new book?"

"Yes."

"You seem to be progressing nicely."

"It's only a first draft. But I thought about it for a long time before I began to write," she said. She glanced at the pile of neatly stacked white paper on the desk. "It's a very simple story, really," she said. "Full of what amounts to homey advice." She looked back at me. "Do you want me to tell you about it?"

I must have looked surprised. "Are you willing to?"

Elena smiled. "For some reason, I'm getting rather talkative these days. There's a Mr. Richardson a few doors down who comes over from time to time. He's a widower. He helps me with things. When I need to go somewhere, he drives me." She shrugged. "Well, to make a long story short, William, I find that I talk to him like a magpie, really, just chat and chat."

"Well, you stayed sort of secluded before you moved here," I said lightly. "It's natural for you to burst out a little."

"Yes, I suppose so," Elena said. She glanced back toward the manuscript. "I like the book. I'm not sure anyone else will." She looked back at me. "It's called *To Define a Word.*"

"I'd like to hear about it."

She made coffee and we sat down in the living room. Then, for almost two hours, Elena described her novel to me, with considerably more grace and affection than I had ever heard her speak of any of her other works.

"It begins simply," she said. "A father, living alone, waits for his daughter to return home. She is fleeing from a bad marriage and a generally disordered life. She has come home to be refreshed." Elena smiled and took a sip from her cup. "She arrives, the daughter, Andrea.

She is mixed-up, confused, and she asks her father — his name is Manfred Owen — she asks him to tell her about his own life. Which is what he does."

I nodded. "Interesting," I said. "So it's the story of the father, not the daughter?"

Elena shook her head. "No. It's the story of how a man chooses to tell his life, of what he draws from it." She sat back and thought a moment. "It's about what can and cannot be taught."

"I see."

Elena then went on to describe the dialogue that develops between Owen and his daughter, the shifting perspectives each of them brings to this long and intense conversation. As she spoke she seemed physically drawn into that ornate, book-lined living room in which she imagined the two of them to sit. I could see the glow from the fire in Owen's hearth light my sister's face. She seemed completely alive, her eyes full of light, her voice firm yet gently passionate. She looked much as Manfred Owen describes his wife on the day she gave birth, "as if she knew where power was."

"More than anything else," Elena said, "Owen wants to give his daughter the benefit of his own experience. Everyone wants that, don't you think, not just every father?"

"Yes."

"At first he fumbles about, spouting homilies and platitudes," Elena continued, leaning forward, her hands squeezed together in her lap. "Andrea thinks all of this just nonsense, that it all boils down to a simple notion that you should think about what you're doing, that sort of thing. Owen becomes frustrated as Andrea continues to dismiss his comments. Finally she asks him bluntly why anyone should bother to think about anything. And it's here that Owen grasps it himself. He looks her in the eye and tells her: 'Because thinking, Andrea, is an act of love.' "

I smiled. "Obscure, Elena, but still interesting."

Elena sat back slightly and looked at me intently. "It's true, William, it really is true." She rose and walked into the kitchen, returning with another cup of coffee. She sat down, glanced out the window, then turned back to me. "I like it here," she said. "I like it here very much."

"You look very . . . I don't know, very uncomplicated, Elena," I told her.

She smiled. "Do I?"

"For you, yes."

"Perhaps it's the ocean."

I shook my head. "No."

"What then?"

"Just a feeling that you've settled in," I said. "That this place is sort of home. At least more than New York."

She took a sip from her cup, then lowered it to her lap. "Jason sent me a copy of his memoirs, a first draft."

"And?"

"He's very complimentary to me," she said. "Self-effacing in everything." She shook her head. "I never meant to hurt him."

For a minute Elena seemed very distant, as if she were going through her life with Jason once again, trying to sort it out. In *To Define a Word*, Manfred Owen advises his daughter to do precisely that, to engage and reengage the past.

"I'd really like to hear more about the book," I said after a moment. "I'm rather captivated by it."

Elena turned toward me. "I'm not much of a quoter, William," she said, "but a few days ago I was reading randomly and came upon a poem by Mark Van Doren." She walked to a small bookshelf near her desk and drew out a thin volume. She opened it, sat down again, and read:

> "Slowly, slowly wisdom gathers:
> Golden dust in the afternoon.
> Somewhere between the sun and me,
> Sometimes so near that I can see,
> Yet never setting, late or soon."

She closed the book and looked up at me. "I read that yesterday, William, and I began to cry." She turned away and looked out over the bay. "It was very cinematic, yesterday," she said with a small laugh. "The sun was going down, the water golden." She looked back at me. "I was overwhelmed."

"I know the feeling."

"I don't mind it at all," Elena said firmly, "this lack of serenity."

Then she continued her guided tour of the new novel. She described very carefully how she wished the tone of the book to follow the mood of the twenty-four hours during which it takes place. She called it a "sunset-to-sunset narrative" and asked if I thought that sounded pretentious. I told her that it seemed to me just the opposite, gracefully modulated. By the time she had finished, I was certain that my sister had in her mind, though not yet on paper, a very remarkable book, one to which she would apply all that she had learned about the process of thought and the difficult craft through which it is offered as a gift to another.

She looked tired when she finished. She removed her glasses and placed them carefully on the desk beside her. Then she closed her eyes and rubbed them softly. Something in her weariness rushed toward me powerfully, and I realized once again what it was to be an artist, to have the talent necessary to bring to life your care.

She went to bed a few minutes later. I read for a while, then went to the adjoining room and lay down as well. Throughout the night I could hear her shifting restlessly. At times she got up, walked around a bit, then returned to bed. I remember admiring her ceaseless agitation. I had sunk into the peace of the elderly, the kind that almost inevitably falls upon those who have achieved a modest reputation, one which the most Herculean efforts could increase but little. Elena, on the other hand, was committed once again to a substantial labor. In my mind, I saw her moving into old age full of relentless energy. It gave me pleasure to think of her sleeplessness in this way, and so I thought of it in no other.

The next morning I left shortly after breakfast. Elena seemed refreshed, though still a bit lethargic. She talked of her book again, though with less animation. Then she walked me to the door, stood at the top of those gray, uneven wooden stairs, and waved good-by as I pulled away.

Two winters later, she sent Christina the completed manuscript of *To Define a Word*. Not long after that, she returned briefly to New York, stayed a few days with Alexander and his family, then packed her things in David's battered Volvo and drove with him back up to Cape Cod. In a letter to me at that time, she wrote that she was "closing down the franchise operation in New York, and now intend to invest my dwindling capital on the Cape." The lightness in her tone was deceptive. I fell for it entirely.

Another year passed, and I found myself sitting with my grandson in Earl Hall. "She's dying," I said, and David's eyes fell toward his cup, while mine fled toward the window and the snow.

For a long time we maintained a delicate silence, the type that turns everything frail and unapproachable. I continued to watch the snow engulfing the ivy-covered walls of St. Paul's Chapel.

He touched my arm and I turned back toward him. He seemed very beautiful to me at that moment. Great care does that to a face.

"How do you know?" he asked.

"Well, I haven't spoken to her doctor, if that's what you mean," I told him, "but there was something in her voice, or her eyes. There was that quote from Jason's memoirs."

David did not doubt my judgment. "She seemed very pensive when I visited her last month," he said. "Of course, *To Define a Word* hadn't been out very long, so I thought maybe she was having some sort of delayed postpartum depression."

"Not Elena," I told him.

David shook his head. "No, you're right. Not Elena." He stared into his cup again. His hair was dark and curly. His skin was very smooth and white. "We're really helpless in a situation like this, aren't we?" he asked as he looked back up at me.

"Yes."

"You know, of course, that if there's anything I can do . . ." he began.

"Yes, I know, David," I said hastily. Then I got to my feet, surprising him with the suddenness of my movement. "I'm going now."

David quickly stood up. "Where?"

"I don't know. Maybe just to walk around a bit."

"But there's a blizzard."

I shrugged and began to walk away from him. "Don't worry about me. This is Manhattan, not the Rockies."

"But you shouldn't be out in weather like this," David said. He grabbed my arm. "Wait, at least let me go with you."

I shook my head. "No. I really need to be by myself for a little while."

I suppose he read the determination in my face. I felt his grip loosen.

"I understand," he said softly.

I took him into my arms, hugged him tightly. "I'll let you know about things, David, about whatever happens." I pushed him away from me and looked him straight in the eyes. "What else can I say?"

I turned and walked back out into the swirling snow. I trudged across Columbia Walk, then, for no particular reason, took the subway to the Village. I got off at Fourteenth Street and made my way down to Washington Square. It was a field of perfect white, with huge drifts piled waist high against the arch. I felt unearthed and thrown into the air, tumbling through space. I was staggering, as if suddenly wounded by a rifle shot. It was a curious feeling that even for me there might be such a thing as an unendurable event. I had seen a few deaths, of course, and as I walked across the park they came to mind: Harry in the Burmese jungle, Elizabeth from her Bank Street window, Miriam, going silently at last after so much tumult. But Elena seemed different from all of these. Not because I loved her more, but because I loved her differently. She was the one great book I had been reading all my life, only to find out with grave alarm and vast surprise that it was coming to an end.

I walked farther south, turned onto MacDougal Street, walked a block or so, then made the old right turn which once led to Miriam's apartment. It was no longer there, that small brick building with the plaster window boxes. It had been replaced by something more sleek and streamlined, a thin glass tower perfect in both execution and design and which therefore failed to engage either the inner or the outer eye. Miriam would have hissed, but the most I could muster was an ancient grouchiness, which I quickly shirked off as I walked away. There is nothing new in despising modern architecture.

What was new was the sense that soon I might be despising it alone, that everyone was fading now — Jason with his creaky bones, Jack with his strokes, and now Elena with something dreadful eating at her life — all of them moving toward their ends, "with death forever snatching pieces from the puzzle," as Kramer envisions it in *To Define a Word*.

I turned around and walked north to a large bookstore on Broadway. Elena and I had rambled through it many times, and as I elbowed my way down aisle after aisle, I half expected to see her darting past, her eyes glimmering with some treasured find. I remembered a day years before when she had stumbled upon *The Landscape Painter*,

Henry James's earliest work, a book which, as she would later write in *Quality*, "suggested all his faults but none of his greatness." But on that afternoon it was merely an object of delight. I had snatched it from her and pretended to run away. She had chased me halfheartedly. To the people around us, we must have seemed two ludicrous poseurs, full of bookish vanities. But for us, I think, it was a moment not only of shared amusement but of that understanding at which we had both arrived: that no matter what our separate paths, the world of letters would always exist as the common ground upon which we could stand together, that though our relationship might fall victim to small hostilities, still in the most important matters we would remain as one.

For a long time I wandered through the store. I knew that I was looking for something that I would never find on these shelves. I thought of my sister, and I could feel the enormity of her impending death growing in my mind beyond all reason, a death that signaled a universe of dying. I thought of her language, her insight, her books, and the approaching unconsciousness of so conscious a mind struck me as an epic calamity. How could milk be delivered the next day, babies blandly fed? For a moment, I entered a state of monstrous unreason, as if beside my sister's death there were no other deaths, as if the world had not been from the beginning the spherical depository of all our endless hope and fear and failure.

Standing rigidly in a book-lined aisle, I opened up unheard-of chambers of exaggeration. I reinvented mankind, reimagined human destiny, in such ways and according to such priorities as would sustain my sister. I remolded the laws of biology, drained chemistry of its impurities, placed all science at the disposal of my sister's life. I turned evolution upside-down so that the mind alone had dominion over every other thing, over age and decrepitude and riotous cells, over the hardening of the lungs and the sluggishness of the heart. Over every infirmity I imagined her triumphant, equal to the new law I inscribed as the central maxim of all nature: that while the mind lives, no lower function shall be allowed to die.

I walked out of the store, slogged my way toward Union Square, then took a cab uptown. I had planned to spend the weekend with David, but that seemed burdensome under the circumstances, so I made arrangements to return to Boston. The plane was delayed at La Guardia for several hours until the snow lifted, so I sat in the lounge and drank a brandy and tried to read a biography of Thomas Gray. It would have been slow going under the best of conditions, but my preoccupation with Elena made it more or less impossible to pay any attention at all to the book, and Gray was left to fend for himself while I searched through my sister's life, looking for the key to all this pain, to the peculiar depth of my grief.

It was almost midnight by the time I got home. I unpacked my bags, hoping that weariness would finally overtake me and I could move into a sound sleep. It didn't, so I decided to work awhile in the darkroom I had set up in a tiny room off the kitchen. I took the film out of my camera and began developing the pictures I had taken during the preceding days. Most of them were of sights around Harvard. One was of a young poet whose work I admired and who at my request had delivered a reading to one of my classes. The rest were mundane shots of buildings and bridges. Except for the last on the roll. It was of Elena. I had taken it while she stood on her porch, wrapped in that enormous scarf. The photograph was very stark in its lines but somehow luminous in its composition. I lifted it from the fixative and placed it under a light. I could feel my breath stop as I looked at it. At that instant I knew the source of all my grief, the element that went beyond my love for Elena and into the love we bear, sometimes grudgingly, sometimes with the highest passion, for all humanity. She stood for those moments of supreme consciousness and understanding when our mercy suddenly overcomes our rancor, and all our sorrow and our jubilation merge into a single sweeping tenderness toward mankind.

She must have been surprised to see me pull up the following Monday morning, the back seat of my car filled with suitcases and pasteboard boxes, but she did not pretend to be surprised as to the reason for my coming. She opened the door and waited until I had gathered up a few of my things and walked up the short span of wooden stairs that led to her house.

"I've come to stay with you awhile, Elena," I said.

She stood behind the screen, watching me carefully. "Is this something you really want to do, William?"

"Yes."

She nodded, then opened the screen and stepped back to let me in. "Would you like a cup of coffee?"

I said yes and put down my bundles. Then I followed Elena into the small kitchen at the back of the house. She was still moving easily at that time, and one would have had to look closely to see any sign of illness or distress.

She sat down opposite me at the table and folded her hands together in front of her. "How much do you know?"

"Only the one basic detail."

"No detective work? No tracking down the physician?"

I shook my head, then took a quick sip of coffee. "Did you think you could keep it a secret indefinitely?"

"Who have you told?"

"Only David. He'll tell Alexander."

"Good," Elena said matter-of-factly. "I wrote to you last night, and to Jason and Jack. I'll mail theirs this morning." She glanced out toward the sea, held her gaze there a moment, then continued. "I've only known for a few weeks myself." She turned back to me. "I have about three months."

I felt a shudder pass over me, but quickly suppressed any outward sign. "You plan to stay here on the Cape?"

"Yes." She got up quickly, walked to the cupboard near the sink, and brought out a box of blueberry muffins. "Would you like one?"

"No," I said. "Look, Elena, what is it, exactly, that you have?"

"It's a problem of the heart," she said. She opened the box of muffins, then closed it immediately and looked up at me. "Congestive heart failure. That's the technical name." She shrugged. "A very advanced case of it, evidently."

"How long have you known?" I asked.

"Not very long at all," she said almost casually, but with a strain in her voice that quite audibly betrayed her fear. "I had noticed a certain weakness for quite some time. Well over a year, at least. I thought it was a part of getting older. But it was this disease." She held her eyes very directly upon my face as she continued, as if by focusing on my emotions she could control her own. "It's a problem in the left ventricle of the heart, Dr. Lawson says, and in many cases it can be helped." She shook her head. "But not in mine."

"How about surgery?" I asked.

"Too late."

"Well, what can be done, then?"

"Not much," Elena said. "I should rest as much as possible. I should stay calm, which is not easy to do. Little things like not eating salt." She stood up, returned the box of muffins to the cupboard, and then sat back down. "One thing, William. I don't want to spend my last days in a hospital, or in a drugged stupor." She reached over and took my hand. "There's relatively little pain. I'll have more and more trouble breathing." She shrugged. "Then I'll die."

She looked calm, matter-of-factly relating what she took to be the routine etiology of her disease as if the life it threatened were that of some distant relative or long-lost friend.

"So, there you have it," she said.

I nodded slowly, then started to speak.

Elena lifted her hand to stop me. "I know. You're sorry about all this. So am I, believe me. But there are other things to think about, now. Some of them are sentimental. Some of them are vain."

"I've come to help in any way I can," I told her.

"I've arranged to give a full interview to the *Saturday Review*," Elena said. "I'd like for you to sit in on it so that you can correct any misstatements I might make."

"All right."

"Also, Martha Farrell is coming to do another interview for the biography. I'd rather she not know about my illness."

"I won't tell her."

"Good," Elena said. "Finally, to the sentimental things. I've told both Jason and Jack I'd like to see them. I'd like you to help make sure that these visits don't become overly mournful."

"That will be hard to do," I told her.

"William, I don't want to get more and more unhappy before I die, do you understand? Certainly these next few months won't be pleasant. But I don't think they have to be morbid."

"So, you're going to a adopt the laugh-death-in-the-face attitude?" I asked.

Elena shook her head. "No, of course not. I'm very glad you're going to be here with me, William," she said, her eyes growing moist. "I know I'm going to be afraid."

Elena was still vigorous a month later when the reporter from the *Saturday Review* showed up on a chilly Thursday morning. He was a trim young man, who had already written a number of articles on my sister and who came with a mind well equipped to probe her.

He looked surprised when I opened the door, though he recognized me almost immediately. "You're William Franklin, I believe?" he said.

"I'm staying a few days with Elena," I explained. "She'll be out in a minute. Would you like a cup of coffee?"

He declined.

"Elena usually likes to sit in the back room by the fire," I said. I motioned toward the rear of the house. "Back here. Come on in."

He followed me into the back room, glancing about, taking it all in — the few pictures Elena had bought, the book on this table or that. It was obvious that the smallest object grew magical because of its association with my sister, and that the young man, whose name was Michael Peterson, as he later told me, intended to soak up the aura.

"Quite modestly furnished," he said as he took a seat in the back room.

"It's just a cottage with heat," I told him. "There's not much room for display."

"But the place in New York, Miss Franklin's apartment, I suppose it's more elaborate?"

I shook my head. "Not elaborate, but well appointed, I'd say. Elena has almost always lived comfortably. In Paris she lived on the Île Saint-Louis."

Peterson nodded quickly. "Yes, I know." He leaned forward, lowering his voice conspiratorially. "I understand a biography is being written?"

"Yes."

He looked disappointed. "Someone from California, I'm told."

"Martha Farrell, the daughter of one of Elena's old friends."

He sat back. "Too bad for me," he said with a slight smile. "I'd hoped to do one myself. I've always admired her work."

"Well, there's probably room for more than one book about Elena."

"Yes, certainly," Peterson said. He stared out the large window. "Nice view of the sea."

"Yes," I said. "Very nice."

"Why has Miss Franklin suddenly decided to give a long interview?" he asked me.

"Maybe because she wants to make things clear."

"Why now, in particular?"

"One gets to a certain age, you know."

Peterson watched me suspiciously. "I'm not a hack journalist, Mr. Franklin," he said. "I'm here because I respect your sister's work. There's no need for you or her to feel cautious with me."

"I don't feel cautious, Mr. Peterson," I told him. "I feel protective of my sister's privacy."

Peterson smiled very gently. "I think I understand."

"Good."

Elena came in a few minutes later. She was wearing a plain dark dress, and her hair was drawn into a bun behind her head. She took off her reading glasses as she sat down opposite Mr. Peterson.

"It's a great pleasure to meet you," he said.

Elena nodded. "Thank you." She seemed unusually tired that morning, and there was a slight trembling in her right hand. During the night she had wandered about the house more or less incessantly. Once I had offered to sit up with her, but she had declined and shuffled back into her bedroom, closing the door behind her.

"I really fought for this assignment," Peterson said.

Elena smiled but said nothing.

"Mr. Franklin tells me that you consented to this interview in order to clear up a few things," Peterson said.

"Yes," Elena said, "and my brother has agreed to sit in on the interview, so that our collective memory might keep matters straight."

She seemed stiff at the beginning, as if determined to maintain a certain distance from the matters she would be discussing, that is to say, the matter of her life. Peterson caught this nuance, and in his introduction to the interview he stated it rather well: "She answered the most intimate questions about her life as if they dealt with someone else's, a person of some renown whom she had known for some time. By pulling away from her life slightly, Elena Franklin entered it more deeply, and for me this transformed an ordinary interview into a uniquely personal experience."

Peterson began with questions about her childhood, and as I sat quietly listening to Elena's replies, Standhope swam back into my memory. I saw the dusty square, heard the Italian cobblers shouting at each other from their upstairs shop, saw McCarthy Pond glittering in the midsummer sun and the large oak that towered over our house on Wilmot Street. It seemed not so long ago that I had lived there.

"There is a sense in much of your writing," Peterson said, "a sense of paternalism, if you will. Was your father a great influence on you?"

Elena answered by describing our father in a way that struck me as surprisingly realistic. It was an honest portrait, warts and all, and yet it was also very affectionate.

"My father was too selective in the things he loved," she said, "and dismissive toward the things he didn't. He loved the road, which could not love him back, and was indifferent to my mother, who loved him all her life." She did not add that he had also loved her, though she was strong enough not to need it, but had not loved me, his son, who had felt at times that he could hardly live without it. "He was faithful to himself," she added in conclusion, "but to almost nothing else. There was rakish courage in his independence, but there was moral failure in it, too." Her eyes moved slowly toward me. "My father had great energy, but it was mostly appetite. He insisted on his freedom but used it chiefly to serve himself. When he touched ground, he destroyed things that did not deserve to be blown apart."

Peterson asked about our mother, her insanity. He wondered if Elena had ever feared that she herself was going mad, and she replied that she hadn't. "Others have found me reclusive from time to time," she said, "and they may have worried about me. But I have never worried about myself in that regard, nor have I ever thought the reclusive impulse to be anything but sane."

Peterson then turned to her life in Standhope, her relationship to the town. Predictably, Elena's attitude had softened with time, a change Peterson noted. "You seem to have grown almost wistful about your hometown," he said lightly.

"Wistful?" Elena said. "No, I don't think I've grown wistful."

"Well, you're certainly not as angry about it as you once were."

"No, perhaps not," Elena said, "but anger is not a sustaining emotion."

"There was anger in *Calliope*," Peterson said.

"That was outrage, not personal anger. There is a difference."

"Which is?"

Elena shifted in her seat. "Outrage is propelled by a sense of justice," she said, "but personal anger is propelled by a sense of personal insult, something like that." She shifted again, and I saw her wince with pain. "I was glad to be angry with Standhope. The anger made me determined to leave it behind."

Peterson nodded. "But what about all those people who feel the same kind of resentment but can't leave it behind, who just smolder."

Elena shrugged. "I would hope that if they come across a copy of *New England Maid,* reading it will help them to turn their phosphorescence into flame."

Peterson then asked my sister about the time she had lived alone in Standhope with our mother. Elena explained that too much had been made of that period of her life, particularly in certain essays about her early work. For the first time, she spoke in some detail about her life on the road with our father. It turned out to have been less sordid than I had imagined, my father ever alert to her protection, steering her away from what he called "low types who just want one thing," men, that is, not very different from himself. Her trips with him were also more rare than I had previously thought, and so for the greater part of those years she had, in fact, remained closeted in the house on Wilmot Street.

"And what about loneliness?" Peterson asked. "Were you lonely during this period?"

"Perhaps."

"There is a persistent loneliness in your work."

"If there were no loneliness in an artist's work, then it would not be true," Elena said. "But again, there is a difference between personal loneliness, which is debilitating, even pathetic, and metaphysical loneliness, the loneliness one feels as one who shares the human fate." She stopped and took a drink from the glass of water beside her. "This second loneliness is something I feel all the time. The first I feel only on occasion, but never with such depth as to make me very knowledgeable on the subject."

Peterson seemed to take this as a final pronouncement and moved on, this time to Elena's early years in New York. Here she seemed almost to glow as she related her arrival, her years at Barnard, the gift she had received from Dr. Stein. "For Dr. Stein, learning was a mission," she told Peterson, "a task of moral passion, something that had to be done not because it was fun, or even because it was noble, but because it was a mitzvah, a requirement of the highest order." She smiled. "Once he said, 'Elena, remember this, when Adam took a bite of fruit from the tree of knowledge, he did the right thing.'"

Peterson continued to question Elena about her life in New York for almost another hour before finally going on to the publication of *New England Maid.*

Elena was surprisingly dismissive about her first book. "It's very dated, now," she said.

"It's still in print," Peterson reminded her. "And very popular on college campuses."

"For me it is dated," Elena said. "And I don't mean simply because many of the things it protested against no longer exist. It is dated as a part of my own development. It seems to me little more than a portrait of a girl resentful of her past and struggling to escape it. As such, it may be useful to people in the same predicament. But as a document of intellectual worth, it is more or less useless. It is filled with passionate attitudes and responses, some of which are legitimate, some of which are not."

It took a moment for Peterson to get into the mood necessary to defend a book to its author. "Well," he said at last, "it seems to be a book that at least suggests some early gifts, literary gifts, that sort of thing. The language is very beautiful in parts."

"And overwrought in others," Elena added. "I know my thundering passages are the ones most often quoted, but I think that my works fail to the extent that I forget that subtlety can be more eloquent than rhetoric."

Peterson seemed somewhat uncomfortable with all this, as if Elena had robbed him of his purpose. "Do you like anything you have written?" he asked helplessly.

"Of course I do," Elena said. "I like much of *Calliope.* I still read parts of *Quality* because I think what I said in certain places was true. I glance through some of my essays and short stories from time to time. I believe that *Inwardness* is a good book, as is *To Define a Word.*"

Peterson clearly had reservations, but he kept them to himself. "Well, since you mentioned *Calliope,*" he said, "why don't we go on to that. Not the book, but your experience in the thirties."

Under Peterson's careful and intelligent guidance, Elena relived the thirties. She spoke of the distress but also of the glory of those times. Following the theme she had established, she said, "There is personal history, which is narrow, and for some of us the Depression will always be the happiest time of our lives, for reasons that could hardly be more obvious. It was a time, as they say, of commitment, and one never entirely forgets one's own commitment. Long after the cause is dead, one's stand is still remembered."

Peterson mentioned Elena's long association with Jack MacNeill. She told him about their cross-country journey in the middle of the Depression and laughed over its more inane moments: Jack passionately speaking to a crowd of farmers who, as he found out later, understood not one word of English; one night in Omaha when they were denied access to a mission soup kitchen because, as the minister explained, "the woman's too pretty, you know, and these men here, they've lost enough"; Jack's being roughed up at a labor meeting because he spoke so well that he was suspected of being a government agent.

It was almost noon before Peterson finally asked his last question about the thirties and Jack and all those things associated with that time in my sister's life. I could tell that Elena was weary, even though her voice remained strong.

"Perhaps some lunch?" I suggested.

Elena nodded. "Yes, that would be good." She turned to Peterson. "You will join us, I hope?"

Peterson agreed, and for the next hour or so we all sat around the kitchen table, talking of various things, carefully staying away from anything having to do with Elena's life or work. By the time lunch was over, I think we were all bored with trivial conversation, and so it was with some relief that we walked back into the other room to resume the interview.

Unfortunately, Elena appeared very tired by the time Peterson began to question her again. Her hand trembled quite noticeably, and after a moment she discreetly tucked it beneath one of the folds of her dress.

Peterson smiled brightly. "Well, I'll start the afternoon with an easy one: Did you like Paris?"

"Yes," Elena said. She bent forward and began to rub her eyes. "Forgive me, but I'm a bit tired."

"Of course," Peterson said. He looked at me. "Should we stop?"

"You should ask Elena," I told him.

He turned to her. "Should we stop, Miss Franklin?"

Elena straightened herself in the chair. "No, I don't think so. I'd rather continue, Mr. Peterson, if you don't mind."

Peterson glanced down at his notes. "Some people have written that your stay in France made you somewhat anti-American, and that this attitude permeates *Quality*. Do you think that's true?"

"I cannot make American writing better than it is, nor American culture more respectable," Elena said. "In *Quality* I tried to perceive the real depth and range of American letters. This was not an easy task. One person, of course, could not really hope to do it. This accounts for lapses in the text, for its spottiness. Still, I did try to give an overview of America's intellectual achievement, such as it is. This meant that some authors, the ones with few ideas, came off rather badly — Jack London, for example, and Hemingway, to some extent, and certainly poor Theodore Dreiser. Some critics thought Jefferson came out looking like an amateur philosopher and Hamilton a cynical genius. The point was to come to grips with what these people had actually said after the flags and drapery had been pulled from the edifice of their work. Some of these esteemed writers came up with very little in the hand and almost nothing in the mind. Some, less well known, came up with a great deal. And still others, like Melville, emerged intact. If any of this makes me anti-American, I don't know why, and really, Mr. Peterson, I don't care. Intelligence is not a soldier to be called forth by the bugle and the drum, nor is it an alchemist whose task is to turn baser metals into gold. To be attacked as an inadequate scholar is one thing; to be attacked as a traitor is another. I take the first criticism seriously, but for the second I feel nothing but contempt."

"Well," Peterson said, subdued, "I have always thought that charge unfair."

Elena looked at him sternly. "So have I."

Peterson cleared his throat nervously and glanced down at his notes again. "Perhaps we should discuss your life in France for a while."

"Fine," Elena said crisply. She looked at me, and I could not keep from smiling back at her. She was still my little sister, throwing her shoe at Dr. Houston.

Peterson then directed Elena through her life in Paris. She had little to say about it, however, and of all the episodes of her life it appeared the one she felt to have been the least significant. "Expatriation is a worthwhile experience, I suppose," she said, "if expatriation is your theme. But it has never been mine." She did talk about certain French writers of the time, however. She had most admired Simone Weil. "*The Need for Roots* has always seemed to me a genuinely remarkable book," she told Peterson. "It has a kind of nostalgia for the good on èvery page. It struck me in reading it that a great moral voice doesn't have to be dogmatic or didactic or even rhetorical."

Elena was rapidly growing weary, but since both she and Peterson knew that this would be her last interview, the two of them pressed on to the fifties — her decision to return to the United States, her first encounter with Jason Findley and the relationship that ensued.

Elena revived somewhat at this point, speaking in a strong voice of her early efforts to write *Quality*, of her conceptual failures, and finally of Jason's role in the making of the book.

"He encouraged me to write something of large scope," she said, "and this was an important step for me. I needed to try something that required concentrated thought, specifically applied to specific works. Imaginative thought is different, so the writing of *Quality* was an experiment in reorienting the nature of my sensibility. The experiment served me very well, I think, because when I came to write a novel once again, it was with a precision that would not have been possible for me before. Whatever worth there is in *To Define a Word* is owed in part to *Quality*, and *Quality* is owed in part to Jason Findley."

It was late afternoon by the time Peterson reached that time in Elena's life which could roughly be thought of as the present. He asked her why she had left New York, and Elena dodged the question, saying only that she was in need of a rest and that Sam had offered this house. This seemed to satisfy Peterson, but I believe he must have known that my sister was gravely ill.

Before he left, however, he engaged Elena in a brief discussion of *To Define a Word*. Again, Elena seemed to revive slightly as she spoke of it.

"The better part of this book," she told Peterson, "is not what Owen tells his daughter. These are often simple things. But the book is also a portrait, I hope, of the impulse to teach through memory and experience, to guide not by rules but by displaying to another

— as Owen displays to his daughter — the fruits of a considered life."

Peterson smiles. "Which are?"

"Complex, to say the least."

"Some examples?"

"Well," Elena said, "Owen understands that to say to an inexperienced person, 'You must think, you must read, you must know, you must not allow yourself to be driven by uninformed impulses' — to say this to the inexperienced is meaningless. So he tries instead to portray his own life in such a way that while he seems at times a failure and at times rather stupid, a nobility still emerges, apparent not in what he does, what he acquires in either wealth or fame, but in what he actually is. His is a plain life that only thought has enriched and made beautiful. In the end, his daughter at last grasps this, that had her father's life been less considered, it would have been less full." She smiled. "Lear is not tragic until he is no longer foolish. He might have died a senile old man, instead, he died a great one. Understanding makes all the difference, not just in a literary figure, Mr. Peterson, but in every human being who ever lived."

Peterson left a few minutes later. He relinquished his formality for a moment and actually kissed my sister on her cheek when we said good-by to him on the porch.

"I hope you don't find that impertinent," he said with a smile.

"Not at all," Elena said. "I have enjoyed this day with you, Mr. Peterson."

"At last, call me Michael."

"And you call me Elena."

"That will be hard, but I'll try," he said. He turned to me and offered his hand. "Good-by, Mr. Franklin."

I shook his hand. "Good-by, Michael."

He laughed lightly, then got in his car and drove away, waving back to us as he disappeared behind a row of hedge.

"Are you tired?" I asked Elena.

"Very."

"Want to go to bed?"

"It's so early."

I started to go back into the house but stopped because Elena lingered outside, still watching the road.

"It went well, I think," I told her.

"So much left out, William," Elena said. "Elizabeth, Harry Morton — so very much left out."

"Still, it was a very good interview," I said.

"I tried to tell the truth."

"That's all that matters."

Elena shook her head. "No, it also matters for you to know just how far that is from what is real."

"You can't ever escape subjectivity, Elena," I said.

"We must, William," Elena said firmly. She turned to look at me. "We must." Then she walked quickly back into the house and to her room.

J ack MacNeill came to visit us a few weeks later. Elena's weakness was more visible by then, and I think that Jack recognized it right away, although he said nothing to Elena about her health. He must have known that he had only a short time left himself. He had already suffered several small strokes, which had left a slur in his speech and had half closed one eye. But his voice was still strong and his mind was as keen as ever.

Elena's face brightened as she saw him ease himself from his car. "Here he is," she called.

I walked out of the kitchen, drying my hands on a dishtowel. "Right on time."

Elena turned from the window. "Remember now that he's not to know about me," she said. She opened the door as he came up the stairs to the porch. When he saw her he straightened himself, then offered her a large smile.

"Elena," he said. "Still radiant. Are you still smart, too?"

"Smarter than ever," Elena said.

Jack stepped into the house and gathered Elena into his arms. "I never found anything better than this," he said, looking at me.

Elena stepped out of his embrace. "Are you hungry, Jack?"

"Damn right, for life and victory."

"I was thinking more along the lines of food," Elena said with a laugh.

"That too," Jack said. He offered me his hand. "Ah, Cold Bill, you must love this northern climate."

"It suits me."

"I knew it would," Jack said. He looked at Elena. "But how about you?"

"It suits me, too."

Jack glanced back and forth from Elena to me. "So, two kids from Standhope begin their bleak retirement," he said. He smiled at Elena. "I read your latest book. Didn't understand a word of it. It must be very great, Elena."

Elena took his arm. "Come into the kitchen. I had William buy some raspberry tarts — your favorite, I believe."

At the table, Jack energetically munched at his tart while Elena and I sat amazed at his appetite.

"I could give you two a good ribbing about leaving New York," Jack said. "Hell, Bill, I might even offer you a quote, the one from Dr. Johnson: when you're tired of London, you're tired of life. Isn't that what he said?"

"Yes. Really, Jack, you don't have to play the illiterate farm boy with me."

"True enough, Bill," Jack said. "But you've always put me in that role."

"Never intentionally."

Jack waved his hand. "Ah, forget it. That's stale bread, right?" He looked at Elena. "Anyway, I can't really rib you too much about leaving New York, because I'm doing the same thing. Only I'm going to Connecticut."

Elena was genuinely surprised. "That's hard to believe, Jack."

"You remember Joe Tully, don't you?" Jack said. "Got his throat cut open on Second Avenue a few weeks ago. Some psycho killed him for the few bucks in his wallet." He shook his head. "An old codger like me, hell, I'm a sitting duck, just like Tully was."

"So you're going to a safer shore," I said.

"Poetically put, Bill," Jack said. "Fact is, I can't just dismiss all this as class war at the level of the street. I know it's true, but it doesn't matter when you're shaking like a leaf every time you leave your lousy little room." A definite sadness moved into his face. "I'd still die on the goddamn barracades," he said. "I haven't lost all my nerve. But I don't want my last minute on earth to be spent staring at some crazy bastard who's about to cut my throat for twenty dollars and a faded picture of my mother."

"I can certainly understand that," I told him.

He didn't seem to care whether I understood or not. He looked at Elena. "So it's Connecticut, old girl. It's the Flight from Egypt, you know?"

Elena reached over and touched his hand. "I hope you like it there. You've earned a little peace, Jack, you have a right to it. Not everyone does."

Jack smiled at me. "All this sentiment must be making you pretty sick, right, Bill?"

"It is rather nauseating, Jack. I prefer you both a bit more crusty."

Jack popped the last of the tart into his mouth. "I'm soft at the core. All us aging Commie bastards are."

I smiled obliquely. "Stalin would be glad to hear it."

Jack laughed and winked at Elena. "Gotten to be a Red baiter in his old age, has he?"

"Just a saintly liberal," I told him.

"You missed something, Bill," Jack said, now serious. "Let me tell you — just one old man to another — you missed something."

"In what way?"

"By standing aloof, by being superior."

"You mean during the thirties?"

"I mean always, Bill."

I looked at Elena. "Do you agree?"

Elena shook her head. "No."

Jack seemed surprised by her answer. "You knew the fire, Elena, don't deny it."

"I'm not," Elena said. "Why should I?"

"When we were on the road, they were the best years, right?"

"I don't think so, Jack," Elena said.

"Really? Why not?"

"We were merely living," Elena said. "That's not enough."

"We were fighting the good fight, Elena," Jack said, "you know that. We were passionate." He smiled knowingly. "Remember that night outside Tucson, remember that?"

"Yes."

"And you tell me that we were merely living that night, just blandly living?" Jack asked vehemently. "No, Elena, we were not just living, we were *alive!*" He stopped, as if to calm himself, then, subdued, went on. "There are things the blood remembers, isn't that right?" Elena nodded.

"Things the blood remembers, yes," Jack said softly. He turned toward me. "Kids today, graduate students, they come to me with their oral-history projects, you know? They ask me questions and I talk about the thirties and the fifties. I talk into their little microphones and I look into their little eyes and I try to get through, somehow, to their little souls." He shook his head. "But I never can. Because they think, you see, that if you didn't win the prize, you never ran the course. To them, we were just a bunch of wild-eyed fools following a stupid dream. That's what they think of me, and Tully, poor Tully, and you, Elena, at least for the few years before you wrote *Calliope.*"

"Yes," Elena said, "I suppose they do think that."

"It's a gap we can't cross and they can't cross," Jack said. "How do you tell somebody that a few thugs beat the hell out of you in Texas one afternoon and left you bleeding in the dust, and you pulled yourself up and realized that, by God, you felt great, just great. You felt like screaming, 'Come on back here, you bastards, come on back and do your worst.' " His eyes shot over to me. "You look me straight in the face, Bill, and tell me that's not something the blood remembers."

"I would never be that presumptuous, Jack," I said quietly.

"Maybe I was a clown for the Party, Elena," he said, turning back to her, "a sucker for the cause, hmm?"

"We are all something like that, Jack," Elena said.

"I guess we are," Jack said, almost wearily. "Except for Cold Bill, here."

"Is this the spot in our program when I'm supposed to admit that yes, even I, have been a fool?" I asked.

"I'd love to hear more, Bill," Jack said. "Please go on." He sat back and folded his arms over his chest. "I'm all ears."

"Well, if you want to know the truth," I said, "I've always felt that I had a great book in me, but evidently I didn't. How's that for soul-rending confession?"

Jack shook his head. "Petty stuff, Bill. You'll have to do better."

"My father didn't love me."

"Nothing new in that," Jack said, grinning fiendishly.

"I was not a perfect husband."

"Oh, Christ, Bill, who was?" Jack asked loudly.

Elena began to laugh, lifting one trembling hand to her lips as she did so.

"I coulda been a contendah," I said, laughing now myself.

"Oh, God, not that," Jack thundered, slapping his hand against his forehead, "not that old Brando line."

"I have measured out my life with coffee spoons," I said.

"No more quoting, goddammit," Jack shouted. He pounded his fist on the table. "No Eliot, no Rousseau, no Augustine."

I looked at Elena. She was still laughing.

Toward evening I began making a light dinner while Elena and Jack went for a walk on the beach. Elena was using a cane by then, but only for occasional support. Jack joked with her about it, calling it a "prop to add dignity to your disreputable life," and he would sometimes snatch it from her and dart away. But beneath all this, I knew, he understood. He thought he might go before her, I think, but he knew nonetheless that she was going.

Dinner was at that small wooden table in the kitchen. I placed two white candles on it. Jack insisted that Elena be the one to light them.

"Forgive my notorious sexism, won't you?" he said. "But I have always found the image of a woman lighting a candle to be very beautiful."

Elena smiled. "Well, I certainly wouldn't want to deprive you of it," she said. She struck a match and lit each of them.

During dinner we spoke casually of the past and the present but carefully sidestepped references to anything but the immediate future. There was no talk of books yet to be written, things yet to be accomplished. We were now concerned with what we had already done, not with what we might yet do.

"At times I think of heading overseas again," Jack said, leaning back in his chair and folding his hands over his stomach, "but it seems so far away, you know. I think Connecticut is about as far as I'm likely to go." He looked at me. "Who do you think will fall most quickly into obscurity, Bill, you or me?"

I shrugged. "That probably depends on which of us has the most pages listed after his name in the index of Elena's biography."

We both laughed, but I think that we both understood that to some extent what I had said was true, that ultimately we were destined to a second-stringer's fame, the men who'd held a towel for the champ.

After dinner we had brandies in the back room. Elena was looking tired indeed by then, and so as casually as I could I suggested that it might be time for all of us to retire.

"There's a pull-out sofa in the living room," I said to Jack.

Elena rose slowly. "But there's a bed in mine," she said to him.

Jack smiled pointedly. "But if we become excited, Elena, we might break something."

"We could take a chance," Elena said.

I remember hearing them talking quietly in Elena's room for almost half the night. There was some laughter here and there, and then the quiet talk resumed.

Jack left early the next morning. I came out of my room and found him all but tiptoeing out the door.

"I thought you'd stay the weekend," I said.

Jack shook his head. "No, I can't. Elena will understand." He lifted his hand to the brim of his hat. "Watch after my old girl, will you, Bill?"

"Yes."

"There's nothing to say, of course."

"No, nothing."

He turned silently and walked down the stairs to his car.

Elena came out of her room, fully awake, as I am sure she had been for some time.

"I knew he'd go this morning," she said as she joined me at the window.

"Well, did you two break anything?" I asked lightly.

Elena took my arm and leaned one side of her face into my shoulder. "Just each other's hearts," she said, "but that was long ago." Then, although Jack could not see her, she stepped to the window and raised her hand to wave good-by.

Toward spring Elena was still able to get around fairly easily. On warm days we took slow strolls down the beach, and often these outings raised her spirits markedly. Having lived for so long in the city, she enjoyed the spaciousness of the sea and the near-empty beach. But there were also moments when she grew remote, lost in thought, as if a vital part of her were already gone.

And yet an element of her character urged her forward, resisting depression and malaise. She continued to write to various friends and associates, even fired off an occasional note to such uninspiring personages as Barney Nesbitt. It was this part of her that provided the energy to continue the long poem she had begun and to make her last public appearance in early May.

She had been invited to address a discussion group at the Brewster Ladies' Library on the subject of *Moby-Dick*, the book they had been reading all spring. Elena agreed immediately. It was held in the mid-morning of a sunny day. The night before had been very restless for her, and I expected her to be dreadfully tired. But when she emerged from her bedroom, her face was glowing with that youthful energy which rose in her from time to time like a sparkling mist.

"You look . . . well . . . very much yourself, Elena," I told her as she walked into the living room, where I had been watching the morning news on the small television set we kept there.

She smiled and gathered her shawl around her shoulders. "I think I look like an old bohemian gone to seed," she said. "Sort of an emaciated Gertrude Stein."

I rose from my chair and walked over to her. "Not at all. You look rather commanding, if you don't mind my saying so. We'd better be going. The friends of the library will be waiting for their star attraction."

Once out the door, I eased her down the front stairs. She was anxious to be on her way but distrustful of her strength. She held on to me like a child afraid to fall, and I realized that she had reached the point where she could not depend upon her own body for support.

She was breathing heavily by the time I maneuvered her into the car.

"Perhaps you'd rather cancel?" I asked as I closed her door.

"No."

"I'm sure they'd set another date."

Elena turned toward me. "Get in the car, William. We will go today."

It was only a mile or so to the library. Even driving at an old man's cautious pace we arrived within a few minutes. Elena spoke very little on the way, though from time to time I could see her lips move suddenly, as if she were in the midst of some silent recitation. In all her life I don't believe she ever gave a purely extemporaneous speech. Others have written of how eloquent she could be, as if her eloquence were utterly spontaneous. It never was. She memorized her speeches and delivered them almost as an actress would. She knew, as she once told Jack, that an address is a performance, and that a good one requires the gifts of a good performer.

The setting for Elena's address at the Ladies' Library was very pleasant. It was a small, book-lined room, in which a few chairs and a lectern had been set up. There were already quite a few people in the room when Elena and I arrived, and they whispered energetically as we moved among them, slowly making our way to the front.

Elena sat quietly in a chair behind the lectern. No one approached her. Perhaps she appeared too imposing, or perhaps too frail. I sat in the front row but she rarely looked at me. She studied the paintings on the wall and then scanned the bookshelves to her right and left. I remember thinking that even in this casual setting she seemed wonderfully engaged.

She was introduced a few minutes later by a man who was no doubt associated in some way with the library. He was tall and thin and suitably bespectacled. His introduction was so full of exaggerated appreciation that Elena later told me she could not imagine such praise for someone who was still alive. It was mercifully short, however. Elena sat mutely behind him, staring straight ahead, as if his remarks concerned someone in another galaxy.

She rose shakily when he stepped aside. The young man offered his hand, but she did not take it. She walked to the lectern and grasped it tightly for support.

"I'd like to thank the library for its invitation," she said. "The staff here has helped me several times since I moved to the Cape. I have learned, at last, to return books relatively near the required date."

There was a patter of polite laughter at this, and Elena added to it with her smile. She seemed genuinely pleased to be able to confront once more that mysterious public which had given her so much. She could never fathom exactly who they were, this unheralded community, but I suspect she knew them to be simply the ones who do not write but ably read, do not speak but wisely listen.

"I am pleased to be here today," she began, "and I am especially happy to be able to talk for just a few minutes about what may be the greatest book written by an American."

She surveyed her audience a moment, and when she spoke again, her tone was more serious.

"Anyone can have an interpretation of a book, and sometimes it seems that the greater the work the sillier some of the interpretations. *Moby-Dick* is one of those great books which has drawn the attention of both wise and foolish commentators." She laughed lightly, then shrugged. "Now it's my turn."

The audience laughed again, warming to her.

"Like all great books, *Moby-Dick* is about many things, and so one finally can't help resorting to impressionistic criticism, that is, to saying that this is what it means to me. With this caveat, then, I will say simply that I think *Moby-Dick* is about striving, that its theme is as old as the myth of Icarus. But Melville attached to this theme elements of tragic grandeur which give the work a special wisdom. This wisdom is something that is felt as powerfully as it is known. I think he knew that great striving is that which both raises man up and sets him apart, isolates him from the family of unconscious life, and by that means lends a special poignancy to his existence. We feel an empathy in the presence of failure that we do not feel in the presence of victory. Victory causes us to celebrate; failure causes us to reflect."

She smiled slightly, then continued. "I believe that Melville knew that it is only those who soar who have a right to fall as Ahab does. And Ahab is part of a long mythic chain. In the cause of human enlightenment, he comes to us both as a hero and as a victim. Adam gave up his innocence, Faust his soul, and Ahab his life, in search of that knowledge which we have every right to pursue. We know this knowledge will finally bring us peace, and that we live sad, narrow, and blighted lives for the lack of it. Without it, we continue to live, generation after generation, shrouded in a darkness which moves only toward a final, endless night."

She stopped again, her eyes searching the room as if looking for encouragement there, that single comprehending face to which every speaker speaks, every actor plays.

"*Moby-Dick* is a great book both in its form and in its content," she said as she began again, "for its notion of titanic striving is embodied both in what it says and in what it is. Melville allowed his book to sprawl in magnificent disorder, to stretch out toward impossible limits; that is, he allowed it to fail in its own mighty endeavor, so that the book itself becomes the physical embodiment of its own extended yearning. Thus, *Moby-Dick* relates Ahab's failure all the more powerfully because it also relates Melville's. In doing both, it is able powerfully to convey two inescapable truths of human life: that our beauty is as inseparable from our travail as our goodness is inseparable from our bafflement."

There was little more than polite applause when Elena resumed her seat. Clearly it had not been the address the group had expected, brief, somber in its tone, unflinching in its manner. The young man who followed her to the podium stammered his gratitude for her having come, rather nervously thanked her for her remarks, then quickly opened the meeting to questions.

For a moment there was nothing but awkward uneasiness. Then a few hands rose tentatively into the air, and Elena answered each question crisply and concisely. Through it all she seemed unusually subdued, as if this speech had somehow drained her of her mission, that now, at last, there was nothing left to say.

"Are you feeling all right?" I asked her as we drove home.

"Yes, fine."

"Tired?"

"All the time, now."

Once at the house, Elena shed her pensiveness a bit. She seemed happy that David was to arrive for a visit a few days later and that Alexander was due the following week. "When you get right down to the core," she said, "they are really the only family we have."

By late afternoon, however, she had weakened, her steady walk becoming a cautious shuffle. She gripped her cane as if it were a life line, and only rarely and briefly did she walk without it again. She ate very little at dinner and retired early. Toward midnight, I heard her pacing the house once again.

I got up and walked out into the front room. She was sitting on the small sofa by the window, her body brightly lit by the reading lamp which glowed brilliantly above her. She looked up as I came in, then took off her reading glasses.

"Is there something you want, William?" she asked pointedly.

"Just to make sure you're all right."

"I am fine."

I must have looked as though I did not believe her, because she repeated it. "I am fine, William."

"Well, it's just that you looked so tired at dinner."

"I *was* tired at dinner, but I am not tired now."

I suddenly felt a powerful desire to rush to her and hold her tightly, but I knew that she would not have liked that. Whatever else may be said of Elena, she demanded that there be a little steel even in another's love.

And so I simply smiled. "You look very lovely under that light, with that open book," I said.

Elena gave me a quick, desultory nod. "Thank you, William."

I went back to my room but could not sleep. Instead, I continued to watch this image I retained of my sister in the other room. Perhaps under other circumstances I would have turned this image into grief, but somehow the vision of Elena so fully illuminated, so resolute beneath the light, filled me with a quiet joy.

In June Elena's interview was published in the *Saturday Review*, and when Jason saw it he telephoned her immediately. Although she had been writing him regularly, they had not spoken to each other in quite some time, and the weakness in Elena's voice must have alarmed him. He flew up from his home in Virginia a week later and I picked him up at the Hyannis airport. He was dressed immaculately as ever, in a dark suit, white shirt, and broad gray tie. He looked like an aging movie actor, the sort who always played the suave sophisticate.

When he saw me, he did not smile. His face was as grave as his tone.

"How is she, William?"

"She is herself," I told him, "but not well."

"How long did she intend to keep her health a secret?"

"I don't know, Jason."

"Well, I can tell you this, I'm not going to pretend that I don't know there's something very wrong with her. I have never believed in that sort of charade."

"I doubt that she would have expected that," I said. "She knows how changed she is, how tired."

I suppose he wanted some sort of denial from me, that she was just out of sorts, that it was just a cold. When I offered no such thing, he looked more shaken than alarmed.

"William," he said, his voice full of disbelief, "my God, is she dying, William?"

"Yes."

He stared at me in silence. Then, in a very odd gesture, he slowly took off his hat. "It doesn't seem possible."

"I'm afraid it is," I said. "Come, let's go. I don't like to leave her for very long."

We drove back to the house in a warm summer rain. Jason was still allowing the news to soak in, and I could tell that it was almost too dreadful to accept.

"She is really looking forward to seeing you," I told him. "She has missed you."

"We should have stayed together."

"Perhaps."

"I don't know what happened to us. Was it just my vanity?"

"Only partly, Jason."

"Yes, you're right. There was something missing between us, but it took me some time to discover what it was."

"But now you've discovered it?"

Jason nodded vigorously. "Oh, yes. It was generosity, William. That's what was missing. She never understood how vulnerable I was."

"When she read your memoirs, she did," I said. "I remember watching her while she read them. She was very moved . . . by your generosity."

"Really?" Jason asked. "That's odd." He thought for a moment. "You know, from the time that I wrote *The American Experience,*

I was considered brilliant by many people. I never believed them, though I tried to live up to their expectations. I knew there was an empty space where all my genius was supposed to be. I covered it up pretty well. After all, I am a very clever man. But Elena saw through it. Then, rather brutally, she exposed it."

"She wrote about a book, Jason, not about a person."

Jason actually laughed. "You've known too many writers to believe that. She attacked my book as if the person who wrote it were no longer alive to read her attacks. But I was alive, William." He smiled. "Listen to me, how shameful. Elena's dying and I'm still nursing my wounded pride."

It struck me then how difficult it must have been for Jason to have written with such beauty and grace about my sister. So much of him had been devastated by what she had written in *Quality* and by the final rejection implied by her leaving him, that it was hard to imagine so kindly a recovery.

"I want to say again, Jason," I told him, "that when Elena read your memoirs, she was moved, not only by the way you treated her, but by the book itself. She believes it to be an enduring work."

He looked at me. "She said that?"

"Yes," I said. "And as you know, she has always said that *Quality* is partly due to you."

Jason gave a sly nod. "A fair exchange, then."

"A fair exchange," I said. He seemed amenable to this judgment, though not exactly satisfied by it.

She was waiting for us in the back room when we arrived, sitting in her chair, facing the bay. Her cane was propped up against the chair and it was the first thing Jason saw. Still, as he stepped around to face her, he put up a determined front.

"I want you to know, dear lady," he said, "that I resent not being told of your ill health. I was your lover until you abandoned me, and I have remained your obedient servant since then. And I resent not being told."

For a moment they simply stared at one another. Elena seemed too weak to offer even the lightest rejoinder.

"William told you?" she asked.

"Yes."

"I suppose it would have been obvious in any event," Elena said. She smiled and held out her hand to Jason. "I'm glad you came."

For the next week the three of us spent all our time together. Neither Elena nor Jason seemed in the least interested in being alone together. It was as if both knew that the real intimacy of their relationship had passed and that any attempt to renew it would prove awkward. Often they seemed like two old soldiers discussing a well-remembered campaign, careful to avoid its grimmer aspects.

Elena was still able to walk on the beach. With some help she could even manage the treacherous path of the jetty. But she also tired very easily and would often return to the house after we had strolled no more than a few yards. She would doze off in the middle of a conversation, leaving Jason and me staring mutely at one another, neither of us able to go on without her.

Yet when she was fully awake, she was very much the Elena of the past, tart and uncompromising. As always, she made little allowance for misplaced sentiment or thoughtless judgment, and she remained as stern as ever in her evaluation and analysis.

One evening, Jason tentatively mentioned that he was thinking of becoming a Catholic, and Elena, who had seemed especially fatigued, suddenly sprang to life.

"For what possible reason would you do that?" she demanded, squinting pointedly. "Is it an old man's panic? Is that what it is? You think you've found a loophole in oblivion?"

Jason shook his head. "I've never been much on immortality."

"So why this sudden religiosity?"

Jason shrugged. "I'm not really sure."

"Don't you think you should be?"

"Some motives, Elena, will always remain mysterious."

"Well, surely you don't believe in the actual tenets."

"You mean the Virgin Birth, the Resurrection, things like that?"

"Well, they do play a rather important part in the faith, don't they?"

"Of course, for some."

"But not for you?"

"No."

"Then what's the point of your conversion?" Elena asked.

"The spirit of the faith," Jason answered.

Elena shook her head. "Not enough, Jason."

"It is for me," he said firmly. "I love the beauty of the story. Surely you of all people should be able to understand that."

"Then say it's a beautiful story, and leave it at that," Elena said. "Myth is all right, as long as it's kept in its proper place."

"And where is that?"

"The imagination, or as part of a symbolic structure. But to believe in it as a reality, I'd say that's making myth carry too much weight."

"But what about faith, Elena? Is there really no room for that in your mind?"

"No."

"Why?"

"It would take up useful space," Elena said.

Jason laughed. "So you have no sympathy for my Christian impulses, then?"

Elena shook her head. "None whatsoever, I'm afraid."

And yet, in a sense, she did, although but marginally. In a letter to Jason a few weeks later, she wished him well on his decision, whatever it might be. "This much I will allow," she wrote, "that Christian irony is very beautiful, especially that humble and glorious idea that he who is most distant from redemption might offer to the saint a true deliverance."

By midweek of Jason's visit, Elena seemed entirely comfortable with his presence in the house. They talked continually, and finally even broached the most sensitive subject between them, what Elena had written about *The American Experience* in *Quality*.

"I can't say it wasn't devastating," Jason admitted, "both to the book and to me."

Elena watched him guardedly. "Well, perhaps it was too severe."

"But you've not changed your mind, have you?" Jason asked.

"No, not on any particular judgment. But I think I should have allowed a bit more for temperament."

Jason smiled. "Mine or yours?"

"Yours in the way you wrote the book," Elena said, "and mine in the way I read it."

"So you still think it's romantic hogwash?" Jason asked.

"I never thought that, and you know it."

"You said as much."

"I said it was a story, rather than an analysis, of the American experience."

"Isn't that the same thing?"

"Not to me."

For a minute, Jason seemed to want to let the subject drop. He glanced away from her, resting his eyes on a vase of flowers by the window. Then he turned back to her. "What do you think, really?"

"I never said *The American Experience* was a bad book," Elena told him, "and I never said that you were a bad writer."

"But what did you actually think?" Jason insisted.

Elena watched him a moment, then answered. "I thought it should have been a poem rather than a history, and that had it been a poem it would have been a great one."

When she said that, Jason's face filled with a grateful peace, as though he had received, at least in part, what he had come for.

Jason left a few days later, on a very warm, sunny day. We had a late breakfast, then Elena sat in the front room and watched him pack. He talked idly about his new home in Virginia, but I knew that his mind was very far from that place. For her part, Elena pretended an interest in her flower garden beside the house. She absently discussed hyacinths and beach plums, while Jason countered with kudzu and boll weevils.

Elena had elected not to drive with Jason and me back to Hyannis. She was tired, certainly, but I think she knew that that short drive would have been pointlessly grueling for us all had she come along. And so she stood at the door, leaning on her cane, as we prepared to leave.

"It was good of you to come, Jason," she said as he stepped up to her and lowered his suitcase to the floor.

He smiled. "I wouldn't have missed it."

They embraced briefly, then parted.

On the way to the airport, Jason talked about an essay he was working on, but it could hardly have been more obvious that his mind was not on it. Finally, in the middle of a sentence, he stopped and looked directly at me.

"Shouldn't we have had just one good cry together, William?" he asked.

"Elena is not too much in favor of that sort of thing," I told him.

"She would think it embarrassing?"

"No," I said, "she would think it redundant."

"So it's still very much as I wrote in my memoirs. Elena is her own best shield."

"Yes, I think that's true," I said. I imagined Elena as she must have been at that very moment, while Jason and I were driving toward Hyannis. I saw her sitting in her back room, the window slightly open, a warm sea breeze ruffling the pages of the book in her hand, and I thought of all the times that Elena and I might have wept unrestrainedly together, and suddenly it seemed to me at least an arguably worthy thing that we had not.

Elena had weakened considerably by the end of summer. She could only rarely manage a short walk on the beach, and she never risked the jetty again. Instead, we would walk to where the first stone rose from the beach, and I would hold her tightly while she peered out, searching the bay as if something might be written there.

It was at this time, in late August, that Elena moved into the quiet, inward seclusion from which she never fully emerged again. It was a kind of gravitational pull that drew her toward the central quarter of her mind. At times she seemed unable to bear any intrusion upon this ultimate privacy. More and more she required complete silence. She found it difficult to listen to music and could not endure the sound of the television at all. Even the whisper of passing traffic disturbed her.

She also fell asleep more often and slept for a longer time when she did. She very much resented these periods of what she called "enforced unconsciousness." "If only I could stay awake until the end," she wrote to Jason a few weeks before she died, "and not be plagued by tiny deaths and petty resurrections."

As her weakness increased, she began to fear what she insisted on calling her "return to infancy." She was especially concerned with the added duties this would impose on me.

"It's all going to get considerably more difficult for you," she told me one evening.

We were sitting in the front room, and she had been watching me silently for quite some time.

I nodded and continued to leaf idly through a magazine.

"Very difficult, William," she said, "I mean physically."

"Don't worry about that," I told her.

"I can still get around a bit, but soon . . ."

I looked at her sternly. "Not another word, Elena."

"You're not a young man."

"I'm young enough to take care of my sister."

Elena shook her head. "I'm not so sure. I was thinking, perhaps a nurse . . ."

"No."

"Someone to help you, William."

"I said no."

"Be sensible," Elena said emphatically. "This is not a matter of pride. This is a matter of physical difficulty."

"I'm aware of that," I told her, "but I am also not at all interested in having a stranger in this house." I leaned forward. "Please, Elena, you and I will go through this ourselves."

Elena persisted. "I think you are being stubborn. You are old enough to know that sometimes the cause may not be worth the stand."

"This one is," I said.

"You'd better be certain of that," Elena warned.

"I am."

There were times during the next few weeks when I had more than a few doubts about the wisdom of my choice. But although some burdens are merely burdensome, others remain works of love. In the days that followed, Elena's condition worsened almost by the hour, and many unsightly duties inevitably accompanied her increasing debility. Despite all that, I still believe — and quite sincerely, without romanticizing the physical ordeal, both hers and mine — that I never learned more about my life than during those weeks I cared for my sister while she died.

By the beginning of September, Elena could no longer go outside, and within a few days of her last halting walk on the beach — no more than a few paces, which totally exhausted her — she found it difficult either to feed or clothe herself. She now spent most of her time propped up in a chair in the back room or lying on a day bed I had moved into it. She no longer wanted to sleep in her bedroom, insisting that the sound of the surf helped her to rest. She slept a great deal, but when awake she remained quite lucid. She continued to work, at least in her mind, on her poem, and from time to time she would dictate some lines to me. Her voice was as strong as ever. She did not slur her words, but on occasion she would rush her sentences forward, as if she thought them written on her breath.

"Dying is full of contradictions," she told me once when I had taken down a stanza or two.

"How so?"

"You feel the need to complete things, so you wish to rush them out," she said. "But at the same time, you want what will surely be your last work to be as perfect as possible, so you do not wish to rush it."

She smiled slightly and closed her eyes. "You will know how that feels one day, William."

I shook my head. "No, I intend to live forever."

"Of course," Elena said drowsily. And then she went to sleep.

David, who had already visited Elena once with Alexander and Saundra, came alone in mid-September. He found Elena's condition so disturbing that he stayed only a single afternoon. Elena sensed his anxiety and tried to soothe it as best she could by talking about his work rather than about herself.

"You must let your research widen continually," she told him. "You must think of it as something boundless, David, so that the investigation of an acre becomes a study of the world." She looked at me. "You remember, Dr. Stein used to talk like this."

"I remember."

She turned back to David. "He was a great scholar, David. Do you know why?"

"No," David said softly.

"Because he never believed that any question could be small."

David left an hour later. When I walked him outside, he begged me to seek emergency treatment for her.

"She decided against that a long time ago, David," I told him.

"But surely something, some experimental drug, something like that . . ." he said desperately.

"Elena is going to die," I told him. "Perhaps within only a week or so."

"But there must be something we can do."

"Yes, there is. And you are doing what is expected of you. And I am doing what is expected of me."

"But, surely there is . . ."

I put my hand gently to the side of his face. "David," I said, "go home."

Elena was strangely invigorated when I walked back into her room. She was sitting up straight in her chair and her eyes were bright, almost cheerful.

"I've written a few more lines of that poem in my head," she said. "I'd like for you to take them down, if you have a minute."

I sat down in the chair opposite her and took up a small notebook. "All right, go ahead."

Elena did not speak. I could tell she was going over the lines again, that she was not satisfied with them. "No," she said finally. "No, I don't like them. Forget it, William. Another time."

With one exception, Elena continued to work at her poem, however weakly, every day from then on. The one exception was the day Jack MacNeill died at his home in Connecticut.

I learned of it early on a rainy morning. Barney Nesbitt called from New York. Elena was still asleep. By then she was so weak that she could no longer feed herself, and I remember thinking as I sat in the front room after Barney's call that this news would surely kill her.

For several hours after she woke up, I kept it from her. I fed her breakfast, then set her up in her chair, as I did each day. She was in fairly good spirits and even commented upon a group of gulls that was swooping up and down along the bay. I busied myself with the morning chores, hoping to conceal my own distress, but something in my manner alerted her. I could feel her eyes studying me as I came in and out of the room.

"What is it, William?" she finally asked.

"Nothing."

"I'm not strong enough to repeat a question endlessly. Now please, what is it?"

I sat down and folded my hands in my lap. "Jack died last night."

Her eyes glistened and she lowered her head slowly so that two long strands of white hair fell forward across her shoulders.

"I'm so sorry to tell you this, Elena," I said.

She remained with her head bowed for a moment, then slowly looked up.

"Wipe my eyes, please," she said.

I took out my handkerchief and did as she asked. She seemed composed by the time I had finished, but her lower lip trembled slightly.

"Give me the details," she said in a very low voice.

"Barney called this morning, while you were sleeping. Apparently Jack died in his bed, during the night. It was a stroke or heart attack, I suppose."

She glanced away from me, out the large window. A sailboat was gliding across the bay. Her eyes followed it. "I'd like to write something about Jack," she said, "but it's too late."

We talked on about him for a few minutes, then Elena asked me to open some wine. I poured each of us a glass, then lifted Elena's to her lips so that together we could toast our old friend.

"I'd like a bath now, if you don't mind, William," Elena said when we had finished.

"Not at all," I told her.

She was very light, no more than a bouquet of flowers in my arms. She seemed almost to dissolve into the water.

"Not too warm, I hope?" I asked as I lowered her into her bath.

"No, not too warm, thank you."

When it was done, I wrapped her up once again in her large blue robe and returned her to her chair. She seemed almost to shrink before my eyes.

"Would you like something to eat, Elena?" I asked.

"No."

"Are you comfortable?"

"Yes," she said, but then she shivered. "I am a little cold."

I brought a large blanket from the bedroom and wrapped her in it very snugly.

"Better now?" I asked.

"Much better," Elena said. She offered me a smile. "Would you mind reading to me awhile?"

I took the copy of *What Maisie Knew* from the table beside her chair and began to read. It was a typical Jamesian scene, so English, and in this case not at all compelling. I kept looking up over the page to see my sister, wrapped in her blanket, her eyes half-closed, and after a moment I found that I could not go on, that my voice was breaking almost with each word.

Elena's eyes shifted slowly toward me, but she said nothing.

"I can't, Elena," I stammered, "I can't."

"Then don't, William," she whispered.

Suddenly I rushed forward and gathered her into my arms. I began to cry, and as I did so, I could feel something shudder in her body. I buried my face into her shoulder, still crying, though almost silently. After a moment, I felt the warmth of her breath upon the side of my face and realized that with great effort she had lifted her head far enough to press her lips into my hair.

The sky was no more overcast than is usual on the Cape in the last days of September. The sea was neither unnaturally calm nor excessively agitated, the wind neither blustery nor subdued. Elena had been sitting in her chair all morning, dressed in her blue robe, her long white hair flowing over her shoulders. She watched the sea, following any movement, a boat or a gull. She had spoken only a few words the entire morning.

Toward noon I carried in a tray with tea and toast, which was about all Elena was able to eat.

"Some refreshment?" I said lightly.

Elena glanced at the tray, then up at me, her eyes barely open, languid. "It will not be long now, will it?" she asked.

"No, Elena, I don't think it will be long."

She turned back toward the window. "I feel cold."

"Would you like a warm drink? Another blanket?"

She smiled softly and closed her eyes.

"You might even like a warm bath," I said.

She said nothing. Her eyes remained closed. I could hear a low murmur in her breath, almost a purr.

"Should I read to you?"

Elena's eyelids fluttered, but she said nothing.

I placed the tray on the table beside her chair and knelt down beside her. "Elena?"

She did not answer. Her face was quiet, calm. She seemed but the residue of an elemental force.

"Elena?"

Nothing.

"Elena?" I repeated. I could hear the edge of panic in my voice. "Elena?"

Her eyes opened very slowly. "Still here," she said very weakly, then she closed them once again.

"Is there anything you want?" I asked desperately. "Is there anything I can do for you?"

She did not answer, nor did her eyes flutter in response. She took in a deep breath, then let it out slowly. Her breathing continued rhythmically. I listened to it for a while, waiting for it to stop. After a time I walked back into the front room and sat down. I could see her sitting in her chair, her hair like a silver fan across her shoulders.

For the next two hours, I made myself busy about the house. I washed things that did not need washing, swept corners already neatly swept. I did not want to go back in that room, fearing the worst, but I did so every few minutes.

She was breathing quite well at three o'clock. The clouds had cleared an hour before, and a slant of sunlight cut across the western corner of the room. It seemed like an impertinence.

I pulled up a small chair and sat down beside her. Then I reached over and took her hand.

"Elena?"

She did not answer. I did not bother to call her name again. She was breathing steadily, but in quick, shallow breaths. I leaned back in my chair, folded my hands in my lap, and waited. A few minutes later, I heard her take in a very deep breath, then the fingers of her hand unfolded and stretched out, as if in search of some final truth. She held her breath a moment, then released it with a sudden rush. She did not draw another.

I sat beside her, studying her face. I thought of various ways that I might describe it in a memoir or to the press. Exalted phrases came to mind, but I remembered that, toward the end, Elena had tried as much as possible to leave mere rhetoric behind.

I lifted her from the chair and brought her over to the day bed. I laid her down on her back, placed her arms at her sides, spread her hair over her pillow, and closed the robe around her throat.

There was still enough light for me to take a short stroll on the beach, so I walked down the stairs and turned right, heading slowly toward the jetty. It was very calm, and I was able to walk out onto the rocks. The water lapped softly at the stones beneath my feet.

At the end of the jetty, the water swirled in a white froth, moving in and out of the crevices like breath. I looked back toward the house, and from that distance I could see her chair sitting by the window, empty now. It seemed very small, and suddenly I remembered that first morning so long ago when they had brought her home, wrapped in a pink blanket, a child no larger than a rolled-up newspaper. I remembered how my father had lifted me into his arms so that I could look down at my sister. They are strange, our first impressions, but they are not as powerful as the last. And in the time that is left to me, I shall continually recall how very large she was.